THOUSAND PIECES OF GOLD

Other Books by Ruthanne Lum McCunn

Fiction

The Moon Pearl

Wooden Fish Songs

Nonfiction

Sole Survivor

Chinese American Portraits:
Personal Histories 1828–1988

Juvenile

Pie-Biter

Thousand Pieces of Gold

a biographical novel
by Ruthanne Lum McCunn

BEACON
150

Beacon Press
Boston

Beacon Press
25 Beacon Street
Boston, Massachusetts 02108-2892
www.beacon.org

Beacon Press Books
are published under the auspices of
the Unitarian Universalist Association of Congregations.

08 07 06 05   6 5 4 3

Library of Congress Cataloging-in-Publication Data
McCunn, Ruthanne Lum.
Thousand pieces of gold : a biographical novel /
by Ruthanne Lum McCunn.
p. cm. (Bluestreak)
Includes bibliographical references.
ISBN 0-8070-8381-X (alk. paper)
1. Bemis, Polly, 1853–1933—Fiction.
2. Chinese American women—Fiction. 3. Women
immigrants—Fiction. 4. Women ranchers—Fiction.
5. Women slaves—Fiction. 6. Idaho—Fiction.
7. China—Fiction. I. Title. II. Series.
PS3563.C353T5   2004
813′.54—dc22
2004047691

To Don
for making it possible

Author's Note

In the years since the initial publication of *Thousand Pieces of Gold,* many readers have asked how I reconstructed the life of Polly Bemis, born Lalu Nathoy. I'm pleased to share that story in the essay "Reclaiming Polly Bemis" at the back of this new edition of *Thousand Pieces of Gold,* and to acknowledge the generous help of friends and strangers.

Ruthanne Lum McCunn
San Francisco, 2004

There is no history,
only fictions of varying degrees of plausibility.
Voltaire

PART ONE

第一部份

1865-1872

ONE

Outwardly they acted the same as any other evening. In the courtyard, between the outhouse and manure pit, Lalu crouched over the wooden tub, washing the pots and bowls from supper. At the opposite corner, near the door to the kitchen, her father, with his queue neatly coiled above his sun-bronzed face, leaned against the crumbling brick wall smoking his pipe. Seated on a stool beside him, her mother nursed the baby while A Cai, her younger brother, showed off, scratching out new characters in the hard dirt beneath her feet. But Lalu, scrubbing and rinsing as quickly as her fingers allowed, knew nothing was the same.

There was the unusual number of bowls and pots to wash, the delicious dinner she could still taste in the linings of her mouth, the sure knowledge that her stomach would know no hunger in the coming year, the hushed expectancy they shared. For the harvest had been exceptional. The best in all Lalu's thirteen years.

Inside the house, the platform suspended above the brick bed curved from the weight of stored sweet potatoes. The huge earthen jars in the kitchen brimmed with salted vegetables. All the baskets overflowed with dried string beans and turnip and sweet potato slices. Bundles of peanut and sweet potato vines and stalks of millet covered half the kitchen in piles higher than Lalu could reach. And, best of all, in the hiding place behind the stove...

Lalu leaped to her feet, frightening the chickens that pecked and scratched in the dirt around her, setting them to a loud squawking. For a moment she tottered on her little four-inch bound feet. Then, regaining her balance, she returned the bowls and pots to their proper shelf in the kitchen, emptied the tub of dirty dish water into the open drain behind the outhouse, and perched herself on the stool across from her father.

"Baba, the autumn breeze is chilly. It must be getting late," she prompted.

Her mother smiled and her father's eyes twinkled as he inhaled deeply, then forced the smoke out of his ears in little puffs.

Laughing, but refusing to be sidetracked, Lalu continued, "Look, the first star is out, and I hear mosquitoes."

She signaled A Cai who, arms whirring, began prancing around them in wild circles. Bewildered by the sudden noise and activity, A Fa stopped nursing and looked around. Lalu scooped him up and circled her father, humming and swinging the child until the baby's puzzled frown became delighted laughter.

Chuckling, her father put down his pipe. "Enough! Enough!" he said, swatting A Cai playfully. We'll go in."

Lalu, tossing the baby triumphantly, followed her father, mother, and brother into the kitchen.

"Let me dig it up!" A Cai demanded.

His mother handed him the metal scoop. "Be careful," she said. "Don't break the pot."

Lalu jiggled the baby. She rested all her weight on one foot, then the other. "What if someone stole it while we were at the threshing grounds?"

Her mother clapped a hand over Lalu's mouth. "Don't even say such a thing."

"Then where is it?" Lalu mumbled through her mother's fingers.

Her father peered over A Cai's shoulder. "A little to the left," he said. "Good. Now up a bit."

"I feel it," A Cai shouted.

He bobbed up, face flushed and streaked with soot, triumphantly cradling the pot of hoarded coins.

"Let me count it," Lalu asked.

"No, me. I go to school, you don't," A Cai said. "I'm older."

"Shh," their mother said. "No squabbling or tears to bring bad luck." She took the pot from A Cai. "If you want the family to have a big ox, a strong mule, two donkeys, three or four good houses, and many large and good pieces of land, you must learn to work hard like your father. It was his skill and labor that earned these coins. He will count them."

Her face glowing with excitement and pride, she handed the pot to her husband. His large brown hands which fit so comfortably around a plow fumbled with the coins as, one by one, he counted them into little piles of ten. A Fa reached out and toppled the piles.

"No, no," their mother said, taking him from Lalu. "This money is not to play with. We will use it to buy two more mu of land."

"And a cow too so I can go to the meadow with the other boys?" A Cai asked.

"Yes, and a cow too," their mother laughed. "But not so you can go to the meadow. A farmer with twelve mu of land should not have to borrow a cow for plowing."

"Is it true, Baba?" Lalu asked. "Do we really have enough for a cow as well as land?"

Her father, his eyes fever bright, scooped up the coins and held them in his upturned palms, like a person testing their weight.

"We will buy no land and no cow," he said. "Not yet. With this money, I'll lease all the land I can get and plant winter wheat. The money from that will make us rich."

ONE

Lalu gasped. Only the big land owners, the ones who could afford risks, planted winter wheat.

Her mother's arms tightened around A Fa until he began to cry. "No," she breathed. "You can't mean it."

"Why not?"

"Because it's crazy. We have pinched and hoarded for four years to get this money, and now you want to gamble it away."

Lalu wrapped her arms around A Cai who had begun to whimper. Together they backed away as their father shouted above the baby's plaintive wail.

"Four years of hard work and doing without to save enough for two mu of land and one small cow. And six years before that for just one mu. And two before that for a donkey! Winter wheat is the best crop there is. One good harvest and we can buy five, maybe six mu. And an ox besides."

"What if the harvest is bad?"

"It won't be. I feel lucky."

"That's what the gamblers in the taverns say while their wives and children beg in tatters on the street." She pulled A Cai from Lalu and thrust him and the wailing baby up before their father. "Think of your sons. What will you leave them?"

"The farm is my concern, not yours. I will hear no more about it."

At home no one dared speak of what her father and Chen, his newly hired laborer, did each day in the fields. But it seemed to Lalu that in the shops, down by the levee walls, at the wells, and in the fields, the villagers spoke of little else.

There was no escaping their talk. Even here, on the river bank where she had come to wash the baby's soiled diapers, she could hear the men's voices drifting from the square where they gathered to smoke, knit straw raincoats, weave baskets, and mend tools.

"Have you heard about Nathoy?"

"You mean that fool that leased all that land for winter wheat?"

"Used up all his savings and mortgaged his own farm besides."

Lalu pounded the rags against the rocks, wishing the slap of wet fabric would drown out their voices.

"What kind of a turtle's egg would stake his farm on such a gamble?"

"Who can say? Maybe he's got the right idea. Already his fields are green with newly sprouted seedlings."

"Yes, and yesterday's rain was perfect. Not heavy, but generous. Just the kind seedlings need to grow strong before the first snow."

"But what if there isn't another rain like the one yesterday? If it stays dry and the seedlings don't grow enough before the first snow?"

"Or if they do grow and the snow doesn't come?"

"Or if there isn't enough snow to cover the wheat and keep it safe until spring?"

"Or if it rains instead? Cold, sleety rain, the kind that kills unprotected seedlings."

The possibilities, one worse than the other, hurtled down on Lalu, pushing her back on her haunches, and all at once she felt paralyzed by the same fear that had gripped her when her father had told the story of Guo Ju, the filial son.

"Guo Ju was poor," her father had said. "Too poor to support his mother, his wife, and his child. So he told his wife, 'The child is eating food my mother needs. Let us kill the child, for we can always have another, but if my mother dies, how could we replace her?'

"His wife did not dare contradict him and Guo Ju began to dig a grave. Suddenly, his spade struck a deeply buried vase which shattered, spilling hundreds of gold pieces, a gift from Heaven to Guo Ju, the filial son."

"What if there were no gold?" Lalu had asked.

"There was gold. More than enough for the rest of their lives," her father had said.

"But what if there wasn't?" Lalu insisted. "Would Guo Ju have killed his child?

"It's just a story from the Twenty-Four Legends of Filial Piety," her mother said. "To teach us we must honor our parents and do whatever we can to make their lives happy and comfortable."

"Would you kill me?"

Her father put down his half woven basket and pinched her cheek. "Of course not. Aren't you my qianjin, my thousand pieces of gold?" he asked.

And he had tickled her until she had laughed, "Yes, yes, yes."

Lalu splashed the rag she had just wrung out back into the icy water. She was being silly. What did that old story have to do with what was happening now? And anyway, hadn't the farmers just admitted that her father could be right? That he might succeed?

One farmer's voice rose above the others. "I can see Nathoy taking a chance with his savings, but to mortgage his farm too!"

"Good thing his daughter is so pretty."

"Mmm. Just the right age to fetch a good price."

"Don't be absurd. Nathoy wouldn't sell her. When his oldest girl died from small pox, he mourned her like a son."

"And when Pan lost all his pigs last year and wanted to sell his youngest girl to buy a new brood sow, Nathoy tried to talk him out of it."

"No, he would never sell his Lalu, his thousand pieces of gold."

"Did you ever think he would risk everything he has on a crop of winter wheat?"

TWO

The winter storm which had raged for almost a
week, continued to rattle the paper that covered
the windows. Rain, forced through the roof of
straw and pine branches, pitted the dirt floor with
little mud puddles. In the only lamp, a dish almost
empty of bean oil, the flame sputtered, casting
strange shadows.

Lalu, seated on her parents' heated brick bed,
shivered. Her eyes were red and weepy from the
smoke which filtered through the tunnels connecting the kitchen stove with the chimney, and she
dropped her sewing to rub them.

Across the room, her mother knelt, stiff as
stone, before the red gilt altar of Guanyin, the
Goddess of Mercy. "Can the Goddess really save
my father's wheat?" Lalu wondered.

Earlier, when her mother was lighting yet
another stick of incense, Lalu had suggested that
perhaps their village was too small and too far north
for the gods to hear their prayers. Her mother had

quickly knocked her head against the dirt floor, calling loudly on Heaven to ignore her daughter who should know better than to question the gods' supremacy and knowledge of everything that went on, even in the most faraway corners of China.

Then she had turned to Lalu and said, "We depend on Heaven and the Goddess Guanyin knows that. After all, it was she who took pity on the Han people when they were still living by hunting and gathering. When she saw how they suffered starvation because their ears of rice were empty, she went secretly into the fields and squeezed her breasts so her milk would flow into the ears of rice plants. Near the end, she had to press so hard that a mixture of milk and blood flowed into the plants, yet she did not stop until all the ears were filled."

Lalu stretched, careful not to disturb her two younger brothers who slept on either side of her. If she were a goddess like Guanyin, she would have filled the empty ears of rice with a mere flick of her wrist, and she would stop this storm at once and replant all of the wheat that had been destroyed or washed away. Then she would make the wheat harvest so plentiful that her father would be the richest man in the whole village. No, not just the village, but the whole district!

The door flew open, letting in a blast of wind and rain that gutted out the last glow of light. In the darkness, Lalu heard her mother rise and move, swift and sure-footed as a cat, into the kitchen. She felt a sudden sprinkle of water as her father shook off his straw rain cloak, letting it fall with a sodden rustle to the muddied floor. The smell of damp clothes mingled with the pungent odor of incense. Lalu sniffed. There was another smell, one of hot gaoliang wine. The kind her father offered to his dead parents and grandparents on feast days. The kind disappointed gamblers used to forget what they had lost.

Her mother returned and the room flared into light. Lalu blinked. Her father stood dripping in the middle of the room, his queue unraveled, his padded jacket and pants covered with mud and bits of wheat, broken twigs, and dead leaves.

"It's all gone," he said.

"Gone?" her mother echoed.

"Everything. Even what was set aside for the land tax."

"What will we do?" she whispered.

From where she huddled under the quilt, Lalu could see her mother's frightened whisper had shocked her father as much as herself. For until this moment, not once, even during the worst of times, had they glimpsed a shadow of doubt in her mother's belief that they would somehow survive.

Years ago, when her father had left for Manchuria, hoping to come back like Old Man Yang with a money belt full of gold, it was her mother who made her believe he would return even though every street in the village had at least one house where a husband, father, or son had gone into the barbaric North with hope, only to disappear forever. Then, during the year of famine after he returned, ragged and disappointed, her mother had quieted their terrible, gnawing hunger with little round bits of yeasty dough which swelled in their stomachs, giving them the illusion of fullness. And when they went into debt for a flock of brood hens and the bandits stole every one, her mother had merely pinched their solemn faces and said, "Heaven gave us life, Heaven will give us succor. We'll manage."

In every crisis, her mother's confident, "We'll manage," had brought them through. Why was she silent now?

"Mama?"

For a moment, before her mother turned and sank before the altar, their eyes locked, and in that brief instant, Lalu suddenly understood the reason for her mother's silence.

Before, they had somehow always scraped together the land tax. This time, with the farm so heavily mortgaged and the extra fields her father had leased, they could not. Unless. What was it the farmers had said? "Good thing his daughter is so pretty." "Just the right age to fetch a good price." Her father was going to sell her, and like Guo Ju's wife, her mother dared say nothing, for if her father did not pay the land tax, he would be sent to prison, and without him, the family would starve.

TWO

All Lalu's training in the four virtues of a woman told her she must accept the inevitable. She must be sold so the family could live. Nevertheless, her mind raced like a cornered rat searching for escape. There had to be some other way.

She crawled out from under the quilt. "We can sell the donkey," she suggested hopefully.

Her father sighed. "You don't know what you're talking about."

"If that's not enough, you can borrow the balance from Shi."

"Shi the Skin Tearer?" her father snapped bitterly. "How would I ever repay that blood sucker?"

Lalu swallowed. It was her life she was fighting for, and her father knew it. Why else was he allowing her to speak?

"You can let Chen, the laborer, go," she said.

"With all the extra fields I've leased? Impossible."

"A Cai can leave school to help."

"He's only eight, too small to do anything except children's work."

Lalu slipped off the bed and stood in front of her father. "I'm not too small. I'll work with you."

Her father brushed loose strands of hair from her forehead, his touch full of tender regret. "Qianjin, in this district women don't work in the fields. You know that."

"They do during harvest."

"That's different," he said heavily. "Only sons become farmers."

"I won't be a farmer, just your helper, and only until A Cai is bigger."

"We'd be the laughingstock of the whole village."

"We already are."

Immediately regretting her words, Lalu burrowed her head into her father's chest. Water squeezed from his rain-soaked clothes, spreading coldly over her, but she felt only the fierce pounding of his heart beneath her cheek.

"Baba, I beg you. Let me help you. I don't want to be..." She stopped, unable to say the word sold. "To go away," she finally whispered.

The muscles above her father's tightly clenched jaws quivered, and for a long moment there was only the sound of wind and rain.

"What about your golden lotus?" he asked.

Lalu released her father and stared down at her feet. Every day for two years, her mother had wound long white bandages around each foot in ever tightening bands, twisting her toes under her feet and forcing them back until her feet had become two dainty arcs. They were not as small or as beautiful as those of a girl from a wealthy family who would not need to use them at all. But they were useless for heavy labor.

Her mother rose and came to stand beside Lalu. "I'll unbind them."

"Is that possible?" her father stammered.

TWO

"We will make it possible," her mother said.

Later, in the quiet darkness of her own bed, Lalu dove under the quilt and felt her feet, no larger than a pair of newborn chicks. Dimly she remembered a time when her stride had been more than a few ladylike inches and she could run across the meadow, teasing a kite into the wind. Could her feet really become large and sturdy once again? Her hands curled around them, just as they had around the little featherless sparrow she had found last spring.

Her father had told her death was certain, and she should drown it so it would not suffer. Obediently she had plunged the tiny creature into a basin of water. Its beak opened and closed soundlessly as it struggled for air and its featherless wings pushed desperately against her clenched fists. She released the bird. But it was too late. Unable to rise above the surface of the water, its wild convulsions became shudders, and one by one, the ripples diminished until the water became as still as frozen ice.

Was it too late for her?

THREE

"Lalu," her father called.

Lalu straightened up from the row of millet she was thinning. She pulled her clinging, sweat-soaked jacket away from her body and wiped the perspiration from her face with her sleeve. Shading her eyes from the glare of the late afternoon sun, she looked over at her father.

"Take that bundle of firewood A Cai gathered to your mother," he said.

"I'll take it, Baba," A Cai said.

"No, this field must be finished today."

Each day her father searched for a new excuse to send her home early so she would not have to mix with the other farmers leaving the fields, and Lalu knew it was useless to offer to stay in her brother's place. Nevertheless, she tried. "A Cai is tired and I am not."

"Your mother needs you," he said tersely.

"Yes, Baba."

Pinching her brother's cheek sympathetically,

THREE

Lalu balanced her hoe and the bundle of firewood on top of the wheelbarrow and started down the terraced hillside to the village.

A colorful patchwork of green, brown, and yellow fields full of farmers with their sons and hired laborers stretched before her. Women washed clothes in the dikes by the willow-lined river bank, and old folks leaned against the levee walls, soaking up sunshine, talking story, and watching their grandchildren play around them. She could hear the laughter of small children, the cries of the peddlers shouting their wares; and when the breeze blew her way, she could smell the smoke that curled above the cluster of houses.

But it was what she could not see that showed the village as it really was. The oxen, mules, and donkeys kept well hidden for fear of bandit raids. The furrowed brows of wives gauging each meal's meager allotment so the carefully hoarded food might last until harvest. The knots of tension in the sun-blackened backs of farmers who knew that all their toil could be swept away in a moment, made futile by flood or drought or bandits or locusts.

From the time Lalu had learned to walk, she had worked: first, following her father's plow and dropping soy beans into the furrows; later, when her father planted the sweet potato vines, filling the holes with water, covering all but one leaf with soil; then, during the harvests, cleaning sweet potatoes for her mother to slice and dry, and picking peanuts off the vines. Even during the two years of foot-binding, when she could not walk, she had not been idle, learning to sew and spin and weave. And after her feet became little four-inch lotus, when she was no longer allowed to work in the fields, she had helped her mother at home. Except for the harvests. Then she and her mother joined the other women and girls, threshing wheat and millet, picking peanuts, and preparing sweet potatoes, turnips, cabbages, and other vegetables for storage. She had thought working as her father's laborer would be no harder. She had found she was wrong.

Her mother had tried to make unbinding Lalu's feet as easy as possible, loosening the bindings gradually, soaking, massaging, stuffing cotton between the toes so they could gradually expand outwards, but the toes had not flattened in time for spring planting. Chewing her lips to keep from crying, Lalu had carried heavy buckets of fertilizer into the fields, making her feet swell. Then, because her father had no stone roller to press the soil down so the young shoots would have solid earth for support, she had trampled the ground with her swollen feet. At night, when she took off the loosened bindings, the smell of decaying flesh had made her too ill to eat. But the ground for the peanut crop needed to be leveled and hardened; ridges had to be built up for planting the sweet potatoes; and the vegetable garden had to be laid out. Then the new seedlings had to be thinned and weeded; and always there was water to be carried up from the river. And when her mother, swollen with child again, neared her term, there were household chores as well, chores her parents said were not fitting for A Cai, a son.

Lalu now knew that her toes would never lie completely flat again, but callouses had formed; and though her walk was somewhat strange and rolling, she felt only pleasure in this her second year in the fields. She paid close attention when her father explained the proper way to fertilize a field or plant a sweet potato vine, feeling enormous pride as he entrusted her more and more with work that needed skillful, knowledgeable hands. There were even guilty moments when she was almost glad the wheat had failed, for she loved everything to do with farming: the preparation of the soil, the planting, the careful nurturing...

"Psssst."

Lalu jumped. A Cai leaped out from behind a grave mound and climbed onto the wheelbarrow, curling up behind the bundle of firewood.

"What?" Lalu began.

"I sneaked off and cut across the fields when Baba wasn't looking. Take me around behind the temple where he won't see me."

"You'd better hurry back before he misses you."

A Cai pouted. "I never get a chance to play with my friends."

Lalu tried to look stern, but his sweaty, dirt-streaked face and babyish pout made the corners of her mouth twitch. "Baba will be furious."

"You can make it all right with him, you always do."

She laughed, knowing her little brother had gotten the better of her again. "Okay, hang on tight!" she cried. And she raced down the hill in her strange, rolling lope, the wheelbarrow hurtling noisily over the bumps, her long, thick braid flying straight out behind.

Lalu, exhilarated from her run, burst through the door, panting. Her mother, face moist and red from the steaming kettles, broke off the folk song she was humming to A Da, the baby strapped on her back.

"Did I see A Cai behind the temple?" she asked.

"He's tired," Lalu defended.

Her mother fed the fire with gaoliang stalks. "But not too tired to play with his friends. You spoil him."

A Fa toddled in from the courtyard. He tugged at Lalu's pants. "Mama has a surprise for you."

Lalu swung her little brother up and hugged him. She pinched his legs which protruded from split pants. "Hmmm, you're getting fat, fat enough to eat," she said, taking a playful bite.

"Come see!" he demanded, kicking.

She set him down. "See what?"

THREE

"Over here, look."

He pulled her out into the courtyard and pointed to the wooden table set for two. "You're going to eat with Baba from now on. Mama said so."

Like all the other men, Lalu's father was fed first, before his wife and children, and with the better food. As a child, Lalu had asked why, and her mother had explained, "Men are the pillars of the family. We depend on them for our lives, so they must be fed well." Now she, Lalu, was to eat first too!

Her eyes brimmed with tears. It didn't matter that the farmers said her father was turning Heaven and earth upside down by allowing his daughter to work by his side. Or that their wives told her mother, "Your daughter's face is passable, but those big feet are laughable." Or that A Cai's friends called her a carp on herring feet, and her own friends avoided her. Her parents understood!

"What's wrong? Aren't you happy" A Fa demanded.

"Leave your sister alone," their mother said. She turned to Lalu. "Come inside, I have something to show you before your father gets home."

A Fa waddled ahead importantly. Their mother pulled a stool out from under the table and set A Fa on it.

"You stay here and keep the flies off the pickles and salt fish," she told him.

Lalu, dazed with pride and joy, followed her

mother inside. Her mother reached into the clothing box and took out a small, fitted under jacket, the kind women wore to flatten their breasts.

"I made this for you."

Lalu blushed. "I don't need it yet."

"You're fourteen, a woman. Look how your sweaty outer jacket clings to you. Do you want to be called a wanton?"

Lalu held the under jacket up against her. "It's too small."

"Try it on," her mother said.

"Now?"

"Now."

Lalu turned to face the wall. Her whole body afire with embarrassment, she unbuttoned her loose-fitting cotton jacket, slipped it off, and struggled into the tight-fitting bodice her mother had made.

"I can't breathe."

"Nonsense, it's perfect," her mother said, tugging it in place.

"How will I swing my hoe?"

Her mother sighed. "The villagers are right. We should have sold you."

"No, Mama. You don't mean that."

As though Lalu were a child again, her mother pulled Lalu's outer jacket over the bodice. "Don't you know I say that for your sake, not mine?" she scolded gently. "If we had sold you, we would have found you a good mistress, one not too far away, and you would be doing decent woman's work in a good household, not bitter labor."

"But I love working in the fields," Lalu protested.

"And when you became of age, your mistress would have found you a good husband, and you would have been free again. Now you're neither snake nor dragon. You are a woman, yet you work like a man, a laborer. Who will marry you?"

"I don't care. I'm happy, really I am."

"You're a woman. You should be growing sons, not vegetables."

"I will, just as soon as A Cai is old enough to really help."

"If it were only that easy," her mother said. "Have you forgotten the saying — A large footed woman tarries, for no one wants to marry her?"

"But you said you would rebind my feet," Lalu stammered.

"I will, but they're ruined. They'll never have the same perfect shape or be as small. Besides, it's not just your feet. You're doing what no woman in this village, this district, has done, and your name is on every gossip's tongue. What decent, modest woman will take you for a daughter-in-law now?"

FOUR

Five years' labor in the fields had given Lalu the experienced eyes of a skilled farmer and she knew as soon as she began spreading the sweet potatoes on the kitchen floor that Old Man Yang had cheated them. Three baskets of undersized and half-rotted sweet potatoes in exchange for a healthy, hard-working donkey! But, in the beginning of the third year of drought, with the mortgage still unpaid, and everything else of value either sold or stolen by bandits, there had been no other way to get the seed potatoes they needed for spring planting. Grimly, she began sorting them into two piles. The better ones for seed. The others to help eke out their diet of dry roots and watery gruel.

Outside, deep-toned drums throbbed like thunder, and Lalu knew without looking that the village leaders were, once again, carrying the Dragon King into the fields to show him the earth, parched and cracked from the angry sun. For two springs and summers they had watched helplessly as the river shriveled into a shallow stream and then a trickle, forcing them to dig deeper and deeper for water. Last year, when the wood buckets dipped into the riverbed began to fill with mud, the village leaders had carried the Dragon King into the fields to show him the stunted crops with deformed, twisted leaves. Men and boys with wreaths of coarse grass on their heads had followed, beating drums and bearing banners inscribed with prayers for rain. The Dragon King had sent no rain then. What made anyone think he would send rain now?

Lalu's stomach gnawed hungrily. She kneaded it, but it only grew more demanding. She picked up another sweet potato and examined it. It already had toothmarks from a rat. Two. If she took a bite, a small one, surely no one would know. Trancelike, she lifted the potato to her open mouth, but before she could bite into it, a drop of saliva fell on it, darkening the skin like blood. She hurled it to the floor. How could she even think of satisfying her own hunger when everyone else in her family was starving?

She rose and opened the door. Dry heat hit her with the force of a blow and she leaned weakly against the door post. The sun-faded strips of red and black New Year greetings crackled beneath her weight, crumbling into dust, and Lalu jerked straight, relieved her mother was not home to witness such a bad omen.

Her eyes adjusted to the glare, and she saw her

father, A Cai, and a few other farmers break off from the tail end of the procession returning to the temple. She knew she would not be permitted to join them, but perhaps she could get close enough to hear what they might say. Anything, rather than hold potatoes she could not eat. She banged the door shut and walked toward them.

Heat enveloped her like a thick winter quilt, and her feet scuffed up clouds of dust, clogging her nostrils, making her eyes smart. By the time she neared the temple, her hair and clothes were sticky with sweat. She thought of her mother's face when A Fa had suggested they water the fields by wringing their sweat-drenched clothes over the dying crops. At the time it had made Lalu giggle, but now, as she crouched down behind the temple wall, she did not even smile. The situation was too grave.

"We must go to the main river for water," she heard her father say.

"But that's over the mountain, half-a-day's journey away," Old Man Yang protested.

"It's the only way," her father insisted.

"Full of ideas aren't you?" the old man said.

"Yes, like winter wheat," someone chortled.

"And making a girl work like a man!"

The farmers, eager for something to laugh at, exploded in a roar.

"This time Nathoy is right. We cannot wait and hope any longer," someone interrupted.

FOUR

"We could try going to the main river," another voice grudgingly agreed.

"What about bandits?"

Lalu felt her sweat turn cold. Ever since she could remember, the village had been threatened by bandits, but since the drought, they had grown in numbers. The raids had been more frequent, and many of the bandits were former laborers who had lived and worked in the village. They knew what to look for and where to find it. And they were completely ruthless.

"Why would they attack us?" her father asked. "We'll be carrying nothing but our buckets."

"They might kidnap one of us for ransom," Old Man Yang suggested.

"Except for yourself, who has money?"

"When they discovered the Pans were too poor to pay a ransom for their father, they made the old man dig his own grave and lie in it. Then they bashed in his skull with the shovel."

"And when Shi was slow paying the ransom for his son, the bandits sliced off the boy's ear."

"It's the women and children I'm worried about. If they're left alone, who knows what we'll find when we return."

"We could take turns going. That way, there would always be men in the village."

"Just having men here is not enough. We must fight them," Lalu's father urged.

"Didn't you see what happened to Fat Wu?"

Everyone grew silent, for Fat Wu had leaped at a bandit's throat only to have his head severed in a single blow. The head had rolled into the gutter and down the street, knocking against sudden curves, splattering blood against courtyard walls until another bandit swooped on it and pierced it with a pole which he stabbed into the ground. The mouth had hung open and the big white teeth had gleamed ghostlike in the predawn darkness while his queue, matted with blood, swayed fitfully back and forth, a warning to anyone else foolish enough to resist.

Lalu's father broke the silence. "Fat Wu tried to fight them alone. We must organize into teams and patrol the streets and lanes."

"Wasn't it your idea to have soldiers come help us? They were worse than the bandits."

"The ones billeted with us ate everything we'd been able to save from the bandits."

"And I was afraid to leave my wife and daughters alone for even a minute the whole time they were here!"

"It's you and your mad schemes that have brought us all this bad luck!" Old Man Yang accused.

"Don't be so foolish," Lalu's father said.

"Look who dares call us foolish."

A shrill, inhuman scream, more terrible than anything Lalu had ever heard, ripped through the cluster of farmers like a crack of lightning, followed by a second, even more piercing, shriek and a rumble like thunder.

Lalu's head jerked up. A thick ochre haze was hurtling down the mountainside toward the village.

"Bandits!"

The farmers scattered, racing for their homes and hiding places. Lalu, her legs weak from months of hunger and cramped from squatting, limped after them. Grit from the swirling dust burned her eyes and rasped down her throat. She covered her face with her hands and struggled on blindly.

A glancing blow knocked her flat. Crawling to her knees, she gaped at the horse that blocked her path. It was the big, handsome stallion A Gao's father had purchased the year of the good harvest. How she had admired its strength and beauty! Now it shook and whimpered above her like a frightened colt. Where his big brown eyes had been were two bloody holes. A long needle, the kind used for making shoes, protruded from the left hole.

A Gao came up from behind and made a grab for the halter. The horse circled crazily, kicking and screaming.

"Help me," A Gao pleaded.

"How could you?" Lalu gasped.

"I had to," he cried, tears streaming down his face. "You know the bandits only take good ɯᴜɪˢes. This way he'll be blind, but he'll still be ours."

"You blundering idiot," A Gao's father panted as he tried to corner the animal. "I told you to tether him tightly."

He leaped up, snatched the needle and hurled it, dripping, onto the ground. The horse screamed and reared, his hooves beating a staccato tattoo against the courtyard walls. Lalu tried to roll away, but the bloodied pits held her in their grip.

"Come on," A Gao said, dragging Lalu to her feet. "The bandits are at the edge of town already."

FIVE

The bedlam inside the house restored Lalu to reality. Their mother, with the newest baby strapped to her back, was throwing sweet potatoes into a basket, half dragging A Da who clung wailing to the hem of her pants. A Fa trailed after them, alternately trying to get their mother's attention and chew on a potato their mother had dropped.

"There's no time to take the little ones away. You'll all have to hide in the fertilizer pit," her father ordered.

Lalu, frantically helping her mother scoop up the sweet potatoes, protested. "There's no room."

"What if the babies cry?" her mother added.

"You'll just have to make sure they don't," he said, hurrying them into the courtyard.

Flies buzzed furiously as A Cai helped their mother and the baby into the pit. He passed A Da and A Fa down to her, then Lalu and the basket of sweet potatoes. Finally, A Cai squeezed into the crowded hole. Manure and refuse swilled around

╌╌╌ ankles. Flies wriggled in and out of their ears and nostrils.

"It stinks," A Fa complained.

"That's what makes it a good hiding place," their mother said. "A Cai, you're too tall. Crouch down."

"There's no room."

"Everyone move back so A Cai can squat."

"He's sitting in shit," A Fa giggled.

"Shh or the bandits will steal you away forever."

"Lalu, rest your basket of potatoes on A Cai so you can carry A Da," their mother said.

"Wait, I'm losing my balance."

The basket slipped and the potatoes slid and plopped into the murky mess. The flies nearest the bottom rose in noisy spirals, causing the ones above to whir and thrum against the closely huddled bodies.

"I told you to wait," A Cai snapped.

A Fa began to cry. "That's the only basket we brought. What will we eat?"

"Never mind," their mother soothed. "We'll fish them out and wash them off."

"I won't eat shit," A Fa sobbed.

A Da started to cry.

"Quiet," their mother commanded in a hoarse whisper. "You'll start the baby crying, and believe me, if the bandits find us, you won't need to worry about eating."

"But I'm hungry," A Fa whined.

"Me too," A Da lisped between wails.

FIVE

"Listen. If you promise to stop crying, I'll bring the other basket," Lalu said.

The children quieted immediately.

"There's no time," their mother said. "I can hear the bandits chopping in doors already."

The children began to snivel.

"I'll go," A Cai sighed, trying to raise himself.

"You're wedged in," Lalu said, hoisting herself up and out of the pit. She leaned over. "Remember, you must be quiet or I won't come back."

She ran across the courtyard and into the house. Her father was putting the last potatoes into a basket. "What are you doing?"

"The potatoes we had fell into the manure," Lalu said breathlessly. The boisterous clamor outside grew louder. She reached for the basket. "Here, I'll take these back."

"No, we must have something to give the bandits or they'll tear the place apart."

"The children are crying. Let me take a few to quiet them."

Her father scooped up two handfuls and threw them into the apron of Lalu's jacket. She turned to run. Bang! The door shook, showering dust and bits of thatch onto Lalu and her father.

"Open up!" a voice roared above the clatter of hoofbeats, splintering wood, and terrified screaming.

"Quick, behind the stove," her father said.

Lalu scrambled up, the potatoes dropping and

_____g across the floor as she squeezed into the narrow crevice. Through a crack, she saw the door burst open and a bandit stride in, kicking aside the splintered crossbar.

"What are you hiding?" he demanded.

"Nothing. See, I've gathered some sweet potatoes for you," Lalu's father said, thrusting the basket toward him.

The bandit's knife slashed the basket from his hands and potatoes spilled all across the floor. "You dare insult me with one basket!"

"It's all we have left."

"Liar!"

Lalu shrank against the wall as the bandit knocked her father aside. Breaking pots, smashing crockery, and upsetting baskets, he strode across the trail of manure to the back of the stove where she hid.

Rough hands yanked Lalu out and threw her down.

Her father bent to help her. "That's my daughter."

The bandit kicked her father across the room. "I know," he leered, jerking Lalu off the floor.

She kicked and drummed her fists against him, but he overpowered her easily, trapping her legs between his and pinning her arms against his side, hugging her to him. She sank her teeth into his arm. He laughed and twisted his arm free, then snapped her jaws between his fingers and forced her to face him. She stared defiantly, screwing up her nose at his stale garlic breath.

His small, sharp eyes glittered. "Don't recognize me, do you?"

The voice was disturbingly familiar. She looked more closely at the swarthy face that loomed above her. Black eyes and long nose were embedded in greasy, pockmarked skin. Stiff black hairs formed a scraggly, off-kilter mustache and beard that hid twisted, misshapen lips. Shave his forehead, comb the hair into a neat queue, take away the mustache and beard, and he would look just like her father's old laborer, the one who had worked for them the year of the winter wheat.

"Chen," she breathed.

"Smart as well as fierce!" he roared.

Her father rose. "Let her go!" he commanded.

"Careful how you speak to me, I'm not your laborer anymore."

Her father stepped forward, raising clenched fists.

"Let's not have any foolish show of bravery," Chen sneered. "A single whistle and my men will come pouring through that door and smash you to pulp, just like this."

Dragging Lalu with him, he swiftly stamped the sweet potatoes until the floor was caked with rusty red smears.

Angry tears spurted down Lalu's cheeks. "How

can you, a farmer, do such a terrible thing?" she cried.

"Quite easily," he said, his voice as cold and sharp as the edge of the knife he held. "I never was a farmer. Only a hired laborer. Someone to get rid of when times are bad. But now I'm a bandit leader. Boss of fifty men."

Out of the corner of her eye, Lalu saw her father reaching stealthily for the sickle. At the same instant, Chen knocked it out of reach.

"You just don't understand, do you? A single whistle. A shout. And your wife and children will be worse than dead. Remember, I know your hiding places." He kicked meaningfully at the closest glob of manure. "Even if I didn't, your little fox has left a trail a blind man can follow."

Lalu's father sank to his knees. "Please, I beg you. Let her go."

"Don't worry, I'll pay you for this little fox."

Lalu gasped.

"She's not for sale," her father said. But his sagging shoulders betrayed defeat.

Lalu stiffened, refusing to give in as easily. She had persuaded her father to allow her to work in the fields, she would persuade Chen not to take her.

"Think of your wife and children," she said.

Chen's knife blade grazed Lalu's neck as he snapped her head back with a yank of her braid. "Did your father think of them when he took away my livelihood?"

FIVE

Lalu bit her lip. She shouldn't have mentioned his family, but it was too late to back down. "There are other farmers to work for."

"Not since the drought."

"We've been hungry too. The younger children are covered with sores and their stomachs are bloated like dead fish."

"But you're alive. My wife and children are dead. From starvation."

"I didn't know."

"Of course not," Chen lashed. "Who cares about a common laborer?"

He burst into ugly laughter, splattering Lalu with a spray of saliva. "Do you really think a sentimental fool can be a bandit chief? When the drought came, I joined the bandits and led a raid on my own village. Sold my children and gave my wife to the rest of the men to use. That's why they made me chief."

He held Lalu at arm's length, examining her like a farmer about to purchase livestock. "Pretty face. Nice white teeth and shiny hair. But such big feet! The brothels in Shanghai like bound feet and smooth white skin. You are burned black." He smiled lasciviously. "Of course, my men wouldn't care. You could be a common wife to them. My wife lasted a week. But you're tough. I'm sure you'd last at least a month." He nuzzled his scratchy beard against her cheek. "Then again, maybe I'll keep you for myself."

Lalu heard her father groan. She gritted her teeth, determined not to show her fear.

Chen raised his head and shouted. "Zhuo."

A short, stocky bandit filled the gaping hole where the door had been.

"Bring me some seed."

Almost immediately, Zhuo returned with two small bags no larger than Lalu's fists. Chen took the bags. "Round up the men and bring me my horse," he ordered.

He threw a bag in front of Lalu's father. It burst, scattering soybeans.

Lalu stared at her father, willing him not to pick them up. He reached out, hesitated, then looked up at Lalu, his eyes pleading for understanding. She twisted her face away, a sob strangling in her throat. Behind her, she heard him snatch the bag and scoop up the spilled seed.

"Two bags," her father begged. "She's worth two bags of seed."

Laughing scornfully, Chen tossed the other bag down, flung Lalu over his shoulder like a side of pork, and stalked out the door.

SIX

The bandits rode silently, in single file, sometimes allowing the horses to walk, other times
breaking into a trot, and occasionally, for no
apparent reason, beating the horses into a gallop.
Lalu's eyes smarted and teared from the gritty,
yellow gray dust that swirled around them.
Squeezed between Chen and the pommel of the
wooden saddle, her pants rubbed like sandstone
between her legs where the soft inner flesh of her
thighs had scraped raw from the long ride. She
strained forward, her collar chafing painfully where
Chen's knife had grazed her neck. A long, low
branch whipped against her. The horse stumbled
and a bolt of fire shot up Lalu's spine. She bit her
lip, tasting blood.

Long after she thought she could not bear the
torment another moment, they halted. Chen dismounted and Lalu sagged with relief. Behind her,
she heard the other bandits dismount, the sounds of
snapping branches and brush being dragged.

The arrogance with which they left her mounted and free to kick her horse into a gallop depressed Lalu more than if she had been tied and heavily guarded, for it confirmed what she already knew. Escape was hopeless. Earlier, she had tried to keep track of landmarks. While there was still some light and they were covering familiar ground, she had been able to tag unusual rock formations, trees, and mountains. But since they had entered strange territory and dusk had deepened into night, it had become impossible. Besides, even if she did somehow elude her captors and find her way home, her parents would not dare take her back. She had not been kidnapped. She had been sold. She belonged to Chen.

A flash of light followed by a burst of flames lit the darkness and Lalu saw the broken columns of a ruined temple. In the distance she saw another fire flare. Seconds later, a third fire sparked on the horizon. Was this some strange bandit ritual of thanksgiving? Then where was their sacrifice?

She trembled as Chen and his men let out a roar and rushed toward her, their faces ghostly pale in the flickering light. She kicked the horse. It reared, and she felt herself tossed into the darkness.

Oblivion, as sweetly warm and comforting as her mother's arms, embraced Lalu. Harsh shouts pricked the edges of her consciousness. Unwilling to give up the peace that had spread like liquid warmth through her tortured limbs, Lalu resisted until stinging slaps and punches pried her eyes open.

She expected a ring of faces. But there was only one. Chen's. The other men were already mounted, restless, eager to leave. Lalu felt foolish relief. The bandits had been rushing for their horses, not for her. The fires were not a religious rite, but beacons to guide them.

"You stupid whore, you could have damaged my horse," Chen snapped, flinging Lalu over the saddle. "If my men didn't need a woman, I'd kill you."

So he had already decided to give her to his men, Lalu thought dully. What was it he had said? "You could be a common wife to them. My wife lasted a week. But you're tough. I'm sure you'd last at least a month." What did he mean?

Dimly she remembered a night as a child when she had wakened to strange, muffled sounds from her parents' room. Frightened, she had leaped out of bed and run to them.

From the doorway, she saw the darkness of her father's larger bulk heave, panting, against her mother, who, flattened against the bed, moaned, then issued the short, sharp cry of a wounded bird.

Lalu scrambled up onto the bed, beating her fists against her father, sobbing, "Leave Mama alone."

Her mother grabbed Lalu's arms and ordered her back to her own bed.

"But he was hurting you," Lalu cried.

Her mother had pushed her away. "You're too young to understand."

Now, years later, she still did not really understand. Vaguely she realized that what her parents did at night was not unlike the coupling that occurred between animals. No one talked about it directly, but from the accumulated knowledge gleaned from years of whispers, she sensed it was something that was all right if it happened between husband and wife, shameful and terrible if the man and woman were not married.

Nevertheless, it happened. In places called brothels. During bandit raids. Sometimes with soldiers quartered in the village. And once, she had heard her mother and some of her friends whispering about a neighbor who had suddenly vanished because she had "disgraced" herself.

Lalu blushed hotly, remembering the time she had studied two dogs locked together. The male had mounted the female. She had quivered dreadfully, but she had not died. Did Chen's wife die because there were fifty men, not one? Then how did women in the brothels survive? Surely they coupled with more than that. Was there something bandits did that made it worse?

After Pan's wife was used by a bandit, she had hung herself. Everyone agreed she had done the proper thing, and her husband had built a paifang to commemorate her courage and virtue. Should she try to kill herself? Was that what Chen's wife had done? Then why had she waited a week? And why did Chen think she, Lalu, would last a month?

She knew it was important for her to sort it all out and try to make sense of it. But her head throbbed from the constant jolting. Her throat demanded water. And her body, exhausted beyond endurance, cried for sleep. Strange night noises were an added distraction. She cocked her ear. Was a wild animal crashing through the undergrowth? Or more than one? From the amount of noise, it sounded like a pack. She glanced up at Chen. It was too dark to see much more than shadow, but he seemed unconcerned, letting the tired horses make their own pace.

Suddenly, there was a rush of dark shadows and excited shouts as bandits greeted cohorts left behind to light the beacons. Lalu clutched the pommel.

"What took so long?"

"We thought the devil had snared you."

"So, you captured a goddess."

"More like a whore!"

The men's voices blared like thunder claps in the quiet of the night. Chen shouted above the hubub. "Silence until we reach camp!"

Immediately, the men stopped their excited talk and only the rhythmic drumming of hoofbeats, the chatter of cicadas, and the hum of an occasional mosquito broke the silence as they headed toward the third beacon.

Lalu had supposed the third fire marked the camp, but it did not. Again, there was a burst of excitement as the bandits greeted each other, and again, Chen ordered the men silent. She was amazed at the way the bandits obeyed him. Obviously his command was absolute. If he decided to take her for himself, surely the men would not dare contradict or disobey. Wouldn't that be better than being thrown like a piece of meat to a pack of starving beasts? And if Chen kept her for himself, wouldn't they be husband and wife?

Her stomach rebelled at the thought of such an ugly old man for a groom. But hadn't her mother warned her that no decent family would take her for a daughter-in-law? That was why, at eighteen, when all her friends were already mothers, she remained unmarried. Unwanted. Besides, even good matches did not guarantee good husbands. Marriage brokers often lied, and everyone knew of girls who thought the red chair was carrying them to rich households with young, handsome husbands only to find they had been cheated.

How would Chen treat her? The winter he had lived with them as her father's laborer, he had never come back from market without a sweetmeat for her and her brother. In the evenings, he had often whittled little toy animals for them or woven delicate balls out of straw, all the time holding them spellbound with marvelous stories of mighty warriors and vengeful ghosts. But he had changed. Sold his own children and caused his wife's death. Still, her mother said if a woman were clever, she could persuade a man to do her will. Could she win Chen over, entice him to be kind?

Lalu swallowed hard and leaned back, soft and cuddly, against Chen. Tilting her face up, she whispered. "Let me be yours."

His hand slid under her jacket, deftly unhooking the buttons on her tight inner bodice. He fondled her breasts. Instinctively, she stiffened. Desperately, she tried to relax. Instead, she felt a rush of goosebumps and a burning redness sweep over her. She forced her body, however unyielding, to remain pressed against him.

Chen twisted her nipple cruelly. "I'm not so easily fooled, Little Sister," he said, withdrawing his hand.

Tears of humiliation coursed down Lalu's cheeks. "I'm a farmer, not a wanton," she wanted to cry. "Then act like a farmer," a voice inside her said. When bandits, insects, disease, rain, or drought wiped out a crop, a farmer did not crumple and cry like a disappointed child, he began the whole process of fertilizing, plowing, and reseeding once again. Even now, with the drought into its third year, the farmers in her village remained undefeated, searching for ways to save their land and their families. Could she do any less? The seed from her sale would save her father's land and her mother and brothers from starvation. Now she had to save herself.

She would find a way to escape. Not back to her village, she knew she could never go home again, but to a large town or city where the bandits would never find her.

SEVEN

Lalu wakened feeling stiff and sore. She stretched. Her arms and legs hit sharp edges. Puzzled, she opened her eyes. She was wedged in by bags, boxes, baskets, and trunks. She reached out to push them aside, then froze as events from the day before crowded in on her: the raid, her sale, her failure to please Chen, their noisy arrival in camp, Chen's orders to dump her with the rest of the booty in this long, windowless room.

She remembered fighting to stay awake as the narrow room filled with fierce-looking camp dogs and men pushing and shoving and all talking at once. The barking and shouting giving way to sounds of eating. And, finally, the agonizing fragrance of the bandits' dinner forcing her to give in to her exhaustion as a means of escape. How long had she slept? Was she alone? Cautiously, Lalu raised herself so she could see beyond the boxes and trunks that surrounded her.

Through a curtain of sickeningly sweet smoke,

she sighted half-naked men stretched in pairs on long sleeping platforms on either side of her. They lay facing each other. Beneath each pair, she saw a small, lighted peanut oil lamp, partly covered with a paper shade. Over the flame, each man held a long, slender wooden pipe with a softly spluttering mass in the bowl. As the dark brown lumps became smaller, the smokers reshaped them into cones and resumed smoking. Lalu's pulse quickened. Concentrating on their pipes, the bandits took no more notice of her than they did of the dogs gnawing on leftover bones. This was her chance to escape.

Her eyes searched the smoke-blackened walls for a door, finding one behind her, to the left, not more than five feet away. Unguarded. She started to climb over the trunks and boxes.

A glitter of gold stopped her. She leaned down to grab it, but it was only a character painted on a red leather trunk. Disappointed, she pushed aside a basket of turnips and squeezed between two boxes. Midway she twisted back to stare at the painted gold. Though she could not read, she knew this pair of characters. Everyone did. Double happiness, the characters used for weddings. This was a wedding trunk, and a wedding trunk meant jewelry, jewelry she needed to exchange for food or pawn for cash.

Lalu crouched beside the trunk. Padlocked. In one swift motion, she removed the brass earring from her left lobe, straightened it, and picked at the clasp. The smoke and shaded lamps made it hard to see clearly, and she fumbled. The lock slipped in her sweaty palms. She wiped her hands dry on her jacket and probed deeper. The earring stuck inside the clasp. She pulled. It would not yield. She twisted it and pulled again, but the end of the straightened earring was too short and thin for her to get a proper grip. Head throbbing and mouth dry, she leaned down, gripped the sliver of wire with her teeth, and pulled.

The wire yanked free, springing the lock. At the same time, the force threw Lalu against a basket which tumbled, scattering peanuts with a loud, dry rustle. The bandits did not look up from their pipes, but the dogs trotted over and sniffed at the peanuts and Lalu. Scarcely daring to breathe, she waited for the dogs to go back to their bones, then pried open the lid.

The trunk was filled with silks and satins. A wealthy bride. She felt around the sides and all along the bottom for jewelry. Nothing. Was she wasting precious time searching for what might not be there? No. She must find jewelry. If not in this trunk, then in another, for without it, she would be helpless, the prey of charletans as evil as these bandits.

Lalu plunged back into the jumble of jackets, skirts, and trousers, tossing out garment after garment until the trunk gaped empty. Nothing. Dizzy with disappointment, she fell back. Something sharp pricked through her thin cotton pants. She pulled it out tiredly and threw it into the empty trunk. It winked up at her. Gold! A gold earring.

She snatched it up and felt around the mess of clothing for its mate. Wildly hurling garments back into the trunk, her fingers knocked against something cold and round. A jade bangle. A silver hairpin. The mate for the gold earring. And three jade buttons. Shaking with relief, Lalu used the earrings and hairpin to hook the bangle and buttons to the wide inside waistband of her pants. She pulled her jacket down over her cache, took one last glance at the bandits, and headed for the door.

The weakness in her legs and the hollow cramping in her stomach reminded Lalu she had not eaten since the bowl of thin gruel at breakfast the day before. She pushed the thought from her mind. She must leave while she still had the chance. Later, when she was safe, she would eat. She edged forward, leaning against the trunks and boxes, grateful for their support. A haze of black and red dots thickened and came together in a solid sheet of black. She shook her head impatiently. For a moment, the darkness faded. Then again it deepened. Tears of frustration pricked Lalu's eyelids. She must eat now.

Sinking to the floor, she searched for some leftover she could grab without upsetting the dogs. As her fingers touched the rim of a bowl, her mouth flooded with saliva. She lifted the bowl to her lips and shoveled in scraps of pork and congealed millet, barely chewing before she swallowed and gulped some more.

Suddenly, the bowl was wrenched from her grasp. She thought at first that the hideous beast who had seized it was a dog, but bony talons clutched the bowl. Could the long tangled hair and matted beard be covering a man? Repelled yet unable to move, she watched the creature lick the bowl clean and hobble away on all fours, dragging a chain and iron weight which left a deep groove in the dirt floor.

"How do you like our bear?"

Lalu whirled around. A small, slightly built man with hollow eyes and sunken cheeks dropped down lightly from the sleeping platform beside her. How long had he been watching? Did he guess she was heading for the door and escape?

He came closer. She must distract him. Talk.

"It's not a bear, it's a man," she said, trying to keep her voice low and steady.

"Once, maybe, but he's been our bear for years. Keeps us entertained with his dancing and tricks during the long winter months when we're snowed in. Of course, we won't need him now that we've got you."

Lalu forced a laugh. "Me?"

"We've drawn lots to see who will get you first. Worst luck I'm forty-three." He lunged and grabbed her to him. "Unless..."

The door burst open. "Soldiers!" the man silhouetted in the doorway shouted. In the rush of stampeding bandits, Lalu found herself seized by a medium-sized, middle-aged man with a long, droopy gray mustache. She dug her heels into the dirt.

"Let me go," she begged.

He hoisted her off the floor. "Believe me, you're better off with us than the soldiers," he said.

Wedged tightly between the bandit who held her and the pommel of the saddle, Lalu listened to the scouts' report. There were soldiers everywhere, they said. And those sons of turtles looked as though they intended to stay.

"This fit of housecleaning won't last. It never does," Chen said.

"What do we do until they leave?" his second-in-command asked.

"Gao and Ma have camps near here. We can take refuge with them," Chen said.

"Wu's camp is not too far either," a tall, thin man added.

"Take some men with you and go see what the situation is with them," Chen ordered. He pointed to a dense thicket about half a li away. "We'll wait for you there."

The trees sheltered them from the glare of the hot afternoon sun, but not from the mosquitoes and horseflies. The horses, nostrils quivering, tossed their heads and flicked their tails, but their necks, legs, and bellies were soon covered with bites. Lalu felt welts rising wherever her skin was exposed. She slapped and scratched until her fingers became sticky with blood, but the itching and irritating buzzing did not stop.

She studied the bandits, wondering if she could crawl away unnoticed. Splotches of blood and flattened insects flecked their backs and faces which glistened with huge blisters of sweat. They swore and slapped themselves angrily.

"A fire would get rid of those blood suckers."

"And bring the soldiers down on us like maggots."

"If they're not deaf, you ignorant bastard, they can hear the horses stamping and snorting."

"But you can see smoke farther away."

"They might think the smoke is from a soldier camp."

"And what do we do if they come? Serve hot wine?"

Chen turned to the bandit who had seized Lalu when the soldiers came. "Ding, build a fire."

"It's too hot," Ding grumbled.

Lalu jumped to her feet. She would quiet Ding's suspicions by gathering brush from nearby, then go farther and farther until she was safely hidden in the forest. "I'll help," she said.

Chen kicked her to the ground. "And fly the coop and spoil our fun?"

The men laughed.

A heavy-set man threw himself on top of her. "How about a taste of swan's meat?" he sneered, ripping the buttons off her jacket.

Lalu struggled, but against his bulk she was helpless. The sharp points from the earrings hidden in her waistband dug into her belly and she felt a strange hardness swell and press against her thigh.

"Get off," she gasped.

"And lose the chance to eat a virgin?" he grinned, his calloused fingers tearing at her flesh.

"Hey, Zhuo, get off her. My number is before yours!" Ding protested.

"Mine too!" another bandit added.

The two men fell on Zhuo, pulling him off Lalu.

"Zhu drew the lowest number, he goes first," Ding said.

"He's with the scouts," Zhuo protested. "I say we draw lots again."

"And lose my low number? Never." Ding laughed scornfully. "You're just afraid that by the time you get her she'll be like a mushy old sweet potato, too much for someone like you with testicles the size of a gnat."

Zhuo sprang to his feet and lunged at Ding. "I'll tear your tongue out, you son of a whore."

Chen jumped between them. "Get the fire

going before the horses bleed to death," he snapped. "The lottery stands as it is."

The scouts returned with the first evening star. Even before they dismounted, Lalu knew from their faces that the situation was desperate. She felt a small flutter of hope. If the news was bad for the bandits, it might be good for her.

"Our rice is cooked," Zhu reported. "Wu's camp is deserted. Ma is taking his men up into Mongolia. And Gao's band, poor bastards, must have been taken by surprise. They're all dead."

"We'll hole up in Shanghai," Chen decided.

"With soldiers crawling all over, we can't make any raids. How will we eat?" his second-in-command asked.

"We'll sell the whore." Without pausing for discussion or argument, Chen continued, "There'll be less chance of getting caught if we travel in smaller groups." Swiftly, he selected four bandits to act as leaders and began dividing the men among them.

"Come here, Little Sister," Ding hissed.

Lalu did not move.

"Come here," Ding repeated more urgently. He edged closer. "Ride with me. I can help you."

Lalu tightened her grip on her torn jacket. "Like you did when you brought me here?"

"You have to trust me. It will be days before we reach Shanghai and you will need my help. Like you did with Zhuo just now."

He had helped her when Zhuo jumped her, Lalu admitted. And later, waiting for the scouts to return, he had stayed close, watching. She had thought he had been watching to see she did not escape. Now she wondered.

"The whore will ride with me," Chen said.

Ding jerked Lalu toward him. "Save yourself the discomfort," he said obsequiously. "I'll make sure our little bag of gold doesn't get lost."

"Or damaged!" Chen warned, laughing.

"Or damaged," Ding agreed, dragging Lalu to the tree where his horse waited.

EIGHT

They traveled hard, following narrow deer
paths that ran along ridges and sides of mountains,
making endless ascents and descents to avoid villages, military forts, and camps, stopping only when
the horses were too exhausted to go any further.
Then, while the horses grazed, the bandits, edgy,
fatigued, and chronically hungry, vented their
frustrations by baiting Lalu. But when they became rough or tried to force themselves on her,
Ding held them at bay, reminding them that their
futures depended on Lalu and the price she fetched.

It was also Ding who found a scrap of coarse
netting to protect her from the mosquitoes, and
Ding who made sure she got a portion of any food
they forced from frightened woodcutters and
farmers in isolated hamlets. Ding. A friend who
cared about her as a person? Or an enemy looking
out for his own interests, protecting her like a
landlord protects his property? She had to find out.

Riding night and day, with sleep coming in

stolen snatches, Lalu lost track of time, and she worried that they would reach Shanghai before she had a chance to speak to Ding without fear of being heard. But finally, on a scorching hot afternoon, as they were ascending a narrow valley choked with sword grass, thorny bushes, and vines, Ding's horse, doubly burdened, fell behind.

Lalu waited impatiently for the distance between them and the rest of the group to widen. Then, relieved and nervous that the opportunity to talk had come at last, she blurted, "Why did you force me to come with you when I might have escaped?"

"Have there never been soldiers in your village?" Ding asked.

"Yes."

"Then you know why I did not leave you."

Lalu thought of the soldiers who had come to their village. She had been a child, too young to remember how they had behaved, but she remembered the farmers' resentful comments to her father just before the bandit raid and Ding's accusing, "You're better off with us." Were soldiers really as bad as bandits? Or, as Ding claimed, worse?

Lalu shook her head. Better or worse, the soldiers were not important. What was important was that Ding had believed he was helping her to escape from them. Would he help her escape now?

"I could have hidden from the soldiers and found

my way to a village or city," she suggested cautiously.

"A girl like yourself does not have one chance in ten thousand of traveling alone safely. But say you had made it to a village or city without being kidnapped or raped or killed, what would you have done then?" Ding asked, imitating Lalu's careful phrasing.

"I would have found work."

"Doing what?"

What kind of work could she do? No one would hire her as a farm laborer, but her fingers, used to a hoe, no longer held a needle with ease, and she had never learned to cook. What else was there? Babies. She loved caring for her brothers, and she was good with them, able to tease a smile from them when no one else could.

"A nursemaid. I could have been a nursemaid for a wealthy family."

"And before you knew what was happening, you would have found yourself with life inside you from the master or one of the men servants."

Lalu flushed. "My parents gave me better home teaching than that."

"It's not a matter of home teaching," Ding said patiently. "You would have had no more choice than I or any of the others here had a choice to become bandits. And when you were discovered with child, it would have been you who were blamed and thrown out into the street. Then what would you have done?"

Lalu ignored his question. "What do you mean you had no choice in becoming a bandit?" she asked, puzzled. "You're educated. I can tell by the way you speak. And your manners. You're cultured, refined. Different from the others. From me."

He hesitated. "I was a magistrate," he said.

Again he paused, and when he spoke at last, his voice was heavy with barely controlled anger and grief. "A sudden change in the political situation forced me to flee for my life. I sent my wife and children back to her parents for safety and joined the bandits to seek revenge."

A magistrate! Lalu twisted round to face him. "Does Chen know?"

"Of course."

"Isn't he afraid of what you might do when you go back to being a magistrate?"

Ding laughed mirthlessly. "Water once spilled cannot be gathered again."

"But what about after you've had your revenge?" Lalu persisted.

"You think I'm different from the other bandits," Ding said harshly. "I'm not. Chen. Zhuo. Zhu. We're all the same. Outlaws. And none of us will ever be anything else."

His voice softened. "Lalu, I know your mother and father did not raise you to be sold to a house of leisure, just as my parents did not raise me to be a bandit, but we have no choice except to follow the paths Heaven has allotted us."

Lalu, facing forward again, said nothing. But as they climbed up the steep trail to the ridge where Chen and the others waited, she vowed she would never accept the path Ding claimed Heaven had assigned her.

She waited until darkness fell on the sleeping camp. Then, hoping the bandits' snores and the horses' restless stomping and whinnying would smother the crunch of broken rocks beneath her feet, Lalu edged past the two scouts keeping watch. Slowly and carefully, she worked her way back to the crest of the narrow valley the horses had climbed with such difficulty only a few hours before. By the time she reached it, the moon had risen, coating the dry, dusty grasses and bushes with a pearl white sheen. She closed her eyes briefly, murmured a prayer to Guanyin, the Merciful One, and began her descent.

The trail was steeper, more treacherous than she remembered. Half walking, half crawling, she clutched the jewelry hidden in her waistband with one hand and reached out the other to steady herself. Thorns ripped her palm. Stifling a cry, she jerked back, slipped, and fell.

Sharp bits of gravel pierced Lalu's thin cotton

pants. Dust and dirt filled her mouth, nostrils, and eyes, making her choke as she hurtled down the sheer slope. She grabbed blindly at a bush, catching twigs which snapped beneath her weight. Skin tore off the sides of her hands, her legs. She felt an ankle lodge in a rut and dug in, reaching wildly for a nearby boulder. The effort pulled her arms half out of their sockets, flinging her sideways, knocking her head against a huge rock face, wedging her right shoulder and hip in a crevice.

The blow stunned Lalu. She lay still, her breathing ragged and shallow. Gradually, the darkness receded and the pain of torn muscles and bruised flesh sharpened. There was the sound of muffled voices.

High above her, spread out around the rim of the valley, pitch pine torches flickered like fallen stars, signaling a search. She leaned back. Solid rock gave way to black emptiness, and she fell again, landing in soft, stinking mire.

She had fallen into a cave, she realized. Was it a lair? Stories she had heard of children carried off by tigers pulled her upright. Hands stretched out before her, she staggered toward the moonlit crack through which she had fallen. Fingers touched wall. Wincing, Lalu leaned her weight against her stinging palms, using the wall for guidance and support as she blundered toward the sliver of light.

Small, soft bodies wriggled beneath her hand, and she heard a curious gnashing like the grinding of hundreds of tiny teeth. Clamping her jaws together to keep from screaming, Lalu crouched low. Her body crawled with gooseflesh and she gagged as the nauseating odor of dung mingled with the stink of fear. Ghostly wings brushed her face and neck. Spirits? Then what were the creatures clustered on the walls?

Through the fissure, moonlight beckoned, promising release from this hideous trap. Lalu dragged herself toward it. Chills racked her sweat-soaked, fiery body, impeding her progress. Then, all at once, the crack of light vanished in a rush of flapping wings, and she found herself trapped in total darkness. Sobbing uncontrollably, she sank defeated onto the muck-covered cave floor.

Just as suddenly as the splinter of light had vanished, it reappeared, with a bat silhouetted against the pale white beam. A bat, symbol of good luck. A sign from the gods? Again wings whirred past Lalu, blocking the opening. Bats. She was in a bat cave!

Relief swept over Lalu in a wash of giggles. She pictured her brothers' faces as she told them the story. How they would laugh! Except, of course, they would never hear her tell the story. "You must be quiet or I won't come back," she had told them. Did they think she had disappeared because of them? Or had her father told them that he had sold her for seed?

"The bitch has got to be around here some-where."

Lalu flinched as though she had been slapped. How could the bandits have come so close so quickly? Her eyes riveted on the only opening through which they could come, she backed crablike into the farthest recesses of the cave. Her limbs, cut, bruised, scratched, and sore from the long hours on horseback and her recent tumble, screamed protest, but she dared not stop. Trembling, slipping, straining, she fell onto her knees and crawled until she hit solid rock. There, huddled against the unresisting boulders, she hugged her soiled knees to her chest and whispered, "The bandits can search for days and never find me here."

Like a Buddhist nun repeating her beads, she said the same sentence over and over. At last, mesmerized by her own whisperings, her tightly clasped arms relaxed their hold, and she collapsed into exhausted slumber.

A piercing, high-pitched squeaking and the furious flapping of wings wakened Lalu. She rubbed her eyes. While she had slept, the sliver of moonlight in the cave opening had turned into a golden beam. And then she realized the golden beam was not sunlight, but a pitch pine torch.

Unable to move, she stared as the flames moved

EIGHT

closer until the light shone above her, blinding, and she heard Ding say, "Don't you understand, you cannot escape your fate?"

NINE

The rickshaw puller stopped abruptly, throwing Chen and Lalu forward. "House of Heavenly Pleasure," he called.

Lalu climbed out onto the hot, dusty street in front of a massive wall the height of two men. She gazed up at the broken glass embedded into the wall's rim. Was it there to keep out thieves or to prevent escapes?

"Come on, come on, stop gawking like a country bumpkin," Chen said, herding Lalu toward the gatekeeper's house.

The gatekeeper's stare made Lalu as uncomfortable as the garish purple jacket, apricot pants, and thick layers of makeup which Chen had insisted she wear.

"A new pullet ready for plucking," Chen said.

The gatekeeper grinned. He opened a small side door. "The Madam will be pleased with this one."

The sight of wide green lawns dotted with rock

gardens, lotus ponds surrounded by graceful weeping willows, and a spectacular main house with carved wooden railings, vermillion columns, and green-glazed roof gave Lalu no pleasure. She knew Ding was pleased that he had persuaded Chen to bring her here, for he had told her in one last conspiritorial whisper, "I know from my days as a magistrate that this house serves only rich, famous, refined gentlemen. Do as you are told, try to please, and you are bound to be bought out soon and installed as a concubine or perhaps even a secondary wife in some wealthy household." But she had her own plan, one that depended on her sale price being kept as low as possible.

Doubling over as though from pain, Lalu felt under her jacket, seeking reassurance from the bulge of jewelry hidden in her waistband. Against the magnificence of the House of Heavenly Pleasure, it seemed abysmally insufficient to carry out her scheme.

"Hurry up," Chen said.

Lalu's hands dropped from waist to feet. "These shoes are too small."

Chen grabbed Lalu's collar and twisted.

"You're creasing my jacket," Lalu said.

He glared down at her. "Don't rub the scales under a dragon's neck," he warned, pushing her past the spirit gate. "One false move and you'll wish you had never been born."

An arrogant housemaid ushered them past

growling guard dogs into a cool, shadowy ante-room. The wood paneled walls, latticed ceiling, painted glass lanterns, and thickly carpeted floor confirmed Lalu's worst fears. Drained of hope, she allowed Chen to propel her behind a heavily carved blackwood chair.

"Now remember," Chen instructed. "When you smile, don't expose your teeth. If the Madam asks you to walk, take small, mincing steps so she won't notice your big feet. If she offers us food, don't wolf it down, take delicate little nibbles."

A middle-aged woman, tall and elegantly dressed, emerged from behind a double panel of embroidered silk. "Is the girl such an ignorant peasant that she needs last minute coaching?" she asked.

"No, no, of course not," Chen said, pivoting to face her and bow.

The Madam turned to Lalu. "Come out from behind the chair so I can see you."

Encouraged by the woman's warm smile, Lalu walked out boldly.

"Small steps," Chen hissed.

"Your feet are not bound," the Madam said. "Why?"

"I was..."

Chen interrupted. "I assure you, they have been bound and can easily be bound again." Under the Madam's icy stare, his voice trailed off weakly.

"I asked the girl."

"I was needed in the fields," Lalu explained.

The Madam walked over to the round lacquer table between the two blackwood chairs. She dipped a square of cloth in a bowl of scented water. Her long tapered fingers wrung out the cloth, and she wiped Lalu's face free of rouge, dye, and rice powder while Chen hovered nervously.

"The girl looks half starved."

"We're from the North where we've been suffering famine from a bad drought," Chen said quickly. "To be very honest, the girl's parents, my brother and his wife, died from hunger. Since the wife and I took her in, we've given her what we can afford, but we're poor ourselves, which is why we're forced to sell the girl much as it grieves us."

"Spare me your fairy tales," the Madam said.

She sat down. As Chen bowed and backed onto the edge of the opposite chair, the Madam reached for the silver waterpipe on the table between them. She opened the lid of the tobacco box. Using little silver tweezers, she picked up a pinch of tobacco which she poked into the pipe. She lit the pipe, drew two leisurely puffs, emptied out the smoked tobacco, and repeated the process.

Watching her, Lalu felt a small surge of hope. She had seen her father act in this same unconcerned manner when he wanted to beat down the price of what he was buying. Pretending to smooth out her jacket, she patted the little cache. If the Madam proved a shrewd bargainer, her jewelry might be enough to buy her freedom after all.

Chen squirmed. His mouth opened and closed like a fish caught in a net gasping for air. He mopped his face with the backs of his hands, his sleeves. Finally, he burst out, "The girl may be thin, but it makes her look delicate. Like expensive porcelain."

"Our patrons are more interested in flesh and blood," the Madam said dryly.

"Oh, you'll find plenty of both. And in the right places too."

"So, she isn't a virgin."

"Oh no, I didn't mean to imply...oh, how could you think?" Chen stammered, horrified. "Of course she's a virgin. My sister-in-law was a pious woman, and the girl has been strictly brought up."

"You all say that, but where will I find you to get my money back if she is not?"

"I'll give you my address in the city."

"You just said you were from the North."

"Look, if you don't want the girl, just say so. There are plenty of Madams that will," Chen snapped.

The Madam set her pipe down. "Perhaps, but none of them can afford to pay the price I can. Isn't that why you're here?"

"I'm asking eighty thousand cash."

Aghast, Lalu cried, "You gave my father two bags of seed worth no more than a small string of cash!"

Chen leaped out of his chair and slapped Lalu.

"You're damaging your merchandise," the Madam said calmly. "And the price you're asking is absurd. Even a goddess wouldn't bring you that much."

Chen drew himself up. He tapped his puffed out chest with his index finger. "I know what you charge for one night with a virgin."

The Madam's brow wrinkled in barely concealed disgust.

"This is not the kind of house you frequent. Virgin or not, we cannot offer our guests an untutored peasant obtainable for free from their own servants' quarters. Before your 'niece' can serve as a daughter of joy, she will need time and money poured into her for lessons in singing, dancing, and all the other techniques of her new profession." She paused. "I can offer you fifteen thousand cash."

Chen stormed toward the door. "Come on. Let's go."

Lalu thought swiftly. If she went with Chen, he would probably take her to a Madam as filthy and coarse as the landlady at the inn where they had spent the previous night. The price of sale would be lower, one that her bits and pieces of jewelry would surely cover, but would she be able to trust the woman not to steal them from her?

She studied the impassive face of the Madam who sat before her. Her eyes glittered as sharply as the points of finely honed needles, yet her touch had been gentle, and she had spoken kindly. She might be hard, but she would be fair.

Chen shook Lalu. "Come on."

She hesitated.

His fingers dug into her shoulders. "Move."

"No, I won't."

"You're mine, you'll do as I say."

As though Chen and Lalu had not spoken, the Madam said, "Twenty thousand."

"Seventy thousand," Chen countered.

"Twenty-five thousand."

"Sixty thousand."

"As you said yourself, there is a famine in the North. Soon girls like this one will be sold for three or four thousand cash, perhaps even a single bag of seed," the Madam said.

"Fifty thousand."

"Thirty thousand. That's my last offer."

Chen released Lalu. "All right, but I might as well be giving her away."

The Madam reached into the strongbox beside her and counted out the strings of cash. Still grumbling, Chen snatched them and left.

As soon as the door closed behind him, Lalu unpinned the gold and silver earrings, jade bangle, and jade button from beneath her jacket. Within the rich grandeur of the anteroom, the earrings seemed tarnished and dull, the jade less green. She rubbed them against her new clothes and held them up to the Madam. "I want to buy myself."

NINE

The Madam rose. "Sit down," she said, guiding Lalu into the blackwood chair across from her.

Lalu thrust the jewelry up at the Madam. "If it's not enough, I'll work off the balance."

The Madam closed Lalu's fingers around the jade and silver and gold, gently forcing the fists onto Lalu's lap. "Keep your jewelry, it might be useful to you someday."

"If it can't buy my freedom, what use can it have?" Lalu demanded.

A twinge of pain flashed across the Madam's face. "The man who sold you called you Lalu. Is that your name?"

Lalu nodded sullenly.

"But he is not your uncle."

Lalu shook her head.

"How did this man who is not your uncle come to sell you?" the Madam asked.

Lalu uncurled her fingers. She stared at the jewelry she had believed would save her, the specks of blood where the sharp points of the earrings had pierced her palms. If the glittering baubles could not buy her freedom, perhaps her story would. Choosing her words carefully, she told how Chen had forced her from her father, her attempt to escape, her capture, and the beating she had received.

In the silence that followed, she heard someone in another part of the house plucking the strings of a lute. The slow, wailing melody fell like a rain of teardrops. Would another girl brought for sale at some future date hear her play or would the Madam let her go?

"Do you know what a cormorant is?" the Madam asked.

"It's a bird that eats fish," Lalu said, puzzled.

"Have you seen how fishermen use them to catch fish?"

"They put rings around the birds' necks so the birds can catch the fish but not swallow them. But what..."

The Madam interrupted. "Like the cormorant, I have a person I work for. You saw me pay for you, but you are not mine to do with as I choose."

Lalu fought back tears. Had she, like her father, gambled and lost? "I don't understand."

The Madam pointed her ringed fingers at the rich silk hangings, bowls of semiprecious fruits, antique vases, and carved jade and ivory bric-a-brac that filled the room. "All this is a result of my labor, yet it is not mine any more than the fish a cormorant catches is his. I work for a high government official who offers me the protection I need to live. But you are fortunate Chen brought you here today."

Lalu leaped out of her chair. "You mean you will let me buy myself back?"

"Lalu, you have great strength. Don't waste it on fighting for the impossible," the Madam said. She pointed to a scroll on the wall. "Look at that bamboo. It's strong, but it bends in the wind, just as you must learn to do."

"Then why did you say I was lucky Chen brought me here today?" Lalu cried.

"Normally, I would not be able to buy a scrawny, dark-skinned girl with feet like dragon boats, but today I have a special buyer who does not care about such things, someone who will take you to America."

PART TWO

第二部份

1872

TEN

Like the hold of the ship, the San Francisco customs shed was dimly lit, but at least the lanterns did not pitch and sway; and the air, though stale and stinking from the press of unwashed bodies, did not reek of vomit or human waste. If anything, the din from hundreds of voices, mostly male, had grown louder. But there was life and excitement in the shouting, joyful expectation in the rush for luggage, relatives, and friends.

Lalu, waiting for her turn to come before the customs officer, caught the contagion of nervous excitement, and she felt the same thrill, bright and sharp as lightning, that had shot through her when the Madam had told her she was going to America, the Gold Mountains at the other end of the Great Ocean of Peace.

"I have never been there, but Li Ma, the woman for whom I bought you, says there is gold everywhere. On the streets, in the hills, mountains, rivers, and valleys. Gold just waiting to be picked up...."

"Gold that will make me rich. So rich, no one, not even Old Man Yang, will dare speak against me if I go home," Lalu had whispered, ignoring the rest of the Madam's words.

Hugging herself inwardly, she had pictured her parents' and brothers' faces when she gave her father the gold that would make him the richest man in the village. The pride they would have in her, their qianjin. And she had held fast to this picture, as to a talisman. First, when the Madam had turned her over to Li Ma, the crotchety, foulmouthed woman who would take her to the Gold Mountains. Then, during the long voyage, when only the men's talk of gold had kept alive her dream of going home. And now, as she folded and refolded the forged papers Li Ma had given her. For the demons who ruled the Gold Mountains wished to keep their gold for themselves, and in order to gain the right to land, Lalu must successfully pretend to be the wife of a San Francisco merchant.

Over and over, during the long weeks crammed in the hold of the ship, Li Ma had forced Lalu and the other five women and girls in her charge to rehearse the stories that matched their papers, sternly warning, "Pass the examination by customs, and you will soon return to China a rich woman, the envy of all in your village. Fail, and you will find yourself in a demon jail, tortured as only the demons know how."

Could the torture be worse than the journey she had just endured? Lalu thought of the sweltering, airless heat and thirst that had strangled the words in her throat, making her stumble when she recited for Li Ma, earning her cruel pinchings and monotonous harangues. The aching loneliness that came from homesickness and Li Ma's refusal to permit the girls to talk among themselves. The bruising falls and the tearing at her innards each time the ship rocked, tossing her off the narrow shelf that served as bed, knocking her against the hard wood sides of the hull. The long, black periods of waiting for the hatch to bang open as it did twice each day, bringing a shaft of sunlight, gusts of life-giving salt air, the smell of the sea. The struggle to chew the hard, sour bread and swallow the slop lowered down as though they were pigs in a pen.

Lalu tossed her head, straightened her jacket, and smoothed her hair. That was all over. Behind her. No more than a bad dream. She was in America, the Gold Mountains. And soon, just as soon as she gathered enough gold, she would go home.

"Next."

Lalu felt herself shoved in front of the customs officer. She had never been close to a white man before and she stared amazed at the one that towered above her. His skin was chalk white, like the face of an actor painted to play a villain, only it was not smooth but covered with wiry golden hair, and when his mouth opened and closed, there were no words to make an audience shake with anger or fear, only a senseless roaring. Beside him, a Chinese man spoke.

"Your papers. Give him your papers," Li Ma hissed.

"My papers?" Lalu said in her native Northern dialect. "I've..."

She stopped, horrified. How could she have been so stupid? True, Southern speech was still strange to her, but during the long voyage, Li Ma had taught her the dialect, for the majority of Chinese immigrants on board came from the Southern province of Guongdong, and her papers claimed her as such. Now she had betrayed herself, proven her papers false. There would be no gold on the streets for her and no homecoming, only jail and torture.

Li Ma snatched the papers from Lalu. "Don't mind the girl's foolish rambling. You'll see everything's in order. Here's the certificate of departure and the slip with her husband's address here in the Great City."

Gold flashed as she passed the papers up to the Chinese man beside the demon officer. "A respected tradesman he is. Could have his pick of beauties. Why he wants this simpleton back is anyone's guess. Should have let her stay on in

China when she went back to nurse his old mother. But you know how men are. So long as the woman satisfies that muscle below their belt, they don't care about anything else."

The Chinese man laughed. He passed the papers to the customs officer. Again gold flashed. They talked between them in the foreign tongue, their eyes stripping Lalu, making her feel unclean. Finally, the demon officer stamped the papers. Smirking, he thrust them down at Lalu. Her face burning with embarrassment, she hugged the precious papers against her chest and followed Li Ma past the wooden barricade. She was safe.

"Look," Li Ma barked, pointing to the huddle of waiting women and girls. "Some of them are only ten, eleven years old. Children. Yet they showed more intelligence and good sense than you. Now you mark my words. That's the first and the last time I put out good gold to save your neck, so watch yourself, do you hear?" Cuffing Lalu's ears for emphasis, she herded her charges together and out onto the wharf.

Lalu, weak from lack of nourishing food and exercise, felt as if the boat were still pitching and rolling beneath her feet. But she walked briskly, not wanting to provoke another storm of abuse from Li Ma who was speeding past heaps of crated produce, sacks of flour and beans, and stacks of barrels. Above her, she heard the screech of seagulls, and beyond the wharf, the clip-clop of horses' hooves, the creak and rattle of wagons, voices deep and shrill. But she could see no further than Li Ma's back, for the same thick fog which had shrouded the Gold Mountains when they disembarked enveloped them, its cold dampness penetrating, leaving the salty taste of tears. Lalu swallowed her disappointment. She would see the mountains soon enough. Meanwhile, she would look for the nuggets the men said lay in the street.

Beneath the sickly glow of street lamps, she saw horse droppings, rats feasting on piles of garbage, rags, broken bottles. Metal glittered. A discarded can or gold? Stooping to grab it, Lalu did not see the rock until it stung her cheek. Startled, she looked up just as a mud ball splashed against Li Ma's back.

Li Ma whirled around. "You dead girl," she screamed at Lalu. "How dare you!"

She broke off as high-pitched squeals and cries burst from the girls around her. Through the heavy mist, Lalu made out white shadows, demon boys, hurling stones and mud, yelling, words she did not understand but she could feel.

"You dead ghosts," Li Ma cried, shaking her fist at them.

Giggling, the boys concentrated their missiles on the short square woman. Without thinking, Lalu picked up the stones that landed nearest her, flinging them back at the boys as fast as they could throw them. Years of playing with her brothers had made her aim excellent and the boys soon fled.

Li Ma fell on Lalu. "Stop that you dead foolish girl or you'll have the authorities after us."

"But they started it."

"Are you so dim-witted that you don't know you're in a demon land? The laws are made by demons to protect demons, not us. Let's just hope we can get to Chinatown before they come back with officers or we'll find ourselves rotting in a demon jail."

Shouting, pushing, and shoving, she hurried them up steep cobbled streets with foul smelling gutters, past wagons pulled by huge draft horses and unwashed demon men loafing on upturned barrels until they reached narrow streets crowded with Chinese men. Chinatown. Even then, she did not permit the women and girls to rest. But the warm familiar smells and sounds soothed Lalu's confusion, and she barely felt Li Ma's parting cuff as she herded them down a flight of stairs into a large basement room with more young women and girls like herself.

"Those with contracts come over to this side, those without go stand on the platform," an old woman in black lacquer pants and jacket directed.

Lalu held out her papers. The old woman took them. She pushed Lalu in the direction of the women without contracts.

"No, I belong over there," Lalu said, trying to take back the papers.

The old woman snorted. "What a bumpkin you are! Those papers were just to get you into the country. They have to be used again."

"But Li Ma said..."

"Don't argue girl, you're one of the lucky ones," the old woman said. She pointed to the group of women with contracts. "Their fates have been decided, it's prostitution for them, but if you play your cards right, you may still get the bridal chair."

A shocked murmur rippled through the group of women. One of them took a paper from an inner pocket. "I have a marriage contract," she said. "Not what you suggest."

"And I! And I!" the women around her echoed.

The old woman took the contract from the young woman. The paper crackled as she spread it open. "Read it!" she ordered.

The young woman's lips quivered. "I can't."

The old woman jangled the ring of keys at her waist. "Does anyone here read?"

The women looked hopefully at each other. Some shook their heads. Others were simply silent. None could read.

"Then I'll tell you what your contracts say." Without looking at any of the papers, the old woman continued, "For the sum of your passage money, you have promised the use of your bodies for prostitution."

"But the marriage broker gave my parents the passage money," the young woman persisted.

"You fool, that was a procurer, not a marriage broker!" She pointed to the thumb print at the bottom of the paper. "Is that your mark?"

Sobbing quietly, the young woman nodded.

"Well then, there's nothing more to be said, is there?"

"Yes there is," a girl said boldly. "I put my mark on one of those contracts, and I knew what it was for." Her face reddened. "I had to," she added.

"So?" the old woman, hands on hips, prompted.

"The contract specifies the number of years, five in my case, so take heart sisters, our shame will not last forever."

"What about your sick days?"

"What do you mean?" the girl asked.

"The contract states your monthly sick days will be counted against your time: two weeks for one sick day, another month for each additional sick day."

"But that means I'll never be free!"

"Exactly."

Like a stone dropped in a pond, the word started wave after wave of talk and tears.

"Keep crying like that," the old woman shouted, "and by the time your owners come to get you, your eyes will be swollen like toads."

"What difference does it make?" a voice challenged.

"Depending on your looks, you can be placed in an elegant house and dressed in silks and jewels or in a bagnio."

"Bagnio?"

"On your way here you must have seen the doors with the barred windows facing the alleys, but perhaps you did not hear the chickens inside, tapping and scratching the screens, trying to attract a man without bringing a cop. Cry, make yourself ugly, and you'll be one of those chickens, charging twenty-five cents for a look, fifty cents for a feel, and seventy-five cents for action."

Slowly the sobs became muted sniffles and whimpers as stronger women hushed the weaker. The old woman turned to Lalu's group. "Now get up on that platform like I told you."

Silently Lalu and the other women and girls obeyed. When they were all on the platform, the old woman began to speak.

"This is where you'll stand tomorrow when the men come. There'll be merchants, miners, well-to-do peddlers, brothel owners, and those who just want to look. They'll examine you for soundness and beauty. Do yourself up right, smile sweetly, and the bids will come in thick and fast from those looking for wives as well as those looking to fill a house.

"When the price is agreed on, the buyer will place the money in your hands. That will make the sale binding, but you will turn the money over to me. Do you understand?"

The women and girls nodded. A few murmured defeat.

The old woman pointed to some buckets against the wall. "There's soap and water. Wash thoroughly. You will be stripped for auction."

"Stripped?"

"Women in the Gold Mountains are scarcer than hen's teeth and even a plain or ugly girl has value. But when a man has to pay several thousand dollars for a woman, he likes to see exactly what he is buying," the old woman said.

She grabbed a tight-lipped, thin, dark girl from the back of the group. The girl stared defiant as the old woman ripped off her jacket and pointed out scars from a deep hatchet wound, puckered flesh the shape of a hot iron. "Look carefully and be warned against any thought of disobedience or escape." She threw the girl's jacket onto the floor. "It will be the bagnio for you. If you're lucky."

She pulled the women closest to her down from the platform and herded them toward the buckets of water. "Now get going, we've wasted time enough."

All around her, Lalu could hear the sounds of women and girls preparing themselves for auction, but she made no move to join them. It had taken all her concentration to make out the words that had been spoken in the strange Southern dialect, and she was only just beginning to feel their impact.

She had been duped, she realized. By the soft voiced, gentle Madam, a cormorant who had nothing to give except to its master. By Li Ma, the foulmouthed procuress charged with Lalu's delivery to the auction room. By the talk of freemen whose dreams could never be hers. For the Gold Mountains they had described was not the America she would know. This: the dingy basement room, the blank faces of women and girls stripped of hope, the splintered boards beneath her feet, the auction block. This was her America.

Through a haze as chilling as the fog that had surrounded her at the wharf, Lalu became aware of warm breath, an anxious nudging. It was the thin, dark girl the old woman had exposed as warning.

"Didn't you hear what the old woman said? You're one of the lucky ones."

"The Madam in Shanghai said that too."

"But it's true. There are women far worse off than you. Like those smuggled into the Gold Mountains hidden in padded crates labeled dishware or inside coal bunkers. Many of them don't survive the journey or arrive so bruised and broken they cannot be sold." The girl leaned closer and lowered her voice still further. "Those women are taken straight to the same 'hospitals' as slave girls who have ceased to be attractive or who have become diseased. There, alone in tiny, windowless cells, they're laid on wooden shelves to wait for death from starvation or their own hand." She brightened. "But you made the journey with papers and a woman to look out for you. You're thin, but beautiful and sound."

"What does that change except my price?"

The girl took Lalu's hands in hers, holding them tight, quieting their trembling. "You must learn as I have to let your mind take flight. Then you won't feel, and if you don't feel, nothing anyone does can hurt you."

ELEVEN

On the auction block, Lalu closed her eyes against her own nakedness and the men who milled around, poking, prodding, and pinching. Bids fell like arrows. Gold pieces, cold, hard, and heavy, dropped into her outstretched palms.

A woman's harsh voice ordered her to dress and Lalu knew she had not been purchased for a wife. She no longer cared. With the heavy lethargy of a sleepwalker, she pulled on jacket and trousers and followed the woman up the steps into the same dirty, narrow streets she had walked the day before.

As they retraced the journey to the wharf, Lalu's nose wrinkled at the stink of garbage and manure, the splatter of mud, but she made no effort to look for promised gold or dodge the stones of demon boys, the drunken leers of demon men.

Vaguely, she realized the vessel they boarded was smaller, less crowded than the one that had brought her across the Ocean of Peace, that the journey was shorter, and Portland, their destination, a sunnier, less hostile demon city. Dimly, she heard a young, handsome Chinese man greet them, felt him take her from the woman and place her on a mule.

He had a packstring of ten mules, eight loaded with supplies, one which he rode, one for Lalu, and as her mule jogged beside his, he attempted to draw her into conversation. He was Jim, he said. A packer Lalu's master, Hong King, had commissioned to fetch his slave.

He spoke kindly and in Lalu's same Northern dialect. But the fragile cocoon she had spun around herself was too warm, too comforting to break with talk, and she did not respond.

Nine days' travel through thickly wooded trails brought them to Lewiston, a strange town made up of tents, makeshift houses of canvas stretched across wood frames, and buildings so new Lalu could smell the rawness of the wood.

"All mining camps look the same," Jim said, guiding the packstring through rutted dirt streets crowded with freighters and horsemen shouting and cracking their whips. "There's a main street, dusty in summer, muddy or snow covered in winter. A few saloons. A dance hall. Two or three stores. A jumble of wooden shacks and tents where everything has to be kept in tins for protection from mice and rats. And Warrens, the mining camp where you will live, is just like that." His arm made a sweeping movement. "Like this. Only smaller."

Languidly, Lalu's eyes followed the sweep of Jim's hand. Hogs rooted in piles of empty tins, potato peelings, old hambones, eggshells, and cabbage leaves. Chickens, pecking and clucking, strutted on and off the boardwalks and around broken pots, shovels, worn-out kettles, boots, and other rubbish, breaking up clouds of flies that covered clumps of stinking manure. A rat burrowed in the spilled-out entrails of a dead dog. From the buildings and tents lining the street came music, raucous laughter, bursts of gunfire, and breaking glass.

"Those are saloons," Jim said. "Wine shops. Like your master's. Only his is empty of customers. That's why he bought you.

"There are sixteen hundred men in Warrens, twelve hundred Chinese, four hundred or so whites. And there are eleven women. Three are wives, two are widows, and a half dozen are hurdy gurdy girls. But they're all white. You'll be the only Chinese woman, an attraction that will bring men, Chinese and white, from miles around."

Like scalding water, Jim's words unraveled the casing of Lalu's cocoon, and she found herself floundering. She halted her mule. From the hitching rack edging the boardwalk, between horses patiently waiting for their masters, she could clearly see the demons inside the saloons. Some simply smoked and drank or competed at squirting streams of brown tobacco juice. Others crowded around gaming tables or hopped and bounded like performing monkeys, their arms around short-skirted, painted demon women whose heeled boots pounded rhythms on crude plank floors.

Did her master expect her to dress like these half-naked, painted demon women? To dance with hairy, unwashed demon men? To lie with them, one woman among sixteen hundred men?

"If you don't feel, nothing can hurt you." She repeated the thin, dark girl's words, reminding. But then she saw again the hurt in the girl's defiant black eyes, the puckered flesh, scars real and deep.

Abruptly, Lalu kicked her mule and urged it forward, galloping past the string of mules and Jim, out of town, and across the meadow, splashing across shallow streams, snapping off low hanging branches in groves of cottonwoods edging the banks, frightening unsuspecting red squirrels, birds, a deer. Finally, the mule staggered, wheezing, blowing, and hollow eyed, its sweat-caked flanks dripping foam. Ashamed, Lalu slowed to a walk.

When the mule's breathing evened, she stopped. Dropping her reins over the pommel so it could drink from the creek, she looked back across the blue green sea of meadow grass and camas. There was no sign of the packstring, not even a faint tinkling of the lead mule's bells. She glanced up at the fiery sun. It would be dark before the pack mules, each one loaded down with five hundred pounds of freight, covered the same length of ground her mule had galloped, and Jim would never dare risk leaving them to pursue her. She could ride on alone, away from the future that waited for her in her master's saloon.

Where would she go? To return to Lewiston or Portland or San Francisco would mean capture, possible mutilation, the bagnio, or perhaps even the "hospital." Yet she could not stay out here on the open prairie or in the mountains skirted and crowned with pines. She had no food and no means to obtain it. And she had no protection against the barbarian demons who made their villages in the open spaces beyond the filthy mining camps.

Dirty and black haired, they wore strange combinations of feathers, beaded skins, and demon shirts and pants, and they lived in tents that looked like funnels turned upside down. Their voices, when they demanded liquor and trinkets, were insolent, their manners arrogant. Yet they seemed sad, their black eyes as mournful as those of the homeless refugees she had once seen pass through her village. But they were frightening too. Armed with bows and arrows, small, sharply honed hatchets, and sometimes rifles, they threatened violent death, and when any approached, she could sense angry fear in the white demons she had run from.

ELEVEN

The woman who had taken Lalu to Portland had said the white demons were merely overgrown children, unable to control their selfish desires and passions. But Lalu knew they could not be dismissed so lightly. Armed with guns and knives, they were as quick to fight and shoot as the bandits who had snatched her from her village. Only these "bandits" had the power to make laws, laws that made people like Li Ma afraid when Lalu had thrown stones back at the demon children who had attacked them.

And there was that first day on the trail with Jim, when he had stopped to read a trail marker carved on the smoothed-out trunk of a cottonwood. The characters had warned of robberies by demons and Jim had led the packstring deep into the woods until he found another, safer trail. As they traveled, his eyes searched out more markers warning of assaults, a lynching. "Out here, there is no law," he had said. "Every man is his own court and his revolver is judge and executioner, especially executioner."

Later, he had pointed out China herders, demons who jumped claims for Chinese miners and guarded them while they worked. But to Lalu, the China herders had looked the same as the other demons: tall, brawny, hairy, and dirty. Like the demons in the saloons in Lewiston. The ones in the saloon where she would be forced to work.

She groaned. If only she could gather up

enough gold, she could go home. But the gold she had expected to find lying everywhere was buried in hard rock or in beds of ice cold mountain streams. She would need pick, shovel, and pan. Her hand dropped to her waist. The jewelry hidden in her waistband might buy the needed outfit and, with luck, she might even find a gulch that had not already been worked clean. But without protection, she would never live to take home the gold she found.

Ding was right. She could not escape her fate. Slowly, she wound her reins around the pommel of the saddle and dismounted so the mule could graze while she waited for Jim.

By the time Jim reached the creek, the cold crescent moon had risen high in a sky bright with stars. Lalu, huddled beneath saddle blanket and bedroll, watched him unload the mules, picket two, and turn the others loose to graze.

From a distance, with his queue coiled beneath the bulge of his Stetson, his red flannel shirt, and corduroy pants stuffed into high leather boots, he could be mistaken for a demon. He even wore guns in his belt and chewed tobacco like they did. And he used a demon name. Yet he had treated her as kindly as he would a younger sister. Until today, when he had talked of Warrens, the saloon where she would work. Then his voice had been cold and hard, deliberately cruel.

He lit the pine knots Lalu had gathered from a distant grove and prepared a simple meal of rice and salt fish. They ate, the silence punctuated only by the click of their chopsticks, an occasional whinnying, the crackle of pitch oozing out of pine knots.

When Jim scooped the last grains of rice from his bowl, he built up the fire until it blazed like a bonfire in the cold night air. Lalu set her bowl, still more than half full, onto the grass and held her hands up to the flames, but they could not warm the chill inside her, and she shuddered.

"Lalu, I know the saloons gave you a bad shock. That what I said and the way I said it was brutal. But when you see a demon, you must confront it. Only then will the demon disappear."

Lalu stared into the red orange flames. "Will the demons in the saloons disappear?"

"Most of the men in the saloons are prospectors or miners, decent men who spend weeks, sometimes months alone in the hills or gulches and canyons, so when they come into camp, they sometimes act crazy. But they don't mean any harm. They're just celebrating or trying to drown their disappointments and fears in drink and gambling."

"Drink, gambling, and me," she said, fighting back angry tears.

Jim cut a fresh quid of tobacco. For a while there was only the sound of chewing, a lone coyote's howl which burst into fitful yaps so rapid the wild bark surrounded the camp. Then, the chaw of tobacco firmly lodged in his cheek, he said, "Eleven years ago, when I came to America, all I had was my strength. So I sold it to a company that contracted labor. At that time a healthy Chinese man marketed for four to six hundred dollars, one with extraordinary ability a thousand. It took me six angry, bitter years to work off my debt, but now I am my own man. And you will be your own woman again, I promise you."

TWELVE

Day after day, as the packstring toiled up the steep mountain trail, Jim told Lalu more about the Gold Mountains and demon customs and drilled her in the English words she would need for her work in Hong King's saloon. But at night, after they had eaten, Jim would build up the fire, cut himself a fresh quid of tobacco, and they would talk about themselves.

Lalu spoke of home, her sale to the bandits, her dream of riches, the auction block. And Jim told of his father's death when he was not much more than a boy, his confusion and fear as each day his mother's touch grew colder and lighter, her eyes more vacant until one day she did not move at all. He had run away then, he said. But her eyes, dark hollows in a face bleached white as mourning, pursued him. So he returned, only to find her dead, buried without her son to mourn her, and he had run again, this time to the Gold Mountains.

Long after the fire had died down, when there

was only the soft crumbling of logs into ash, the tinkle of a mule's bell, Lalu would lie wide awake, savoring the shared closeness of their talk, promise of a deeper intimacy. A promise all the more precious as each night the moon grew larger, the distance separating her from her master shorter.

Resentment swelled in her at the thought of Hong King. She had not been sold to pay for her father's mistake, why should she now pay for the mistake of a stranger? A greedy old man who had scorned the miserable, ill-paying jobs permitted Chinese for the gamble of a demon saloon.

"He's old, he will not misuse you, his last hope," Jim had said. But she had heard the concern in his voice and she knew he was not sure. Nevertheless, she understood honor demanded Jim deliver her to Hong King. He was a packer. She was his freight.

In the darkness, listening to Jim's soft, steady breathing, she thought of his promise that she would be free. He intended to buy her. Of that she was sure. But Hong King had paid twenty-five hundred dollars in gold for her, more than the cost of Jim's entire packstring. Was that why Jim was teaching her vocabulary for use in a saloon, drilling her with an almost frightening urgency? Because he could not pay for her now? And why, when he talked of everything else, was he silent on this?

The questions tore at Lalu, surfacing each time she woke from thin, fitful slumber. But when

Warrens' unpainted shacks came into view after twelve days' hard travel, she was as empty of answers as she had been the afternoon she had urged her mule into the futile gallop across the prairie.

"These first cabins are the Chinatown," Jim said, bringing the packstring to a halt. He pointed across the creek to a huddle of irregular, steep-roofed shanties set down in a clearing surrounded by mountain and forest. "That's the white section of Warrens. Hong King's saloon is the first one on the left-hand side of the main street. You can't miss it."

Lalu's eyes widened in panic. "You aren't coming with me?"

"It wouldn't look right if I brought my string into camp when the stores I deliver to are here."

"But I'm part of your goods."

Jim's face, strong as newly carved rock, darkened as though shadowed by a cloud. "You know you're more than that."

"Then ride in with me now."

"I'm a packer," he reminded. "In camp for two, three days, gone for three weeks, a month. If you're to survive, you must stand alone."

So he couldn't buy her. At least not yet.

Disappointment and fear stuck like fishbones in her throat. "Tonight, in the saloon..."

"I'll be there."

Lalu pulled short her reins, dropped them.

Swift as a bird's wing, Jim's hand reached out. Their eyes locked.

"Remember," he said, his voice husky. "You have a friend in me. Always."

Not trusting her own voice, Lalu nodded. She pressed her knees against the mule. It trotted forward obediently, its hooves drumming across the wooden bridge, the sound a hollow echo in the painful emptiness of her heart.

Dust rose from the garbage-strewn, unpaved main street, but it did not hide Lalu from the knots of demons idling on the raised boardwalks, and they crowded round her, jerking the mule to a halt.

A demon lifted Lalu off the mule and set her on the ground. "Here's Polly," he said.

Remembering Jim's admonition that there was nothing demon men admired so much as pluck in a woman, Lalu fought down a rising panic and drew herself up straight. "Lalu. Me Lalu."

The men laughed. "The China doll talks." One of them pushed open the swinging doors behind him. "Hey, Charlie," he called. "Here's Polly."

A demon, bearded like the others but shorter and hatless, emerged, squinting in the sudden glare of light.

"Lalu." She pointed to herself. "My name Lalu."

From behind, bony hands seized her, and Lalu found herself looking into a Chinese face as cracked and creased as parchment. The fleeting moment of relief as she took in skullcap and silk robe, the dress of a gentleman, vanished when the man spoke.

"A slave does not choose her own name," he snapped in Chinese. "From now on you are Polly. Is that understood?"

Lalu knew this man must be Hong King, that she should lower her eyes and bow assent, yet she could not. His grip hardened, the long nails digging through the thin fabric of her jacket and into her flesh.

"Yes, I understand," she said.

Twirling the hairs sprouting from the wart on his chin, Hong King turned to the crowd that had gathered. His thin, white lips spread in a satisfied smile, exposing black stumps of teeth and sour breath. "You want look see, you come Hong King's saloon tonight," he said.

He turned back to Lalu. "The first taste will be mine."

In the pale afternoon sunlight that filtered through the filthy upper window of Hong King's shack, Hong King looked more than old. He looked dead. His skin, stretched taut over fragile bones, was the color and texture of old wax, and his mouth gaped wide, drooling spittle onto Lalu whom he clasped tightly, his long, brown stained nails scraping her flesh raw.

He blamed Lalu for his lack of arousal. Her feet were so big and her hands so coarse he thought he was in bed with a man. And her ignorance was not to be believed. Did he have to tell her everything?

Finally, his loins stirred weakly and he mounted her. And in the stain of blood that proved his victory, Lalu saw the death of yet another dream.

THIRTEEN

That night, in the narrow room behind Hong King's saloon, the hurdy gurdy girl Hong King had paid to dress Lalu applied the last of the makeup. She stood back and admired her handiwork.

"Good. Now hair," she said.

She crimped Lalu's hair in the front, parting it in the middle and drawing it back behind the ears, making the ends into finger puffs on top of the head, then indicated Lalu should remove her jacket, the restrictive bodice underneath.

Lalu hesitated, thinking of the day her mother had told her she must wear the bodice to flatten her breasts or be called a wanton. What would her mother say if she knew her daughter had been forced to submit to an old man's feeble, humiliating rutting?

She closed her eyes, trying to shut out the memory of Hong King's demands, his naked, withered flanks, and shriveled manhood, picturing Jim instead. His skin, a pale ivory above the line of his

Stetson, a dark golden beneath. The gleam of his teeth when he laughed. The ripple of his muscles when he lifted heavy packs. All warmly familiar. All lost to her now.

The hurdy gurdy girl tugged at the bodice. "I help?"

"No," Lalu said. "I do."

The corset which replaced her Chinese bodice squeezed the breath out of Lalu, and the whalebone stays cut into her flesh. Did demon women's bodies naturally curve like the necks of vases or did the lacing of the corset work like footbinding cloths, changing the shape of the body after years of suffering, Lalu wondered.

She looked at the tightly corseted girl with renewed interest.

The girl smiled. "Small pretty. Good for catch husband."

Jim had told Lalu that the hurdy gurdy girls in Warrens were recruited from Germany, that they owed the price of their passage to an agent, and that they paid it off by working at the saloon, dancing, encouraging the customers to buy more drinks. But often, a miner wanting a wife would pay off the balance due, making her free to marry. Was this girl trying to tell Lalu that tiny waists, like bound feet, were necessary for a good marriage? That marriage was still possible despite Hong King?

The girl smoothed Lalu's red silk skirt. "My dress too long for you. I make short."

THIRTEEN

"No." Lalu opened the back door, letting in the sweet scent of pines. "You go. I do."

The girl drew a derringer from inside her bodice. She nodded toward the door that led to the saloon. From the other side came the sounds of stamping feet, table thumping, shouts for Polly. "You need."

Lalu gaped at the tiny gun. Jim had said the hurdy gurdy girls were not required to give favors. He had not told her that they had to carry guns to ensure it.

"I get," Lalu assured the girl.

She closed the door and leaned against it. She had hoped this narrow room with just enough space for a small potbelly stove, chair, bed, and commode would be hers alone, for Hong King lived in a cabin in the Chinatown. Now she wondered if he expected her to entertain in it. A fist pounded on the opposite door, the one that opened into the saloon. She could not delay her entrance much longer.

In three steps Lalu crossed the width of the room and picked up the high-heeled boots the girl had left. Like the dress, they were too long. She wadded rags into the toes, slipped them on, and clumsily hooked together the long rows of tiny buttons.

She stood, took a step, teetered precariously, and fell. Leaning heavily on the commode, she pulled herself upright. A painted, frizzy-haired stranger with bare shoulders frowned at her from the mirror above the commode. Lalu stared. She was Hong King's slave, his to use as was his right, but she had not yet become a whore.

Dropping back down onto the chair, she unhooked the high-heeled boots and slipped on her soft cloth shoes. She took out pitcher and washbowl from the commode and scrubbed her face clean of rouge, powder, and paint. She recombed her hair, smoothing out the silly finger puffs. Finally, she wrapped a lace shawl around her naked shoulders.

She looked at her image in the mirror. The sad-eyed woman she saw was not the girl her family had known, but the face was clean and honest. With a toss of her head, she strode to the door, twisted the knob, and plunged into the saloon.

"Hey Polly, where you been keeping yourself?" a high-pitched voice piped above the indistinguishable roar.

Tanned arms swept her off the floor. "Been waiting for me, huh, kimono girl?"

Stronger arms in red flannel snatched her away. "No, me. I'll make her queen of the bull pen."

Lalu forced herself to smile at the demon holding her. "Put me down. I working girl," she said, using the words Jim had taught her.

"So what're we waiting for?" he slurred, burying his beard in her neck.

Lalu did not understand the words he used, but she could feel their meaning, the scratch of his beard. She pushed the demon's head away. "You wrong idea. I waiter girl. Nothing more."

"Sure," he said, swinging Lalu on top of the bar. "And here's to the darlingest, sweetest fairybelle that Warrens ever saw."

As he lifted his glass in a toast, she sprang free and dropped behind the bar. She crouched low, listening to the rapid pounding of her heart, the catcalls, shouts, finger snapping.

Hong King set down the scales he used for measuring the pinches of gold dust miners used to pay for their drinks.

"I didn't pay twenty-five hundred dollars plus freight just for you to hide," he snapped.

Ripping off her shawl, he yanked Lalu to her feet. Immediately she felt herself swung back on top of the bar. Through a gray haze of cigar smoke, she looked down at the men crowded into the saloon. Bearded demon miners in faded flannel shirts and worn corduroy pants stuffed into heavy, mudcaked boots. Smooth-faced Chinese in traditional blue cotton jackets and pants or full-sleeved, long-tailed Chinese shirts hanging out over coarse demon trousers. Gamblers and speculators gaudily dressed in satin coats and colorful vests with gold watch chains hanging across well-padded bellies. Adolescents suddenly become men bursting out of ready-made suits too tight and short. They were all the same. Hungry. Like the coyotes she heard howling in the night. And she was their prey.

"Why she's pretty as a heart flush!"

"A little doll, no taller than a broom."

"Give us a dance, doll!"

Lalu stood paralyzed.

"Hey booze boss, make her dance," a demon shouted.

Hong King tapped the counter. "The men told you to dance."

Didn't he realize she couldn't? That her deformed feet would not let her dance?

A demon pulled out a harmonica. "Name your tune."

In the crowd of upturned faces, Lalu saw Jim's. Relief washed over her. And then embarrassment. How could she meet his gaze?

Eyes downcast, she lifted her hem and pointed to her feet. "No good. No can dance."

"Look at those chinee feet!" the demon directly in front of Lalu marveled.

He grabbed a foot and snatched off her shoe. A second demon seized her other foot and another lifted her off the bar. Pressed close to the demons, the stink of sweaty underwear and liquored breath overpowered the less offensive smells of sour tap drippings and smoking coal oil lamps.

"Put me down," Lalu said, kicking.

"She got her spunk up!" the demon holding her laughed. He tossed her in the air.

"Wild as a mustang," the demon who caught her agreed.

She drummed her fists against his chest, but it only made him squeeze her tighter. She squirmed, straining to see over his shoulder. Where was Jim? She knew her refusal to meet his gaze had betrayed her shame. But he had said he was her friend. Always. Then why wasn't he helping her?

Suddenly, as she was being tossed to another demon, Lalu realized he was gone. All the Chinese had vanished. Except Hong King. And he was red with fury. At her, not the demons, she was sure.

She was alone. Just as she had been this afternoon when she rode into camp. Just as she had been since Chen took her from her home. Frantically, she searched for the word Jim had said she might need. What was it? Move? With the men tearing at her, she could not think. Run? Go? No, git! That was it!

"Git," she cried. "Git up and dust!" But the demons only laughed harder.

"Put the girl down."

Narrow chested and round shouldered, the demon who had spoken was shorter and far less brawny than the one holding Lalu, but as he walked toward them, his gun drawn, a path opened for him, and Lalu felt the grip on her loosen. She slid to the floor.

"No need to pull your iron Charlie, we just joshin' her."

Charlie's eyes, blue as camas, flashed. Startled, Lalu recognized the shaggy red brown hair and beard, the skin more pale than the sunburned leathery faces surrounding her. He was the demon who had been called to come out and gawk at her when she arrived, the one whose eyes had flashed when Hong King shouted at her.

"You've had enough funning for one night," Charlie said.

"She's the Chinaman's girl and he don't mind."

Angry voices murmured agreement. Hong King scowled. Charlie tossed a buckskin bag of gold dust onto the bar.

"Step up and liquor at my expense," he invited.

During the rush to the bar, Charlie whisked Lalu back into her room behind the saloon. Jim was there waiting.

"Are you all right?" he asked anxiously.

"Yes, but I don't understand."

Jim smiled. "This is my friend, Charlie Bemis. He owns the saloon next door."

"I've got to get back to the saloon," Charlie said. "But you tell Polly to holler any time those fools get too liquored up and start getting rough and I'll be right over." Flashing Lalu a smile, he slipped out the back.

Jim translated. Then he explained how when he had seen her in trouble, he had gone to fetch Charlie. "No one dares mess with him, he can keep a tin can dancing in the air with his six-shooter and everyone knows it."

"So can you."

THIRTEEN

Jim pointed to his belt. It was free of holster and pistols. "It isn't wise for me to wear my guns in camp."

"Not wise? Everyone out there had a gun! Or two. At least the demons did. Even the hurdy gurdy girl Hong King paid to dress me had a gun. And she told me to get one."

"Lalu," Jim interrupted. "If I had tried to help you, I couldn't have just walked in like Charlie did and say, 'Put her down,' I would have had to shoot to kill, and you can be sure I'd be strung up on a tree by now, with a half dozen Chinese beside me."

"But you said the Chinese in this camp outnumber the demons."

"The white men have the power."

"How can you call them men when they act like demons?" Lalu exploded.

"Would you call Hong King who used you like a whore a man and the man who saved you tonight a demon?" Jim retorted.

Lalu's eyes stung with tears. "How could I stop him?"

His voice softened. "Lalu, you did, and you will continue to do what you must in order to live. There's no shame in that. But Charlie is a good man. Trust him, he'll be a true friend to you."

FOURTEEN

Lalu's life fell into a strictly circumscribed routine revolving between the saloon and Hong King's shack. Though she slept in her own room behind the saloon, Hong King refused her permission to talk to anyone except customers from whom he could profit and Charlie and Jim whom he did not dare refuse. But in the five months since she had ridden into Warrens, Jim had returned only four times, a total of twelve days. She lived for those days.

And her day of freedom.

Each night, after the saloon emptied, she carefully swept up the dirt clotted with tobacco juice, cigar butts, ashes, and spittle from the rough planked floor. Then, in her own room at the back of the saloon, she panned the sweepings for the gold dust the men dropped when they dipped into their pokes to pay for their drinks and gambling. Occasionally, like today, there was a nugget.

Using her hairpin as a tweezer, Lalu picked it up

and added it to her cache. She ran her fingers through the little pile of clean gulch gold. In the glow of the coal oil lamp, the cold flakes glittered like stardust and the nuggets jingled merrily as they hit the jade button and bangle at the bottom of the leather pouch. It had taken Jim six years to buy his freedom. Would it take her as long?

"Lalu."

She knew the person knocking was Jim, only he called her that anymore, but she could afford to take no risks. Quickly, she hid her poke in the chamber pot and shut the door of the commode before she called, "Come in."

Frosty October wind and fallen leaves gusted into the room with Jim. He hung his hat on the nail behind the door and stamped his feet, blowing into his cupped fists. Lalu pushed the wooden box of floor sweepings and pan of water from the floor in front of the stove.

Jim stoked the fire. "Mining?" he asked with a chuckle.

Lalu laughed. "White men mine the rich claims. Chinese mine the ones that have been worked over, Hong King mines the miners, and I mine Hong King."

Jim laughed with her. "A few years ago, in Virginia City, a man bought a saloon and burned it down. Then he hired two men with a rocker to work his claim while he stood guard with a shotgun. At the end of ten days he'd reclaimed ten thousand dollars in dust that had spilled through the cracks in the floor."

"I'd like to burn this place down," Lalu said, setting the chair in front of the stove for Jim.

He sat down and cut a fresh quid of tobacco. "Be careful. If Hong King finds out you're cheating him, there's no telling what he'll do."

"Every time that old fraud takes a pinch of dust for a drink, he makes sure some gets wedged beneath his long nails!" Lalu blazed. "But don't worry, Charlie says the number of customers has quadrupled since I came, and there's so much more dust in the sweepings I'm sure Hong King doesn't realize I'm taking some for myself."

Jim worked the lump of tobacco in his cheek. "You're planning to save enough to buy your freedom and then go home, is that it?"

Lalu sat down on the bed. The ticking, stuffed with hay, rustled, making sounds like dry, anxious sighs. From the day she had run from the saloons until this moment, Jim had never again mentioned her freedom, and since her delivery to Hong King, the unkept promise had lain like a stillborn child between them. Why was he bringing it up now? How should she answer?

"When my father came back from Mongolia," she said at last, "he made my brother and I learn the saying — The copper corner of one's hometown is more precious than the gold or silver corner at the end of the earth."

FOURTEEN

Jim spat. The wad hit the red-hot side of the stove, making it sizzle. "Did he also teach you— The moon is not always round, flowers do not always bloom, and men do not always have a happy reunion?"

"No, he didn't."

"Lalu, you think of your family as they were when you left them, but by the time you've saved enough to go back, your brothers will be grown men, your mother and father, grandparents."

Lalu picked at the quilt covering the bed. "So?"

Jim leaned forward. "When we were on the trail, I heard you call in your sleep for your father, and I've seen your face when you sneak out to hold Mrs. Saux's baby. It's not Melina you're crooning nursery rhymes to, it's your baby brother. And when you look at the sky and sniff the air and feel the wind, you're halfway round the world again, in your father's fields. Your family means everything to you. But you're dead to them."

Lalu jumped to her feet. "That's not true."

"Then why haven't they responded to the letters you asked me to have written for you?"

"It's only been five moons."

"That's time enough for a reply," Jim persisted.

"The letters might have been lost. Or maybe they're dead, or they've become landless refugees."

The excuses she had rehearsed over and over to herself tumbled out in desperate denial.

Jim walked over to Lalu and gripped her

shoulders, forcing her to look him in the face. "Your father sold you."

"He had no choice," she defended.

He shook her, his voice hard and cold as the hoarfrost coating the ground outside. "Face it! You're dead to them," he repeated.

"No," she cried. "I'm their qianjin."

He released her. "If you still believe that, you're as much a slave to your own falsehoods as you are to Hong King."

For a long time, neither one of them moved or spoke. Finally, Jim reached for his hat. "I just came to say goodbye. It'll start snowing soon and Warrens will be snowbound. I won't pack in again until the trail clears. Maybe May or June."

"So long?" Lalu said, her lips quivering.

"With all my trips, I'm hardly here anyway," Jim said. "Charlie will look out for you."

"He watches over me like a China herder. If there's any trouble, I just run out the door and wait in his back room until he straightens it out." She paused. "But we can't talk. Not like you and I do."

"That way you can't argue."

For a moment, Lalu felt an urge to break through the veneer of their argument to the real feelings and issues running like deep currents beneath. Feelings and issues she could not label but which she sensed were far different from those their words expressed. But when she took Jim's hat and hung it back on the nail, she simply said, "Don't let's part with bitter words between us."

She poured tea from the pot on top of the stove and handed the cup to Jim. "I know you're right. No letter is going to come."

Small dishes of food, spirit money, smoldering incense, and freshly turned earth marked Jim's grave. Lalu knelt and knocked her head on the ground.

Three days ago he had been alive. Then his mule had stumbled on French Creek hill near Secesh Creek. She pictured the worn trail they had traveled together. The steep ascent. The broken ridges, dark ravines, and densely wooded gulches. The bleached out bones of horses in purple canyons, the remains of those who fell. And she remembered the way her heart had lodged like a lump in her throat as the mules' steel shoes clinked against the rocky ledges where a single misstep meant certain death. Still, she could not believe Jim's broken body lay rotting beneath the damp earth and decaying leaves on which she knelt. He was too experienced a horseman. Too careful. Too alive to become mere memory.

She thought of their last night together, the dark sadness she had seen in his eyes. Had his mother's eyes looked like that? Had hers when she had retreated from a reality she could not bear? The angry words they had hidden behind haunted her. Had she unwittingly helped weave his shroud?

Footsteps crunched on gravel. "When do you suppose Jim will come back to eat all that food?"

Lalu jerked up angrily. Charlie, a spray of faded, windblown columbine in one hand and fiddle in the other, loomed over her.

"When Jim come smell flowers?" she snapped.

Charlie laid the scarlet blooms beside the dishes of food. He leaned against a fallen tamarack and clinched his smooth brown fiddle between shoulder and bearded chin. "If Jim can eat and drink and smell, do you suppose he can hear too?"

"Of all my tunes, I think he liked this one best. Said it reminded him of the river near his village."

The tune Charlie played was not mournful, but as the high, clear notes danced through the air, Lalu felt the tears she had struggled to hold back trickle down her cheeks. She wiped them off impatiently. But like a dam finally, suddenly burst, the tears became a steady stream.

Without a word, Charlie laid down his fiddle and took Lalu in his arms. She leaned against him, shaking, her body racked with huge sobs as she wept.

For Jim.

And for Lalu.

Both dead forever in a strange land.

PART THREE

第三部份

1875

FIFTEEN

In the chill of predawn darkness, all Warrens slept. But inside Hong King's saloon, the coal oil lamps blazed and Polly, her face and dress damp with perspiration, searched for something else she could clean or wash or scrub.

The bottles, cigar vases, and glasses on the shelves behind the bar glittered, and the bar itself, polished until it was slick enough for skating, glistened darkly. The towels customers used to wipe foam from mustaches and beards hung, pressed and folded, from the edge of the counter, and Polly could see her own distorted image in the shiny brass rail around the bar's base. Beside the windows on the side and front of the saloon, the four gaming tables sat squarely, the chairs tucked beneath green felt coverings brushed up like new. The stove, freshly reblacked, gleamed in the center of the room, and the deep wooden boxes the men spat in were filled with fresh sawdust.

The odor of whiskey and stale tobacco lingered,

clinging like an indelible brand to the walls and Polly's clothes and skin. But there was nothing left to clean. To keep her from facing the black man's words.

"You ain't no slave, honey," he had said. "They is no slaves in America, not fo' ten years."

The words should have filled her with joy. Instead, she felt a sense of betrayal as strong and deep and painful as when her father had picked up the bags of seed. For if the black man was right and she was not really a slave, why hadn't Charlie told her?

Her limbs, overcharged with energy a moment before, felt weak, and she jerked out a chair, upsetting the piles of chips stacked at the center of the table. Automatically, Polly restacked them, then sank limply onto the chair.

She could understand why no Chinese had spoken. Those loyal to Hong King would not, and the others either did not know or did not dare to speak. And the white men and women had no reason to interfere. But Charlie? He was always reading books and newspapers so he had to know the law. In fact, he was often asked by miners to solve minor disputes, for his knowledge and reputation for honesty made his judgments respected even when disliked. Yet he had remained silent on this. Why?

She had trusted him, given herself to him, at first because he was kind and gentle and she was lonely and afraid, and then because she believed he cared. But he had betrayed her.

The door swung open, and Charlie walked toward her, his footsteps loud and unnatural in the quiet. "When you didn't come, I thought you'd gone down to Chinatown. Then I saw the lights and got worried."

She looked up at him, her eyes dark bruises of pain. "Why you not tell me I not slave, that I not belong Hong King?"

The hesitation before Charlie spoke was fractional but Polly, her senses scraped raw, felt it.

"Who said you're not?"

"Black man come to saloon tonight. He tell me his people come from Africa. Like me, stolen from village and bring here, but man name Lincoln make war and they free. He free, I free," she said, her English deteriorating under the strain.

"The Civil War was fought to free Negroes."

"You mean law for China people not the same?"

Charlie pulled out a chair. "It's more complicated than that."

He took out his tobacco pouch and pipe, stuffed the bowl, tamped it down, lit it, and took a deep drag. The smoke drifted between them.

"Years ago, special laws were passed in California to forbid the kind of auctions and contracts that made you a slave, but the laws only raised the price of slave girls."

"How law make black man free and raise price for me?" Polly demanded.

"Because girls started running away and it cost their masters a great deal of money to get them back."

She shook her head. "I not understand."

"I don't understand it myself," Charlie sighed. He puffed thoughtfully.

"The system works something like this," he said at last. "If you ran away from Hong King, he would trump up some charge that would force the sheriff to come after you. Then, when you were caught, Hong King would get a friend of his to bail you out, and once he got you back, he would drop the charges."

"You tell judge Hong King make me slave."

"I wish it were that simple, but judges and lawyers are not always indifferent to bribes, and there's a problem with language and translators, and technicalities in the law. There are the high-binders from the tongs as well. They've been known to kill those who've tried to escape and those who've helped them too."

The words Charlie used were long and he spoke quickly, but Polly understood only too well what he was saying. Striving for control, she balled her hands into tight fists beneath the green felt table covering. "So you not tell judge."

Charlie walked over to the stove. He finished his pipe, knocked the ashes onto the grate, and sat down again. "I will if you ask me. But you should know that the majority of women who have braved the courts have lost, and of the few that have won, most have been deported. Do you want to take that chance?"

"What 'deported' mean?"

"Sent back to China."

Polly's fists tightened, her nails dug into her palms. What would happen to her if she were sent back to China? Though she had told Jim she knew no letter would come, each New Year, under the pretext of illness, she had gone to Li Dick, the herbalist, and given him money to send home for her. Three New Years had come and gone without reply, and she could no longer avoid the truth. Either her mother and father were dead, or she was dead to them. Either way, she could not go home.

But the gold she had saved would buy some land. Land she could farm like her father had taught her. If the villagers permitted. She thought of the widows' struggles in her own village. The suspicion and hostility a single woman would arouse. And she knew if she went back to China, she would have to marry.

All through her childhood she had believed what her mother had told her, that getting married and birthing children were a woman's happiness. Even after she had begun working in the fields and doubts had seeped in like dust from a summer storm, she had not really questioned the truth of what her mother had said. Wasn't marriage for a woman as inevitable as birth and death? That was why, when Chen had bought her, she had tried to offer herself to him, to be his wife, thinking that would make everything all right. And during the journey into Warrens she had hoped and even prayed that Jim would buy her for his wife. Now she was not sure. Her mother had said a woman belongs to the father of her sons. If she married, wouldn't she be exchanging one master for another?

She looked up at Charlie, saw his lips move.

"The Negroes had terrible lives," she heard him say. "They came to America in chains and were forced to work under conditions you can't begin to imagine. Many of them barely had enough to eat. They were at the mercy of their masters and overseers. Whipped. Raped. Sold at will. Things aren't so bad for you here.

He lifted a corner of her silk skirt, rubbed it between his fingers meaningfully, pointed to the snow white petticoats beneath. "You have beautiful clothes and plenty to eat. I keep the men in line and Hong King..." He paused.

"You're better off than a lot of free people," he finished abruptly.

Polly stared at the man who sat before her. Was this the man she had allowed herself to love? This man who did not seem to care that he had to share her with another. This man who dared look her in the eye and say she should be content with her lot.

She turned from him and walked to the window. For more than two years now, they had shared the same bed. But what did he know of her life beyond his bed and cabin and Hong King's saloon? She had never told him about the long weeks crammed into the hold of the ship, scarcely able to breathe the stale, stinking air. The humiliation of standing naked on an auction block. The way her gorge rose each time Hong King mounted her. Her fears that if she did not obey she would be sold to a bagnio or sent to a "hospital." She had not told him because she had thought he could understand without words. She had been wrong.

Polly laid her forehead against the cold pane of glass. Outside a meadowlark sang, its haunting melody reminding her of the three robins she had saved after Mr. Grostein's cat had killed the birds' mother.

At first, they were content to fly around her room, but soon they began pecking at the window, demanding to be let out. So Charlie built a cage for them, and she hung the cage on a tree outside. But their cries tore at her, and finally she opened the door, letting them fly where they pleased. Then one day Mr. Benson, the butcher, came to the saloon and handed her a cigar box with three stiff bodies crusted with blood.

He was sorry, he said. He knew how much the

birds meant to her, and he had reprimanded his clerk severely. But the way they hovered, demanding scraps, had been annoying, and if she had kept them in the cage Charlie had made for them, his clerk would not have killed them.

Charlie had told her the same thing, and she had tried to explain why, even though she mourned the birds' deaths, she did not regret leaving them uncaged. But he had not understood. Then how could she make him understand her own need to escape the cage that held her?

Slowly, Polly turned and walked back to the table. "Charlie, your father doctor, and you have fine education and beautiful home in Connecticut. But you run away because your father try make you surgeon and you not want. You work as deck hand on ship, and when you reach San Francisco, you hear about gold rush, and you try mining. Now you saloon keeper and gambler. But if you want change again tomorrow, nothing stop you. You free.

"I only daughter of farmer who cannot read or write. But I too want be free."

Charlie took Polly's hands in both his own. "Do you think I want anything less for you?" he asked sadly. "But it just doesn't seem possible."

She pulled away. "Maybe not now, but I will be free. Now, please leave. I must lock up."

Charlie started walking toward the door, then wheeled about sharply. "Polly, I know you're skimming off gold from Hong King, that you're saving it so you can buy your freedom like Jim did, but it won't work."

"You need not worry," she said coldly. "I not ask you to help."

He ran his fingers through his beard, tearing at it. "Listen to me. Jim tried to buy you. Not once, but three times. At first, Hong King said Jim could have you for ten thousand dollars, four times what he had paid for you. But at the end of the summer when Jim went to him with the money he had borrowed and saved, Hong King laughed in his face. So Jim came to me and borrowed three thousand more. Still he refused. Then Jim asked me to try. That's when Hong King said he would never sell you, not at any price."

Too late, she understood the dark sadness in Jim's eyes, the reason for the angry words. And yet she could not believe it. "Why Jim not tell me? Why you not tell me?"

"Jim made me swear I wouldn't. He said hope was all you had to live for, and he couldn't rob you of that."

SIXTEEN

They talked until dawn, but it changed nothing. Jim was still dead, the gold Polly had labored so hard to save simply so much dust.

As they walked back to Charlie's cabin, Polly pieced together bits and pieces of conversation she had overheard about Hong King. He had come to the Gold Mountains more than twenty years ago when gold was more plentiful, the laws against Chinese less severe, and it had taken only seven years for him to mine enough to go home a rich man. But on his way back to San Francisco to buy his passage, he was persuaded to join a game of fan-tan, and he had lost everything. Twice more he had saved enough for a comfortable retirement, and twice more he had gambled it away, the last time on renting the saloon in Warrens and buying her.

His gamble had paid off. She had made him rich, more than rich enough to retire. Yet he never talked of going home. And why should he? Home meant a wife as old as himself, household responsibilities, a siege of requests for help from poor relatives. Warrens meant gold, an enviable life of self-indulgence. So long as he had his slave.

She should have seen that long ago. But she had not wanted to. Wasn't that why she had not confronted Jim during their last night together? That night he had accused, "You're as much a slave to your own falsehoods as you are to Hong King." And she had been. All through her years in Warrens. How else could she have endured Hong King's sour breath and clawing hands, his blind rages when he lost at gambling, his pleasure when he caused her pain. But now there could be no more turning away from the truth.

She would never be free. Not until Hong King was dead.

With that realization, Polly became silent. Then, while Charlie slept, she slid out of bed, dressed, and took his Winchester off its rack.

She had never learned to shoot. Jim would not teach her, and she had never asked Charlie. But she had gone with Charlie on hunts, and she knew from the trampled brush and grass, small sunken rocks, and bushes stripped of leaves and berries, that the trail she was following had been made by bears. Large rocks overturned in search of insects, a dead tree trunk clawed wide open in play, and long streaks of plowed up ground where cubs had romped confirmed her suspicions. Then, in the distance, she saw a brown she-bear streaking along, her cub not far behind.

She did not follow them. Neither did she attempt to shoot the deer stealing silent and ghostlike through the brush. Nor the wild goats, some as big as ponies. For this, her first attempt to shoot, she had decided on a fool hen, a bird too stupid to fly from danger.

She knew the birds' brownish gray feathers blended so skillfully with the texture and color of bark that they were almost impossible to spot. But she also knew that the cock liked to beat its wings against its breast and that the noise would betray its location. She stopped to listen.

Squirrels, mere flashes of red against moss green trunks, chattered as they ran from tree to tree. Bees from a nearby hive hummed as they competed with yellow butterflies for the little blossoms that flowered between the gnarled roots of giant pines. But there was no sound of wings beating against breast.

Wishing more sunlight penetrated the hoary weave of firs, larches, cedars, and pines, Polly searched the branches methodically, the closest ones first, then farther and farther. Nothing. Disappointed, she turned to go, then froze. There, on a branch not thirty feet from where she stood, a fool hen's gray brown tail feathers drooped over pine needles.

Pulse quickening, Polly lifted the rifle and pushed ten long, soft nosed shells into its magazine. She sighted her target and fired.

The explosion split her head into a thousand brittle fragments of pain. The smell of burned powder, bitter and acrid, filled her nostrils. She lowered the rifle. Squirrels scolded alarm. Wings flapped as birds, sounding shrill warnings, made good their escapes. But the fool hen sat on the same branch. Unaware of danger, it blinked stupidly, as though annoyed by the sudden noise.

Its tiny beadlike eyes made Polly think of Hong King and his refusal to let her go. Abruptly, she lifted Charlie's rifle. Just as abruptly, she lowered it, swallowing, her mouth suddenly dry. Hong King was not a bird, but a man. An old man who would surely die before many years passed, leaving her free, without blood on her hands.

Insects hummed, distracting, and she thought of the dragonflies her brothers used to catch and tie with thread then force to fly from one boy to the next. After a while, their gossamer wings would fall off but, captives still, they could not stop. So they crawled from one master to the other until, exhausted, they died.

Polly's hold on the rifle tightened. Hong King was not just any old man. He was her master. And if she wanted her freedom, she would have to kill.

For the third time, she lifted the rifle. She blinked, willing the myriad of red dots that clouded her eyes to disappear. Concentrate. She must concentrate. And steady herself.

She breathed deeply. The soft, damp, loamy smell of the wild filled Polly's nostrils. She sighted the bird and fired.

Again she felt the rifle recoil, the explosion shatter the peace. Heart pounding as savagely as her head, she forced herself to look at the branch, the bird she had aimed for. Empty.

For a moment, she thought the bird had flown. And then she saw it. Caught in a bush where it had dropped. Dead.

And Hong King would be next.

SEVENTEEN

Polly hid the rifle under her bed. She wished she had a smaller, less obtrusive gun like the hurdy gurdy girl's derringer or Charlie's pistol, but she would not be able to get one without attracting attention and the key to her success would be surprise.

As she washed and changed, Polly planned her strategy. It should not be difficult, for like the fool hen, Hong King had grown complacent, leaving her to run the saloon while he played fan-tan or poker. If she waited until he came to pick up the night's earnings, she could shoot him without witnesses, and he would be dead before he realized that behind his slave's placid mask lay a woman scheming for freedom. Fixing a bright smile across her face, Polly opened the door to the saloon.

It was crowded, but strangely silent. Except for a tremulous, pulsating murmuring. Had Charlie discovered his rifle missing? Had he guessed her intention to shoot Hong King and come to give warning? No, he would never give her away. Not after all they had said and shared only that morning. Then what? Grimly maintaining her fixed smile, she jostled through the press of bodies.

From the way the men surged near the windows, she thought perhaps the attraction was in the street, but when she finally squeezed her way through to where she could see, she realized they were jammed around the gaming tables. One gaming table. The gaming table where Hong King and Charlie sat hunched over cards.

The lamp above the table flickered, then flashed suddenly bright, and she saw that Hong King's skin, usually dry and cold as a snake's, gleamed with perspiration as he spread his cards on the table.

"Two pair," he said.

Charlie exposed his last card. "Three aces."

The men packed around them breathed a collective sigh of release. "That a way, Charlie." "Go to it." "Show the chink!" they shouted as Charlie scooped up the pokes of gold dust from the middle of the table, adding them to the extraordinary pile already in front of him.

Dismayed, Polly watched Charlie gather the cards and shuffle for another hand. Her plan required Hong King to stay out of the saloon until closing and then to come in feeling amiable and self-satisfied, not agitated over heavy losses. Somehow she must signal Charlie to stop.

"Drinks," she called, her voice unnaturally high

and shrill. "Tangleleg, beer, champagne, brandy, forty-rod! You call, I get."

"Here's two sacks on Bemis."

"Put my bet on Hong King."

"Don't be crazy chink. Poker's an American game."

"Put mine on the Chinaman too."

"Yeah, Hong King's shrewd."

"But Charlie's the best."

"His luck can't hold much longer."

Charlie slapped the deck down. "Cut."

The men quieted. From within the wide sleeve of his dark blue robe, Hong King reached out his long, bony hand. His nails scraped across the green felt cloth, straightening the cards into a neat stack, then cut the deck precisely. Charlie licked his thumb and dealt. One card each, face down. One card each, face up.

As Hong King and Charlie tipped the edges of the hidden cards, the men pushed closer, their breath hot and damp against Polly's neck and shoulders. Anxious as they were for a glimpse, she craned forward. But already Hong King was tossing a poke from his pile of three, Charlie matching it and flicking two more cards off the deck.

Hong King's hooded eyes barely flickered as he studied the cards: his three and ace of hearts, Charlie's two of diamonds and four of clubs. But Polly knew from the way his fingers were stroking the hairs sprouting from the mole on his chin that he was well pleased by the ace, the turn in his luck.

He pushed another poke into the pot. Again, Charlie matched it and dealt: a five of spades for Hong King, a four of hearts for himself, making one pair.

All eyes turned to Charlie. He tapped the deck lightly on the tabletop, set it down, and pondered his cards, his fingers drumming silently on the mound of gold he had already won. The battered piano from Al Ripson's saloon tinkled and someone sang in a drunken quaver. The flumes by the river moaned. A lamp gurgled.

A film of perspiration covered Polly's body and she felt alternate waves of fire and ice. It was just another game, she told herself. One with only a small pot. But the tense silence, the piercing concentration on heated faces swollen ugly with anticipation insisted otherwise.

She looked at the single bag of gold in front of Hong King, then raised her eyes to look at him. Once again his fingers were entwined in the hairs from his mole, but they were tugging, not stroking. Was that one poke all he had left?

"Pass," Charlie said.

Hong King's hand dropped to the table. With the edge of his nails, he lined up his cards. "Pass," he agreed.

Sighs of relief and disappointment rippled through the crowd like shudders. Charlie reached for the deck, slid off the last cards for the hand: four of diamonds for Hong King, two of spades for himself, making two pair.

A burst of last minute betting ruptured the quiet.

"Two more on Charlie."

"Are you crazy? He's only got two pairs. The Chinaman's got a straight."

"You're guessing. Charlie's got two pair I can see."

"No guess. The Chinaman's got a two in the hole I tell you."

As Charlie threw a poke into the center of the table, talk vanished. But when Hong King pushed his last poke across the table, Polly heard a renewed stirring.

Her eyes darted from one player to the other. If Charlie's pair could win the game, why was Hong King pushing his last poke across the table into the pot? Could he possibly have a straight? Then why was Charlie tossing in three buckskin bags, matching Hong King's bet and raising him two? Was he testing, checking to see if Hong King was bluffing?

Nails pierced Polly's flesh, twisting her wrist. "I told you to bring me today's take."

Though his voice was even, cool almost, Polly could feel Hong King's anger seething beneath the surface. And all at once she understood. Hong King really did have a straight. A straight that

could win back what he had lost. A straight he
would forfeit if he did not match Charlie bet for bet.

A path opened for her and she fetched the
strongbox from behind the bar. Hong King un-
locked it and pried open the lid. With a fury he
could no longer conceal, he weighed the contents,
hurled them into the pot.

"You covered and raised one," he said, the
words spewing out in a sour, frustrated hiss.

Two pokes thudded down, scattering loose
dust. "I see you, and raise you one," Charlie said.

Hong King scraped back his chair and a ripple
ran through the crowd. Was he throwing in his
hand? Slowly, deliberately, he loosened three side
buttons, withdrew a piece of paper from an inner
pocket, and spread it on the table. The paper
crackled in the quiet. "I bet lease for saloon."

Charlie leaned back in his chair. "I already have
a saloon."

Hong King's lips tightened. His tongue darted
out, licking dryly. "I give you paper cover half my
take for next six months."

"I'd be a fool to risk gold for paper, and you
know it," Charlie said quietly.

Again Hong King's lips tightened.

"I have nothing else," he said at last.

Charlie nodded casually toward Polly. "Stake
the girl."

Polly bit her lips, choking off a cry, but Hong

King's eyes gleamed bright as the dust he was fighting to win.

"How much you stake me for her?"

Charlie hesitated. "Everything on the table."

The men around them gasped, but Polly, burning with the same anger and shame she had felt on the auction block, barely heard them.

"Final bet?" Hong King asked.

Charlie pushed all the gold into the center of the table. "Yes."

Hong King's lips twitched into a broad, toothless grin. "Agreed."

Swiftly he flipped his final card: two of hearts, a straight; then stood, knocking over his chair in his eagerness to scoop up his winnings.

Without a word, Charlie turned over his hidden card: two of clubs, a full house. He had won.

EIGHTEEN

For Polly, Charlie's cabin with its glowing stove and two chairs pulled close, the dresser made of packing crates, and the bed they shared had always been a refuge. Now, as Charlie lit a lamp and the room flared into light, she saw it as simply another shack.

Charlie wrapped his arms around Polly. His belt buckle dug into her, and she felt a wave of disgust as his body quivered with the same drunken exhilaration she had detected in Hong King after a big win. But she did not move. Even if he were not her new master, she could not stop him. He was too big. Too strong.

"Hey, you're supposed to be happy," he said, taking Polly's face in both his hands and kissing her full on the lips.

She flinched.

"Okay, so I don't rate a hallelujah chorus, but what about a simple thank-you?" he said.

A thank-you? For what? For humiliating her?

EIGHTEEN

For forcing her to break her promise that when she left Hong King it would be as a free woman. Or for teaching her that a slave had no right to make promises, especially to herself.

He took the pins out of Polly's bun. Her hair rippled down her back, a sheet of black silk.

"Tonight I ruined a man for you."

"Not for me. For the game. Because you gambler."

"It was the only way to free you."

"That what you believe. Just like Jim believe I better off if I not know Hong King not sell me. Maybe Jim right. Or maybe you right. But this my life. Not Jim life. Not yours. Mine."

Charlie strode over to the dresser and poured himself a drink, downing it in a single swallow. "All right. What would you have done?"

"I shoot him," she said, knowing even as she heard the words out loud that she could never have done it, knowing that was not the point, the reason for her anger.

"There are more ways to kill a man than with a gun," Charlie said, setting his glass down. "Hong King's lost so much face, he'll have to leave camp. For you, for us, he's the same as a dead man."

Polly slumped onto the bed. Again he had not understood, had not seen beyond her words. "You could have lost," she said tiredly.

"I didn't."

"And when you play again?"

Charlie lifted Polly off the bed and hugged her to him. She felt the worn flannel of his shirt against her face, soft as a caress.

"I would never stake you," he said, his voice surprised and hurt.

She kept her back taut. "I your slave. You can do anything."

He stood back, holding her at arm's length. "I didn't win you from Hong King so you could be my slave. You're free."

She looked down at his arms.

He dropped his hold, but the marks from his grip remained, deep red purple like the bruises from Jim when he had shaken her, demanding she face a reality neither one of them was able to confront. Rubbing the tender new bruises, she thought regretfully of the rich promise her first days with Jim had held, a promise unrealized in part because of circumstances, but more because, for all their talk, they had kept too much hidden from each other, from themselves. Was she to suffer the same loss again? And for the same reason?

In front of her, she could see Charlie, shoulders slumped, his head tossing back as he downed yet another drink. And in the mirror above the dresser, she could see his hands clasping bottle and glass. But she could not see his face, for he had lowered the mirror long ago to a height appropriate for her. Suddenly, all around her, Polly noticed similar instances of Charlie's thoughtful concern, the curtains nailed up to shield her from prying eyes, the second chair made smaller, the shelves and hooks lowered, and she found herself wondering if he had indeed forced the final bet to win her freedom and not the game.

Tonight, and the night before, she had been hurt by his apparent betrayals, angry because he could not understand her. But did she understand him? From the day she had ridden into Warrens, he had protected her, and she had accepted his help without question, as though it were her due. Now, for the first time, she asked herself why he had come to her rescue in the saloon. Had he interceded out of some strange sense of Western chilvary? Or pity? Or because he was Jim's friend. And after Jim's death, had he continued to protect her out of loyalty to Jim, or because he had come to care for her, or simply to keep her in his bed?

She did not even know how or why he and Jim had become friends. Like a frog at the bottom of a well, she had seen nothing beyond the small circle of blue sky that meant freedom, concentrating all her thoughts, all her energies toward piling up the gold she needed to reach it, never once considering it might be gained another way. And now she could lose that freedom which Charlie had put within her grasp, and with it, Charlie.

Searching for words that would clear away the misunderstandings, she began haltingly. "Charlie, sometimes I angry with you and you with me. But

I know anger is only because you and I not understand, not believe the same way. Please, try understand this." She paused, waiting for acknowledgment.

He did not speak, but she saw his hands on bottle and glass freeze, breaking the steady drinking. Taking heart, she continued, "All my life I belong someone. My father, the bandits, Hong King. And I promise myself when I free of Hong King, I belong no man, only myself.

"You know I have gold I save to buy myself from Hong King. I want use that to build a house, start my own business. A boarding house like Mrs. Schultz."

Charlie poured another drink, gulped it. "You can't."

"You worry I not know how to cook? I watch Mrs. Schultz and I learn plenty quick."

"It's not that," he mumbled.

"Then what?" Polly demanded. "Because you think I not wife like Mrs. Schultz, not respectable, people say it bawdy house? You see, I show them they wrong."

Charlie turned to face her. "A Chinaman can't own land," he said, so softly she could barely hear him.

"But you say America have land for everyone. That people from all over the world come for the land. Rich. Poor. All the same. Anyone can have land. You said."

"Any American. You're from China."

She opened her mouth to shout denial, but the pain in Charlie's face told Polly his words had cost him too dearly to be negated by mere anger, and she sank silent onto the bed. She must think carefully, make sense out of Charlie's contradictions, her own confusion.

She knew the Chinese in Warrens did not own the stores and laundries where they worked, but she had thought that was because they planned to return to China as soon as they made enough money. Weren't the ones who came to Hong King's saloon always complaining about the loneliness of lives without wives and children, the brutish manners of white men, unfair taxes, and harsh laws? And didn't they always end their grumbling with talk of home, their eagerness to return to families left behind? But she had no family, no one to go home to.

Of course. That was it. Charlie didn't realize that she intended to remain in America. She would become an American and buy the land for her house. Land that would keep her free and independent always.

She leaped up, ran to Charlie, and crooked her arm through his. "You not understand. I never go back to China. I become American."

He pulled away. His fists clenched and unclenched. He took his pipe out of his pocket, rotated it in his hands, studying it, then tossed it onto the bed, and reached for the bottle.

Polly grabbed his arm. "What is it? What wrong?"

"The only way a Chinaman can become an American is to be born here."

She laughed. A short, bitter laugh. Here or in China, slave or free, it was the same. She needed a protector. She rubbed her hands across Charlie's back, unknotting the tight muscles. He turned. Mechanically she began unbuttoning his shirt.

He took her hands in his, holding them still. "Polly, I meant what I said. You're free. Let me be your China herder and build a house for you. You can do whatever you want to in it, invite anyone, refuse anyone. It's yours, I promise you." He smiled weakly. "You don't even have to have me."

"I..."

His fingers brushed her lips, gently silencing. "And yes, you can pay for it too."

She laughed, a joyous peal clear as ringing bells. Hearing it, Charlie's smile grew stronger, deepening into laughter that became one with Polly's. And suddenly, within the circle of their laughter, she felt finally, wonderfully free.

PART FOUR

第四部份

1890-1894

NINETEEN

Rockets whistled past the window, exploding in showers of lemon yellow sparks against the cloudless July sky. A string of firecrackers burst, then another, and a smell of burned powder drifted through the open window, mingling with the fragrance of baking and cooking. From the main street came the sounds of last minute hammering, the gathering of men, women, and children from outlying ranches and mines come to celebrate.

In her tiny bedroom adjacent to the larger one in which her boarders bunked, Polly hurriedly stitched the final gold button onto her tight-fitting basque. Charlie had taught her to goldsmith, and she often hammered out trinkets for sale in Mr. Grostein's store, but these buttons made out of five-dollar gold pieces were made for her by Charlie.

In the fifteen years since he had won her freedom from Hong King, the barriers of misunderstanding which had been torn down that night had never again come between them, for they spoke openly of everything to each other. Neither had Charlie once wavered from the promise he had made, building her this boarding house beside his cabin and giving her the protection she needed while respecting her independence. And so, to Polly, these gold buttons which Charlie had made were special, tangible evidence of his love and understanding and she changed them from dress to dress.

Downstairs, the kitchen door slammed. She bit off the thread and dressed swiftly, her fingers managing the hooks, laces, and buttons with practiced ease. Then, giving waist and skirt one last tug, she grabbed her hat off the top of the bed and ran down the stairs into the combination sitting-dining room.

Of the four rooms in the house, this was her favorite. The windows, filled with plants and flowers, sparkled behind white curtains trimmed with crocheted lace. The wood planks beneath the bright hooked rug were oiled smooth, and the room was made cozy with cross-stitched pillows and runners, and crocheted antimacassars, all of her own making. She walked past the round oak table covered with shiny white oilcloth and peered into the mirror beside the kitchen door to adjust the angle of her hat.

The face she saw was not much different from the one that had gazed out at her that first night in the room behind Hong King's saloon. The youthful freshness was gone. But the planes of skin beneath the high cheekbones were still firm and golden, and the eyes had lost their fear, the mouth its anxious quivering. Yet beneath the sparkling humor and warmth which now graced eyes and mouth was an intensity not immediately apparent, shadows of the past, the pull of unacknowledged tension.

Hat straight, Polly turned, saw Charlie stooped over the stove, licking his fingers appreciatively. She rapped her knuckles on the doorjamb. "Food is for the dance later, no snitching. Also, I promise Frank and some other boys who dance through the night that they can come for breakfast."

Charlie, fiddle and bow in hand, strode into the room. "You have enough food for a dozen dances and breakfasts, and the other women will be bringing more," he said, throwing himself onto a chair.

Wrinkling his nose, he shook his fiddle at the dirt-caked shirts in Polly's sewing basket beside the chair and said, "If you must take in laundry from miners, why on earth do you insist on doing the patching while they're still dirty?"

"Because when I get them clean and iron, I don't have to muss them."

"That's crazy."

"More crazy than you changing your saloon, where no lady is allowed, into a 'dance hall' where everyone can come, just by hanging up a canvas curtain to cover the bar and turning the pictures to face the walls?" she retorted.

Laughing, Charlie opened the door. "Come on, I can hear the fellows tuning up."

"Hey Charlie, the parade's starting without you," called Three-Fingered Smith.

Squinting against the glare of the afternoon sun, Polly could see a cluster of women in white already marching down the opposite end of the main street. "You better hurry," she told Charlie.

Nodding, he dashed across town, his boots scuffing up small puffs of dust. Polly, joining the crowd already gathered, sensed the same excitement she had once felt celebrating New Year. Of course, she was wearing white and navy blue instead of red, the breeze blew dust instead of snow, and there was no lucky New Year cake. But the festive air filled with the happy crackle of exploding fireworks, laughter, and talk was the same.

The band marched past. There were five: Charlie and Rube Bessey on fiddles, Brown at the accordion, Jenkins on the banjo, and Peter Beemer playing the flute and conducting. Polly found her feet tapping time to the music.

George Dyer, the blacksmith, clapped admiringly. "That Charlie sure can make his fiddle talk."

"Can't wait for the dance tonight," Benson agreed.

Mary Dawson nudged Polly. "You don't know how lucky you are your poor feet don't allow you to dance. After each one of these all night marathons, I walk for a month like a horse with stringhalt."

Polly laughed. "That is because all the men want a chance to dance with a lady and ladies are so few." She felt a tug on her skirt and looked down.

It was Katy, Mary Dawson's five-year old. "I can't see," Katy complained.

Polly lifted the girl. "You sit on your daddy's shoulders," she said, passing her up to her father.

Katy bounced happily. "Look at the flags!" she shouted.

Behind the huge star-spangled banner held aloft by freshly scrubbed prospectors and miners, dragon flags fluttered above two hundred Chinese marching to the crash of cymbals, gongs, and stringed instruments. Watching their proud, clean-shaven faces and handsome black queues swinging below their waists, Polly felt a rush of nostalgia for her village, the processions which ended at the temple where soul tablets marking generations gave an aura of permanence and security.

The Chinatown in Warrens was as large as her home village, and the sounds and smells were the same. There was even a small temple. But without any women or children, the men drifted in and out, always hoping that the next camp, the next job would be able to satisfy the false promises that had brought them to the Gold Mountains, and the Chinatown they created was an echo of their loneliness and disappointment, a hollow imitation of the villages they had left behind.

"It won't last," a voice said in Chinese.

Startled, Polly looked away from the twisting, swirling dragon to see Li Dick, the herbalist, deep in conversation with A Sam, the laundryman people called Mayor of Warrens.

"What do you mean?" A Sam asked.

"There's trouble ahead."

Polly looked at the smiling, cheering crowds lining the sun-washed street, the weathered buildings gaily festooned with red, white, and blue bunting, the creaking wagon beds made into colorful floats. What kind of trouble was Li Dick talking about?

"The Chinese coming in from the coast say the demons are trying to pressure the government into kicking us out," he continued.

"They tried that in '86 and we're still here," A Sam said.

"Those of us who weren't burned out, beaten, or killed."

"None of that happened in Warrens."

"No," Li Dick admitted. "But people and places change."

Despite the hot rays of sun beating down on her, Polly shivered, remembering Charlie's worried frown when he had read about the formation of Anti-Chinese Associations that vowed to force all Chinese to leave the Territory, her own agitation when news came of boycotts against Chinese merchants, laundries and stores in Chinatowns blown up, entire populations of Chinese marched out of towns at gunpoint.

Through all of it, there had been no real violence against the Chinese in Warrens, and now the troublemakers had turned their fury against a group of white people called Mormons. But she could not forget the resentful talk against the Chinese that had spilled out of the camp's saloons. Could that resentment be simmering, waiting for an opportunity to explode?

Long strings of firecrackers burst in a series of ear-splitting explosions, signaling the end of the parade, and Polly found herself pushed away from A Sam and Li Dick in the press of the crowd headed for Warrens Meadow. But the uneasiness their words had evoked remained.

She looked for Charlie, but the men and women surrounding her were too tall, and she saw only stiffly starched shirtfronts, the backs of dark suit jackets graying with dust, frilly laces, ribbons, the bobbing heads of small children. There was a determined squirming: Katy, climbing off her father's shoulders, wriggling to the ground and Polly's side.

"Are you going to come watch me race?" she demanded, wrapping her sticky fingers around Polly's.

Looking down at the candy-smeared face flushed with excitement, Polly smiled, welcoming a return of holiday spirit. "Of course. And you must help me cheer for Charlie in the horse race. Then we will go see the drilling contest, and after that you can help me get ready for the dance."

While the men and women jammed into Charlie's "dance hall" raised dust pounding schottishes, quadrilles, polkas, mazurkas, and waltzes, Polly laid out the midnight supper on the counter. With each dance, the air grew warmer, steamier, more redolent of sweaty bodies than perfume. Scarcely able to breathe, she left the platters of meat, bread, cakes, and pies, and worked her way through the crush of swirling skirts, stamping boots, and clicking heels to the window.

She pushed up the sash. Fresh air drifted in, and with it, the clink of bottles, the scratch of matches lighting cigars or pipes, for neither smoking nor drinking were permitted in the "dance hall."

She turned, waved to Charlie, nodded at friends dancing past. There was Pony Smead, the justice of the peace. Miss Benedict, the young, good-looking school teacher all the eligible young bachelors were sparking. Three-Fingered Smith who had accidentally blown off his own finger and thumb. John Long, her former boarder, whose handsome face with kindly gray eyes and neat, well-trimmed mustache towered above his wife's. Through the crook of his elbow, Polly caught Bertha's impish wink, and she laughed, glad of the dance that had brought Bertha to Warrens.

Long before they met, Polly and John had heard about Bertha's pretty brown hair, light blue eyes, and fun-loving ways from her proud older brother who boarded with Polly whenever he was in Warrens. Yet it was quite by accident that John and Bertha became acquainted. He had stopped in Florence on his way back to Ireland to see his mother. Bertha was there with her father who had traveled from Grangeville to trade his farm-cured ham and bacon for gold dust. There was a dance. The two met. Three months later they were married, and last spring John had brought his bride to set up housekeeping at a cabin near the Little Giant Mine where he worked.

Though separated in age by seventeen years, Polly had felt an immediate, special kinship with Bertha, and they visited daily, with Bertha making the mile journey into Warrens in winter on skis.

The set ended and Mary Dawson spun to a stop beside Polly. She sank onto the bench pushed against the wall. "First the parade, then the races, the drilling contest, tug-of-war, and now this," she gasped. "If you hadn't taken Katy off my hands so I could rest up, I don't know how I'd make it."

Her baby, swaddled in shawls and tucked out of

harm's way beneath the bench, whimpered. "Oh no, not now," she groaned.

Polly swooped down and picked up the baby. "You rest, I take care of Henry," she said. The baby, burbling bubbles, grasped one of Polly's shiny gold buttons and smiled.

"You're a lifesaver!"

"That's what old Mr. McGuiness tells me," Bertha giggled. "Swears the medicine Polly gave him for his rheumatism makes him feel twenty years younger."

Polly laughed with her. "You know he just like the whiskey in it."

"Get your partners," Rube Bessey called.

Bertha and John swept back onto the floor. The music started and a nervous young man approached.

"Oh no," Mary groaned again. "I can never turn down the ones just out of diapers."

Polly, bouncing the baby in time to the music, chuckled as the pimple-faced boy dragged Mary onto the floor. Eyes riveted to his feet, his arms pumped up and down like bellows, and Polly could see him counting steps under his breath. Snatches of talk drifted through the window.

"Looks like the district's about mined out."

"Said that years ago when we voted to let the Chinamen in."

"And now most of the money in circulation is theirs."

The words brought back Li Dick's somber

warning, her own fears of a simmering resentment, and suddenly Polly realized that in this brightly lit room alive with music, laughter, and goodwill, there were no Chinese except herself.

No matter how often it happened, the realization caught her off guard, leaving her feeling cut adrift, acutely alone. She hugged the sleeping baby to her, hungry for his warmth, his innocent trust. But the baby, not hers, only underscored her loneliness.

Leaning down, she tucked him back under the bench and slipped outside.

As Polly climbed the hill to her special place beneath the grove of pines that surrounded the cemetery, the men's words and Li Dick's warning became less real, but she knew from experience that the feeling of loneliness would take longer to subdue.

Since her freedom from Hong King, she had determined never again to suffer the ignorance in which he had kept her. She had become knowledgeable of Western foods, customs, and laws, a part of the community, counting the dancers, the men on the porch outside the "dance hall" as friends. Yet she was a stranger to them. Just as she was to Li Dick and the men of Warrens'

Chinatown who could not forgive her past, her choice of Charlie for a mate.

A twig snapped, and she shrank back into the shadows. Hidden behind a bush, she listened to boots tearing through brush, the rasp of labored breathing.

"Polly, wait up. It's me, Charlie."

She stepped out into the open. The same kind of wordless communication that had brought Charlie out of the dance to find Polly flashed between them, and they climbed silently. When they reached the top, they turned and looked down at Warrens.

Directly below and to the left, cabin windows glowed honey yellow, splashes of color flitted across the squares of light, and music blared from Charlie's "dance hall" as the camp celebrated. But to the right, in the Chinatown beyond the musical murmuring of Warrens' Creek, no band played, and the only sounds were the ordinary ones of heavy irons banging on clean clothes, the rattle and scraping of beans for fan-tan.

A thrush on a nearby branch began its night song. The soft, low notes rose higher and higher until they became a strong, beautiful melody. And then, without warning, the song ended, leaving a sad, ringing trill that accentuated Polly's loneliness, a loneliness Charlie's caring presence could ease but not entirely vanquish.

"I remember one time a man bring a performing monkey to my village," Polly said. "The man divide the audience in two and give each side one end of a rope to hold. Then the monkey walk carefully back and forth between the two sides. At each end, he stop a little bit, but he cannot stay, and so he walk again until he so tired, he fall."

She pointed down to Warrens, so clearly divided into two camps. "Sometimes I feel like that monkey."

TWENTY

A cloud of pungent steam burst from the kettle of herb tea as Polly lifted the lid and sniffed professionally. Just right. She replaced the lid, eased the kettle into a basket padded thickly with straw and newspapers, and bustled around her tiny kitchen assembling the rest of the things she would need for her patient, Mary Dawson's girl, Katy. Coconut candy. Porcelain spoon. Doll.

Bertha took the doll and spoon, wrapped them in an old washed out salt sack, and passed the bundle back to Polly who placed it in a nest of straw above the kettle.

"After you finish at Mary Dawson's, would you come over to my house and help me pick up the stitches I dropped in the sweater I'm knitting for John?" Bertha asked.

"Sure," Polly said, clamping down the basket and opening the door.

"Good. Then you can show me how to cook my

rice properly. John says it still doesn't taste like yours."

Polly smiled at Bertha, so slender, frail, and anxious to please. "I think it's time we play a trick on John. I will come make the rice for your supper tonight, but you don't tell him. Then we see what he has to say."

Laughing, they set off at a leisurely pace, enjoying the September sunshine, the comfortable silence of good friends.

As they neared the Dawson cabin, Bertha pointed to the teams of Chinese miners working the flatter spaces of Warrens Meadow, their picks and shovels clanging on bedrock, the gravel rattling in sluices beside neatly stacked tailings.

"I wish John worked above ground like they do," she said.

Polly thought of the one time she had gone down into a mine, the feeling of being buried, the sound of dripping water, the smell of burned powder and bad air, the rats. "He make more money," she comforted. "And he is a foreman, not have a dirty job like the muckers."

"He says miners, whether they're foremen or muckers, die young and quick or old and broke, so he's used the money he saved for his trip to Ireland to buy a farm near my father's."

"He quit his job at Little Giant?"

"Not yet. We've got to save up some money first."

Polly dug the toe of her boot into the rich black soil beneath their feet. "This dirt is the real gold in these mountains."

"That's what John says." She hesitated. "Polly, anyone can see you love the soil. Why didn't you start a farm instead of a boarding house?"

"Warrens is snowbound six months a year. The growing season's too short."

"Sell the boarding house," Bertha said impulsively. "And Charlie can sell his saloon. That will give you enough to buy a farm in Grangeville. Near us."

Polly laughed. "Charlie love gambling too much to leave his saloon, and I love Charlie too much to leave him."

Mary Dawson, eyes red and hair uncombed, greeted them at the door. "Oh Polly, Bertha, thank God you've come. I've tried everything I know and she's still burning up. I'm afraid the baby will catch it."

"Don't worry," Polly soothed, setting down the heavy basket on a table piled high with bottles, dishes, pans, and uneaten food. "I use this tea many times and it always bring the fever down."

While Polly unpacked and poured the herb tea into a bowl, Mary rocked the fretting baby and picked ineffectually at the clutter.

Bertha took the baby and led Mary out of the room. "You rest now. Polly and I will take care of everything."

Polly slipped the candied coconut into her apron pocket and carried the bowl of tea into the curtained alcove behind the stove. How small the child looked under the pile of heavy quilts. And how flushed. She laid a hand on Katy's forehead. Hot as a cookstove after a day of baking.

The child's eyes fluttered open, green and fever bright. "Polly? I want Polly."

"Polly is here," she said, brushing the tendrils of damp hair from Katy's face. "And Polly bring medicine to make you feel better."

Katy pushed her face into the pillow. "No. No more medicine," she whimpered.

Polly sat down beside her. "You get better, I take you to fly kite."

Katy twisted back to face Polly. "A dragon kite?"

Polly, nodding, dipped the porcelain spoon into the tea.

"As big as the one you made for Mike?"

"Bigger," she promised, holding the spoonful of tea in front of Katy's swollen, blistered lips.

Katy swallowed the tea. Her face puckered. "I don't like it."

Polly dipped the spoon into the tea, then turned it so the handle touched Katy's lips. "Watch the muddy brown water go down the sluice box into the gully," she said, tipping it so the liquid poured through the curved handle into Katy's mouth.

Katy giggled. "Again."

Polly obeyed, again and again, until the herb tea was almost gone.

"No more," Katy said, sliding under the quilts.

Polly reached into her pocket and took out a piece of coconut candy. She laid it on her lap where Katy could see it. "For you when you finish."

The child peered into the bowl. "Okay," she agreed grudgingly.

Swiftly, Polly administered the rest of the tea and popped the candy into the child's mouth. While Katy sucked contentedly, Polly brushed out the tangled hair and changed the soiled nightgown.

She pinched the child's cheeks lightly with both hands. "Now you sleep, and when you wake up, I give you surprise," she said, tucking the child back under the quilts.

Watching the tiny, fever-ravaged body relax into sleep, Polly felt a familiar flash of regret that the children she nursed so lovingly were never her own, and she began a lullaby her mother had sung, beating back the shadow on her happiness with song.

Above the melody, she heard the whirring and honking of geese flying overhead. She imagined the birds dipping and soaring with her song, keeping their perfect wedge-shaped formation as they flew south for the winter.

TWENTY

She loved the winter. The pure whiteness of the snow. The trouble-free months of isolation from the outside world. The funny, strange activities. Like the Hocum Felta Association whose members each took turns trying to be as funny as possible while the rest of the club attempted to remain poker faced until, finally, someone's mouth would twitch, issuing short, sharp splutters which eventually exploded into helpless laughter.

Hoofbeats thundered outside, breaking Polly's reverie, drowning the quiet inside sounds of Bertha tidying the kitchen, Katy's uneven breathing, Polly's song.

The pounding hooves stopped. A door burst open. Slammed. And suddenly a white-faced Bertha was standing beside her, saying, "Come quick, Charlie's been shot bad."

TWENTY-ONE

Too stunned to speak, Polly allowed Bertha to lead her outside, Benson to pull her up behind him on his sweat-soaked horse. He kicked the tired beast into a gallop.

Shot bad, Bertha had said. What did that mean, Polly wanted to ask, but she did not dare, for the exhausted horse told her Benson had looked elsewhere before he found her. How long had it been since Charlie was shot? What if she was too late?

She had to talk. Anything rather than think of Charlie lying in a pool of blood. Dying. Possibly dead.

"Where?" she asked.

"In the head."

Polly closed her eyes, shutting off the images and thoughts his words conjured. "No. Where is Charlie?"

"In the saloon."

The drum of hoofbeats, her own loudly beating

heart, and screaming fears made it impossible for Polly to hear properly. "Where?" she repeated.

"Saloon. The room in the back."

He had said saloon. The room in the back. But who would shoot Charlie there? And why?

As though she had spoken the questions out loud, she heard Benson shout, "Johnny Cox did it."

Johnny Cox? That didn't make sense. Or did it? She remembered how Cox had swaggered into camp the night before with his poke full of dust from a cleanup on Crooked Creek. Intent on a bust, he had gone straight to Charlie's saloon to drink and play poker. But after he had lost two hundred and fifty dollars, Charlie had refused to play another hand until Cox sobered up. Had Cox thought Charlie was trying to cheat him? Denying him a chance to win his money back? She had seen men get shot for less. And she knew Cox was a bad man to fool with. Yet she could not believe he had shot Charlie. Not when he had asked Charlie to watch out for him. To make sure he didn't lose his whole poke.

"Charlie is too good a shot. You sure he's hurt?"

She felt Benson's body twist around, his spurs dig into the horse. "Charlie was taking a nap so Cox had the drop on him," he shouted. "Told Charlie he'd give him the time it took to roll a cigarette to get the money out of the safe or he'd shoot Charlie's eye out. There was no way for Charlie to get his irons from the end of the couch so he called Cox's bluff. Shut his eyes and rolled over. That's when Cox shot him."

Polly listened disbelievingly. Only the mob of angry miners outside the saloon convinced her of the truth.

"Don't worry Polly," the sheriff said, helping her dismount. "Cone's gone after Cox like a coyote after a jackrabbit."

He pushed wide the swinging doors and followed Polly into the saloon, his footsteps reverberating in the unnatural quiet. "He'll get that killer, make no mistake."

Killer? Then she was too late. Her knees wobbled like those of a newborn calf, and she was glad of the knob to lean on when she opened the door to the back room.

There was blood everywhere. On the couch. The floor. Its pungent, metallic odor overcoming the familiar smells of tobacco and liquor. How could there be so much blood and Charlie still live?

He was lying on the couch. Covered. Except for his face, yellow gray and waxy. A death mask. Polly signaled the sheriff she wanted to go in alone.

She leaned over Charlie. A black hole gaped beneath his right eye and beads of sweat trickled between ridges of clotted blood. There was a dry rattling. The quilt rose imperceptibly, then fell. He was alive!

"Charlie!"

Beneath the quilt she saw movement, a feeble

groping. She lowered the quilt and took his hand. "First thing we take you home and clean you up," she said.

"No. Stay here." Blood seeped out of his mouth into his beard.

"Shhh. Don't talk now."

"Must. Running out of time." His eyes, dark caverns of pain, opened. "I love you Polly. Marry me."

The constriction in her chest was unbearable. She lifted a corner of the quilt and wiped the blood from his lips, his beard. "Shhh. Later. We talk later."

"The saloon, the gold in the safe, everything I have is yours."

Struggling, he lifted his hand a few inches before it dropped back onto the couch. His eyes rolled and Polly, following his gaze, saw they were not alone. From out of the shadows, Pony Smead, the justice of the peace, stepped forward.

"Doctor. Charlie need a doctor."

"Troll's already sent to Grangeville for one, but even riding hard it will be night again before he gets here. By then it might be too late."

She bit her lips to keep back the sob that choked in her throat.

"No one I know in Warrens would want to cheat you," Smead continued. "But you know what the law is. It'll be safer if you marry."

Polly sank to her knees beside Charlie. "You

listen to me, Charlie. You get better. I promise you."

His eyes, black with defeat, closed. "No."

She laid her head against his chest. "You got to let me try."

He did not answer.

She turned to Smead. "You find Troll. Then take the door down and use it for a stretcher to carry Charlie home. I will go ahead and get ready."

Stumbling back through the crowd to her boarding house, Polly closed her ears to the remarks, angry and sympathetic, forcing herself to think only of what she would need. Something to clean the wound. Cloths. Plenty of clean cloths. And herbs. To stop the bleeding. To replenish the blood he'd already lost. To give him strength. Quickly, she gathered all she had.

She ran over to Charlie's and put a kettle of water on to boil. Smead and Troll eased Charlie onto the bed. Polly poured some whiskey into a glass and gently lifted Charlie's head.

"Drink this," she said, holding the glass to his lips.

She tipped the glass. The liquor spilled into his mouth and over his beard. He did not swallow.

"He's unconscious," Troll said.

"I help Smead hold Charlie while you get the bullet out," she told him.

"Don't you think we should wait for the doctor?" Troll asked.

Polly, taking a reading of Charlie's feeble pulse, shook her head. "We lose too much time already."

Still Troll hesitated. "We have no instruments."

Polly glanced around the cabin. She picked up her crochet hook. "Use this."

Troll paled. "A crochet hook?"

"You and Smead hold Charlie. I will clean," she said.

She worked silently. Digging. Daubing. Staunching. Desperately pretending the tortured moans did not come from Charlie. The hole was closer to the eye and larger than she had thought, and the crochet hook sank deeper and deeper, but she could not find the bullet. Bits of flesh and splintered bone gleamed whitely on cotton swabs blackened with powder and blood. The pile grew. Blood spurted freshly from the wound. She packed it with a poultice of herbs and fresh cloths. The wound was clean, but the doctor would have to get the bullet.

"Thank you. I will wait with Charlie for the doctor," she told Smead and Troll.

Wearily Polly closed the door behind the men and sank into the chair beside the bed. Charlie groaned.

"Polly's here," she soothed. "You okay."

He tossed restlessly. She cradled him in her arms. He quieted. Dusk deepened into night. The saloons closed. There was a burst of footsteps and noisy talk, the soft whinnying of horses. Hoofbeats. A door slammed. Crickets chirped. A coyote howled. The lamp spluttered, went out. Intending to relight it, Polly half rose.

"No," Charlie moaned. "No."

She stayed, not moving, willing her breath, her strength, to flow into Charlie. Light, dusky gray, filtered through the windows. She heard the town come to life. Still she did not move. Sunshine, honey golden, flooded the room, warming her, and through her, Charlie. Friends came and went. But concentrating on pouring all her strength, her life into Charlie, Polly did not speak, did not move. Then, as dusk came again, she heard horses pounding to a halt. Footsteps. The doctor.

Troll held the lamp above Dr. Bibby as he worked on Charlie. The doctor's three-hundred-pound bulk cast deep shadows, and Polly lit a second lamp and brought it close. On the packing crate beside the bed, metal and bits of bone glowed like red hot coals.

The doctor, his giant body sagging from exhaustion, dropped his instruments into the basin of hot water. "The ball must have hit the cheekbone and split. I can only find half of it."

"What does that mean?" Troll asked.

"Unless Bemis' system is strong enough to expel

the other part of the bullet, the fragment will induce blood poisoning."

He washed his hands and dried his instruments. Polly set the lamp down. "You finish, you will not look for it?" she asked, alarmed.

The doctor shook his head. "I've probed as deep and as long as I dare."

"No," Polly protested. "You can find it. I know. You're tired. You rest. Then you look again."

Dr. Bibby snapped his case shut. "I've done all I can."

"No," Polly denied. "You're the best doctor. I know. I never see you before, but I hear. I know one time you need special instrument for operation at ranch and you make it yourself in the blacksmith shop. You can do anything. I know. I hear."

"And I've heard what an excellent nurse you are. Too good for me to lie to."

He took a bottle of laudanum from the table. "The wound will probably be fatal, but this will ease the pain and make the going easier for the both of you."

She backed away, refusing to take the bottle he offered. "No. He will get well, I tell you. He will."

TWENTY-TWO

Polly had smelled the stink of death before. Only a faint, teasing whiff two days ago, the sickeningly sweet odor of rotting flesh had become distinct. Soon it would begin to cling, becoming as impenetrable and inescapable as a shroud.

She fell to her knees beside Charlie. He was lying as he had since the shooting. Silent and inert. Only now the gaping hole in his cheek oozed yellow green pus. She laid her hand on his.

How often she had felt this hand. This hand which danced in the air when Charlie spoke, split logs for her woodbox, and turned fallen leaves to study the insects below. This hand, familiar and smooth as worn leather, which stroked her body, playing it like he played his violin, making it come alive with joy and longing.

There was a knock at the door. Polly ignored it. She wanted to see no one. Except Charlie. Charlie come alive again, his deep-throated laughter washing over her like clear spring water.

Behind Polly, the door opened. She recognized Bertha's light tread, but she did not turn.

"Have you heard? Mr. Cone's arrested Cox! He tracked Cox to Salmon Meadows, found he'd sold his horse and gone by stage to Weiser, so followed him there. Someone in Weiser had seen Cox catch a train, but no one knew where the train was headed. Luckily, Mr. Cone heard it was paytime in Pocatello. He guessed Cox would go there to try and pick up some cash gambling, and that's where he was! Going by the name of Eaton, but Mr. Cone got him."

Reaching Polly, Bertha's excited chatter trailed off into silence. She knelt beside her friend. "What is it?"

Polly laid Charlie's hand back beneath the quilt. "It's three weeks, more, since the shooting. The hole should begin to heal, not have pus and smell."

"What does Mr. Troll say?"

"He think Charlie will die."

Bertha winced. "What about Li Dick?"

"He give me special white powder, mold, to kill infection. Always before on other people it work. But not on Charlie."

"Does Li Dick know why?"

"He say the same as Dr. Bibby. The bullet inside Charlie make his blood poison."

"Then we have to find the rest of the bullet," Bertha said simply.

Polly fell back on her heels. "How? I look, Dr. Bibby look. We cannot find it."

Bertha gazed thoughtfully at Charlie. After a few minutes, she turned back to Polly and said, "It was right after the shooting when you and Dr. Bibby tried to find the bullet, and you both looked in Charlie's cheek. Didn't Dr. Bibby say the bullet could work its way to another part of Charlie's body?"

"But where?" Polly, exasperated by Bertha's naive, well-meaning questions, snapped. "I cannot cut Charlie open to see."

"No, but you can feel."

Polly closed her eyes. An overwhelming tiredness pressed her down and she could not move. She felt Bertha's hands on her shoulders.

"Polly, you were only a girl when your father sold you, but you were strong. Strong enough to cross the ocean to a new world. Strong enough to forge a new life for yourself. Aren't you strong enough to keep fighting for the life of the man you love?"

Wearily Polly opened her eyes. "My strength is all used up."

"You've both hung on this long, you can't give up now," Bertha pleaded, her passion as sincere as Polly's had been when she had cried, "He will get well. He will."

She had believed it then. Now she was not

sure. The doctor had been right about the laudanum Charlie would need to escape the pain. Was he also right about the blood poisoning? Certainly Troll and Li Dick agreed.

Bertha walked to the foot of the bed. "Charlie was lying down when Cox shot him," she said slowly. "And Dr. Bibby said the bullet hit the cheekbone. Is it possible the other part went past the bone and down to the back of the head?" She walked back around until she stood opposite Polly. "Let's turn him and see."

Unable to prevent the tiny flicker of hope Bertha's words had ignited, Polly leaned heavily on the bed and pushed herself upright. Together, they turned Charlie. She probed the skull beneath his hair. Nothing. Her fingers worked their way down to his neck. His skin, fiery hot to her touch, was moist. How thin he had become. All bone and flacid muscle. She felt the faint beginnings of a lump. Bone? She brushed aside his hair. Near the center of his neck the skin swelled discolored over the beginnings of a hard, ungiving ridge.

She looked at Bertha. "Is this bone or bullet?"

"It's close to the backbone but off center from it," Bertha said, feeling in the area Polly pointed to. Her eyes brightened. "I think you've found it. Shall I fetch Mr. Troll?"

He had been unwilling to clean the wound without the doctor. How would he feel about digging for a bullet fragment they only believed was there? Would he insist on sending for Dr. Bibby again?

"I do it," Polly said, assembling Charlie's razor, scissors, clean cloths, herbs, and Li Dick's mold on the dry goods box beside Charlie's bed.

Bertha put the kettle on to boil. "What about Li Dick?"

"He does not believe in cutting people," she said tersely, testing the edge of the razor.

She reached for the strop which hung above the washstand and moved the razor across the leather, back and forth, back and forth, the smooth, rhythmic stroking a soothing contrast to the rapid beating of her heart.

"Won't we need help holding Charlie down?"

Polly tested the edge of the razor. It needed no further sharpening. She dropped the strop. "Charlie is full of laudanum. But to be safe, we can tie him down."

They tied him down with sheets twisted into soft ropes. Polly gathered back his hair from around the ridge of skin, cutting and shaving the soft tufts she could not pin. She scrubbed her hands in the basin of scalding hot water, turning them a mottled red.

Bertha stationed herself across from Polly, hot water and cloths on the stool beside her.

A loud croaking broke the hard silence, followed by another and another. Cranes migrating south.

Croaking orders down the line. Cranes. Birds of Death.

"Ready?" Bertha prompted.

Polly, shuddering at the omen, hesitated. Then deliberately she wiped her hands, dipped the razor into the water and wiped it with a cloth soaked in whiskey. "Ready," she breathed.

The razor sank into Charlie's neck, letting loose a gush of red black blood which soaked the pads of white cloth Bertha held ready. Polly dug deeper. The tip touched something hard. Bullet or bone? She withdrew the razor and forced a finger into the hole she had made, trying to ignore the blood spurting over everything. She felt sweat beading her forehead. A wave of faintness washed over her. She forced her finger deeper. It hit something solid. Something small and smooth. Or was it blood that made it slick? She crooked her finger around the object but could not move it. She would have to use the razor to dislodge it.

She withdrew her finger and wiped it clean on the towel Bertha passed her, then picked up the razor. Let it be bullet and not bone, she prayed, easing the razor back into the wound. She felt a slight movement beneath the razor. Her own trembling, Charlie moving, or the bullet loosening? She heard Charlie groan deeply. She would have to hurry.

"Hush," she soothed, as much for herself as Charlie. "I almost done."

She probed deeper, forcing the razor against the bit of hardness, jiggling it slightly. Drops of sweat splashed from her forehead onto her hands. Should she have waited for the bullet to surface on its own? Gritting her teeth, she forced the razor against the hardness and pushed up. Charlie groaned.

"You have it," Bertha said.

Through a haze of moving gray dots, Polly withdrew the razor and bullet fragment. She dropped them into the basin of water. Pink swirls floated from the razor and bullet fragment, turning the colorless water into deepening shades of red, like the sky at dawn.

Again Charlie groaned. Polly quickly rinsed her hands, dried them, and mixed a poultice which she packed into the wound. "You okay now Charlie," she whispered. "You okay."

TWENTY-THREE

Polly looked up from the gold pin Bancroft had asked her to make for his daughter, Caroline. A simple pick and shovel, it did not require enough concentration to distract her from her concern for Charlie.

Still weak, but completely healed, he sat hunched close to the stove, smoking his pipe, his forehead creased with worry Worry about what? Though he had not been to the saloon since the shooting, business had continued brisk, so he could not be fretting about money. The stream of visitors was constant, so he could not be lonely. And he was not a vain man, so it could not be the horribly disfiguring scar, red and raw beneath his right eye. Then why was he becoming increasingly withdrawn?

The off-key strains of a violin tuning up sounded faintly outside the tightly closed windows of Charlie's cabin. A flute quavered, followed by a series of disjointed spasms from an accordion.

Incoherent caroling mixed with drunken laughter rose above the sounds of the orchestra.

Polly pushed back her stool and walked to the window. Her breath added to the opaque film created by the steamy warmth. She lifted her apron and wiped a pane clear. Ice crystals frosted the outside corners of the glass and a layer of fresh snow covered the town, but the night was clear, and she looked expectantly in the direction of Charlie's saloon.

Since the Christmas Eve dance had broken up two days ago, the Old Crowd Club had been using the saloon to celebrate, and now they were spilling out onto the snow, reeling in a drunken procession. Pony Smead, the torch bearer, keeled over. His torch, fizzling in the snow, was seized by John Divine.

Polly turned from the window. "They will never make it all around the camp," she laughed.

Charlie, tamping his pipe, gave no indication he had heard her. He knocked out the unsmoked tobacco, refilled the bowl, tamped it down, knocked it out again.

Polly stoked up the remains of the pine knots alight in the stove. She rummaged in the wood box Taylor was keeping filled and added more kindling, a small log. The fire crackled to life, and she inhaled deeply, relishing the fragrant wood smoke.

"Remember the winter of '88 when it was so cold the horses freeze standing up and you let the fire die? By morning your breath make icicles on your beard, all across the blanket and under your nose," she chuckled.

The words fell like pebbles into the tense silence. She wiped her hands on her apron, leaving sooty streaks. "I know something is bothering you, Charlie. Why don't you tell me?"

"It's nothing," he said, playing with his beard, the tender flesh around his scar. "I just want to say something and I don't know how to begin."

Polly massaged his back. Beneath her fingers she felt him seething, like a pot of boiling water. "You know you can say anything, I will not mind."

He refilled his pipe, stopped, let the tobacco spill unheeded, took a deep breath, and blurted. "I haven't forgotten I asked you to marry me the day I was shot."

"I know you say that to protect me," Polly said, carefully keeping her fingers kneading in an even rhythm. "But you are well now, so there's no need."

"You don't understand," Charlie countered, face flushed, hands fidgeting with bits of spilled tobacco. "I love you, Polly. I want to marry you."

He was serious. But why? After all these years. She put her hands over his, stilling his twitching fingers. "We fine like we are."

"What about children? If we don't marry, we can't have children."

She laughed. "I'm thirty-eight. In China, I be a grandmother."

Charlie laughed with her. "So here you'll be a mother!"

Polly walked over to the washstand and straightened the towels. "No."

"Why not? Plenty of women have children in their thirties, forties even. Look at old Mrs. B. Her last child, what's his name, the fourteenth one, you know the one I mean, you helped birth him. Why, when he was born, she must have been close to fifty!"

So it was children he wanted. Why? Because he had come so close to death? For all their talk, their professed frankness with each other, this was the one subject they had never discussed.

Stalling for time, she emptied the wash basin into the slop bucket. As she poured in fresh water from the pitcher for rinsing, images crowded in on Polly. The special smell of a baby. The warmth of a child's arms wrapped around her legs, her neck. The trust in their eyes. The emptiness in her arms when she returned a child to its mother.

She swilled, emptied, and polished the basin dry. "No, Charlie. Not me."

"You mean you can't?"

For a moment Polly was tempted to let him believe that. But she had not lied to him before. Not even when she was Hong King's slave. She would not begin now. "I mean I will not have children because I do not want children."

"I can't believe that. You love children. You

take care of them when they're sick, play with them when they're well. Every time I turn around you seem to have a baby in your arms or pulling at your skirts."

"Other people's children. Not mine." She swallowed hard, her throat a raw lump of pain. "I decide long ago."

Charlie's voice softened. "I can understand why you didn't want children when you were Hong King's slave. Or even these last years. But if we marry, it'll be different."

Polly stared unseeing out of the window. "I know what people call men with Indian wives. Squaw men. They do not live in town and not with the Indians. They belong nowhere. Their children too. Strangers to their father's people and their mother's."

"You're not Indian, Pol."

"It's the same."

"No, not at all. The white people in Warrens have never treated Chinamen badly. Doesn't everyone call A Sam Mayor of Warrens? And in the eighties, during the height of the troubles, when the League was trying to run Chinamen out of Idaho, Warrens stayed peaceful."

They were the same arguments, almost the same words A Sam had used when Li Dick had warned of trouble. But even as Charlie spoke, she felt the same unease, the same pull of the tightrope and wash of loneliness that had come over her during the Fourth of July dance.

She felt his hands on her shoulders, turning her around. "And if there were trouble, don't you know I'd protect you and the children?"

Her fingers reached up to smooth out the deep furrow between his eyes. "I know you try. Just like my father try. But he not save me from the bandits."

TWENTY-FOUR

The stiff pose captured on the pasteboard by the studio photographer could not hide the obvious pride and joy radiating from the happy parents: John Long holding Edward, the first born, already a year old, and Bertha holding Mary, the new baby.

Polly pointed to Mary's lacy dress and bonnet peeping from beneath layers of finely crocheted shawls. "That's the same dress I made for Edward," she told Li Dick proudly.

His cabin was so small that, seated across from each other, their knees almost touched. Nevertheless, he set down his long-stemmed Chinese pipe and leaned closer, his tongue clicking the appropriate noises of admiration Polly demanded.

She rewrapped the photograph carefully in paper and slipped it back into her pocket. "It's been two years since Bertha and John moved to their farm in Grangeville, but I still find myself walking halfway across Warrens Meadow to the Little Giant Mine for a visit before I remember."

"Seems to me there are other things you've forgotten too."

"Don't start that again."

Li Dick relit his pipe. The smell of tobacco mingled with the fragrance of the herbs and roots hanging from the ceiling. "I can't seem to get through to you. The new law from Washington requires all Chinese laborers to register or face deportation." His right hand sliced the air between them. "There are no exceptions."

"If I register and admit I was smuggled in, I'll be deported. If I don't register and I'm found out, I'll be deported. But if I don't register and I'm not found out, I'll live like I've lived for the last twenty-one years."

"You think because we're high up in the mountains the government won't come after you? When they wanted the Sheepeater Indians they sent troops up here to chase them down. They can do the same to us."

She thought of the naked, unreasoned anger of the government troops unleashed against the Sheepeaters who had sought refuge in the high-timbered mountains near Warrens, the willingness of the townspeople to join the battle. "That was different. The Sheepeaters had murdered two white men."

"Only a few committed the murders. The troops went after them all. The whole tribe. And got them. Just like they can get you."

Polly forced a little laugh. "You're as vinegar-faced as a hired mourner."

"And you're behaving like a fool hen." He shook his pipe at her. "If you're so safe in Warrens, why did Bemis have to build your boarding house for you? Why do you have to keep it in his name?" He set his pipe down.

"Look, you and Bemis have lived together almost eighteen years. You're husband and wife by common law. A five-minute ceremony, a piece of paper, and you're safe from deportation forever."

"Leave Charlie out of it," Polly said, twisting the heavy gold buttons Charlie had made her.

Fists pounded against the door, shaking the bundles of herbs, showering Polly and Li Dick with bits of dried leaves and dust.

"Li Dick, open up! It's me, Bemis!"

Li Dick unbolted the door. Charlie and Talkington, crouching low to avoid damaging the herbs, squeezed through the narrow opening. Snow blew in from small drifts piled up against the cabin, and Li Dick quickly slammed the door behind them. The bottles, jars, and tins crowding the shelves that lined his cabin shook and rattled.

"There's a Chinaman, a stranger come in to winter, who's in a jackpot. He's been accused of stealing a pair of boots from a white man," Charlie said.

Li Dick nodded. "I already went up to jail to see him. Mr. Skinner said the men who brought A Foo in threatened to hang him if he did not return the boots, but A Foo insists he did not take them."

Polly slid off the packing crate. "I take him some supper."

"He's not in the jail. I just checked," Talkington said. "Some men Skinner had never seen before came and took him away. They told Skinner they just wanted to scare the truth out of the Chinaman, but they haven't come back. I'm afraid they've gone and done something stupid."

Polly pulled on coat and gloves. "We go look for them."

"No, you go back to your place or mine," Charlie said. "Li Dick, Talkington, and I will take care of this."

"Sometimes men will listen to a woman, not other men." She traced the scar on Charlie's cheek. "I don't want you to risk another shooting," she added softly.

Li Dick gathered lanterns, a knife. "They'll be gone by now."

"The men weren't on horseback. I figure they didn't intend to take the Chinaman far," Talkington said.

He opened the door. "Skinner says he saw them headed for the river."

Their lanterns held high, they walked in the direction Talkington suggested. Snow, like a fresh lime coating, covered the garbage strewn mud paths that twisted through the huddle of window-less shacks, purging the air of familiar odors, smothering the usual cacophony of night sounds.

It was like a ghost village, Polly thought, goosebumps rising beneath her warm flannel dress and wool coat. A ghost village hoping to escape notice, hence wrath.

Their boots crunched through the thin crust of ice above the first snow of the season. Loose snow rippled like sea sand.

"We can cover more ground if we fan out," Li Dick suggested.

"It's safer if we stick together," Charlie said.

Polly plucked Charlie's sleeve. "Li Dick is right."

Reluctantly, Charlie agreed and they spread out, leaving the town behind them.

Closer to the river, the snow was slick with treacherous ice patches. Wind whipped Polly's skirts, twisting them around her legs, and each step became a battle for balance. The sky, pitch black, threatened a second storm, but she needed support more than she needed light. She set down her lantern.

With one arm, she gripped the ice-sheathed trunk ahead and stepped carefully toward it. The next tree was too far to reach with her hands, but she could grab a branch. Her gloved hands crushed the tiny, glittering icicles shrouding the branch, and she edged forward without falling. Slowly, laboriously, with wind-carried spray stinging her face with fine hard crystals of ice, she worked her way from one tree to the next, leaving the pale glow of her lantern farther and farther behind.

A quarter moon, struggling from behind black clouds, cast gloomy shadows through thickly intertwined branches. From below came the sounds of water smashing against rocks, pulling fallen branches, debris. Closer, she heard a faint rustling. Almost a sigh, it might be the wind or a small wood animal. But the moaning. Was that the wind? Or a human, a man in pain?

She stopped. Not far from her, Charlie's, Li Dick's, and Talkington's lanterns bobbed, their twinkling lights reassuring her of help nearby. But in her own immediate area, there were only shadows.

A snowshoe hare skimmed across the snow, its white winter coat startling in the darkness. A wolf howled, the sound wild and drawn out. Owls hooted. The moon disappeared and the black sky released its snow, dusting the pine branches. She would have to start back before the light powdering became a blinding whirl.

Head bent against the wind, she turned and worked her way cautiously up the ice slick slope toward the barely visible glow of her lantern. A broken branch dangled dangerously. She pushed it aside.

TWENTY-FOUR

It swayed stiffly. Not a broken branch, but a broken man wrapped in a new shroud of feathery white flakes.

TWENTY-FIVE

The dream, when it came, was always the same. The tightrope stretched taut. Herself edging forward. Tired. Anxious to reach the end.

She could not see the place she was struggling to reach. But she could feel its contentment, a sense of repletion. And then, without warning, a branch snapped, knocking her off balance. She fell. The bark peeled off the branch, and she found herself staring into eyes, red and bulging, in a face swollen black, the tongue, distended, choking off a silent scream.

"No," Polly shouted. "No."

Charlie shook her. "Wake up, Pol."

A match scratched against flint and Polly became aware of a sudden glare beyond the darkness of eyelids squeezed shut. Hands straightened her twisted nightgown, stroking, soothing, forcing the dream to recede until she finally dared open her eyes.

There were their two chairs pulled up to the

stove. Charlie's fiddle. The tablecloth she had embroidered. Her plaid dress, gold buttons gleaming, hanging on a nail. Charlie's corduroy pants and flannel shirt tossed on a chair. His boots. Pipe.

Charlie picked up the quilt from the floor where Polly had kicked it, tucking it around her. "Pol, the hanging was terrible, but it's been eight months."

"The men who hang A Foo are still out there."

"They were outsiders Skinner had never seen before."

"Now snow is gone, they can come back. Why you think Chinatown is almost empty?"

"For the same reason white men are leaving Warrens. There's no gold and times are bad."

"Maybe. But Li Dick say, and you know it's true, bad times are when trouble always begin."

Charlie smoothed the hair from Polly's forehead. "Let's close down the saloon and boarding house and take a trip."

"What?"

"There's a place I want to show you."

"Where?"

He smiled. "Not far, just a day's ride. But I can't tell you about it, you have to see it for yourself."

His eyes shone with excitement, like a young man's. A young man with a secret.

"Okay," she agreed. "We go."

Polly took a last bite of the trout Charlie had caught earlier. She had coated it in yellow cornmeal and fried it crisp, serving it sizzling hot with the dandelion greens she had found while Charlie fished. The fresh, tender meat contrasted perfectly with the crunchy casing, and she glowed with the satisfaction that comes at the end of a meal enjoyed. Careful not to disturb Charlie, napping in the shade of a mahogany bush, she gathered the tin plates, forks, and pans and headed for the river to wash.

How deceptive the river was. At first, near Warrens, it had been only a faint rustle. Then, gradually, as they descended the gorge, the rustling had become a rushing roar. Now, at the water's edge, she could see arcs of broken rainbows curving across falls, foam beads glittering like fiery opals, awesome in their colorful beauty. But it was the sound the water made as it crashed against the huge rocks rising dark and treacherous from the Salmon's depths that amazed Polly the most.

A few yards away, a creek, a mere silver streak winding through stands of firs and pines, broadened into shallows, then suddenly narrowed, gushing into the deep, boiling eddies of the Salmon. Across the river, a second, larger creek did the same. And the sound of all the tumbling, boiling water was mesmerizing, washing away any thought of the troubled world beyond the canyon walls.

Impulsively Polly bent and took off her shoes and stockings. The ice cold water lapped against her toes as she strolled along the sand bar, adding her own footprints to the peppered impressions and trailing quill lines of porcupines and, farther on, the tracks of bobcats, minks, otters, and deer.

At the end of the bar, she turned and went back, scuffing up the hot sand, feeling it slide off her feet. She dipped the dishes and pan into the river. A beaver stuck its sleek, dripping face up from the water and eyed Polly inquisitively. Playfully, she splattered it with water. For a moment, it did not move, staring, defiant. Then it dove out of sight. Chuckling, she finished the washing, laid the dishes, pan and forks beside the dying embers of the cooking fire, and dragged her saddle near Charlie.

It was hard to believe that this canyon, so wild and secluded, was only eighteen miles from Warrens, but she could fully understand why the Mallicks, the Nez Perce family across the river, had chosen it to farm. The land, a wilderness of cheat grass, vicious nettles, sumac, and prickly blackberry thickets, was free for the taking; the soil rich, the growing season ample.

She stretched out, her head pillowed in the satin smoothness of her saddle. Above her, in a pocket of the canyon wall, mountain sheep searched for grass, their slate-colored hides barely discernible against the rock. Closer, on a rocky outcrop streaked with bands of grass and trees, she found the big head and horns of a ram feeding, and near it, two brown spots, one larger than another, a ewe and her lamb. They saw her, but did not run, continuing to eat, confident of their safety. All around them dragonflies flashed. Smaller insects hummed. A squirrel scampered up a nearby trunk rich with yellow and green lichen. The sun felt warm, the peace palpable.

"You see why I couldn't tell you about this canyon, why I had to show you?" Charlie said.

Polly, suffused with a sense of contentment she had never known before, rolled over. "Let's stay a few more days."

Charlie propped himself up on his elbow. "Pol, when I asked you to marry me before, you said there was no reason to. But now, with the new law, there is every reason. Let's get married and come here and start a new life together."

Polly catapulted to her knees, showering Charlie with sand. "You don't mind leaving Warrens?"

"It's only a day's ride. I can rent out the saloon, you can rent out your boarding house, and we can always go into town if life gets too dull."

She laughed. "Dull? Too much work on a farm to be dull!"

"Then you agree?"

She pictured the photograph of Bertha's family, only it was she and Charlie with their own babies, children who would know only the joy and peace the canyon offered. After all, hadn't her father and his fathers before him lived in the same village for generations? But her mother, like the other women, had come from another village and, if she had not been sold, there would have come a day when she would have had to leave her family to go to a husband's home and village. And Jim, Li Dick, A Sam, the hundreds of Chinese men in the hold of the ship, in Warrens, and all the other towns and camps, hadn't they left their fathers' villages like Charlie had left his?

The Gold Mountains teemed with men and women on the move, chasing dreams from coast to coast, city to city, mining camp to mining camp. Her dream, the end of the tightrope, was here. But she could not answer for the dreams of the children she and Charlie might have.

She scooped up a handful of sand. It glittered like the copper coins in her father's hands when he had gambled and lost, the gold Charlie had gambled with Hong King and won. And now she too must gamble.

The sand filtered through the cracks of her fingers, sending sand crabs scurrying out of reach. She tightened her hands into fists. How could she bear to lose this canyon, Charlie.

He tipped her chin. "What is it?"

She looked at her twin reflections in his eyes, the one that yearned to say yes, the one that could not. "Children." She shook her head. "No children."

Charlie took her fists, loosening the fingers until her hands lay open in his. "It's you I want, Pol, nothing more."

Her eyes misted, blurring her twin reflections, making them one. "Then yes, Charlie. Oh yes, I marry and come live with you here."

PART FIVE

第五部份

1898-1922

TWENTY-SIX

The ground cherries rustled in their paper shells as Polly tossed them into the five-pound lard bucket beside her. Their first fall in the Salmon Canyon, she had only had the cherries and wild thimbleberries, huckleberries, and blackberries to can. But each year, as her garden expanded and the trees she had planted in her orchard matured, her harvest had increased, and by the time the first snow fell on this, their fourth winter, the shelves that lined her root cellar would be crammed with bottled bear cracklings, plum butter, canned peaches, apricots, garden truck, venison, and grouse.

In addition to fruits and vegetables, she grew her own wheat and ground her own flour to make bread. The single cow and the hens provided all their dairy needs, and she rendered her own grease and made soap from the occasional bear Charlie shot.

On his trips to check on his saloon in Warrens, Charlie traded Polly's produce for the few necessities they could not grow or make, like coal oil, fabric, thread, and shoes. Polly did not accompany Charlie on these trips, for she had sold her boarding house. Everything and everyone she wanted was either already in the canyon or would come to her here.

During the spring, summer, and fall, there were only the occasional prospectors and adventurers Charlie ferried across the river. But in the winter, when the river froze over with huge chunks of ice, ranchers and old friends from Warrens would come. They would stay up all night, getting caught up on news, retelling old stories, playing poker, eating, and drinking whiskey made from her own rye and hops. Then Charlie would bring out his fiddle, and there would be singing and sometimes dancing, and for days, their snug, two-storied log cabin would fairly shake from all the laughter and foot stomping.

"Polly, come here," Charlie called.

Polly tossed a last handful of cherries into the bucket, rose, and stretched, proudly surveying Polly Place. Slender green tips of asparagus peeked above flat gray boulders at the base of the steep canyon slope. Grain hay, sowed to rest the soil, spread a golden aura around long rows of dark green cornstalks, beds of lettuce, cabbage, carrots, turnips, and the special herbs she grew for Li Dick. Roosters strutted among the hens which cackled as they scratched in the straw beside the stable.

Meadowlarks sang above the roar of the river, and from the trees beyond the creek, pheasants drummed on a log.

Across the river, the Mallicks' farm stood empty, for they had left for a homestead near Grangeville where their children could attend school. Polly would like to have been nearer to Bertha and Bertha's children, and a farm anywhere would probably give her many of the same pleasures. The feel of rich soil crumbling between her fingers, the warmth of the sun on her back, the ache of muscles after a day's weeding, the steamy fragrance of cooking fruit, the pungent odor of pickling spices. But only this canyon could infuse her with such deep contentment, and she would never leave it. Never.

"Over here," Charlie said.

She could not see him, but his voice came from the direction of the chestnut and mulberry trees she had planted that spring. Polly walked toward them. A big, bald squash peered out from a few dry, hairy green vines which had fought their way through the willow fence enclosing her garden. She took out her bowie knife and cut the stray squash from the vine, rescuing it from the chipmunks and porcupines which came in the night.

"Just look at this nest of ants," Charlie said from where he lay, belly down, studying the ants scurrying around a mound of pine needles and fallen leaves.

Polly set the squash down beside him and dropped to her knees. An earthworm, half buried in the rich black soil, caught her eye. She plucked it out, dusted it free of clinging dirt, and deposited it in her apron pocket.

"If you work like these ants, I have time to go fishing later," she said, lightly patting the worm wriggling in her pocket.

His blue eyes danced. "You want me to plow?"

They both laughed, remembering their first spring in the canyon and the steer Charlie had purchased to break for the plow. Expecting resistance, he hitched the animal to the top of a fallen tree so that if it ran, the branches would gouge into the earth and stop it. The beast ran as predicted. But the branches, instead of gouging into the earth, slid like runners of a sled over the hard ground and Charlie, too surprised to jump out of the way, was knocked down and pushed under the limbs. When the steer finally stopped, Charlie had emerged clothed only in scratches and bruises. And one sock.

"It's the wrong time of year for plowing," Polly said when she stopped laughing. "But you can help me bring up my buckets of cherries."

He retrieved his hat from beneath a bush and put it on. Two large cabbage leaves covered the crown of the hat, and fluttering over the back of his head and neck was a large white handkerchief fastened to the hat band. Polly, pointing to Charlie's hat, burst into a fresh fit of laughter.

Charlie drew himself up. "This book I read said it's important to shade the neck from the sun." He took a few steps. "See how the handkerchief moves? That keeps a constant current of air passing through to cool the neck and head."

"Charlie, it's October, almost winter, not August," Polly gasped, using her sleeve to wipe the tears streaming down her cheeks.

"I'm trying it out," he said with mock dignity.

"Even in the summer you don't stay out in the sun long enough to need that."

"I will be."

Trying desperately to keep a straight face, Polly said, "Yes?"

"I'm going to rock for gold."

"You give up mining years ago," Polly reminded. "You say it's too much work."

"Maybe your industry is rubbing off on me."

"Good. Then after you take the cherries up to the house, you can chop wood for my wood box and hull the corn."

"Can't. Got to start staking my claim."

"Right today?"

"You remember the prospectors that came down from Buffalo Hump in August, the ones that were in such a hurry they didn't want to stop to eat or talk?"

She nodded.

"Rumor has it the ore they carried will assay enough gold to start a whole new rush."

A chill ran down Polly's spine, raising the soft, downlike hairs at the back of her neck. A rush would mean men pouring into the canyon on their way to the Hump, destroying the peace, the land. And though she was protected by her marriage certificate and her new certificate of residence which Charlie had sent for from the government office in Montana, there was nothing to protect her home, the farm she had carved out of wilderness no one else had wanted. Until now.

"The ranch?"

Charlie waved his hat at her, laughing. "Don't you see? That's why I'm going back to mining. You can't be a partner in a homestead, and you can't own land, but plenty of Chinamen hold claims. So I'll stake out the ranch as a mining claim and file it the next time I go to Warrens."

TWENTY-SEVEN

They worked well together, Charlie fitting the crude wooden box he had made out of a coal oil crate around the tenderfoot's crushed leg and foot, Polly padding the box with cotton ripped out of old quilts, then binding the leg and box in place with long strips of torn sheets.

As soon as she tied the last knot, the boy swung his good leg off the bed.

"No, no," Polly said. "You must rest five weeks, maybe six, before your leg is strong enough for you to leave."

Holding on to the edge of the mattress with both hands, the boy raised himself off the bed. "Haven't you heard about the strike at Buffalo Hump? If I wait six weeks, there'll be no claims left."

He rested his weight on his good leg, took a step, and winced.

Charlie gripped the boy's shoulders and pushed him back on the bed. "You don't know it, but you've got the Angel of the Salmon River caring for you, and if she says five to six weeks before you're fit to move on, that's how long it will be."

The boy propped himself up on his elbows. "But this is a chance in a lifetime."

"You already used up your chance in this lifetime when you tumbled down the mountain and lost your outfit and your horse. If I hadn't happened on you by accident, you would have lost your life too. Don't tempt fate twice," Charlie said, swinging the boy's legs back onto the bed. "Besides, you can't cross the river if I don't row you."

"They say the strike at the Hump is so rich you only need a few days with a shovel and gold pan to get enough dust to be a millionaire!" the boy pleaded.

His eyes, his face, his whole person shone with the same naive hope that had buoyed Polly and all the other men and women crowded into the hold of the ship which had brought her to America, and she knew there was nothing either she or Charlie could say that would deter the boy.

Smiling, she pulled a quilt over him. "With this bad leg, it will take you one week, maybe two to reach the Hump. If you do not die first. On a horse, with Charlie to show you the way, you can get there in two days. So you stay here two weeks, then Charlie will take you."

From the moment Charlie had come home with the tenderfoot across his packhorse instead of a deer, Polly had realized that the winter snows would not protect them from the rush for Buffalo Hump, and Charlie's trip to the Hump with the boy had confirmed it.

The vein of ore was huge, fully visible for five miles, and its course ran down through the Salmon. Despite several feet of snow, more than one hundred prospectors were already living in tents along the vein, and every day more arrived. They came on horseback, often two men on a horse. Or on foot, with huge packs on their backs. And they all had one thought. To have Charlie ferry them across the river so they could climb up to the Hump and stake a claim before all were gone.

The ranch, the only claim Polly and Charlie cared about, was staked out, the claim form completed. But it was not filed, for the ten-foot deep ditch required by law had not been dug.

They had cleared an area near the creek where their sluice boxes would go, and they had started to dig, swinging their picks into the, by then, frost-hardened, ungiving earth. But as the four-foot-square shaft deepened inch by inch, the weather worsened, and Charlie's cough grew more worrisome until Polly insisted he stop.

Coughing and panting, his wet clothes frozen stiff, he refused. "You've heard the men coming through. Grangeville's a madhouse, and Florence and Elk City and a lot of other camps are empty because people are rushing to the Hump. They're staking claims in ten, fifteen feet of snow."

"Most of those claims won't hold up."

The scar from the shooting stood out harshly red in a face gray with exhaustion. "Exactly. This one will," he coughed.

Polly covered Charlie's mittened hands with hers, preventing him from lifting the pick. "You think I care about the claim if this is your grave we are digging?"

That night she wakened to feel Charlie burning with fever. In a voice hoarse from coughing, he complained of tightness in his chest. For days Polly made hot mustard and linseed poultices for his chest, simmered herb teas for him to drink, and brought up kettles of steaming hot water for him to inhale. His cough worsened, his nose bled, and she ran up and down the stairs cleaning the slop bucket, changing the sweat-soaked sheets. Finally, in the second week of illness, his fever broke. But it was almost a month before he was well enough to go down-stairs again.

He sat hunched over the stove, puffing on his pipe, staring through frost-crusted windows at a world turned white as mourning. Across the river which crashed and roared beneath slabs of con-gealed ice, the fires of prospectors camped along Crooked Creek winked, mocking.

Polly rammed her fist into the dough she had

left to rise. While Charlie had demanded her constant attention, she had not had time to think of the ditch left unfinished, the claim not filed. But now, with his recovery assured, fears she had refused to acknowledge surfaced.

She pounded the dough with calloused brown fingers balled into fists, kneading, pressing down unwanted thoughts as well as dough. Then she shaped the formless mass into loaves which would rise and fall and rise again. Like lives.

Was that the reason for the New Year cake families in her village made each year? It was the one time her father supervised the cooking, shutting all the doors just before her mother eased the dough into the huge boiler to steam. Then he would light the incense to time the cooking, hovering as it smoldered into ash. Finally, as he lifted the lid, waving away the cloud of steam which burst out like a winter mist, they would all crowd around, anxious to see if the cake was a fluffy, delicious omen of good luck or a flat portent of disaster.

Polly set the pans of light bread on the stove to rise. Her mother's cake had always risen. Even the New Year before the winter wheat. The New Year before she was sold. It was not luck that determined the rise and fall of cakes or bread or lives, but skill, strength, the right ingredients.

She wiped her floury hands on her apron and wrapped herself up in coat, scarves, boots. She had skill and strength. And she would create the right ingredients.

Alternately urging him to hurry and to walk slowly, Polly led a well-bundled Charlie toward the frozen creek. The wind-whipped mountain slopes glared a painful white against the sunny blue sky, but dark shadows slashed the snow-covered floor of the canyon, and the sharp frosty air, fragrant with wood smoke, stung Charlie's sallow cheeks into a chapped red. From the hen house came the sleepy clucking of chickens jostling in their roosts, and from the stable the tinkle of the cow bell, the restless nickering and pawing of horses.

Their boots crunched in the ice-crusted snow.

"The canyon is not the same when the river is frozen silent," Polly said.

"Makes travel to the Hump easier," Charlie said gloomily, his breath puffing out like smoke.

Polly playfully caught at the wispy streamers of white breath. "The Hump is not the only place people go."

"This winter it is."

"Not you," she said, bringing them to a sudden stop. "You will go to Warrens."

"What for?"

"To file the claim."

Stooping, she dragged away broken pine branches laden with clumps of new snow, revealing a ditch exactly four feet square and ten feet deep.

Charlie gaped. "That's impossible! The ground is frozen solid."

"Not when I dig," Polly chuckled, enjoying Charlie's astonishment. "Each day I build a fire in the hole and warm the top of the ground. Then I dig. When I reach frozen earth again, I stop and build a new fire."

"This calls for a celebration!" Charlie said.

"Not yet. When you come back from Warrens."

TWENTY-EIGHT

During her twenty-two years in Warrens, Polly had observed that there were five types of miners. The happy-go-lucky prospectors, men of few words who roamed the forests and mountains with boundless patience and optimism. Placer miners who drifted from stream to stream, seesawing between poverty and riches, hardship and hard living. Promoters, flabby and soft, who were not above salting samples before assaying in order to attract investors. Financiers, capitalists who knew little and cared less about mining and miners, but whose money bought the machinery, organization, and engineering necessary for proper development. And hard rock miners, men like John Long, courageous and reliable, who brought the leavening influence of wives and children into the camp.

The strike at Buffalo Hump, advertised as "the greatest gold camp on earth," brought men from all around the world. Men with the same hopes and fears, greed and generous good natures, rugged individuality and prejudices as the ones Polly had observed in Warrens. And at first, during the tense months before Charlie successfully filed the claim for Polly Place, she had felt the tightrope returning. But with the ranch secure, the fears and bad dreams which had returned vanished.

By July of the following year, the only claims left were those invented for sale to suckers, and the steady stream of hopeful men trudging through the canyon on their way to the Hump dwindled to a trickle. But promoters enticed capitalists from the East, and a year later, mill operations were started at the Big Buffalo, Crackerjack, Badger, and Jumbo Mines, and development began in earnest.

Then in July of 1901, there was a new rush, this time for Thunder Mountain. "The gold on that mountain is skin deep," Charlie said scornfully. Nevertheless, optimistic prospectors, miners, and smooth-talking promoters were able to keep rumors and mines alive for almost a decade until a slide in 1909 created a lake, putting Roosevelt, the supply camp, underwater.

Traffic through the canyon shrank back to the occasional prospector and adventurer, and the peace Polly loved so well returned, more satisfying and deeply valued than before.

There were a few permanent changes. In order to keep the claim on the ranch valid, she and Charlie now placered each spring when the creek was at high water. And they had new neighbors, Charles

Shepp and Pete Klinkhammer, who had bought the Mallick's old farm across the river.

They had met Shepp, an old Klondike argonaut, near the start of the Buffalo Hump rush when he filed a claim on the west fork of Crooked Creek and rode down to buy produce from Polly. Two years later, Pete, a young man who had left his parents' Minnesota farm to seek adventure in the West, joined Shepp. Unlike Polly, Pete had wanted to leave farming behind him, but neither the mine nor the brewery company he and Shepp started was successful, and when the Northern Pacific made a survey for running a line through the canyon, they bought Tom Copenhaver's claim on the Mallick farm.

"You think the railroad will come to the canyon?" Polly asked.

Charlie pushed Teddy, their black and white terrier, off his chest and rolled over in the grass. "We'll never see the railroad here."

Teddy scooted over to Polly. She scratched his ears with her left hand, continuing to paint the hen house with her right. "Pete say he and Shepp homestead one hundred thirty-seven acres."

"One hundred thirty-seven," she repeated, shaking her brush for emphasis. "I busy all day with twenty."

Charlie snatched his fiddle out of reach of the drops of carbolic acid and coal oil sprinkling from Polly's brush. He tucked it under his chin. "Don't forget they have two men working the place. You only have yourself. Besides, Pete is less than half your age, and both Shepp and Pete are twice your size," he said, drawing the bow across the strings.

"Pete handle the stock and the team for plowing and haying, but he still do assessment work to bring in cash. Shepp take care of all the garden work by himself and he is also carpenter and cook," she said, squirreling inside the hen house to paint the mite-infested roosts.

"Makes a fellow tired just thinking about it."

Polly stuck her head out. "Not too tired to hunt, I hope. I tell Shepp and Pete since they have so much work, you will hunt fresh meat for us all."

Lifting her hems, damp from the last traces of morning dew, Polly skirted a thorn bush and took Charlie's hand. Clammy. She reached up and felt his forehead. Beneath a fine film of perspiration, it was cold to her touch. He had told her his eyes were weakening and he needed her to sight the game for him to shoot, but he had not said how difficult the climb uphill had become for him.

He coughed. In the aftermath, Polly detected the same rattle that had worried her during his attack of pneumonia the winter of the Buffalo Hump rush.

"You okay?" she asked.

"Fine," he panted, propping his Winchester

against a pine and collapsing onto a soft bed of ferns. "Just need a few minutes to catch my breath."

Polly knelt beside him. "You sure?"

"Polly, I'm sixty-three years old and winded. That's all."

Teddy hurtled back down the steep wall of the canyon. Panting, he threw himself down at Polly's feet.

"See, even Teddy needs a break," he said, stretching out.

Polly leaned back against a fallen log, thoughtfully chewing a blade of sour grass. Beneath them thundered the Salmon. Swollen ten, twenty feet above its summer level, it swept along fallen trees, rolling rocks, the last few blocks of unmelted ice. In the distance, a lone buck rubbed its new antlers against a pine tree, scraping off the velvet, polishing. Closer, on the creek bank, a beaver sat, combing its fur with its toe nails. Everything smelled alive, fresh, newly green.

Teddy, eager to be off again, nuzzled inquiringly, his nose wet and cold against Polly's cheek. She scratched behind his ears, burying her face in his fur. Perhaps Charlie was right and she was just over anxious. Wasn't she almost sixty herself, her hair white, her brown face wrinkled as a walnut, her fingers beginning to gnarl?

"Look," Charlie said, pointing to a golden eagle circling the sky above a rocky ledge.

TWENTY-EIGHT

As Polly's eyes followed Charlie's finger, the huge bird tucked in its wings and dove. When the distance between ledge and bird narrowed, it spread out its wings. Then, barely touching the ledge, it soared back up, its claws weighted down with a yellow bundle.

Charlie stood. He dusted off dirt, bits of twigs and dead leaves. "What is it?" he asked, squinting.

"Some kind of cub I think."

"Any sign of a mother?"

She caught a quick movement on the ledge, but it was far too small to be a grown cat. "No. Maybe another cub."

"Not like a nursing mother to leave her babies, let's go check it out."

TWENTY-NINE

Charlie picked up the cub. "A cougar. She can't be more than six weeks old."

"I make a bottle for her."

"She might refuse cow's milk. Like those motherless lambs you tried to raise," Charlie warned.

But unlike the lambs which had stubbornly locked their jaws against the bottle, letting the milk spill into their tight curls until they reeked of sour milk, weakened, and died, the cougar cub sucked until her stomach bulged, then yawned and stretched. Teddy, his furry brow wrinkled comically, hovered while the cub sniffed at the furniture and the plants outside, turning over pinecones, tossing leaves and feathers, and tumbling over fallen branches. When she strayed, he picked her up by the scruff of her neck and brought her back, dropping her at Polly's feet, and as the cub grew, they romped together, wrestling.

By the time the cottonwoods turned yellow and

gold, the cub was the same size as Teddy. By midwinter, stretched out, she was as big as Polly, and by spring thaw, larger than Charlie. Sitting on the floor, she could reach and eat from the tin plate Polly had nailed onto the table for her, and when she raked her claws along the trunks of trees, the marks ran deep.

"It isn't natural," Shepp said, pointing to the cougar sitting across from him, licking her plate clean.

Polly, coming in from the kitchen, set generous portions of peach cobbler in front of Charlie, Pete, and Shepp. She poured fresh coffee all around. "Amber make you nervous?"

"Any animal that can break a buck deer's neck with a snap of its jaws makes me nervous," Shepp said, digging into the cobbler.

"She won't hurt you."

"Try telling Tom that," Charlie laughed. "He came down from Warrens last week. Got here after dark and before he knew what was happening, Amber had leaped out of a tree, knocked him off his horse, and pinned him to the ground."

"She only want to play."

"Well, get her to play outside," Pete said.

He shoved back his chair and opened the door. Charlie grabbed Amber by the scruff of the neck. She arched her back and hissed. Teddy rose to his haunches and growled protectively.

Charlie dropped back onto his chair. "You get her," he told Polly.

Polly stroked Amber's arched back, smoothing the fur which had bristled. The cat licked Polly's face wetly.

"Outside," she ordered.

Amber padded obediently toward the open door, her claws clicking on the plank floor. Teddy followed. Polly shut the door behind them.

"There, now you feel safe?" she asked the three men.

Grinning sheepishly, they concentrated on their cobblers and coffee. Pete held his mug out for a refill.

"If prohibition goes through, you could take that cat up to Warrens to guard Charlie's saloon from federal officers," he said.

"Only problem is, she'd scare the customers away too," Charlie said. "But no need to worry, winters will be no problem. The officers, no matter how zealous, will never brave twenty-foot drifts, and in the summer, there are telephone lines between most of the ranches, so it'll be easy to give warning of anyone coming in who looks suspicious."

"A telephone's not too different from the crystal set I made," Shepp said. "I could put a line between our two ranches."

"What for?" Polly asked.

"Maybe they're thinking of going back into the brewery business," Charlie said.

Pete shook his head vigorously. "Never!"

"But a telephone could come in handy," Shepp persisted. "Just think, if we have a line, we can call ahead and have Polly get Amber out of the way before we cross the river."

Teddy, his muzzle spiked cruelly with porcupine quills, squirmed under Charlie's firm grip while Polly tugged at the quills with a pair of pliers.

"Poor Teddy," she sympathized. "You think just because Amber can jump a porcupine and eat the quills, you can."

"Maybe Shepp's right," Charlie said.

The quill Polly was pulling snapped off close to the flesh and Teddy whimpered. "You want to get rid of Amber?"

Perspiration from the strain of holding Teddy mottled Charlie's forehead. "No, of course not. I mean about the telephone. Some day, if we really need help, that signal we use, the white towel on the bush, might not be fast enough."

"They get over here plenty quick enough for fish fries."

Charlie coughed. "Polly, be serious. We're not getting any younger, you know."

She worked the broken quill free. "Years, white hair, and wrinkles mean nothing. They're just a way to mark time. Like the rings in a tree.

Uncle Dave Lewis is more than seventy and he live alone on Big Creek and run a pack string and hunt cougars. And Goon Dick is older than that, but every spring he come back all the way from Seattle to placer in Warrens."

She extracted the last quill, dropped the pliers, and rubbed Teddy's nose tenderly. "Sure I need spectacles for close needlework, but I still farm a big garden. And," she added, laughing, "your fingers are still mighty quick with cards and fiddle."

"Look at me," Charlie said. "I mean really look at me and tell me what you see."

The intensity in his voice startled Polly. She released Teddy and studied Charlie's face. Each morning, when she woke beside him, she was surprised anew at the dark smudges beneath pale, watery blue eyes, the thin wisps of hair, the shock of white beard, the way bones protruded under finely wrinkled skin. But then, during the course of the day, when they talked and laughed, he became the same Charlie who had saved her that first night in Warrens, camas blue eyes dancing, coppery hair and beard a blaze of flame, and she allowed herself to forget how easily he tired. How he made fewer and fewer trips into Warrens. How his pale cheeks flushed as afternoon wore into evening. How her cough syrups and herb teas were losing the fight against the cough which had become a part of him.

She looked away. Amber, head lowered, crouched in the grass, creeping along noiselessly, her tawny fur a slither of gold in the waves of green. She leaped on top of Teddy and they tumbled down the slope, a blur of black and white and gold.

Polly had seen the same scene reenacted many times, and it always made her laugh because she knew Teddy saw Amber long before she jumped. But she did not laugh now. For like Amber, she had allowed herself to be fooled. Refusing to acknowledge what her eyes, her years of nursing the sick had told her.

Polly turned to face Charlie. "We tell Shepp yes, we want the telephone," she said.

THIRTY

The sun dipped behind the canyon walls, its afterglow casting a silvery sheen on the bleached roof shingles still steaming from an unexpected afternoon shower. Polly, laughing, wiped her hands clean on a tuft of damp sour grass. She leaned on the lard bucket, half full of chestnuts, and pushed herself upright.

Pete eyed her quizzically.

"When a person start picking up horse nuts instead of chestnuts, it's time to quit," she chuckled.

Pete picked up the two lard buckets of chestnuts. "I'll take these up to the house for you."

Teddy, his gait stiff and awkward, hurried after Polly and Pete. She slowed, partly to accommodate him, partly because her own feet pained her now after a full day's labor.

"Your harvest good?" she asked.

"Better than our first one."

Polly laughed. "I remember. You plant too

early and everything come up and just sit. You have enough seed for ten years!"

She opened the door for him. "You say you pack produce up to the Jumbo tomorrow?"

Pete set the buckets down. "Yes."

"You have room to take a few things to friends for me?"

"Sure."

From the shelves beneath the stairs, Polly brought out jars and bottles, a crocheted cap. "This liniment is for Jessie, the preserves are for Nellie Shultz, and the crocheted cap you give Four-Eyed Timothy to take to his mother in Dixie."

She wrapped them up in clean flour sacks, tucked them into a well-lined coal oil tin, and headed for the kitchen.

"Whoa!" Pete said. "I'm only taking one mule, not a whole string."

"You mean you have no room for sauerkraut I make like your sister teach me?"

"Well now, that'll just go across the river and I didn't say there wasn't room in the boat," Pete said quickly.

Chuckling, Polly wrapped two jars of sauerkraut and added them to the tin. She followed Pete back out onto the porch. "Thank you for bringing the mail. Charlie like to keep up with the news."

"How is he?"

"Last year, after he give up his saloon and stop going to Warrens, he eat a little more, and drink a little less. For a while, I think he get better. But this year is almost over and he not come downstairs one time. And this month he not get out of bed at all."

"Well, remember, anytime you need help, you give us a ring. That's what the telephone's for."

She glanced up at the thin black wire suspended between the two ranches, thinking of how she had joked when Shepp had suggested it four years ago, how grateful she was for it now.

"You and Shepp already do too much," she said. "You order my seeds, my spectacles, my shoes." Laughing, she pointed to the stream of clear water now officially designated on maps as Polly Creek. "You even order survey men to make me a famous person!"

Pete nodded at the tin loaded with Polly's gifts. "Small payment for this, all the surprise fish fries, and good suppers," he said.

"You come over after you get back from the Jumbo, I make you a chestnut pie and good venison jerky to take with you when you go set your trap line."

Pete patted his stomach. "Don't worry, I will."

Back inside, Polly chopped some leftover chicken for Teddy who had grown toothless, then took down a clean jar to make gum arabic water to soothe Charlie's cough. She poured water, sugar candy, and gum into the jar, set it in a saucepan of water, and stirred.

As she waited for the gum and candy to dissolve, she thought of all the remedies, Chinese and Western, which had failed to cure Charlie's cough or restore his strength. Not for the first time, she wondered if the cough was perhaps a symptom of a more serious illness and not the illness itself. If only Li Dick had not left Warrens, she could ask him, but he had gone back to China and A Can, the retired packer who had taken his place as herbalist for the dozen or so remaining Chinese, did not have Li Dick's skills. Nevertheless, she tried the powders and herbs he ordered for her from the Big City, just as she tried the medicines friends and strangers suggested, the receipts for cures Charlie found in his books.

Steam rose fragrant from the saucepan and she poured the mixture into a mug to take up to Charlie. At the bottom of the stairs, Teddy raised his forepaws expectantly. He was too old, too stiff to climb more than one or two steps, and he pawed at the treads, whining, begging Polly to carry him up too.

Careful not to spill the gum arabic water, she leaned over cautiously and scratched behind his ears, his chin, ruffling his fur. "I come back for you," she promised.

Charlie was asleep. Polly set the steaming mug down on the table beside him and laid the back of her hand against his forehead, his sunken cheek. How thin he had grown, his flesh melting despite custards and rich broths, leaving mere skin over bone. And his cheek, falsely rosy, burned to the touch.

His eyes opened, brightened at the sight of Polly beside him. He pulled her down onto the bed and pointed to the photograph album propped open on his chest. "Look," he said hoarsely.

It was her wedding picture. She stood, stiffly corseted, dress dark and sober, face serious, sad almost, right hand resting awkwardly on Charlie's thick family bible. But underneath, where no one except Charlie and herself would see, she had been afire in scarlet. From her long crimson petticoats to her embroidered corset cover and ruffled drawers.

Polly smiled, remembering. "I dare not wear red outside or everyone think I am shameful, but in China, red is a happy color, a wedding color, so I want to wear it. That's why I look so serious. I'm trying not to laugh and give away our secret."

"It's been twenty-seven years," Charlie said. "Fifty if we go back to the day you first rode into Warrens, trying to act brave when any fool could see how scared you were." A spasm of coughing shook him.

Polly propped him up on his pillows and rubbed

his back. She passed him a square of clean sacking. He spat into it. Phlegm threaded with red wisps. Blood.

She felt the moment freeze. Blood meant the spitting blood disease. The same spitting blood disease she had seen kill men much younger than Charlie.

Blinking back tears, she snatched the soiled piece of sacking and threw it into the can already spilling over with phlegm-stiffened squares of cloth, some traced with the telltale brown of dried blood.

"If only life could be held captive like memories," Charlie sighed.

Unable to speak, Polly closed Charlie's wasted fingers around the mug of gum arabic water and walked over to the window opposite the bed. She rested her forehead against the chilled panes of glass.

Outside, dusk gathered into darkness. Soft and gentle, it rolled down the canyon walls, obliterating the mahogany and scrub oaks flamed red between blue green spruces and lemon yellow aspens and willows. It marched on, relentless, devouring her garden, the vine-covered hen house, the porch, until there was only blackness. A bit of gold flashed, Amber hurrying home? But Amber, shot by a faceless stranger, was dead. Like Bertha Long's second son, a soldier in France, and her husband, John, snatched by death at the end of a dance.

The bit of gold flickered, leaped into a tongue of

fire, and she saw the room and Charlie, ghostly white, reflected in searing flame. A dog howled.

"No," Polly cried, spinning around.

She realized immediately the flame was only Charlie lighting the lamp, the howl Teddy reminding her of her promise. But when she took the empty mug from Charlie, it shattered in her grasp.

A shard pierced her palm. Instinctively she brought it to her lips and sucked the wound. The blood tasted of salt. Like tears.

THIRTY-ONE

During the long winter months, the red stains in Charlie's phlegm had grown larger and darker, his cough more deep seated. But with the coming of the dry summer heat, his cough had eased up, and though he was still too weak to walk, Polly was confident he was on the mend.

She set his empty dinner dishes on the tray. "You know, Bruce Crofoot at Sheep Creek have the spitting blood sickness like you and he come to Salmon River to die. Now he is more healthy than me. You know why? Because he eat mold. All the mold he can find. Especially bread mold."

Charlie dealt out a game of solitaire on the light summer quilt Polly insisted he needed. "Don't get any ideas about feeding me mold," he said.

"What do you think stop your infection when Cox shoot you?" she said, retrieving Teddy's empty bowl from where he lay at the foot of the bed.

"That wasn't any old mold. It was Li Dick's. And I didn't have to eat it."

She peered over Charlie's shoulder. "Put the three of spades there and that queen here," she advised, pointing.

"I thought you were going fishing," he said.

Laughing, she picked up the tray. Teddy pawed at the edge of the bed, silently begging to be carried down and taken with her. She rubbed his nose. "No, Teddy. You stay with Charlie," she said, scratching his chin, his twitching whiskers. "You too old to climb over rocks."

She was getting too old for climbing over blisteringly hot rocks herself, Polly realized, puffing, her heat-swollen feet chaffing against the stiff leather of her brogues. But by August, Polly Creek was too low for good fishing and, with Pete in Dixie, she did not want to disturb Shepp for something so trivial as rowing her over to Crooked Creek.

Scrambling over one final boulder, she set down her rod and tackle, wiped her face free of perspiration, took a few minutes to catch her breath, then unlaced her brogues, pulled off her stockings, and soaked her burning feet in the ice cold water of the Salmon.

The swift current swirled around her feet, soothing, and she closed her eyes and settled back against the smooth hollow of a sun-baked rock. The lacy fronds of willow shading her from the sun created a cool blue green world, and inside Polly, peace and contentment brimmed replete.

THIRTY-ONE

When Polly woke, the air had become heavy and threatening, and the sun had already begun its descent in the arc of sky above the canyon rim. She dried her feet quickly on her apron, pulled on stockings and shoes, attached bait to hook, lifted her rod, and cast out. The line curved, sure and graceful, into the gittering white water of the Salmon.

The glare of sun on water hurt her eyes, and she looked beyond the silver streak of river to the sparsely wooded slope rising from the stretch of rocks and sand. In the open space around a deer lick, three or four doe and a young buck became suddenly still, then darted from the hollow. Their big ears and long slim necks flashed between rocky outcrops as they disappeared into tall grasses and pines, leaving Polly jumpy, her senses fractured, yet keenly aware.

She felt the stifling heat that bounced off the canyon walls, heard the nervous chatter of squirrels. Bird cries. Flapping wings. Crackling. The acrid smell of smoke. Her eyes scanned the tree- and brush-covered slopes ahead of her. All clear. She turned. There, rising from behind the thick copse of trees screening the house was the smoke, a thin, innocent spiral. A cooking fire started by a prospector or friend? Then why the flight of deer and squirrels and birds?

The rod slid from Polly's fingers and she scrambled back over the rocks, heedless of the sharp edges that snagged her stockings and scraped her hands.

Her legs, hampered by skirts and fear, grew heavy. Her rock-torn palms stung. Throat and lungs burned. Heart pounded, threatening to burst through chest. But now she could hear Teddy's mournful wailing, the pounding of hooves against stable doors, frightened neighing, Charlie's hoarse cries, and she dared not stop.

At last she was past the rocks and blind of trees and on the grassy slope to garden and house. A small tongue of flame licked the peak of the roof nearest the chimney. A roof fire? And the cedar shakes drier than the kindling she used to light the stove. How bad was it? How fast was it spreading? What was happening on the side she could not see?

Her thoughts raced past her feet. The pole ladder. The one in the shed. Water. Too far to the creek. Use the water in the barrel first. Then the creek. Can't do it alone. Shepp. Telephone him first. Then the ladder, then the buckets.

Cut across the vegetable patch. Shorter. Can't. The deer fence. She tore at the poles. Too deeply embedded. The gate too far. Squeeze through. Not enough space.

Splinters pierced her skirts, her flesh.

"Polly!"

She whipped around. Shepp was in his rowboat, already halfway across the Salmon. He knew. He was coming. Help was coming!

Hope surged through Polly, giving her the strength to burst through the fence. Her feet crushed cabbages, squashes, melons. She pushed through rows of corn. And then the earth exploded, throwing Polly to the ground. A rifle cracked. And then another, and another, the sharp reports of pistol and rifle ammunition exploding one shell at a time. Dirt filled Polly's mouth, her nose, her ears, her eyes. Fragments of vegetables. Grit. Screams. Drumming hooves. Teddy's barks. The frantic squawking of chickens.

Dazed by her fall, choking from the dust and smoke, Polly pulled herself to her knees. The cabin was completely enveloped in flames.

"Charlie!" she screamed, scrambling to her feet. "Charlie."

With a fierce energy she thought lost forever, Polly broke through the fence, rushed across the strip of yard and tore up the stairs, heedless of the flames that leaped around her.

The smoke upstairs was far thicker and blacker. She covered her nose and mouth with her apron, dropped to her knees, and crawled to their bedroom. Her eyes, unprotected, smarted and teared. Groping, she found the bed. Empty.

"Charlie," Polly called through her apron. "Where are you?"

Smoke burned her throat raw. She coughed. Above the crackle of flames she heard Teddy whimper, felt his tongue wet against her arm. She hugged the dog to her.

"Where's Charlie?" she asked.

Teddy tugged at her sleeve. She crawled behind him. Around the bed. Past the dresser. To the desk beside the washstand. He stopped and pulled feebly at a crumpled quilt beside the open trunk.

Polly fell on the lifeless form beneath it. "Charlie!" she cried.

He stirred, struggling to reach the desk. "Papers. Must get papers," he whispered.

"We have to go," she said, tearing a towel from the rack above the washstand and dunking it into the pitcher of water. "Get out. Now." She wrung out the towel. "You hold towel over your mouth with one hand. Wrap your other arm around me, and..."

Charlie pushed the towel away. "No. Got to get certificates. Claim."

Polly staggered to her feet. "Charlie, please. Help me," she pleaded, trying to pull him upright.

Glowing cinders and ash showered down, sparking small flickering fires. Teddy frisked like a puppy, yelping in pain. Polly, choking from the smoke, the smell of singed fur, and burning flesh, released Charlie to stamp and beat out the flames on the floor, Charlie, Teddy, herself.

"Polly? Charlie?"

"Shepp," Polly called. "Over here." She patted Teddy. "Fetch Shepp," she commanded.

She tore a second towel off the rack and dunked it in the pitcher.

"Here," she said, handing the towel to Shepp. "You take."

Shepp draped the wet towel over his head and shoulders. "Hurry," he said, hoisting Charlie to his feet. "The staircase will go any minute."

Charlie struggled. "No," he coughed. "Papers. Must get papers."

Polly jerked open the drawer of the desk, grabbed a sheaf of papers and waved them in front of Charlie. "I have papers," she said, stuffing them into the bib of her apron.

Quickly, she covered his face with the wet towel and lifted the hem of her apron, making a sling for Teddy.

"Charlie's passed out," Shepp said. "He's dead weight."

"I help," Polly said. Cradling Teddy with one hand, she tried to lift Charlie's legs with the other. She could not.

"Drop the dog," Shepp said.

"No." She stuffed the bunched up apron into her mouth and held it with her teeth, leaving her arms free to lift Charlie's legs.

She backed toward the door. The heat in the hallway was intense. Polly twisted her head to see behind her, but the smoke and flames had created an impenetrable black and orange wall.

"Left," Shepp shouted above the roar of flames and falling timber. "Right. First stair."

Hardly able to breathe, her jaw straining from Teddy's weight, her arms from Charlie's, Polly felt warily for the edge of the stair, lowered one foot, then the next. And again for the second stair. The third.

The awkward angle pushed Charlie's feet against Teddy, tearing at the taut stretch of apron. Polly clenched her teeth tighter. She thrust Charlie's legs stiffly forward from Teddy's bulk, dropped onto another stair, snapped her head back, pulled Charlie's feet back against her belly, and lowered Teddy onto Charlie's legs. Immediately, the pressure on her teeth, jaw, and neck lifted.

She continued the torturous descent. Right foot feel, drop. Left foot follow. Right foot feel, drop. Left foot follow.

Her skin blistered from the profusion of falling cinders. Her eyes teared. She gagged from the choking black smoke, the apron stuffed into her mouth. The weight on her arms, her jaws, and neck became unbearable. She tried pushing Charlie's legs onto one side of her so she could wrap her arms around them more fully, but the movement threatened Teddy's precarious balance in the slackened folds of her apron. Almost there, she told herself, tightening her grip. Right foot feel, drop. Left foot follow. Right foot feel, drop.

Her foot plunged through the stair. Jagged, splintered wood tore through her stockings. Flames seared her scratched flesh. She hurled herself forward, reaching for the banister, pulling her leg back through the charred stair. Teddy squirmed, yelping, burrowing. There was a sudden release of pressure on her teeth and jaws, an emptiness, a long mournful howl. The crash of a falling beam. A shower of cinders. The awful stink of scorched fur and flesh.

"You all right?" Shepp shouted.

Tearing the now useless apron sling from between clenched teeth, Polly coughed a faint, "Yes."

Grimly, she hoisted Charlie's legs back up, clutched the bannister, and half slid, half fell to the bottom of the stairs, staggering around fallen timbers, raging flames, outside to air. Life. And a rain of ashes cold as her own heart.

THIRTY-TWO

From the spare bedroom of Shepp and Pete's house, Polly could not see what was left of Polly Place. Yet there had not been a moment, day or night, in the seven weeks since the fire when the events of that afternoon did not replay themselves in her mind's eye.

Exhausted, choking from smoke and fear, their clothes scorched, and their singed hair and blistered flesh stinking, she and Shepp had carried Charlie to safety, released the horses and cow, and run back and forth from the creek, pouring bucket after bucket of water, stamping and beating out new bursts of flames. The fire had not spread beyond the sheds. But the house was a black skeleton above dead embers, Teddy and twenty-eight years of her life buried in its ashes. And Charlie?

In the gloomy yellow puddle of light cast by the lamp, his bearded face peered corpselike above the bright patchwork of borrowed quilts, radiating questions which haunted like spectres.

What if she had not gone fishing that afternoon? What if she had not fallen asleep down by
the river? What if Charlie had not been so worried
about the papers needed for her protection? Would
he have tried sliding down the stairs on his own
before the explosion, escaping the clouds of black
smoke that had filled his weakened lungs? Or what
if she had not tried to save Teddy, a toothless dog
already close to death? Would Charlie then be free
of this terrible gurgling that sounded increasingly
like a death rattle?

Only an hour ago, when his coughing had
become so severe that breathing became impossible, she had thrust her fingers down his throat,
allowing the phlegm, blood, and corruption to spill
out in curdled lumps, clearing the clogged passages. But already they had refilled, and again his
chest was heaving, his lungs straining for the small
bits of rank sickroom air that grated through the
blocked passages of his nose and throat.

Polly fumbled for the bottle of oil among the jars
and bottles that crowded the nightstand. When she
had inserted her fingers in Charlie's mouth before,
his teeth had clamped down involuntarily, and she
had had to pry open his jaws with her other hand in
order to force her fingers into his throat. She knew
he would not let her try again, yet it was the
constant struggle for air that used up his strength.

She rubbed the oil into the blue gray ridges and
fissures of Charlie's swollen fever-cracked lips,

remembering their smooth, gentle warmth, their ability to please, love, and hurt.

His eyelids fluttered open. He lifted his arm and reached for hers. "The laws haven't changed," he whispered, just as he did each time he woke.

She took his hand, the flesh so shriveled, so cold she could almost feel the pull of death. "I know, but you not worry. I have papers. See?"

She picked up the wedding certificate, certificate of residence, and claim for the ranch, and held them close. He strained forward. The gurgling deep in his chest intensified, and he fell back against the pillows, gasping for air. Polly dropped the papers and added another pillow to the already large pile beneath his head.

"It's no good," he panted. "I'm drowning. Drowning in my own juices."

He coughed. Polly pulled a wad of clean sacking from her apron pocket. She wiped the blood from Charlie's mouth and beard, the perspiration from his forehead, neck, and chest, grieving for his loss of strength, his regression to the helplessness of a child, a baby.

A baby. Hadn't she once saved a baby by taking a reed, pulling out the pithy center to make a hollow tube, working the reed down the baby's throat, and sucking out the mucus? Then why not Charlie? She threw down the soiled sacking. "Charlie, I go get a reed to make tube that can help you breathe."

He clutched her sleeve, his eyes dark pits of fear. "No. Stay."

"I won't be long. Just a few minutes."

"Pol, you can't save me," he rasped, the rattle from his chest and throat muffling his words so she could scarcely hear him.

Her eyes glistened. "You say that when Cox shoot you. I pull you through then. I can get you through this." Out of the corner of her eye, a tear trickled.

Charlie's fingers touched the tear, traced its passage down her wrinkled cheek. "Let me go."

Unable to speak, Polly stroked his sunken cheeks, his wisps of white hair, and beard.

"Remember how you held me all through the night after Cox shot me?"

She nodded.

"Hold me now."

She climbed onto the bed beside him

"Hold me tight. Like you did then."

Polly wrapped her arms around Charlie, cradling him, making his strangled fight for breath become her own. For a long time, her chest strained, struggling. Then their breathing became one, and together they sank into a soft, feathery darkness.

When Polly wakened, the moon had risen, filling

the room with its cold white light, turning the rock face of the canyon a gravestone white. From far away, she heard a loon cry, the sound a lonely haunt against the rushing roar of the Salmon. Closer, she heard the half-audible call of cow to calf, the sharp, harsh quack of a duck. A dog growled.

She shuddered. Nightsounds, she told herself. Ordinary nightsounds. And then she understood. It was not the animal cries that made her shudder, but the silence. The absolute quiet that had come while she slept.

She tightened her arms around Charlie, comforted by the real presence of his weight. Then, resting her face against his, she began to speak, filling the silence with words.

"Once, a long time ago, a goddess give a man a pill. She tell him if he eat the pill, he can live forever. But first he must build up body strength. So he hide the pill in a ceiling beam and wait.

"One day, his wife see the pill shining in the moonlight like a pearl. She not know what it is and she curious, so she put it in her mouth. A noise frighten her, and she swallow the pill. Straightaway, she fly out of the window to the moon.

"There, she lonely for her husband, and he lonely for her. So the goddess give him a charm which let him visit his wife on the fifteenth day of each month."

She paused and stared up at the moon, a perfect white circle of light against the pitch black of the night sky. "That is why one time each month the moon is especially big and bright.

"Like tonight," she whispered. "Like tonight."

THIRTY-THREE

The chicken, onion, garlic, and parsley Polly needed for croquettes had been diced sufficently fine long ago, but she did not stop chopping, for as long as she kept knife striking meat, vegetables, and board, she could not hear the sounds of death. The whine of Shepp's saw. The pounding of his hammer as he constructed Charlie's coffin. The clang and ring of shovels as Pete, Shultz, and Holmes dug Charlie's grave.

The door to the kitchen swung open, and frosty, late October cold sliced through the warm, nutty smells of corn bread and baking pie. Shepp strode in, a long, narrow plank beneath his left arm. Shultz and Holmes shuffled in behind him, a raw pine coffin awkward between them. Pete shut the door.

They paused a moment, and through the beating of her knife, Polly heard Shultz and Holmes murmur condolences. She wanted to thank them, to tell them she appreciated their coming down from War

Eagle to help, but the lump in her throat refused speech. Instead she merely nodded and increased the frenzied rhythm of knife against board.

The men climbed the stairs. The clump of their boots and the sharp slap of board and coffin against stair treads and walls reverberated through the kitchen. Above, the floorboards creaked, then were silent. The men had reached the bed. The bed where Charlie lay cold and dead. Straining, Polly heard muffled directions. A sudden, concerted heaving. The dull thud of human flesh against wood. Hammer blows.

Stop, she wanted to call. Charlie can't breathe. He won't be able to breathe. But that was foolish. As foolish as thinking she could block out the reality of Charlie's death by pulverizing chicken into inedible mush.

With a single sweep of her knife, Polly scooped the meat and vegetables into a bowl, added a buttery flour paste, seasonings, lemon, a dash of wine. Her hands moved mechanically, molding the mixture into large balls, rolling the balls in cracker crumbs, dropping them into boiling lard. The grease sizzled, splattered against her hands, stinging. But she felt only the painful scraping and bumping of coffin against stairwell walls, the sudden pause at the turn, suppressed curses.

And then the men were in the kitchen beside her, their breathing heavy, like Charlie's. No, not Charlie. Never again Charlie.

Polly set the croquettes in the warming oven and pulled on coat, gloves, hat. She opened the door and followed the men and Charlie out across the yard, around the house, and behind the root cellar to the grave, an open wound in the hard earth beneath the pines.

Feeling as dry and brittle as the dead leaves scattered in the dirt, she stood at the foot of the grave, longing for the comforting fragrance of incense to smother the smell of raw pine and freshly dug earth. The shrieks and wails of mourners so she would not hear the slither of coffin grazing rope, the sudden banging of wood against rocky outcrops, the soft roll and thud of Charlie within.

Pete cleared his throat. "The Lord giveth, the Lord taketh away, blessed be the name of the Lord."

He hurled a thick clod of soil into the narrow rectangular hole. "From earth to earth, dust to dust, ashes to ashes." He crossed himself.

The men reached for their shovels. Rock and dirt fell on wood, the sound heavy, final. A mist of dust rose around Polly, thickening, like the haze of fine soot that had coated her as she sifted through the charred remnants of her life with Charlie.

There was the elk antler which had hung over the door of Charlie's saloon. The range with the high warming oven and reservoir which she had bought when she first started her boarding house. The bed she and Charlie had shared for almost fifty years. The bowl that had been Teddy's. Charlie's fiddle. The coffee pot kept ready for passing prospectors, friends. All burned, melted, and twisted into shapeless, broken bits of rubbish which crumbled beneath her shovel like so much dust.

Suddenly, through the mist of dust and years, she saw her father crumbling the brick from the kang, mixing it with sooty scrapings, ashes, ground bone, and gristle, shoveling the lot into the narrow hole that had been their fertilizer pit.

She darted to the edge of the half-filled grave. "Stop."

Taken by surprise, all four men stopped their shoveling.

"What is it?" Shepp asked.

Polly thrust her gloved hands into her pockets to hide their trembling. "You tired. Walk all the way to War Eagle for Shultz and Holmes," she told him.

"I'm fine."

"Shultz and Holmes have a long way back."

"It's all right. We're almost done," Holmes said.

"You're hungry, must eat first. Go eat the dinner I make."

"She's right," Pete agreed. "You three go ahead. I'll finish."

Polly seized his shovel. "No, I finish."

"You can't do it alone," Pete protested.

"I plow. I dig the garden. I can bury my man."

Shultz and Holmes looked from Shepp to Pete, questioning.

"Please, I want to be alone."

The men left reluctantly. She waited until they filed past the corner of the root cellar and out of sight. Then, leaning her whole weight against the shovel she held, she gave in to exhaustion and grief.

Late afternoon shadows stained the pines ink green. The canyon walls, imprisoning as the walls of Charlie's grave, closed in on Polly, suffocating, refusing comfort, their dark pockets somber echoes of the frozen emptiness that held her fast.

She heard footsteps crunch against gravel, shovels scraping into earth, realized Shepp and Pete had come to finish filling Charlie's grave. She wanted to help. To make Charlie safe from scavenging coyotes. But she was too tired. And so she remained standing, stock still, like the long-legged wading birds with webbed feet and slender bills that she and Charlie watched in winter.

Sometimes singly, sometimes in pairs, they stood absolutely motionless on the rocks at the edge of the Salmon, waiting to regain their strength. She had seen a full day pass, even two, before a bird took wing again. But always, no matter how tired and faltering their first nervous flutters, the birds pressed inexorably back into flight.

Clumsily, she pressed cold, cramped muscles into motion, and above the noise of scraping shovels and falling earth, she said, "Tomorrow I go Warrens."

PART SIX

第六部份

1922-1923

THIRTY-FOUR

The children, their coats, hats, scarves, and stockings streaks of color against the mourning white of winter, ripped through the gash in the timber on their homemade skis, some tumbling, others expert, their laughter shrill, their wind-whipped faces flushed with fierce, energetic delight. A bundle of fur, wool, and two long, slender pieces of planed wood rolled into the soft drift of snow near Polly. She heard muffled sobs.

"You okay?" Polly called.

The shapeless bundle shaking off loose snow laughed. "Sure."

"Who cry?" Polly asked, puzzled.

The bundle cocked her head. "Sound's coming from the back of the school house so it's probably Gay Carrey. She's always hiding behind the wood pile to cry."

Her walk rolling and awkward, Polly stumbled across the gray brown snow trampled hard by dozens of booted feet to the narrow path cleared between the school house and the woodpile stacked high as the roof. In the shadows, a girl, no more than five or six, crouched on a fallen log, tears streaming down chapped cheeks.

Above her, a boy only a few years older, hovered, pleading. "It's no use crying. You know you can't go home."

Polly rummaged in her coat pocket. Out came handkerchief, fish hook, candies. "You the Carrey children from South Fork?"

The boy, eyeing the candies in Polly's gloved hand, nodded.

His cheeks, red and bulging as though he had swallowed two apples, and his big eyes, transparent with desire, made Polly smile. "Then you are Johnny," she said, extending her hand.

He took a candy. "Thanks. Who're you?"

His question, innocent and ordinary, hurt Polly deeper than she would have guessed possible. There was a time when there would have been no need for questions, when every child knew her just as she had known them, their birthdays, their likes and dislikes. But after almost thirty years absence, only a few were faintly recognizable as children of the children she had nursed and loved. More were as unfamiliar as Warrens itself, with the hundreds of Chinese who had placered Warrens Meadow gone, the meadow carved into craters by steam-powered shovels, and the buildings in the camp all new since the fire in 1903.

She popped a candy into Gay's mouth. Too startled to object, the child sucked noisily, her sobs diminishing. Polly squatted on the log beside her. She wiped Gay's eyes and nose, straightened the knitted stocking cap.

"My name is Polly," she told Johnny. "One time five years ago, you play the fiddle with my husband, Charlie Bemis, in his dance hall. I not there, but he tell me about it. He say you play real good."

Anxious to waylay questions about Charlie, she rushed on. "This your first winter in school?"

"Not mine, Gay's. She's homesick."

Fresh tears spilled down Gay's cheeks. She smeared them with the back of her mittened hands. "I am not, I just hate her!" she declared vehemently.

"Who?"

The boy pointed to the teacher who had come out to the yard. Tall, rawboned, and sternly gaunt, she rang the bell, signaling the end of noon recess. "I board with Francis's mother, Mrs. Rodin, the lady that runs the big hotel," Johnny explained. "But Gay boards with the teacher. She's horrible. Can't boil water and says we get on her nerves. Poor Gay has to sleep in her bed, and she has garlic breath and snores and takes up all the room!"

The yard filled with chatter, laughter, the clatter of skis, the stamping and scraping of boots. As the teacher shouted at the stragglers, Polly felt the child tremble beside her, saw the lips quiver, threatening the fragile dam of tears.

She pinched the child's cheek tenderly. "The teacher frighten you?"

Johnny took Gay's mittened hands and pulled. "Come on, we'd better go or there'll be trouble."

Gay slid off the log reluctantly. Eyes riveted on Polly, she trailed behind her brother, her little legs in their high buckled overshoes making two steps for his every one. Polly started after them. But before she reached the schoolhouse door, the teacher slammed it.

Walking back to the one-room cabin Pete had rented for her, Polly wondered if her own loneliness for Charlie and their life together in the canyon was clouding her judgment, making her see an urgency in the child that did not exist.

Ever since the school in Warrens had been built, families in outlying ranches who wanted educations for their children had boarded them out for the school year. The separations were hard on parents and children, but unavoidable, and Gay, like her brother, would adjust if only she did not have to live with that grim-faced tartar.

The thought brought Polly to a halt. Why did Gay have to stay with the teacher when she could come live with her? Of course, they would have to share the one bed in the cabin, but she was much smaller than the teacher. And, Polly chuckled softly, she was sure she didn't have garlic breath. Or snore.

Gay's tears vanished once she moved in with Polly. At noon recess and after school, she and Johnny joined the other children skiing down the mountain slope, playing dare base and pullaway, and in the late afternoons and early evenings before Johnny went back to Mrs. Rodin's hotel and Gay slept, Polly's cabin filled with laughter, the warm buttery fragrance of popping corn, the sweet stickiness of taffy pulls.

With the children, Polly found even the most ordinary tasks took on new color and life. They dyed eggs with onion and walnut shells and cut cookies in the shapes of animals and clouds. While Polly dressed a hen for supper, Johnny blew up the cleaned-out chicken crop, tossing it like a balloon. And when Polly made bread, Gay, her face and long-sleeved gingham apron streaked with flour, stood on a chair, neighing, while her hands, pretend horses, plunged into dough, then pawed their way back up the steep sides of the bowl and down again.

Often, Johnny would make the mile walk to Slaughter Creek to borrow a fiddle from the Adams children. Then, face fixed in serious concentration, he would tuck the fiddle under his chin and, as bow flew across fiddle turning out merry tunes, Polly would find herself back in time with Charlie.

The days, golden as sunbeams, slid into weeks and months, and winter gave way to spring. Long underwear, leggings, thick-ribbed stockings, flannel petticoats and heavy wool dresses peeled off layer by layer, and they gave up indoor baking, story telling, singing, and stereoscope views for kite flying, fishing, and picnics. Soon, spotted trout, too tiny to eat, swam in jars on window ledges spilling over with cans of sprouting seeds and bouquets of wild flowers gathered on long rambles. And soon, all too soon, school would be over, and Gay and Johnny going home.

Polly's fingers lightly brushed the child sleeping beside her. If her days and nights after Charlie's death had been long and dark before Gay came to brighten them, how would she bear them when Gay left?

Abruptly, she rose and padded across the cabin to the stove, opened the damper and draft, and shook the grate. The coals flashed sparks which, shiny as false gold, crumbled into ash. Like her few fleeting months with the child, Polly thought as she built a new fire.

For a long time, she stood, staring into the bright new flames, holding her hands out to them, warming. Then she turned, lit the lamp, and carried it over to the dresser. The old Bull Durham tin she took from beneath the fabric scraps in the bottom drawer was cold to the touch. She held it lightly, reluctant to open it, knowing she must. Finally, she pried it open.

The lingering, bittersweet fragrance of Charlie's favorite tobacco assailed Polly's nostrils. She inhaled hungrily, but the scent was too thin and too soon gone to satisfy. Feeling cheated, she took out the papers she had stuffed inside after Charlie died. Brittle with age and too much folding, they crackled as she spread them out. Her wedding certificate. Her certificate of residence. The mining claim for the ranch. The papers for which Charlie had been willing to give up his life. The papers she would gladly surrender to bring him back.

Unwanted tears blurred the papers, the child on the bed. Polly rubbed her eyes, impatient. After Gay went home, she would go to Grangeville to visit Bertha and get fitted for new spectacles.

THIRTY-FIVE

In the far corner of Bertha Long's kitchen, Polly, the parrot, strutted across its cage, jumped onto its perch, ruffled its brilliant green and gold feathers, and pecked at its empty dish, demanding, "Polly wants breakfast. What does Polly want for breakfast? Polly wants something for breakfast!"

Polly, slicing cherries at the work table between the stove and sink, shook her knife at the bird. "Polly be quiet or Polly be breakfast!" she warned.

Bertha laughed. "Do you remember when Brown complained about your coffee and you jumped out from behind the stove, waving your cleaver, and shouting, 'Who not like my coffee?'"

Chuckling, Polly stirred the chopped cherries into the bowl of cookie batter. "Brown tell me my coffee is too strong. Your husband say it's too weak. After I shake my knife, they both say my coffee is the best!"

"Having you here is like having the old times back," Bertha said, still laughing. She pulled a handkerchief from her pocket and dried her eyes. "I can almost believe my John and your Charlie aren't dead, and that I'm not a fat old woman with stiff rheumatic knees."

"I'm glad I come. Grangeville have so many old friends and at the same time so many new things I never see or try before."

"What have you enjoyed the best?"

"Let's see," Polly said, dropping teaspoons of batter onto a cookie tray.

There was the excitement of her ride in the stage, one of the new wagons that needed neither horse nor mule to pull. The warm welcome of old friends. The unexpected kindness and curiosity of strangers like Mr. Shaffley, the editor from the Idaho Free Press who had come to interview her at Jennie Holmes' house; the school teacher who had brought his daughter to see her; the little girl, Verna, who had walked all the way across town just to take her photograph and ask a few questions. And of course, there were the fine shops where generous friends reawakened her vanity by buying her new clothes. The new gold-rimmed spectacles that made the hills and wheat fields look freshly washed and her friends and herself twice as old. The trips to the nickleodeon and, even better, the moving pictures.

"Mary Pickford," she decided, scraping the last of the batter from around the bowl. "We go see 'The Love Light' again, okay?"

"I thought you found 'The Love Light' embarrassing," Bertha teased.

"Never mind, I cover my face with my hands and only look through my fingers."

Bertha, shaking seed into the bird dish, began to laugh, scattering the seed over the linoleum floor. The bird flapped its wings furiously. "Polly's breakfast," it squawked. "Where's Polly's breakfast?"

Polly swept the seed up and poured it into the bird's dish. "There, you silly old bird."

"You mean you'd rather see 'The Love Light' than go on a train ride?" Bertha said.

Polly's eyes widened. "Train? Here? Charlie say we never see the railroad."

"Not in the Salmon Canyon maybe, but we've had the railroad here for years."

Polly whipped off her apron. "Then what we wait for? Let's go."

When the trainmen heard that Polly had never seen a locomotive or cars before, they lifted her into the engine cab and opened the firebox. The blast of hot air sprayed soot all over her starched white dress, but she was too excited to care. As long as she had been in America, she had heard of the iron road. Charlie had told her that there were tracks laid all across the continent, and she knew many of the Chinese in Warrens had helped build it. Now that she was finally going to ride in one, she wanted to see everything. The great solitary reflecting lamps in front above the cow guards, the seething, roaring furnace that fed the engines, the baggage cars loaded with produce and grain, the smoking cars, sleeping cars, even the tiny, cramped lavatories.

A bell tolled. With a shriek of the train whistle, the metal wheels ground against the tracks, and she and Bertha were flung against the prickly green plush seats. Trees, mountains, wheat fields, horses, and wagons flew past in a blur.

"Now you've done everything," Bertha shouted above the rhythmic clickety-clack of wheels.

"Oh no," Polly shouted back. "I only just begin. After I go back to Warrens, my old boarder, Jay Czizek, and his wife take me to Boise."

Boise was a spectacular city of tall buildings with moving boxes which took the place of stairs, street cars, gas and electric lights, and a huge park complete with joy wheel, fun factory, miniature railroad, ostrich farm, picture show building, and a natatorium where men and women, practically naked, swam in a huge, steamy enclosed pool. But, pacing the thick pile carpet of her room at the Idanha Hotel, it was none of these wonders that

Polly thought about. Instead, a conversation she had overheard replayed itself.

She had been on the street car leaving Chinatown after her visit with Bob No. 2 who had worked for Bob Katon in Warrens, and there had been two male Chinese voices, low and intense.

"When I was a young man, there was no food in my village. I had to come to America, but China is different now. Won't you change your mind and come with me?"

"No, Uncle. This is my home."

"I have worked here forty of my sixty years, but I do not call it home."

"I was born here"

"An old man like me goes back to China to die. But you are young. You can help build our country, make it strong."

"My country, my home is here."

"And where is my home?" Polly had whispered. Not in China, a faded memory. Or Warrens. Or Grangeville. Or Boise. Then where?

The question had repeated itself during her tour of the big city stores, the White City park, even during the motion picture with the short, funny-looking tramp called Charlie. His tiny black mustache, bowler hat, and crazy antics had made her laugh. Yet there had been a frantic sadness about him, as though he dared not stop.

Like herself.

The unexpected comparison caught Polly short.

She stopped her pacing. The room with its bright fire, heavy drapes, and clutter of furniture closed in on her, and she lifted the window sash and leaned out.

It was late, but the street and buildings were brightly lit, voiding the sky of stars, and though she could see the faint glow of moonlight, the height of the buildings blocked the moon itself.

All at once, a wave of homesickness engulfed Polly, sweeping away doubts and fears in a crest of longing. She knew where she belonged.

THIRTY-SIX

Bird song woke Polly. She had arrived too late
the night before to see anything more than deep
shadows and starlight, but the warm embrace of the
canyon walls and the welcoming roar of the Salmon
had told her she was home, and she had fallen
asleep dreaming of the rustle of wind through tall,
healthy corn stalks, the smell of new cut hay, the
taste of bread made from her own wheat, milk
warm from her own cow. Now, eager to see the
ranch in daylight, she threw off her shawl and
stretched.

The seventeen mile walk down the steep trail
from Warrens and the night spent on the cold, hard
ground of the root cellar had taken a deeper toll
than she anticipated, and her muscles, cramped and
sore, resisted movement. Unalarmed, in fact rather enjoying the teasing suspense the delay
evoked, Polly worked the knots in her arms and
legs loose, then rose and pushed open the door.

At first she thought her eyes, dazzled by the

sudden light, deceived her. Then she realized she had merely deceived herself. Polly Place, like Charlie, was gone forever. Angrily, she ripped at the dew wet weeds and brittle grasses around her.

"Polly! What are you doing here?"

She looked up at Pete, startled, forgetting how the night before she had playfully spread her white hankerchief on a bush facing the river to announce she was back.

"I couldn't believe it when I saw your old signal for help, but I thought I'd better check it out. When did you get here? Is something wrong?"

Polly's fingers closed around the black earth beneath the pulled weeds and grasses. She smelled its dampness, felt its heavy richness, the warmth of the sun sweeping down the pine-clad canyon walls, the rushing roar of the Salmon.

"For a long time, yes. But not now, not anymore," she said.

"Polly, you're not making sense."

She smiled. "You see, after Charlie die, I hurt so much, I think I must get away. But I wrong. Charlie's not just here in the canyon. He's inside me, and it does not matter where I go, Warrens, Grangeville, or Boise, he be there. There and not there. That is what hurt. But nothing will change that, and this canyon is my home. Our home. So I come back."

Pete's arms made a wide sweep, taking in the fences torn down by bears, the garden trampled back into the earth, the sagging chicken house overrun with trailers of hops, thirty years' work work reclaimed by the canyon in one. "There's nothing left."

She opened her hand, revealing the rich black soil. "I have the land."

"You know how much work it took to make your ranch," Pete said gently.

"And I'm too old to start over," she said for him.

"Yes."

"I know I never have big ranch like before, and I not need. All I want is a small house and help with heavy work."

She reached into her pocket, pulled out Charlie's old Bull Durham tin, forced open the lid, and took out a piece of paper. "This is Charlie's mining claim for twenty acres. Help me build a house and make a small garden, and when I die, bury me next to Charlie. Then the claim is yours and you can homestead the land."

"You don't have to do that," Pete said gruffly.

Polly smiled. "You think when I die I can take the land with me?" She spread the claim open and held it out to Pete. "You agree?"

For a moment the paper fluttered in the morning breeze. Then Pete reached for it, folded it, and put it in his pocket.

"Welcome home," he said.

PART SEVEN

第七部份

1933

THIRTY-SEVEN

The salmon thrashed, jerking against the line that meant its certain death. At the same time, Polly, wedged firmly behind a rock, whirled the reel, rapidly letting out more slack. Then, at just the right moment, she tightened the line until it became taut. Again the fish fought hard, threatening to snap the slender strand that snared it, and again, Polly's fingers twirled expertly to release the tension. Like a cat with a mouse, she continued to play with the fish until, exhausted, it offered no resistance when she wound in her line.

Laughing at the contrast between the ten-inch squaw fish at the end of her line and the salmon of her daydream, Polly unhooked the fish and threw it in the creel with the five she had caught earlier.

"Never mind," she told the fish. "You small and you bony, but you just right for old lady."

She threw her unused bait into Polly Creek, picked up creel and rod, and started up the grassy slope to the cabin Shepp and Pete had built for her. It was not far, but she climbed slowly, studying the wild sumac, buttercups, towering pines, and firs like a person scrutinizing the face of an old friend, for beneath the blue canopy of sky and within the rock face and timbered slopes were countless memories. Memories she had tried to run from, but which she had learned to treasure, mulling over them, in conversation or alone, just as she and Charlie had once reviewed the photographs in the album the fire had destroyed.

She sank down on the porch steps to catch her breath. Sunshine poured down on her, penetrating the lightly quilted percale dress lined with outing flannel that she had made for summer wear. The rays warmed, easing the rheumatism that had settled in her joints, and once again Polly congratulated herself for choosing a site where the sun, as soon as it rose over the rim of the canyon, would shine through her curtainless loft window, and where, from her porch, she could catch the last rays as it sank out of sight. She closed her eyes, basking like a contented cat until her breath returned. Then she picked up creel and rod and went inside.

Pete said the cabin was not much more than a doll's house, with space downstairs only for the smokey wood stove she kept threatening to replace, and the chairs and table Shepp had made, and upstairs, in the sleeping loft where only she could stand completely straight, a bed and dresser, also made by Shepp. But with the lace-trimmed muslin curtains she had made for the downstairs windows, the rag rug she had hooked, the photograph of Charlie, and bundles of fragrant herbs and spices, it was home, and she had lived in it well content for ten years.

Not waiting for her eyes to adjust to the dim light, she fumbled for the telephone Shepp had installed. Cradling the receiver, she turned the crank and shouted into the speaker.

"Shepp? How many eggs you get today?"

"Six? I get ten," she countered proudly. "How many fish you catch?"

"None? You no good," she chortled. "Never mind, you and Pete come over, I cook squaw fish I catch today, okay?"

"Good. See you later."

She hung the receiver back in place and bustled out to the vegetable patch to pick vegetables to cook with the fish.

With each passing year, her garden had shrunk as her strength had waned. Now she cultivated barely half an acre, and the hen house sheltered only a handful of chickens. But Pete and Shepp brought her wild game and she had more than sufficient food for her needs and those of visitors, old and new. She surveyed the rows of melon, beans, corn, and cabbages drooping in the August heat. Before she picked anything, she would have to water.

Fetching water from the creek had become an increasingly difficult chore, so she watered sparingly, a dipperful at the base of each plant, just as her father had taught her. At the end of each row, she straightened slowly, kneading the small of her back. Halfway through, her head grew swollen and heavy. Black spots danced before her eyes. She pushed on stubbornly. The spots receded, then surged forward, becoming red and gold, then black again.

Then it was all black.

A numbing heaviness sealed Polly's lids so she could not see, but the steady buzzing seemed like the drone from one of the new flying machines that sometimes soared above the canyon. Faint at first, it became louder and louder, rising above the thunder and crash of the Salmon.

She knew she must signal it. She opened her mouth to shout. No sound came. She struggled to rise, but her limbs refused to obey. The droning became faint, then louder, then faint again, until finally it faded, and there was only the familiar roar of the Salmon.

Then there were voices. Shouting. She felt herself gathered up. Bound. Trussed like a chicken for market.

"No, Baba. No," she cried, straining against the

arms that held her. "Some other way, Baba, I beg you. I don't want to go."

His voice, warm and kind, began a comforting murmur, but the grip that held her remained as tight. She knew she was lost, her efforts too feeble against his strength. Still she struggled until, once again, darkness overcame her.

A sudden fierce jolting shot vicious bolts of fire through Polly, shattering the numbing darkness. She mourned it like a lost lover. Why the agonizing punishment when she had given up the struggle long before, she wanted to ask. But her tongue, thick and swollen, prevented her, and she suffered in silence, yearning for the darkness to return and smother her pain.

It came and went, like surf against the shore, sometimes generous, sometimes meager, sometimes simply hovering on the edges of her pain, its promise of relief cruelly tantalizing.

A star glittered silver bright and she searched for moon glow.

"Charlie?" she whispered.

"He's dead, Polly. You know that."

She forced her eyes open. Above her loomed a white man's face, weathered and bearded, no different from the faces of a thousand others, except, on his chest a bit of silver flashed. Silver, sharply edged. A star. The sheriff.

"Paper," she croaked through cracked lips. "I have paper."

He seized her arm. Silver glittered, pierced her skin, bringing peace.

THIRTY-EIGHT

A heavy weight bore down on Polly's chest and limbs, making breathing difficult. Impossible. So this was death, she thought. Confinement in a narrow, airless coffin pressed down by six feet of earth. But if she were dead, then surely she would not be able to feel pain. Doubt bubbled, bursting into panic. It was a mistake. They had thought her dead, buried her too soon. Her arms flailed weakly, ineffectually, against the constricting boundaries.

"Polly! Polly! Can you hear me?"

With a tremendous effort of will, Polly reined in her terror so she could think. She had asked Shepp and Pete to bury her beside Charlie, next to the river they both loved, but the voice calling her was not his. It was a woman's.

"Wake up, Polly. Wake up now," the bodiless voice urged.

Wake up? Then she was not dead, not buried. She struggled to open her eyes. The lids burst open, fluttered against the painful glare of light, and closed again.

"That's it. Come on, you can do it."

Using her lashes to shield her eyes from the hurtful brightness, Polly opened them a little at a time.

Above her, a big strong woman with curly brown hair hovered, encouraging. "That's it. A little more. Come on.

Pale blue walls. White ceiling. Wood stove. Chair. Curtains rippling in a cool breeze. The harsh smells of antiseptics, medicine.

"Hospital?" Polly croaked, her voice as much a stranger's as the woman's.

The woman smiled. "You're in the County Hospital in Grangeville. I'm Eva Weaver, your nurse."

Broken pieces of memory surfaced briefly, blindingly. Men. Horses. Pain. Darkness. A sheriff. Fear. Sirens. Polly struggled to fit the pieces, but reaching for one, she lost another.

"When I come?" she whispered.

The nurse smoothed the sheet that covered Polly, pulling it taut. "You've been here three days. There for a while we thought we would lose you, but you'll be fine now."

Three days! Again, Polly fought to remember. Bits and pieces glimmered, teasing, then vanished, swept away by black waves that, even now, threatened to pull her down.

"I not remember."

"You must have been working in your garden when you took sick," the nurse explained. "Mr. Shepp and Mr. Klinkhammer found you there unconscious. They took you to the War Eagle Mine by horseback though how they got through those steep trails without falling and breaking everyone's neck is anyone's guess. Then the Deputy Sheriff and Nurse brought you here in Glen Ailor's ambulance."

Heat. Thirst. Weariness. Memory or reality? Her head hurt.

"Tired," Polly murmured.

The nurse leaned over Polly, starched uniform crackling. "Of course. You go back to sleep and rest. You have lots of people asking for you. Mr. Klinkhammer, Mr. Shepp, Mrs. Holmes, Mrs. Shultz, Mr. Cyczik, Mrs. Long..."

The names trailed off, disappearing as Polly sank into a deep, restful sleep.

When she woke again, late afternoon sunshine streamed through the open window. While the nurse's daughter held Polly, Mrs. Weaver plumped her pillows, propping her up so she could drink the beef broth they had brought. Polly held the bowl, but feeling no hunger, looked out the window, feasting instead on the cloudless blue sky, the wide expanse of golden prairie rimmed by big buttes, the mountains beyond.

And then she saw them. The gray granite slabs just beyond the picket fence. Headstones. A graveyard. What had Mrs. Weaver said? Struggling, she forced the words to surface. "You're in the County Hospital." The hospital for indigents. Where old men and women went to die.

She thought of her small hoard of nuggets, the gold buttons Charlie had made her, the ones she changed from dress to dress. She dipped the spoon into the soup and drank. She was not indigent. And she was not going to die. Not here.

"Put my shoes next to the bed," she told Mrs. Weaver.

"You're too weak to walk yet."

"Today. But I want shoes there ready for when I can."

The doctor came. Old friends and curious strangers visited, smiling encouragement as the days inched into weeks, the weeks into months. But the shoes beside Polly's bed remained untouched.

"You'll soon get well," Bertha said.

Polly looked at the shoes on the floor, the graveyard outside covered with snow. "I'm too old to get well," she said.

"Don't give up now."

Polly patted her friend's hand. "After Charlie shot, you tell me the same thing. You help me to save his life that time. I know you want to do the same now. But it's not possible. We young then, old now. I have to go to the other world to get well."

Her grip on Bertha tightened. "When I am dead, help me to find Shepp and Pete. Remind them I want bury beside Charlie."

"I will."

EPILOGUE

On November 6, 1933, Polly Bemis died at the Idaho County Hospital in Grangeville. Due to heavy snows, all trails into the Salmon River were impenetrable and neither Charles Shepp nor Pete Klinkhammer could be located. With the City Council of Grangeville acting as pallbearers, Polly was buried in the cemetery she could see from her window.

Her gold nuggets, the gold buttons Charlie had made her, and other effects were donated to St. Gertrude's Museum by Pete Klinkhammer who homesteaded Polly Place.

When he died in 1970, Klinkhammer's sister, heir to his estate, purchased a stone for Polly's grave. The marker reads:

POLLY BEMIS
Sept. 11, 1853 - Nov. 6, 1933

PHOTO CREDITS

Part I — Chinese girl with bound feet. Courtesy of the Bancroft Library.

Part II — Chinese slave girl in a Chinatown bagnio. From *Pigtails and Gold Dust* by Alexander McLeod. Courtesy of the Caxton Printers and the San Francisco History Room, San Francisco Public Library.

Part III — Warrens, Idaho. Courtesy of the Idaho Historical Society.

Part IV — Lalu/Polly Nathoy's wedding photo-graph.[1] Courtesy of the Idaho Historical Society.

Part V — Polly Place, the Bemis ranch. Courtesy of John Carrey.

Part VI — Polly Bemis, Grangeville, 1923. From *The River of No Return* by R. G. Bailey. Courtesy of the Idaho Historical Society.

Part VII — Polly Bemis. Courtesy of the Idaho Historical Society.

1. According to Gay Carrey Robie, Polly referred to this picture as her wedding photograph. Hence the citation above. It has since become clear to me that this is the same photograph that is on Polly's certificate of residence, so it was most likely taken by Hanson, a newspaper photographer who went to Warrens on May 4, 1894, to "(shoot) celestials for registration purposes." (*Idaho County Free Press,* May 4, 1894.)

Reclaiming Polly Bemis: China's Daughter, Idaho's Legendary Pioneer

When I set out to reclaim the life of Idaho's legendary Polly Bemis in 1979, I had no training in research and very little experience. "Don't worry," a psychic told me. "She's holding your hand." Two years later, *Thousand Pieces of Gold* was completed and published.[1] But I have yet to stop work on reclaiming the life of Polly Bemis, born Lalu Nathoy.

Beginnings

I first came across Lalu/Polly in Sister Mary Alfreda Elsensohn's *Idaho Chinese Lore*.[2] Even in this brief sketch, Lalu/Polly struck me as extraordinary, for she had not only overcome great hardships but had survived with her humanity intact, her spirit undiminished. To me, her life cried out for a book-length biography, and I wrote to libraries and historical societies throughout the Pacific Northwest for anything they might have about her.

Back came numerous photographs, newspaper and magazine articles, a pioneer's unpublished memoir, references in books, and a master's thesis. The wealth of material was gratifying. Unfortunately, there were many conflicting "facts" and huge gaps of information, especially about her life in China. It soon became clear that unless I passed over those years, I could not write a nonfiction book. I felt very strongly that in order to understand Polly in America, it would be crucial for the reader to know about Lalu in China. Instead of a biography, then, I decided to write a biographical novel. That did not mean I was willing to take liberties with the truth. Rather, it meant I threw myself into the kind of intensive research that would, I hoped, help me sort through the disparate facts and fill in the gaps.

I read dozens of books, particularly those dealing with village life, bandits, and the flora and fauna of nineteenth-century Northern China. I studied the crops, when to plant, when to harvest, the various cycles of cultivation, the farm implements used, daily routines, and the holidays and folklore of the area until I knew it as intimately as if I had lived there myself. Similarly, I steeped myself in the history and geography of Idaho, especially of Warrens and the Salmon River, where Polly had lived.

It should be noted that these histories, even those sympathetic to the Chinese, did not include their viewpoint. And one of the many long-range effects of the intense anti-Chinese violence and legislation (both local and national) that prevailed in nineteenth-century America is the complete absence of Chinese pioneers (or descendants) still in the area. But I located white people who had known Polly and went to Idaho to interview them.

Then I began reconstructing Lalu/Polly's life.

The Basis for Thousand Pieces of Gold

Most of what we know about Lalu/Polly's early life can be traced to an interview she gave Countess Eleanor Gizycka in 1922 and three newspaper articles published in the next decade.[3]

From these accounts, it would seem Lalu Nathoy was born on September 11, 1853, in Northern China, near one of the upper rivers, in an area frequently ravaged by bandits.[4] Although Lalu's parents were impoverished farmers, her feet had been bound, then unbound. And when Lalu was eighteen, there was a prolonged drought, during which her father was forced to sell her to bandits in exchange for enough seed to plant another crop that would, he hoped, save the rest of their family from starvation. Since Lalu said she'd been in Shanghai, that may have been her port of departure for the United States.

As to how Lalu came to Warrens, the *Oregonian* claims, "The bandit leader took Polly down the river to one of the big seaport cities, whence he sailed to San Francisco. Soon afterwards the gold rush around Idaho City lured him to Warrens, where he either died or deserted Polly, who operated a restaurant for several years." But Gizycka quotes Polly as saying, "Old woman smuggle me into Portland. I cost $2,500... Old Chinee-man he took me to Warrens in a pack train."[5]

Idaho's gold rush had begun in 1861, and Warrens was one of many "rip-roaring" camps that had sprung up in the territory. As in most camps, Chinese were initially prohibited from holding claims or working as hired men, and it was 1869—seven years after James Warrens had accidentally uncovered gold in the district—before the white miners, believing most of the gold gone, decided by majority vote to allow Chinese into Warrens (now known as Warren).[6]

Mining was then an almost exclusively male activity that involved moving from place to place in search of the most productive site. Few men of any race or nationality brought their families with them, and among the earliest female arrivals were those who hired themselves out for dances or sex—or both. Some of these women were Chinese. Of the Chinese women who labored as prostitutes, however, very few were free agents. Indeed, the majority worked as chattel for masters who had bought them. Beginning in 1861, California passed a series of codes aimed at restricting the importation of Chinese women for prostitution. As a result, the enslaved had to be smuggled in, sometimes "disguised as boys, hidden in buckets of coal, or concealed in padded crates labeled as dishware." Furthermore, losses (through discovery or death) and the need to bribe officials raised the prices for the women, with the sum paid for Lalu on the high side of the one- to three-thousand-dollar range.[7]

Warrens, northeast of McCall, has an elevation of 6,000 feet, and the snow is so deep in winter that it is sometimes completely inaccessible. Not surprisingly, the population has always been greater in summer than in winter. Historically, the population also fluctuated depending on the amount of gold being recovered. Shortly after Chinese were allowed into the camp, they became the majority. Yet they did not live in the town proper but just below in tiny, windowless cabins "not much larger than doghouses."[8]

The town proper had a single crooked street parallel to the gold-bearing gulch. Each side of this street was lined with saloons, dance halls, bunkhouses, hotels, and stores. All the structures were built of logs— even the floors were hewn logs. Hong King, who had purchased Lalu, was an old man who ran a dance hall/saloon/gambling house here. Charles Bemis, the man she later married, did too. And this is where the pack train must have brought Lalu on July 8, 1872, because "she was greeted by a stranger who said, 'Here's Polly,' as he helped her from the saddle." Then somebody called for Charlie Bemis to come outside and "introduced the slave girl to him in this way, 'Charlie, this is Polly.'" Thereafter, Lalu was called Polly.[9]

When recalling her arrival in Warrens, pioneer A. W. Talkington added, "Polly was a good woman and entitled to a good deal of consideration because of her upright conduct in rather difficult circumstances." Perhaps as part of that consideration, he did not elaborate on those circumstances. Similarly, the articles published in Polly's lifetime did not delve into her first decade in Warrens. To my knowledge, George Bancroft is the only pioneer who has ever claimed Polly "got money from women's time-honored methods." He did not condemn her for it. Indeed, he described her as having "shy, modest ways," clearly thought highly of her, and considered himself a good friend. But he did not meet her until the early 1900s, and all the pioneers I contacted insisted Polly had never worked as a prostitute, although they acknowledged that she may have been purchased by Hong King for that purpose. As the daughter of Polly's longtime friend Bertha Long put it, "Polly Nathoy was brought from China to Warrens for the world's oldest profession. When taken to [Hong King's] saloon, she was terrified! Charlie Bemis was present and protected her from unwanted advances."[10] How was Bemis able to accomplish this? Bemis's "fearless personality, coupled with his skill at shooting, enabled him to maintain order without getting into trouble."[11]

Just the fact that Bemis was a white man would probably have been sufficient for him to enforce his will on Hong King. During the ten years Chinese had been migrating to the Idaho Territory (mostly from the California gold fields and points along the Central Pacific railroad), they had not only been prohibited from working rich claims but forced to pay a "miner's tax" of four dollars a month regardless of their occupations. They had also been subjected to random and orchestrated violence throughout the territory. In one camp, children were not allowed out of the house on Saturdays for fear of being accidentally shot by white miners using Chinese for target practice. In Warrens, Chinese did interact with whites—bringing in supplies for both, working in mines operated by whites—and news articles over the years indicate there was limited mingling in some activities, such as Fourth of July celebrations. But a Chinese man accused of stealing a pair of boots was lynched.[12]

Slavery was then against the law, yet Bemis apparently did not challenge Polly's status as Hong King's slave. And since she did remain chattel, Polly most likely had to grant Hong King sexual favors as well as do any necessary cooking and cleaning. She must have served drinks to his customers in the saloon, and she may have danced with them, too, despite her peculiar rolling gait (a result of her childhood experience with foot binding).

All the descriptions of Polly in her youth are those of a beauty, and she was renowned even in her old age for her wit and charm. On those occasions when Polly's wit was not enough to keep her out of trouble or "things got too rough" in Hong King's saloon, she would call for Bemis, or she would fly out of Hong King's back door and in through Bemis's, and "he never failed her." The back door of Bemis's saloon opened into his bedroom. Polly, "always industrious and noting the untidiness of her neighbor's bedroom, used to slip over during the early afternoon to tidy up. This of course pleased Bemis."[13]

At what point the two became lovers is not known, but by the 1880s they were living together. Polly was not financially dependent on Bemis—she took in laundry from miners and ran a boarding house that Bemis had built for her beside his own, a short distance from his saloon. Where Bemis's house was a single room, Polly's boarding house had a small kitchen and a combination sitting/dining room downstairs, a bedroom upstairs. She had taught herself how to cook Western food by watching the white women in Warrens, and young people liked to eat at her place, especially after a dance. Polly had her own inimitable style. When doing laundry, she would mend before she washed. And she once silenced her boarders' complaints about her coffee by waving a butcher knife while asking, "Who no like my coffee?" Little wonder she seemed to make a lasting impression on everybody who met her, and many of her boarders and their families became her lifelong friends.[14]

Legend has it that Bemis and Hong King were playing poker together one day. Bemis was having a run of good luck, and Hong King, bad luck. Finally, Hong King had nothing left to stake except Polly, which he did, only to lose her as well. Since both Bemis and Hong King were dedicated gamblers, this tale seems plausible. Besides, if there was no poker game, how did Polly get free of Hong King? Bringing Chinese women into the country had become so difficult that men with women already in their possession refused to sell them. It does not seem likely then that Hong King would have allowed Polly—who must have been drawing customers to his saloon with her beauty, wit, and charm—to buy her freedom, let alone give it to her.[15]

There are some who suggest Polly and Bemis married as the result of a poker game in 1890 in which Bemis won $250 from John Cox, a known troublemaker. The next morning, Cox demanded his money back. Bemis refused. Cox said he'd give Bemis the time it took to roll a cigarette to hand over the cash. If Bemis failed to comply, Cox would shoot his right eye out. When Bemis did not return the money, Cox fired. Luckily, the shot missed Bemis's eye, but it tore into his cheek, shattering the bone. A doctor was quickly sent for. Dr. Bibby, who came eighty-seven miles by horseback from Grangeville, enjoyed a reputation for being dedicated and inventive. The bullet, on striking Bemis's cheekbone, had split, and although Dr. Bibby was able to find and extract one half of the ball and fourteen pieces of bone, he feared the wound would prove fatal from blood poisoning, unless Bemis's system proved strong enough to expel the remaining fragment of the ball.[16]

While there was no Western doctor in Warrens, there were two Chinese, Ah Kan and Lee Dick, who were credited as healers by whites as well as Chinese, and "one of their unusual methods of treatment was the use of mold for the curing of infection." Whether Polly used this mold or a concoction of her own devising is not known, but she did clean out Bemis's wound with her crochet hook, then packed it with an "extract of herbs," and within a month, her patient was sitting up, dressed, able to talk and smoke, although "looking ghastly." Still the wound continued to discharge pus, and Polly never left Bemis's side. Finally, she found the remaining piece of bullet embedded in the back of Bemis's neck and cut it out with a razor.[17]

At least one account of this incident ends with, "Afterward Bemis married her," as though he did not recognize Polly's value until she saved his life, or he married her out of gratitude or a sense of obligation. But Bemis and Polly had already been living together for years, and they did not marry for another four.[18]

I believe the true impetus for legalizing their relationship came as a result of the 1892 Geary Act, which required Chinese legally living in the U.S. to carry a certificate of residence at all times. Polly, by her own admission, was in the country illegally, and there was a very real fear that she would be deported. "To prevent Polly from being sent back to China as an alien, Bemis was married to her August 13, 1894 at Warrens." And, as a result of "continued efforts by her husband," Polly received her certificate of residence in 1896. There are no specific details about these efforts, but the photograph on Polly's certificate of residence appears to have been cropped from the full-length portrait that she said was her wedding photograph. Ironically, Idaho law at the time prohibited whites from marrying nonwhites, but the justice of the peace who performed the ceremony for Polly and Bemis, A. D. Smead, was himself a white married to a Sheepeater Indian.[19]

After their marriage, Polly and Bemis left for the Salmon River (popularly known as the River of No Return because it could only be navigated in one direction), where he had built a two-story house directly across from the river's Crooked Creek, seventeen or so miles by trail from Warrens.[20]

Periodically Bemis would return to Warrens to sell the produce they raised, check on his saloon, or play at a dance. Polly remained at the ranch to care for their cows, horses, chickens, ducks, and extensive garden and orchard. The canyon, thousands of feet deep, was mostly too steep for farming. For years, however, Chinese had been raising vegetables on terraced slopes near the South Fork to sell to mining camps in the vicinity. At the base of the canyon, Polly grew herbs for Lee Dick and Ah Kan in Warrens, but most of the tillable land was given over to cherries, pears, plums, grapes, blackberries, raspberries, chestnuts, mulberries, watermelons, clover, a variety of root vegetables (including purple potatoes), corn, and other garden truck, some of which the couple sold, much of which they gave away or fed to strangers and friends passing through.

Bemis, who refused money for ferrying folks across the river, would invite them to enjoy Polly's cooking and spend the night. Departing guests would be loaded down with pies, cakes, fruits, and vegetables to be delivered to old friends, or with delicacies for the sick. And in the winter, when the river was frozen over, "people would come down from Warrens to gamble and stay a few days because Polly's cooking was so good and her company too."[21]

The couple became renowned for their generous hospitality, but it was Polly's bright-eyed warmth and humor that people talked about most. She would take in those who were injured or ill and nurse them back to health. As pioneer John Carrey put it, "There was nobody in my day who carried the respect Polly earned through her kindness to everybody." Not surprisingly, the Bemis ranch soon became known as Polly's Place, and a government survey party named the creek running through the property for Polly in 1911.[22]

There are many stories of how Polly hoed while her husband fiddled, how she would come upon Bemis playing cribbage and order him to go fill her woodbox, how he would call her over to watch ants at work and she would tell him he would do better to emulate them. Her own hands seemed ever occupied with chores, making silk scarves, knitting, crocheting, even goldsmithing. While working in her garden, though, Polly would pick up worms and slip them into her apron pocket so that, without fail, she would be ready at three o'clock to go fishing. And, much as Bemis avoided physical labor, he filed a mining claim in February of 1899 in which he noted he had "opened new ground to the extent or depth of ten feet as required by the laws of Idaho."[23]

Polly loved animals and often made pets out of wild creatures. While still in Warrens, "she took a nest of baby robins and raised them, letting them come and go as they pleased. When they found fresh meat at a nearby market . . . they spent so much time there that a French clerk killed them. This made Polly very angry." But after Bemis's eyes dimmed, she, with her sharp eyes, would sight the animals for him to shoot. Once, when hunting, the two came across an orphaned cougar cub, and they brought it home for a pet. To the dismay of subsequent visitors, the cougar would sometimes leap on them as they approached the ranch. Visitors had to eat with the cougar, too, Polly having nailed its metal plate in place at the table. Only if the cougar began snarling would Polly—who could handle the cat even when it "got ugly"—take the animal outside.[24]

In 1909, Charlie Shepp purchased the ranch across the river. Later that year, his partner, Pete Klinkhamer, joined him from Buffalo Hump. Shepp was the gardener and carpenter, and he built a fine two-story house for them. Pete, who was much younger, took care of the stock and brought in cash by doing assessment work on mines for companies and individuals who wanted to keep their claims valid. He also made the six-day round-trip journey to Grangeville once a year to pick up necessities (sugar, coffee, tea, flour, lamp oil, and the like) for themselves and for Polly and Bemis.[25]

From Shepp's diary, we know that Bemis's health, never great, continued to deteriorate. By 1919, Bemis was bedridden, most likely with tuberculosis. Countess Gizycka, stopping at the ranch in July 1921, asked Polly where Bemis was, "and she said, 'Abed. He bin abed most two year now. He pletty closs, too. I gotta pack grub all time—all a time.'" But Polly clearly had not lost her sense of humor. For when Gizycka said, "'You'd better get another husband,' [to see how Polly would take it], she laughed, coy and amused. 'Yas, I tink so, too.'"[26]

Polly was illiterate. "When school come to Warren, I can't go," she explained. "I got to make money." So Shepp helped by writing away for seeds Polly wanted, glasses she needed, measuring her for a new dress that he sent for from Montgomery Ward. Shepp, Pete, and Polly also arranged a signal for when she and Bemis needed them: a dishtowel spread on a bush facing the river. Then Shepp and Pete strung a telephone line between the two ranches, and the neighbors spoke daily.[27]

At least one pioneer claimed, "No one, but no one, could fry fish and make biscuits like Polly," and she would boil squaw fish in a salted bag so that "the flesh just fell off the bones." Her favorite fishing spot was at Crooked Creek on the Shepp Ranch side of the river. After Bemis was no longer strong enough to row Polly over, Shepp or Pete would come for her. And when the Bemis house caught fire in the summer of 1922, it was Shepp who helped Polly drag Bemis out to safety. With Pete away in Dixie, Polly and Shepp were unable to save the house or her dog, Teddy. Shepp noted in his diary that "everybody's feet burned." After Pete returned, he was able to round up thirty of Polly's chickens; otherwise, they failed to save anything. But Polly had the gold buttons that Bemis had made her and which she moved from dress to dress, her certificate of residence, marriage certificate, and the mining claim. To me, the survival of these documents indicates the couple's recognition of their importance for Polly.[28]

For the next two months, Polly and Bemis lived at Shepp Ranch. On October 29, 1922, Shepp wrote in his diary: "Bemis passed in at 3 a.m. I went up to War Eagle camp at 5 a.m. to get Schultz and Holmes. We buried the old man right after dinner." A few days later, he noted: "Polly going to Warrens. Took her stuff over river. Pete went to Warrens with Polly." Polly took her husband's death very hard. And Pete later explained that he had taken Polly to Warrens because he and Shepp thought she would be happier among other Chinese.[29]

Warrens, completely rebuilt after a devastating

fire in 1904, would have been unrecognizable to Polly. But she knew the name and date of birth of every child that had been born in the camp. And Bemis and Polly, while living in Warrens, had been "like father and mother" to at least one child, Taylor Smith, who had come to Warrens as a twelve-year-old. Now Polly took in six-year-old Gay Carrey to live with her.[30]

Like other children from outlying ranches, Gay and her brother, Johnny, had to board out while attending school in Warrens. "Polly took good care of me," Gay recalled. "I loved her." Since Polly's cabin was tiny, Johnny stayed with Ethel Roden, who was running the hotel. But he visited his sister and Polly frequently. "I'd borrow a fiddle and walk up to Polly's house. She was very appreciative. More so than anybody else in town. She would stop [whatever she was doing], sit down, and listen." Her favorite tunes were "You've Got to Quit Kicking My Dog Around," "Where Has My Little Dog Gone," and "The Chinese Breakdown."[31]

Polly was homesick in Warrens. One morning, Pete and Shepp woke to see smoke rising from Polly's chicken house. Rowing across to investigate, they found that Polly had walked the seventeen miles from Warrens to offer them her property in exchange for their making it possible for her to come back and live in the canyon. Both men agreed, and Shepp began building a cabin immediately, but he didn't finish it until 1924. Meanwhile, Polly remained in Warrens.[32]

The cabin Shepp built for her—a single room with a sleeping loft—was on the site of the house Polly had shared with Bemis, where sunlight touches earliest in the morning and lingers longest in the evening. Shepp installed a cookstove and furnished the cabin with a bed, table, and chairs that he'd made. He and Pete reconnected the telephone line between the two homes, and the men did all the heavy work, chopping wood and bringing Polly game.

Polly and her neighbors exchanged daily telephone calls. When she failed to answer the phone on August 6, 1933, they rowed across the river and found her ill. Unable to care for her themselves, Shepp and Pete took her on horseback to the War Eagle Mine, where they were met by an ambulance that drove Polly to the Idaho County Nursing Home in Grangeville. She was said to be unconscious during the grueling, nine-hour journey.[33]

Polly had many visitors at the nursing home. And although Polly recognized she was "too tired, too old" to get well, she remained interested in life, especially in children.[34]

On November 6, 1933 at 3:30 in the afternoon, Polly died. She had wanted to be buried in the canyon she loved, but winter had set in, and neither Shepp nor Pete could be located. So, with members of the Grangeville City Council acting as pallbearers, Polly was buried in the Prairie View Cemetery. Before Shepp died in 1936, he signed everything over to his partner, and on December 8, 1936, Pete filed a U.S.

Patent (#210249) for Polly's land. Pete donated what he had of Polly's belongings to St. Gertrude's Museum. He also shared what he knew of Polly with Sister Mary Alfreda and with Paul and Mary Filer, with whom he lived on Shepp Ranch for many years. After he died in 1970, his sister—who inherited his estate —purchased a stone for Polly's grave. The marker reads:

Polly Bemis
September 11, 1853–November 6, 1933.[35]

Subsequent Discoveries

After *Thousand Pieces of Gold* was published, readers who had known Polly sent me personal or family memories. There were also readers who directed me to additional sources or undertook new avenues of research themselves, then shared their discoveries with me.

More startling than any discovery about Polly in Idaho were revelations about her origins. The name Lalu Nathoy had always puzzled me because it does not sound Chinese. But many a Chinese name has been changed beyond recognition when transliterated from characters. Wondering whether there might be a different explanation, Tsoi Nuliang—the translator for *Thousand Pieces of Gold* in Guangzhou —wrote to a contact at Beijing University's Research

Institute of Chinese Nationalities, who forwarded the inquiry to Huang Youfu in the Research Department on Northeastern and Inner Mongolian Nationalities. Huang recognized the name immediately: Lalu means either "Islam" or "long life" and Nathoy is pronounced *Nasoi*. Then, based on her name, her northern China origins, and a photograph of Lalu, Huang determined she was not Chinese but Mongolian, quite likely a Daur, a minority in Mongolia that is related culturally and linguistically to the Mongols and Tungus—Manchu-speaking peoples.

In the mid-nineteenth century, Huang explained, many Mongolians, previously nomadic, settled in Han areas to farm. Some of the settlers adopted Han customs, such as foot binding. When living among people who professed Islam, some even gave up the Mongolian faith, Lamaism, and became followers of Islam. This, Huang speculated, had been the case for Lalu's family. Regrettably, too many years had passed for him to find a precise location for Lalu's family. Nor could he ascertain how much, if any, of the Daur culture Lalu's family might have retained.[36]

The Daur wore buckskin tunics with pants and underclothes made of cotton. Their winter clothing included leather gloves, boots, and leggings. Their houses—sturdy, rectangular, one-story log structures—were considered ideally situated when there was a mountain rising behind them and a river flowing in front. They farmed grains, vegetables, and tobacco. They also fished and hunted bear and deer. A generous people, they would ostracize any hunter who did not share his kill, and strangers were always welcome.[37]

Familiarity with even a few of these characteristics would certainly explain the ease with which Polly seemed to have adapted to living in Idaho, her apparent alienation from most of the Chinese in Warrens, and her affection for her home in the Salmon River canyon. But was she, in fact, Lalu Nathoy?

In Polly's testimony for her deportation case in 1894, there is space for her signature, which has two characters that are difficult to decipher because the ink was blotted, yet they are written with a sure hand: 恭享, Gung Heung. Below these characters is the signature of W. A. Hall, U.S. Circuit Court Commissioner for the District of Idaho; it seems doubtful he would have permitted somebody else to sign on Polly's behalf. Besides, the calligraphy for "Gung Heung" does not match that of any other Chinese who gave testimony—some before W. A. Hall, others before A. Kavanaugh, justice of the peace in Warrens—at the same time as Polly.[38]

Given her background and the absence of any evidence to the contrary, I'd assumed she was illiterate in Chinese as well as English. But was she? When I revisited Polly's cabin in June 2001, I noticed two Chinese characters, 觀迎 (welcome), carved on a piece of wood above her door. The area, under an overhang, is dark, and I may have missed them during my visit in 1980. Or, they may have been added later. In any case, the first character, 觀, *gwoon,* should be 歡, *foon.* Despite this error, the calligraphy is well rendered.

Adding to the puzzle, Terrie Havis—who was showing me around the restored cabin—pointed out nine notches on a windowsill that were said to have been made by Polly, one for each year she lived there. I had not noticed these during my 1980 visit either. And if Polly was illiterate, she might well have made them. If she was literate, however, why would she have used such a crude method for marking time?

Regardless of who signed the two characters on Polly's testimony, why don't they sound out as any of her known names? A Mongolian living among Han Chinese might well have had both a Mongolian and a Chinese name—in which case Gung Heung could have been Lalu Nathoy's Chinese name, or Gung Heung might have been the name under which she was smuggled into America. According to Professor Marlon Hom, Gung Heung is a man's name, not a woman's. Does that mean she was smuggled in as a man?

Translator Tsoi Nuliang contends the characters were written by a man as a deliberate act of malice. "'Heung' means 'enjoy' (and) the sound 'Gung' can mean 'public' or 'provide.'" Acknowledging that the character on the form is for a name, Tsoi maintains it was chosen for its sound, so "'Gung Heung' would mean the woman is 'provided for public enjoyment,' in other words, a prostitute."[39]

Final Thoughts

With imperfect records and memories and the virtual absence of her own voice, it seems unlikely that the facts of Lalu/Polly/Gung Heung's life will ever be completely recovered or without contradictions. Her incredible spirit, which made her noteworthy in life and memorable in death, has never been contested, however. Not even by the new discoveries. And it was this spirit that I wanted to honor and attempted to convey in *Thousand Pieces of Gold*.

It was also this spirit that inspired Jim Campbell, when he owned the Polly Bemis Ranch, to bring her remains back to the canyon, restore her cabin, turn it into a museum, and nominate it for entry into the National Register of Historic Places. In 1987 the Department of the Interior deemed the cabin significant in Idaho's heritage, and at the museum's dedication ceremonies, Governor Cecil Andrus declared, "The history of Polly Bemis is a great part of the legacy of central Idaho. She is the foremost pioneer on the rugged Salmon River.[40]

Although the Polly Bemis Ranch is privately owned, the seventy-one owner-members are committed to maintaining the cabin museum and keeping it open to the public. And Polly's spirit seems to linger—with characteristic good humor—in her cabin. In 1999 Kathy Schatz was struggling to reach a high shelf when she distinctly heard Polly say, "Ha ha! You short like me too."[41]

Notes

1. In print since its publication in 1981, *Thousand Pieces of Gold* has been available from Boston's Beacon Press in trade paperback since 1988, and it has been translated into six languages. The title is a Chinese term of endearment for daughters.

2. Sister M. Alfreda Elsensohn, *Idaho Chinese Lore* (Cottonwood: The Idaho Corporation of Benedictine Sisters, 1970) (hereafter cited as *Chinese Lore*).

3. Countess Eleanor Gizycka, "Diary on the Salmon River, Part II," *Field and Stream,* June 1923 (hereafter cited as "Diary"); "Woman of 70 Sees Railway First Time," *Idaho County Free Press,* August 16, 1923 (hereafter cited as *Free Press*); *The Idaho Statesman,* August 8, 1924, reprinted August 8, 1954 (hereafter cited as *Statesman*); Lamont Johnson, "Old China Woman of Idaho Famous," *Oregonian,* November 5, 1933 (hereafter cited as *Oregonian*).

Note: Since I was writing a novel, I did not copy down page numbers when taking notes, and my notes from Sister Mary Alfreda Elsensohn's letters, articles, and books sometimes simply reference "Elsensohn." These decisions, made over twenty years ago, now make for incomplete footnotes, and for this I apologize.

4. This is the date on Polly's tombstone. If Lalu did arrive in Warrens in 1872 and was eighteen when sold and nineteen when landed, she would indeed have been born in 1853. On Polly's 1896

certificate of residence, however, her age is forty-seven, making the year of her birth 1849.

5. Johnson, *Oregonian*; Gizycka, "Diary."

6. Sister M. Alfreda Elsensohn, *Pioneer Days in Idaho County,* vol.1 (Cottonwood: The Idaho Corporation of Benedictine Sisters, 1947) (hereafter cited as *Pioneer*); Eileen Hubbell Macdonald, "A Study of Chinese Migrants in Certain Idaho Settlements and of Selected Families in Transition" (master's thesis, University of Idaho, 1966) (hereafter cited as "Study"); Johnson, *Oregonian*; Elsensohn, *Chinese Lore.*

7. Lucie Cheng Hirata, "Free, Indentured, Enslaved: Chinese Prostitutes in Nineteenth-Century America," *Signs: Journal of Women in Culture and Society* 5, no. 1 (1979) (hereafter cited as "Free, Indentured") and "Chinese Immigrant Women in Nineteenth-Century California," in *Women of America,* eds. C. R. Berkin and M. B. Norton (Boston: Houghton Mifflin Co., 1979).

8. Iris Anderson, "Life at Warren Today Is Shared with Ghost of Her Colorful Mining Days," *Lewiston Morning Tribune,* September 4, 1960 (hereafter cited as "Life at Warren"); G. M. Campbell, "A Chinese Slave Girl Charmed an Idaho Town," *Salt Lake Tribune,* July 9, 1972 (hereafter cited as *Tribune*); Elsensohn.

9. George J. Bancroft, "China Polly (Lalu Nathoy): A Reminiscence" (unpublished typescript, Denver Public Library) (hereafter cited as "Reminiscence"); Louise Cheney, "China Polly Was a Pioneer" (Idaho Historical Society) (hereafter cited as "China Polly"); Grace Roffey Pratt, "Charlie Bemis's Highest Prize," *Frontier Times* 36, no. 1 (Winter 1961) (hereafter cited as *Frontier*); Campbell, *Tribune*; Elsensohn; *Free Press.*

Note: Gizycka's claim that Polly said an old Chinese man brought her to Warrens seems implausible because running a pack train that carried supplies was physically demanding work performed by young men. For this and other reasons, I created Jim, the packer, in my novel. (See my article, "Reclaiming Chinese America: One Woman's Journey," *Amerasia Journal* 26:1, p. 167).

Although all sources on Lalu's arrival in Warrens seem to stem from the eyewitness account of pioneer A. W. Talkington, one of Elsensohn's several reconstructions has Lalu arriving with two other Chinese girls, a claim also made by Otis Morris and George Bancroft, neither of whom was present. Since the one Chinese woman in the 1870 census might have been gone by the time Lalu arrived, I opted in my novel for Lalu to arrive alone and be the only Chinese woman in Warrens.

All sources using the name with which Polly arrived, Lalu, and the name of her owner, Hong King, seem to originate from Elsensohn. Having failed to ask for her source while she was living, I can only speculate that she got this information from Talkington as well. The name Nathoy appears on Polly's marriage certificate.

10. Elsensohn, *Pioneer*; Bancroft, "Reminiscence"; Mary Long Eisenhaver, letter to the author, October 8, 1980.

11. Elsensohn; Bancroft, "Reminiscence"; Taylor Smith, preface to "Original Music Manuscript," by Peter Beemer (Idaho Historical Society, November 2, 1961); interview with John Carrey, July 18, 1980; John Carrey, letter to the author, September 15, 1980.

Note: In *Thousand Pieces of Gold,* Bemis's background only comes up during an exchange about freedom on p. 144, where Polly refers to Bemis as being the son of a doctor and having worked as a deckhand. The former came from Fern Cable Trull, "The History of the Chinese in Idaho from 1864–1910" (master's thesis, University of Oregon, 1946) (hereafter cited as "History");

the latter came from Robert G. Bailey, *River of No Return* (Lewiston, Idaho: Bailey-Blake Printing Co., 1935) (hereafter cited as *River*).

12. Betty Derig, "Celestials in the Diggings," *Idaho Yesterdays,* Fall 1972 (hereafter cited as "Celestials"); Macdonald, "Study"; Trull, "History"; Elsensohn.

13. Elsensohn; Cheney, "China Polly"; Gizycka, "Diary"; Pratt, *Frontier*; interview with Vera Weaver Waite, July 15, 1980; Verna McGrane, letter to the author, August 24, 1980; interviews with John Carrey and Gay Carrey Robie, July 18, 1980; *Free Press*; Johnson, *Oregonian*; Polly's dresses in the Polly Bemis Collection, The Historical Museum at St. Gertrude, Cottonwood, Idaho; Gizycka, "Diary"; Johnson, *Oregonian*; Bancroft, "Reminiscence."

14. Bertha Long, "Polly Bemis—My Friend" (typescript written for Clara Landrus, a niece in late 1930s, in possession of author) (hereafter cited as "Friend"); *Statesman*; Elsensohn; Campbell, *Tribune*; *Free Press*; interviews with John Carrey and Gay Carrey Robie, July 18, 1980; interview with Vera McGrane, July 20, 1980; interview with Vera Weaver Waite, July 15, 1980; Denis Long, letter to the author, September 18, 1980.

15. Elsensohn; Trull, "History"; "Polly Bemis, 'Poker Bride' of Salmon River County, Expires," *Lewiston Tribune,* November 7, 1933 (hereafter cited as "Expires"); Pratt, *Frontier*; Cheney, "China Polly"; Trull, "History"; Hirata, "Free, Indentured"; Campbell, *Tribune*.

16. Elsensohn; Johnson, *Oregonian*; Bancroft, "Reminiscence"; *Free Press*; *Idaho County Free Press,* August 16, 1923 and September 26, 1890; Campbell, *Tribune*; Denis Long, letter to the author, September 18, 1980.

17. John Carrey, letter to the author, December 9, 1980; An-

derson, "Life at Warren"; Elsensohn; Bancroft, "Reminiscence";
"Mountain Notes," *Idaho County Free Press,* October 24, 1890;
Johnson, *Oregonian;* Campbell, *Tribune.*

18. *Free Press;* Polly Nathoy and C. A. Bemis, Certificate of
Marriage, August 13, 1894, The Historical Museum at St. Gertrude, Cottonwood, Idaho.

19. Interview with Gay Carrey Robie, July 18, 1980; Ann
Adams, "The Legend of Polly Bemis Retold," an undated, unattributed article that quotes extensively from the *Idaho County
Free Press* and may actually be from that newspaper; John Carrey, "Moccasin Tracks of the Sheepeater" in *Sheepeater Indian
Campaign* (Grangeville: Idaho County Free Press, 1968); Polly
Bemis, 1896 certificate of residence, The Historical Museum at
St. Gertrude; Johnson, *Oregonian;* Campbell, *Tribune;* Elsensohn.

20. Johnny Carrey and Cort Conley, *River of No Return* (Cambridge, Idaho: Backeddy Books, 1978) (hereafter cited as *No Return*); Elsensohn, *Polly Bemis;* Bob J. Waite, letter to the author,
May 29, 1980.

21. John Carrey, letters to the author, September 15, 1980,
December 9, 1980; Trull, "History"; *Free Press;* Johnson, *Oregonian;* Carrey and Conley, *No Return;* Bailey, *River;* Bancroft,
"Reminiscence"; Elsensohn; interview with Mary and Paul Filer,
July 20, 1980.

22. John Carrey, letters to the author, September 15, 1980,
November 21, 1980, December 9, 1980; Bailey, *River;* Bancroft,
"Reminiscence."

23. John Carrey, letter to the author, December 9, 1980; Mary
Long Eisenhaver, letter to the author, October 8, 1980; Carrey
and Conley, *No Return;* Trull, "History"; Elsensohn; Bancroft,
"Reminiscence"; Placer Location #522, Idaho County Records.

24. Johnson, *Oregonian;* Gizycka, "Diary"; interview with John

Carrey, July 18, 1980; John Carrey, letter to the author, November 21, 1980; Elsensohn, "Memories."

25. Interview with John Carrey, July 18, 1980; interview with John Carrey, Paul Filer, and Mary Filer, July 20, 1980; Carrey and Conley, *No Return.*

26. Elsensohn; Gizycka, "Diary."

27. *Free Press*; Elsensohn; Inez Wildman, letter to the author, September 16, 1980.

28. Inez Wildman, letter to the author, September 16, 1980; interview with Mary and Paul Filer, July 20, 1980; Carrey and Conley, *No Return*; Elsensohn.

29. Elsensohn, *Chinese Lore*; Johnson, *Oregonian*; interview with Mary and Paul Filer, July 20, 1980.

30. Elsensohn, *Polly Bemis*; *Free Press.*

31. Interview with John Carrey and Gay Carrey Robie, July 18, 1980; John Carrey, letter to the author, November 21, 1980.

32. Interview with John Carrey, July 18, 1980; interview with Mary and Paul Filer, July 20, 1980; Frances Zaunmiller Wisner, "Simply River Women," *Incredible Idaho,* Spring 1972, vol. 3, no. 4 (The Idaho Department of Commerce and Development); Elsensohn; Carrey and Conley, *No Return.*

33. Interview with John Carrey, July 18, 1980; Johnson, *Oregonian*; Elsensohn, *Polly Bemis*; "Expires."

34. Long, "Friend"; Johnson, *Oregonian*; Elsensohn; Mary Long Eisenhaver, letter to the author, December 8, 1980.

35. "Expires"; interview with John Carrey, July 18, 1980; Elsensohn; Mary Long Eisenhaver, letter to the author, December 8, 1980; interview with Paul and Mary Filer, July 20, 1980.

36. Tsoi Nuliang, letter to the author, June 27, 1984; Tsoi Nuliang, translation of letter from Huang Youfu to Tsoi Nuliang, October 1, 1984.

37. *Daur Folk Tales: Selected Myths of the Daur Nationality,* trans. Mark Bender and Su Huana (Beijing: New World Press, 1984).

38. *United States v. Polly Bemiss* [*sic*].

Note: Since I am illiterate in Chinese, I could not read the characters myself and I am indebted to Marlon Hom, Wei Chi Poon, You Shan Tang, Tsoi Nuliang, Ellen Lai-shan Yeung, and Judy Yung for their help. Because of the blotted ink, the characters were read differently by the individuals listed here. "Gung Heung" was the most frequent reading.

39. Tsoi Nuliang, email to author, October 16, 2001.

40. Associated Press, "Old Cabin Becomes Museum," June 6, 1987; Alice Koskela, "Polly Bemis finally rests at homestead," *Star-News,* June 10, 1987, 1; Bill Loftus, "Salmon River Museum Dedicated to Pioneer Polly Bemis," *Lewiston Tribune,* June 6, 1987, 6A.

41. Conversation with the author, June 28, 2001.

42. This essay is adapted from an article originally printed in *Frontiers: A Journal of Women Studies* 24, no. 1 (2003), published by the University of Nebraska Press.

DISCUSSION QUESTIONS

1. In chapter 8, Ding says to Lalu, "Don't you understand, you cannot escape your fate?"(p. 77). How does this book embody the debate on predestination vs. free will?

2. Discuss the various meanings behind the title *Thousand Pieces of Gold*. Do you think it is an appropriate title for this book?

3. Do you think the author presents a realistic portrait of race relations in a small yet polarized nineteenth-century American community? How about the role of women in a largely male community?

4. "For the Gold Mountains they had described was not the America she would know. This: the dingy basement room, the blank faces of women and girls stripped of hope, the splintered boards beneath her feet, the auction block. This was her America."(p. 102). This small passage touches upon the idea of the American Dream and how reality is often very different from the way immigrants imagined life would

be. Do you think immigrants still experience these same feelings in America today?

5. During the course of the book, Lalu/Polly's status changes from that of a daughter to a slave to a free woman. What events and character traits help facilitate these transformations?

6. What limitations did Lalu/Polly face as a Chinese woman living in nineteenth-century America?

7. Explore Lalu/Polly's relationships with other Chinese in Warrens and what, besides her gender, might have had an impact on them.

8. Compare Lalu/Polly's relationships with Ding, Jim, and Charlie. Discuss the similarities and differences.

9. Charlie tells Polly that a Chinese person in America cannot own land. Considering Polly's love of farming and the land, does she ever accept this concept? Give examples of her defiance and perseverance.

10. Discuss Charlie and Polly's relationship. In what ways was it atypical of relationships of that era?

11. Discuss the daily discrimination Lalu faced in China and how it differed from the discrimination she faced in America.

DISCUSSION QUESTIONS

12. In what ways does the enslavement of women continue in America and around the world today?

13. In the nineteenth century, some Chinese women bound their feet while some Western women bound their waists with corsets. How do women today alter their bodies to achieve an idealized appearance?

ACKNOWLEDGMENTS

For their help while I was researching and writing *Thousand Pieces of Gold,* I am indebted to the following: Lalu Nathoy/Polly Bemis, for her inspiration; Don McCunn, without whose contributions at every stage this book would still be a dream; the pioneers who cared enough about Polly to record her story in private papers, newspapers, journals, and oral histories; Sister Mary Alfreda Elsensohn for introducing me to Lalu/Polly and directing me to numerous sources; all who agreed to give interviews, provided additional leads to other persons and source materials, and continued to answer my questions via correspondence, especially Jim Campbell, John Carrey, Mary Long Eisenhaver, Marybelle and Paul Filer, Denis G. Long, Verna McGrane, Gay Robie, June Sawyer, Vera Weaver Waite, and Inez Wildman; Nellie McClelland at the *Idaho County Free Press,* Bob Waite at the Idaho County Recorder's office, and M. Garry Bettis, Jim Davis, Karin E. Ford, and Kenneth J. Swanson at the Idaho State Historical Society for uncovering critically needed information; Bob Hawley at Ross Valley Books for introducing me to books about the real West; the librarians at San Francisco

Public Library's Interlibrary Loan Department, who never failed to secure the books and papers I requested from libraries all across the United States; the many friends who gave their time and talents to the critical reading of my manuscript, especially Beverly Braun, Hoi Lee, Ellen Yeung, and Judy Yung, whose insights and specialized knowledge contributed largely to the final form of this book; John Carrey and Bob Hawley, who read the manuscript for historical accuracy; Lynda D. Preston whose editorial skills gave my prose needed polish; Jeanne Wakatsuki Houston, James D. Houston, Joan Levinson, Diane Levy, and Alice Van Cleef for their early support.

For their contributions to the essay "Reclaiming Polly Bemis," I thank: Valerie Matsumoto for encouraging me to share the story of my research; Terrie Havis for inviting me back to the Polly Bemis Ranch in 2001 and, together with Steve Havis, Mike Sohrakoff, and Dixie Weber, making available opportunities for further research during my stay; all those named in the footnotes, especially Tsoi Nuliang and Judy Yung; also Sue Armitage, Katie Gilmartin, Patricia Hart, Yvette Huginnie, and Jan Venolia; again and always, Don McCunn, for his unflagging support and concrete help, and Lalu Nathoy/Polly Bemis/ Gung Heung, who continues to inspire me—and to hold my hand.

For their assistance with this new edition, I am

ACKNOWLEDGMENTS

grateful to: Joanne Wyckoff for her editorial acumen and direction; Brian Halley for his commitment, gentle insistence, and attention to detail.

I also wish to thank Brad Bunnin and Dale Minami for their wise counsel.

Ruthanne Lum McCunn, a Eurasian of Chinese and Scottish descent, has published eight books on the experiences of Chinese people on both sides of the Pacific, including W*ooden Fish Songs, Sole Survivor: A Story of Record Endurance at Sea, Chinese American Portraits: Personal Histories 1828–1988,* and, most recently, *The Moon Pearl.* Her award-winning books have been translated into nine languages and adapted for stage and screen. A former teacher, she currently resides in San Francisco and lectures extensively at universities, schools, and community organizations.

Writing Across the
Chemistry Curriculum

An Instructor's Handbook

Jeffrey Kovac
University of Tennessee

Donna W. Sherwood
Knoxville College

Prentice
Hall

Upper Saddle River, NJ 07458

CIP Data is available upon request

Executive Editor: *John Collier*
Manufacturing Manager: *Trudy Pisciotti*
Manufacturing Buyer: *Lisa McDowell*
Supplement Cover Manager: *Jayne Conte*
Supplement Cover Designer: *Kiwi Design*
Electronic Page Makeup: *Joanne Del Ben*

Printed in the United States of America

10 9 8 7 6 5 4

ISBN 0-13-029284-2

Prentice-Hall International (UK) Limited, *London*
Prentice-Hall of Australia Pty. Limited, *Sydney*
Prentice-Hall Canada, Inc., *Toronto*
Prentice-Hall Hispanoamericana, S.A., *Mexico*
Prentice-Hall of India Private Limited, *New Delhi*
Pearson Education Asia Pte. Ltd., Singapore
Prentice-Hall of Japan, Inc., *Tokyo*
Editora Prentice-Hall do Brasil, Ltda., *Rio de Janeiro*

Table of Contents

Foreword   *v*

Preface   *vii*

chapter 1   Introduction   1

chapter 2   Designing Effective Writing Assignments   6
Characteristics of a Good Assignment   6
Topic Types   8
Conceptual Levels   8
Formality and Informality in Writing Requirements   13
Constructing a Good Assignment   18
Summary   20

chapter 3   Using Writing in the Chemistry Curriculum   23
Using Writing in an Individual Chemistry Course   23
Using Writing Across the Curriculum   30
Summary   33

chapter 4   Grading Writing Assignments   35
Weighting Writing   35
Holistic Grading   37
Analytical Approach   44
Ungraded Writing   48
Training Graders   49
Summary   52

chapter 5   Responding to Student Writing   54
Written Responses   55
Peer Evaluation   58
Conferencing   62
Summary   64

chapter 6   Assignments   65

Content-Specific Assignments   65
Reintegration/Enrichment Assignments   69
General Chemistry   70
Exam-Preparation Assignments   73
General Chemistry   75
Form-Specific Assignments   76
Professional Advancement Assignments   77

chapter 7   Annotated Bibliography   81

Style Guides   81
Dictionaries and Usage Guides   81
Internet Resources   82
Professional and Technical Writing Guides   82
Other Resources for Writers   83
Resources for Teaching Writing   84

Index   89

Foreword

by
Robert L. Lichter
Executive Director
The Camille and Henry Dreyfus Foundation

Music that is not heard, literature that is not read, and art that is not viewed do not enhance the human experience and thus do not justify the efforts of their creators. Similarly, new scientific (and, more generally, scholarly) knowledge that remains uncommunicated is of no value to the human enterprise. Unlike artistic communication, which is more affective than expository and hence can be indirect, scientific communication has to be direct and lucid. At the same time, scientific communication that has these properties does not have to be dull. Indeed, good scientific communication will engage readers as compellingly as good artistic communication. The best flows like poetry; the worst, as noted by physiologist Jared Diamond,[1] actually impedes the progress of science.

Regrettably, and undoubtedly for many reasons, most undergraduate science curricula exclude written and oral communication skills as an integral part of undergraduate science education. Many science faculty members, while admitting how important it is for students to have these skills, nonetheless also acknowledge their frustration in being unable to incorporate them broadly into the curriculum. Often they assume (read: hope) that students will get these skills in other courses. In doing so, they fail to recognize that general principles of communication are best realized in specific contexts, very much as music theory plays itself out differently on different musical instruments. In other cases the task is left to an occasional written assignment that may be included in an advanced course. Here, however, it is not clear that students will necessarily get the constructive feedback that is so essential to effective learning. Exceptions to these observations are frequently found among the minority of students who take part in original research projects.

Another significant barrier to incorporating communication skills into science curricula is the lack of experience among science faculty in teaching them. Even faculty members who understand and practice the elements of good communication may lack appropriate teaching skills and understandably find it daunting to spend the time and effort required for developing them. It is to these faculty members, and specifically in chemistry departments, that Jeffrey Kovac and Donna W. Sherwood direct *Writing Across the Chemistry Curriculum: An Instructor's Handbook*.

Unlike a number of books on the practice of teaching communication skills to science students, many of which are given in the extensive bibliography, Kovac and Sherwood's short and eminently readable how-to book is literally designed to walk the novice instructor through the tricky thickets of the writing adventure. Based on a curriculum that the authors have tested at the University of Tennessee, the book brings the scattered literature on science communication together in one source and draws upon the literature efficiently and effectively. It is chock full of practical advice and replete with real examples and analyses of both good and bad writing. Its self-contained chapters, which eliminate tedious page flipping, are easy to follow and use. While the book focuses on writing for a technical audience, it addresses the importance of writing for a non-technical audience as well, an issue that is critical for scientists to embrace. Presented in a non-pedantic style, the book's many offerings include exemplars of student chemistry writing assignments that anticipate student resistance to writing; templates for analyzing papers; practical tips about grading papers (sit in a comfortable room, and don't do it after a heated faculty meeting!), and multiple ways of staging writing throughout the chemistry curriculum as a function of student technical and rhetorical sophistication. Users will be able easily and with little financial expense to adopt the book's suggestions or adapt them to their own circumstances and objectives.

The authors cleverly make no presumptions about the settings in which the book might be used. Indeed, *Writing Across the Chemistry Curriculum* is written in a way that should allow it to fold seamlessly into undergraduate curricula at institutions from research-intensive universities to two-year colleges. I have no doubt that many graduate programs will benefit from the book as well.

The next step, of course, is for Kovac and Sherwood to write a comparable book on oral communication.

REFERENCE

1. Jared Diamond, "Kinship With The Stars," *Discover Magazine*, May 1997.

Preface

This book derives from three insights. First, and most important, is the fundamental principle of the writing across the curriculum movement: writing is thinking. Perhaps the best way to develop a new idea is to write about it, to put one sentence after another, then revise and revise until what was once poorly understood is finally clear. Second is the realization that conceptual understanding in chemistry and other technical subjects is neither well developed nor assessed through the usual numerical problems that comprise the homework assignments and examinations in undergraduate courses. Often these problems can be solved algorithmically without yielding much conceptual insight. Writing, on the other hand, facilitates conceptual learning. Finally, we recognize that chemistry instructors need both a theoretical framework and practical advice on how to use writing effectively in their courses. Even though all working scientists are writers, few have had any experience or training in the teaching of writing.

It is easy to find excellent books on writing, including books on writing in chemistry; we have listed some of our favorites in the bibliography. While these books give excellent advice on all aspects of the writing process, they are usually silent on the teaching of writing. Books on how to teach writing are usually addressed to English composition instructors. This book is unique in that it is written for chemistry instructors who would like to help their students use writing as an effective learning tool. While we do provide a theoretical framework, the book is intended as a practical handbook addressing the "nuts and bolts" issues of assignment construction and grading. The ideas and sample assignments can be used immediately. We have applied our experience in teaching chemistry and writing to distill the best thinking from both the English composition and science education literature.

Many people have helped along the way. We are grateful to Dan Apple (Pacific Crest, Inc.), Janet Atwill (University of Tennessee, Knoxville), Terry Carlton (Oberlin College), Brian Coppola (University of Michigan), R. J. Hinde (University of Tennessee, Knoxville), Libby Jones (Berea College), Roger Jones (Berea, Kentucky), Michael L. Keene (University of Tennessee, Knoxville), Celeste Shibata (St. Andrews Episcopal School), and Jack Steehler (Roanoke College) for reading drafts of this handbook and making valuable suggestions for improvement. Valarie Breeding proofread the preliminary edition, and Peter Kovac designed the cover.

A number of colleagues around the country provided assignments. We appreciate their willingness to share ideas and experiences.

We are grateful to the University of Tennessee students in Chemistry 120 who generously allowed us to use samples of their writing.

In the summer of 1996, E. Cathleen Foster, an undergraduate research student supported by the UTK/ORNL Science Alliance, did important preliminary research for this project.

Financial support was provided by The Camille and Henry Dreyfus Foundation; The University of Tennessee, Knoxville; The Hodges Better English Fund; and the Knoxville-Oak Ridge Chapter of the Society for Technical Communication.

We thank John Challice at Prentice Hall for believing in this project and Kristen Kaiser and Blake Cooper for making the book a reality.

Finally, friends and family sustain authors with support and encouragement. JK would like to thank Roger Jones for twenty-four years of conversations on science and science education that have influenced my thinking profoundly. Our families have sustained us with love, laughter, and, above all, patience.

JEFF KOVAC
jkovac@utk.edu
DONNA W. SHERWOOD
sherwood@utk.edu

chapter 1

Introduction

A Writer is not so much someone who has something to say as
someone who has found a process that will bring about new things
that he would not have thought of had he not started to say them.
—William Stafford, *Writing the Australian Crawl* (1977)

Like controlling the weather, teaching chemistry students to write well may seem to be a problem without a solution. For nearly two decades, teachers of writing have heard professionals in industry and the natural sciences saying loudly and often that a chief weakness of both students and professionals seeking positions is their inability to write well. Chemistry faculty have received the same complaint from their colleagues, both in industry and in graduate departments. Meanwhile, writing has been incorporated into the science and technical curricula slowly and in a series of disconnected and wavering lines. The writing across the curriculum movement, based on the philosophy that writing should not be the sole possession of the English department but should be an integral part of how every subject is taught, stimulated a few science and engineering faculty to take writing seriously enough to assign it in their courses.[1] Chemistry instructors at a variety of institutions have used writing in their courses, often in creative ways, but these efforts are usually isolated.[2] Similarly, English departments have made tentative efforts to link English faculty with science programs, but such efforts too often have been underfunded and short-lived. Consequently, the development of professional writing skills is still a serious issue in the chemistry community.

The recent national discussion of undergraduate chemistry curriculum reform has highlighted the issue of conceptual understanding. While chemistry students often can solve the usual numerical problems posed on examinations, they are less able to provide coherent verbal explanations of chemical and physical phenomena. Some chemistry faculty who are developing innovative pedagogical techniques to address this problem have realized that writing can be a powerful tool to facilitate student learning.[3] Productive scholars have long known that "writing is thinking." Ideas are often best clarified through informal writing in a private journal or letter, or in the preparation of a formal paper for publication. The key pedagogical question is how to help students understand and take advantage of this important insight.

Writing, then, has two complementary functions in chemical education. First, it is an essential professional skill. A chemist, even at the Bachelor of Science level, must be able to write in a variety of forms such as scientific and technical reports and proposals. Second, writing is a powerful active learning tool that can help students achieve a deeper understanding of chemistry. The two functions are synergistic. As students write informally to construct an understanding of a concept, they develop their ability to communicate in clear prose. As Stafford points out, writing is a process that leads to insight.

Chemistry instructors who are interested in using writing in their courses face several obstacles. The first is the problem of assignment design. Beginning faculty members learn how to write problem sets and examinations by modeling them on examples from their own education or using the problems conveniently placed at the ends of chapters in standard textbooks. These models are developed and refined with experience. Although occasional articles on the use of writing in chemistry courses do appear in the *Journal of Chemical Education* and other publications,[4] analogous models for writing assignments are rare. The experiences of writing teachers in the English department can be helpful, but they are often difficult to translate into practical advice on assignment design for chemistry courses.

A second obstacle is the development of a strategy to use writing effectively in an individual course and throughout the four-year chemistry curriculum. Questions that arise include the following: What kinds of assignments are appropriate for the first-year general chemistry course? What should be postponed to senior elective courses? What kinds of learning objectives are best addressed through the use of writing? Are there ways to develop writing skills systematically? Efforts to incorporate writing into chemistry curricula would be facilitated by development of a general strategy to address these and related questions.

The final obstacle is evaluation: how to grade writing. Chemistry instructors ordinarily are not well trained in the subtleties of grammar and style and have a natural fear of attempting to evaluate student writing. The usual chemistry problem can be graded "objectively" in that points can be assigned to various steps in the solution and to the correct answer. The evaluation of an essay entails much more ambiguity. Not only must the scientific content be correct, it also must be communicated well. While mechanical elements such as grammar, spelling, and punctuation are important, less quantifiable elements such as organization, coherence, and style also affect the overall impact of a piece of writing. Chemistry faculty need a practical guide to assessment and evaluation as well as advice on how to respond effectively to student writing.

This handbook addresses these three issues by providing a theoretical framework and practical advice on assignment design, a strategy for using writing in the chemistry curriculum, guides for grading and responding to student writing, and a collection of model writing assignments that can be used in core chemistry courses. We have taken the best thinking from teachers of writing and from chemistry faculty who have employed writing in their courses and distilled it into a form that can provide a starting point for faculty who have not yet assigned and evaluated a paper and for those who have used writing in their courses but are looking for new ideas and suggestions for using this tool more effectively.

A properly designed assignment can stimulate students to think and write creatively. Much has been learned by teachers of writing and those who design standardized tests, such as the Advanced Placement examinations, about developing questions to prompt student writing. It is essential that questions be clearly written, interesting, and pitched at the correct level to motivate the best students to do their best work but not overwhelm the weaker students. Students must know whether the primary emphasis is the subject, the audience, or the writer, each emphasis leading respectively to explanatory, persuasive, and expressive prose. The first two are common in formal scientific writing, while the third is useful in "writing-to-learn" assignments in which students are asked to write in personal terms about a subject in a journal or other informal assignment. Expressive writing can be a useful learning device as well as a way to develop ideas for a subsequent formal paper.

Designing writing assignments at the correct level of conceptual and rhetorical sophistication for the student is a challenge. To provide guidance we have adopted an eight-fold hierarchy of conceptual tasks, analogous to Bloom's taxonomy, introduced into the composition literature by Kiniry and Strenski.[5] The hierarchy, described in detail in Chapter 2, both classifies the conceptual levels and provides a set of rhetorical building blocks used routinely for constructing larger pieces of writing. It begins with fairly simple tasks such as listing and definition and ends with the construction of scientific arguments. Not only does this classification help in the design of individual assignments, it also provides a development strategy. Assignments can be increased in sophistication during a single course and over the four-year curriculum.

Writing can be introduced into chemistry courses in a wide variety of ways. Informal assignments include journals in which students write personal accounts of their attempts to understand the course material, short in-class assignments, or out-of-class papers of varying lengths. Informal assignments are excellent tools to develop conceptual understanding. In Chapter 2, we present a large selection of formal writing assignments that traverse the spectrum of writing tasks undertaken by professional working scientists, with options for every course and for essentially every instructional objective.

In designing an assignment, four factors must be considered: (1) instructional objective, (2) audience, (3) process, and (4) evaluation. The final section of Chapter 2 discusses these four factors in detail and shows how all the pieces can be put together into effective writing assignments.

Even the chemistry instructor who is convinced that writing is important might ask, "How can I best use writing in my courses?" We have tried to answer this important question in Chapter 3. Writing is an effective way to approach at least four different instructional objectives: (1) conceptual understanding; (2) skill development; (3) reintegration of knowledge, by which we mean the connection of chemistry to other sciences and engineering and to the broader liberal arts; and (4) enrichment. Each of these objectives can be approached by a wide variety of writing strategies depending on the nature and level of the course, the kinds of students enrolled, and the interests of the instructor. We outline a strategy for the use of writing in individual courses and an approach to the systematic incorporation of writing in the four-year chemistry curriculum.

Perhaps the biggest barrier to the use of writing in chemistry is the matter of assessment and evaluation. A lack of experience makes many chemistry faculty uncomfortable with the prospect of grading writing, and the time it takes and the ambiguity attached to grading writing assignments are also likely to give a chemistry teacher caution. Chapters 4 and 5 offer a practical guide to grading and responding to student papers. We outline the two major approaches to grading: holistic and analytical. Holistic grading is based on an overall reading of the paper that focuses on total impact and can be done rather quickly.

With some experience and an appropriate set of criteria, holistic grading is both fair and accurate. In fact, this system is used to grade all standardized tests like the SAT and the Advanced Placement Examinations. Analytical grading, on the other hand, is similar to the usual grading of problems in a chemistry course. In this system points are assigned to particular features of the paper, both content and form, and the grader evaluates the success of the paper in meeting the preassigned specific criteria. This more time-consuming system provides detailed feedback to the student and is particularly useful when applied to a draft that will be revised.

No matter which system is chosen, it is also important to provide students with appropriate guidance to help them improve their writing. Chapter 5 provides advice on how to respond to student writing based on the idea of developing a dialogue between the instructor and student about writing. Several possible ways of responding to students are presented, ranging from one that takes very little instructor time to those that require substantial effort. Written, oral, peer, and consultant responses are discussed.

Finally, in Chapter 6 we provide a collection of specific writing assignments for all the core chemistry courses. Our goal is to provide a set of model assignments that can be adapted for immediate use as teacher and student begin to explore writing as both process and product.

All chemistry professionals need to be able to communicate in clear, concise prose. Productive scholars have long recognized that writing is a powerful aid to thought. Our goal is to provide a handbook that will allow chemistry faculty to use writing effectively in their courses because writing is too important to be left solely to the English department.

REFERENCES

1. W. Zinsser, *Writing to Learn.* Harper & Row: New York, 1988.
2. H. Beall and J. Trimbur, *A Short Guide to Reading and Writing about Chemistry*, 2nd ed. Longman, New York, 2001; N. P. Shires, "Teaching Writing in College Chemistry: A Practical Bibliography 1980–1990," *J. Chem. Educ.* **1991**, *68*, 484–495.

3. D. Hanson and T. Wolfskill, "Improving the Teaching/Learning Process in General Chemistry: Report on the 1997 Stony Brook General Chemistry Teaching Workshop," *J. Chem. Educ.* **1998**, *75*, 143–147.
4. N. P. Shires, see note 2.
5. M. Kiniry and E. Strenski, "Sequencing Expository Writing: A Recursive Approach," *College Composition and Communication* **1985**, *36*, 191–202.

chapter 2

Designing Effective Writing Assignments

Faculty and students read typical writing assignments with very different eyes. Even experienced instructors underestimate their students' difficulty with the usual writing topic. Often students are assumed to understand unstated criteria, such as the nature of the audience and the assessment standards. The topic may require a higher level of intellectual sophistication than most students possess. The student may not understand the relevance of the writing assignment to the overall objectives of the course. The instructor may then blame the poor writing that results on the students rather than on the nature of the assignment.

The purpose of this chapter is to outline some principles of writing assignment development. Much has been learned about this subject in the process of developing standardized essay tests such as the Advanced Placement examinations.[1] Ideas about the design and proper sequencing of writing assignments within a course or curriculum can be adapted from the design of freshman composition courses.[2] Instructors in writing across the curriculum and technical writing programs also provide guidance.[3] We have tried to distill the best ideas from these disparate sources into both a theoretical framework and a practical guide for the design of writing assignments for chemistry courses. First, we list the general characteristics of a good writing assignment. Next, we present two important considerations in assignment design: topic type and conceptual level. This is followed by a detailed list of the kinds of assignments appropriate for chemistry courses, which have been divided into two categories: informal or writing-to-learn assignments and formal assignments. The final section is a practical guide to the process of assignment development.

CHARACTERISTICS OF A GOOD ASSIGNMENT

Teachers know that a good assignment is the one that helps the largest possible number of students to achieve the highest possible standard of learning and expression. But it is more difficult to know when a particular assignment is likely to achieve that end. Committees that develop standardized essay examinations have learned to require four characteristics of the questions they approve: clarity, validity, reliability, and interest.

Clarity. Students will not need to puzzle over what is required, but will be able to begin to work immediately. A course assignment is unclear if a large number of students feel they need to ask the instructor for clarification. Lack of clarity can be a result of an assignment that is too brief, but can also result from one that is too discursive and contains ambiguous directions and irrelevant and distracting details.

Validity. Students will have little cause to speculate about whether the topic or question is "fair," and readers readily can justify marks and scores. For writers of standardized test questions that are designed to evaluate and separate students according to ability and accomplishment, validity is important. Although the term *validity* is usually applied to evaluation, its importance here implies its consideration in the creation of an assignment as well. A carefully constructed topic allows for the prediction of valid results. Good students should generally receive high scores while poor students receive low scores. There should also be a good range of scores without too many in the middle. If you are using writing as an evaluation tool, you must be concerned about the issue of validity, but even ungraded writing-to-learn assignments should be designed with grading validity in mind. A question that produces responses that are all the same with all the scores in the middle range is neither a good evaluative question nor a good writing-to-learn assignment. Questions that are too difficult will bewilder all but the best students; questions that are too easy or boring will not inspire good students to produce their best work.

Reliability. If the topic is both clear and specific, readers will be able to come to reasonable agreement on the assessment or scoring of the papers, and a guide can be constructed to describe the differences between the different assessments or scores. The major culprit in lack of reliability is vagueness of the question or topic. Guiding students to produce better writing requires that the instructor provide clear and comprehensible criteria for success.

Interest. The question offers enough intrinsic interest that the students will become engaged in the writing task and the graders will not become so bored that their reading accuracy declines. Although grader boredom is a small concern when assigning papers to a class of twenty, it becomes important when a much larger number of essays on the same topic are read and is a serious problem in assigning writing in science. This issue is complicated by the fact that students may not be very interested in the explication of the technical topics that comprise the usual undergraduate course. Finding a question that stimulates students to write engaging and creative papers that are still scientifically correct is a challenge.

While these criteria have been established for the construction of standardized tests, they also make sense for course assignments. As a classroom instructor you do not have a test committee to consult, but you can refine your assignments over the years to meet the four criteria better. You can clarify the goals of your courses and curriculum and try to make your assignments reflect those goals. As you listen to your students' responses, you can revise your assignments in light of their comments and your own assessment of the results.

In this handbook we provide suggested assignments for chemistry courses, and we encourage you to use and to refine them. Since we cannot possibly provide an exhaustive list, we will present some systematic principles for the design of writing assignments.

TOPIC TYPES

Writing topics can be classified into three types based on the three components of the writing process: the writer, the subject, and the audience. If the focus is on the subject then the writing is called explanatory. This kind of writing is the most common in chemistry courses, where the student is asked to explain clearly some technical subject, such as the Lewis theory of acids and bases or the chemistry of the alkali metals.

If the focus is on the audience, the writing is called persuasive. Persuasive writing is also important in science. Both proposals and research articles are exercises in persuasion, so it is important that students learn to write in this form.[4] For example, students in an advanced laboratory course might be asked to propose an independent project in a format based on National Science Foundation guidelines.

Finally, if the focus is on the writer, the writing is called expressive. Expressive writing is rare in a professional context, but it can be useful to have students write in this mode, particularly in personal journals. You might have them read a passage or two from Primo Levi's *The Periodic Table*[5] or Roald Hoffmann's *The Same and Not the Same*[6] to show them how and why to write expressively. As they develop their careers, they will want to be able to incorporate expressive writing in their correspondence.

While it is impossible to separate the three components, each must be assigned a relative importance. All good writing is personal and expressive, though in technical writing the style is more constrained. Every writer must keep the prospective audience clearly in mind and have command of the subject. The interplay of the three components in writing in chemistry is discussed by Beall and Trimbur,[7] and Booth, Colomb, and Williams[8] provide excellent advice on connecting with the reader.

It is important that your assignment clarifies the topic type in both the formulation of the assignment and in the assessment criteria. You should also specify the nature of the audience; otherwise students will write for you only or, worse, for what they imagine you to be.

CONCEPTUAL LEVELS

As noted in the section on characteristics of a good assignment, a writing task is most successful when its difficulty level is appropriate for the students. An assignment that is too easy will be boring; an assignment that is too difficult will be frustrating. If writing is to be a tool for developing intellectual skills, you must have a strategy for taking students from the college-entry level to the level of sophistication required of a graduate student or working professional. Also, a technical writing program should equip students with the rhetorical skills necessary to perform the writing tasks expected of a professional.

As a strategy for sequencing assignments in a course or the curriculum, we have adopted a system originally suggested by Kiniry and Strenski[9] and introduced into chemical education by Rosenthal.[10] In this system, writing tasks are classified into a small set of expository forms of increasing abstraction and conceptual sophistication: listing, definition, seriation, classification, summary, comparison/contrast, analysis, and academic or scientific argument. These basic rhetorical forms, briefly described in Table 2-1 and further described below, encompass the principal professional writing tasks for students to master, and classification by cognitive difficulty level provides a natural strategy for developing thinking and writing ability in a course and across the curriculum.

Assignments on essentially any subject can be written at every level of the hierarchy. To illustrate this fact, we will provide sample writing tasks at each conceptual level on a limited number of chemical subjects: atomic theory, acids and bases, chemical formulas, and chemical bonding. It is also important to note that assignments of varying difficulty can be written at every level, so the scheme is applicable for seniors as well as freshmen. Examples of assignments of varying difficulty, but at the same level of the conceptual hierarchy, are given in Table 2-2, which follows the detailed description.

A major challenge in designing assignments is ensuring that the question cannot be answered satisfactorily with a response at a lower level of the hierarchy. Thus a carefully formulated assignment must be combined with clear assessment criteria. Intellectual growth requires both challenge and guidance.

The eight conceptual levels in order of increasing difficulty are

❶ Listing. At its most basic level, listing merely asks for a rote display of memorized items. A sample assignment is "List the postulates of Dalton's

TABLE 2-1 Conceptual Hierarchy

Form	Definition
❶ Listing	Display of important items
❷ Definition	Brief or extensive explanation of a word or concept
❸ Seriation	Ordered list or description of a procedure
❹ Classification	Application of specific categories to specific data
❺ Summary	Identification of important facts and ideas in a reading
❻ Comparison/Contrast	Listing and perhaps analysis of similarities and differences
❼ Analysis	Breaking down a complex idea into its constituent parts
❽ Academic or Scientific Argument	Use of facts and theories to support a proposition

atomic theory in your own words." Listing, however, can provide the backbone of more complex papers where the list provides the paragraph or section topics as in the assignment "List and explain the three major theories of acids and bases: Arrhenius, Brønsted-Lowry, and Lewis" or a historical assignment such as "List and explain the major contributions of R. B. Woodward to organic synthesis."

❷ **Definition.** Clear definitions are essential to chemistry. Assignments in definition can result in a short paragraph or can be expanded into a more extensive essay. An example concerning Dalton's atomic theory is "Give a clear definition of a chemical element based on Dalton's original atomic theory. According to Dalton what are the essential characteristics of an element?" A second example involving chemical bonding is "Write clear definitions of covalent, polar covalent, and ionic bonds."

❸ **Seriation.** This step-by-step format of the laboratory report is clearly an important form in scientific writing. A seriation assignment can be as simple as an ordered list or as complex as the description of a complicated experimental procedure or theoretical algorithm. A rather challenging example from general chemistry is

> In a coherent one-page essay describe how you can use combustion analysis and gas density to determine the molecular formula of an organic compound consisting only of carbon, hydrogen, and oxygen. As part of your paper you should briefly describe the experiments that must be performed; then thoroughly describe the analysis of the data obtained. Be sure to list the assumptions that are made in the data analysis. Use mathematical equations where appropriate, but also describe the procedures clearly in words.

❹ **Classification.** Ordinarily the application of established categories to specific data, easy classification assignments ask the student to list the categories and provide examples or to restructure lists. More sophisticated assignments might encourage the students to extend or refine categories or even to create them. A simple assignment is

> Essentially all simple inorganic reactions can be classified either as precipitation, acid–base, or oxidation–reduction reactions. Provide a clear definition and examples for each category. Identify the basis for classification of each example.

❺ **Summary.** Summarizing and abstracting are important in scientific writing. An easy summary assignment asks students to identify and pull out the thesis and topic sentences from an article or other reading. More sophisticated summary assignments involve inferences and clarifications. A simple summary assignment is

> Summarize the Bohr theory of the hydrogen atom.

A more challenging assignment for a major paper is

> Summarize the development of the concept of an atom beginning with Dalton's original atomic theory and ending with the quantum theory of the electronic structure of atoms.

This topic offers a sophisticated or advanced form of seriation.

    ❻ **Comparison/Contrast.** Compare and contrast topics are widely used in college writing because they provide a simple and useful framework for students to begin to think more deeply. Assignments of this type can vary in difficulty from the simple listing of points of similarity and difference to tasks in which the student must first invent the bases for comparison and then convey the significance of similarities or distinctions. A simple assignment concerning acids and bases is

> Compare and contrast the three concepts of acids and bases: Arrhenius, Brønsted-Lowry, and Lewis. What essential features do they have in common? How do they differ?

A more complicated question concerning atomic theory is

> In a coherent essay compare and contrast Dalton's theory of an atom with the modern theory. In what ways are they similar? In what ways do they differ? Begin your essay with a concise summary of the two theories.

    ❼ **Analysis.** In its simplest form, analysis requires breaking down an idea into its constituent parts. An example concerning acids and bases is

> Using chemical examples, show how the concept of acid and base was made more general and powerful as chemists moved historically from the simple Arrhenius concept to the Brønsted-Lowry and finally to the Lewis theory. What explanatory power is gained as the concept is generalized?

More sophisticated analysis questions require an application of a theoretical framework such as

> In a short essay show how the postulates of Dalton's original atomic theory are consistent with the empirical law of definite composition and how they explain the empirical law of multiple proportions.

    ❽ **Academic or Scientific Argument.** An academic argument brings together facts and theories to prove one or more propositions. An example that could be used in general chemistry is

> Using your understanding of the chemical bond, construct an argument either supporting or refuting the statement that van der Waals interactions are bonds.

This form also includes problem solving in which students are asked to propose and defend solutions to open-ended problems.

    This eight-fold hierarchy provides a framework for incorporating writing into chemistry courses (see Table 2-2). First, it offers a natural order for sequencing assignments. Since cognitive models suggest that listing is simpler than defining, it should come first so that students can build skills and confidence. Second, the forms that come lower in the hierarchy are used in higher-level tasks. For example, listing is integral to comparison/contrast, and summary is certainly used in both analysis and academic argument. In this view the forms developed in the lower part of the hierarchy can be seen as building blocks for the complex tasks of analysis and academic argument. The scientific paper is usually an academic argument and usually uses most or all of the lower levels to achieve a larger purpose. In this sense, the hierarchy can be seen as recursive, by which we mean that the conceptual tasks can be revisited at increasing levels of sophistication.

TABLE 2-2 Sample Assignments at Ascending Levels of Difficulty

Form	Level of Difficulty	Explanation
Listing	*Easy:*	List and explain the three theories of acids and bases: Arrhenius, Brønsted-Lowry, and Lewis.
	Intermediate:	List the important categories of Brønsted-Lowry acids and bases in inorganic solution chemistry.
	Advanced:	List and explain the various concepts of acids and bases that chemists have used, beginning with the original definition of acids as oxygen-containing substances by Lavoisier and ending with modern concepts based on electronic structure exemplified by the Lewis theory. Describe the essential features of each concept, its historical origin, and its subsequent development (or abandonment). What are the strengths and weaknesses of each concept?
Definition	*Easy:*	Write a clear, concise definition of a covalent, a polar covalent, and an ionic bond.
	Intermediate:	Write a definition of a delocalized chemical bond based on the concept of resonance.
	Advanced:	Develop definitions of covalent, ionic, and metallic bonds based on the relative electron distributions around the bonding atoms.
Scientific Argument	*Easy:*	Based on your understanding of covalent bonds, develop an argument to defend or refute the proposition that the most important factor in the strength of a covalent bond is the bond order.
	Intermediate:	Using your understanding of the chemical bond, construct an argument either supporting or refuting the statement that van der Waals interactions are bonds.
	Advanced:	Construct an argument to explain the experimental observation that the volume of decane increases much more strongly with temperature than does the volume of high molecular weight polyethylene.

Within any level of classification, writing tasks can be more or less complicated. Definitions can range from simple sentences or paragraphs to major essays. In planning a sequence of writing assignments for a four-year chemistry curriculum, an instructor can use the same forms in each course but increase the sophistication of the assignments from year to year, perhaps culminating in a senior thesis. In a major project, such as a senior thesis, the various rhetorical forms introduced in the hierarchy are used as building blocks to produce an effective scientific argument.

FORMALITY AND INFORMALITY IN WRITING REQUIREMENTS

Writing tasks can be divided roughly into two types: formal and informal. By formal writing we mean the standard forms of professional writing such as abstracts, laboratory reports, proposals, research papers, resumes, and, of course, essay examinations. Formal assignments are always read and graded, although the writing can be significantly improved if the evaluation occurs after a process in which initial drafts are assessed by the instructor, a writing coach, or a peer reviewer and then revised by the students. By informal writing we mean writing tasks designed to help students (and working scientists) think through and learn complex material. Examples of informal writing include journals, short in-class writing assignments (the "five-minute" paper), or out-of-class writing assignments of various lengths.

Informal writing might be assigned for the student's benefit and not read or graded (except perhaps as complete or incomplete), may be read and assessed by the instructor and not graded, or may be read and formally graded. Informal writing assignments are an effective prelude to a formal assignment; the ideas generated in a journal or an in-class assignment can be further developed in a more formal paper. As students begin to see how informal freewriting feeds into their formal assignments, the habit of informal writing will become more self-sustaining.

All these forms have been used by chemistry faculty in a variety of contexts. We will describe each one and provide suggestions for its use and references to the literature for further detail. Sample assignments can be found in Chapter 6. A bibliography on teaching writing in college chemistry, listing articles published between 1980 and 1990, is available[11] as is a bibliographic essay on "writing across the curriculum."[12]

Informal Writing Assignments

Personal Journal. Journals are widely used in college courses in the humanities, but rarely in science. In a personal journal students are encouraged to write about the course material using personal language. In a chemistry course the personal journal can be thought of as an annotated set of lecture and reading notes. In introductory courses it is useful to give the students some structure to guide their writing of journals—a suggested format or a set of questions to be answered and a clear set of success criteria. For many students writing can be a valuable learning tool if they use it to summarize, paraphrase, and organize the course material. Productive scholars often develop their ideas in private journals.

If a journal is required, it should not be formally graded, except for completeness. The instructor can offer to read students' journals and comment on the writing, and students can be encouraged to exchange journals for peer critique. More information on managing, reading, evaluating, and responding to student journals can be found in Chapters 3 (p. 24) and 4 (p. 49). You can find other ideas for the use of journals or annotated lecture notes in Powell,[13] Hermann,[14] Beall and Trimbur,[15] and Malachowski.[16]

Short In-class Writing. In-class informal writing has been used effectively in a variety of chemistry courses.[17] Students are asked to write for one to five minutes on a well focused question. When used at the beginning of a class, in-class writing can focus the students on the day's learning task. When used in the middle or at the end of class, it provides students with an opportunity to process the course material and raise questions. Such writing is rarely graded. Some instructors ask students to exchange papers for peer critique. Others collect and read the papers, perhaps appending comments. Some instructors post or project the best student papers as models. For the instructor, the short in-class essay reveals how well students are comprehending the course content.

Summary. In his general and physical chemistry courses, Kovac has used summary assignments as effective active learning tools. In general chemistry he asks students to prepare a one-page summary of the material to be covered on each of the in-class exams. Writing a summary provides students with a structured process for reviewing the important ideas in the course. As an incentive, students are allowed to use the summary as a reference during the exam. The summaries are then stapled to the exam paper and evaluated for bonus points that are added to the exam score. In a physical chemistry course with a guided-inquiry cooperative learning approach, students were regularly asked to write two- or three-page summaries of the course material. These summaries were read and graded holistically. In the course evaluation students commented that the summary assignments helped them to organize the course material into a coherent whole.[18] These are only two variations of the possible uses for a written summary assignment.

Microtheme. Microthemes are short out-of-class writing assignments[19] in which students are asked to explain some idea introduced in the course. Generally, these assignments are confined to one typewritten page or less, so they can be used in large-enrollment classes without creating an enormous grading burden. If a holistic grading method is used, it is possible to read and evaluate 150 student papers in about four hours. The microtheme, however, can also be used as an ungraded writing-to-learn assignment in which the papers are read by the instructor and the best papers posted or in which the papers are subjected to peer review. Chapter 4 suggests processes for peer review.

Concept or Project Paper. In his organic chemistry courses, Powell has used "concept" papers of two to three pages and "project" papers of five to eight pages.[20] The terms *concept* and *project* were introduced to eliminate the anxiety that science students often feel when descriptors such as essay, term paper, or research project are used. Like microthemes, these are out-of-class writing projects in which students are asked to explain an idea introduced in the course or to pursue some topic in greater depth. Powell and his students agree on whether the paper will address a lay or technical audience. The shorter, more focused concept papers are used to explain a principle or describe a reaction. A longer project paper treats broader topics such as the separation of complex biomolecules using molecular sieves or the scientific background of the disaster in Bhopal, India.

Formal Writing Assignments

Abstract and Summary. Writing concise, informative abstracts is an important professional skill. An assignment asking students to write an abstract can be used in any course as long as a suitable article can be found. In lower-division courses, finding articles that the students can read and understand is a challenge, but more accessible publications such as *Chemical and Engineering News, Science News, New Scientist, Endeavour,* and *Scientific American* should provide sufficient materials. In advanced courses students can be asked to read articles from the research literature.

Unfortunately, these articles usually come with abstracts written by the authors. One strategy is to provide students with photocopies of the articles with the abstracts removed. You may also want to remove journal title and volume number from the citation and running heads so that the clever students do not just go to find the published abstract. Alternatively, students can be asked to write one-to-two-page extended abstracts or summaries that contain the additional details that a research scientist might need, perhaps including a critique of the article.

Annotated Bibliography. Since constructing a good annotated bibliography is often part of a major research project, chemistry majors should undertake this writing task several times during their education. To develop bibliographic skills, small-scale annotated bibliography assignments can be made in conjunction with library research projects. A large-scale annotated bibliography is a logical part of a senior research project or thesis.

Literature Review. The next step beyond the annotated bibliography is the literature review, which surveys the research on a particular topic. A literature review assignment provides a means for introducing students to the primary research literature in chemistry as well as a number of cognitive tasks such as listing, summary, seriation, and comparison/contrast. Beall and Trimbur provide a detailed discussion of literature reviews in chemistry as well as suggested assignments.[21]

Laboratory Report. Laboratory reports are integral to an undergraduate education in chemistry. The laboratory report is a logical place to develop writing skills, but in many chemistry departments this opportunity is wasted. Often when lab reports are assigned, students pay lots of attention to data analysis, but little to prose. Since the lab report contains many of the basic rhetorical forms in the hierarchy, it can be used to reinforce and extend the writing skills developed in other courses or to develop new ones. For example, students can practice their skills in writing abstracts by providing them for their own lab reports. An experimental procedure is usually an exercise in seriation, while the theoretical background is usually summarized. If an independent project is part of the course, a short research proposal can be assigned as a prelude. Olmsted has described an upper-division laboratory course with many of these elements.[22] Bailey and Geisler describe the use of writing consultants to help students improve their laboratory reports.[23] Beall and Trimbur provide an excellent overview of the writing of laboratory reports.[24]

Proposal. Proposals, of course, are the lifeblood of science, so learning to write them should be part of any chemistry curriculum. While the eight basic forms in the hierarchy can provide the building blocks, a proposal must be written in a persuasive mode. As noted above, laboratory courses are an excellent venue for proposal assignments, particularly if an independent experiment or project is required. Students can be asked to write a proposal to the instructor for their independent project, justifying it in terms of predetermined criteria. Writing projects in upper-division courses can be framed as proposals rather than as reports. Guidelines for proposal writing in chemistry can be found in Beall and Trimbur.[25]

Research Paper and Technical Memorandum. Among professionals, science is communicated in research papers and technical memoranda. Undergraduates are often asked to write research reports but are seldom exposed to the rather rigid forms of professional journals and the style guidelines of the American Chemical Society. Again, laboratory courses, particularly in the upper division, are good places to introduce students to the professional journal and technical memorandum forms. Detailed guidelines for writing scientific papers can be found in books by Porush;[26] Booth;[27] and Ebel, Bliefert, and Russey;[28] and in *The ACS Style Guide.*[29]

Resume, Curriculum Vitae, and Cover Letter. Working professionals use well-written resumes in a variety of circumstances. Students should be introduced to the resume and curriculum vitae forms early in their undergraduate education and then should return to their personal resumes to update and expand them year by year. They can write cover letters to real or imaginary companies. The American Chemical Society has produced an excellent booklet on resumes and cover letters.[30]

Professional Biography. Like a resume, a professional biography is often useful to a working chemist. This writing project also can be initiated early in a student's education and revisited yearly.[31]

Popular Article. It is increasingly important that scientists communicate effectively with the public. Moreover, careers in technical communication or science journalism are interesting options for chemistry majors. Hence, writing assignments that ask students to write for a lay or a scientifically educated, non-expert audience are appropriate for chemistry courses. Developing a good popular article is both interesting and challenging.

There are a number of good options for assignments of this type. An obvious example is to ask students to write about a current issue involving science and society: acid rain, chemical weapons, drug design, or ethics, for instance. Good suggestions can be found in the ACS textbook for non-majors, *Chemistry in Context.*[32] Another possibility is to explain an important concept or recent discovery in an article suitable for a publication like *Discover* or *The New York Times*; future teachers might enjoy writing an article for a middle-school audience or for a juvenile environmental publication like *Ranger Rick*. A third option is a profile of an important chemist's life and scientific work. All of these assignments can be customized for use in any course in the undergraduate curriculum. Suggestions about the writing of popular articles in science can be found in Beall and Trimbur[33] and Porush.[34]

Historical and/or Philosophical Paper. Many students find the history of chemistry interesting and will welcome a writing assignment that allows them to explore the development of the field. Historical assignments generally take one of two basic forms: a profile of an important person, such as a Nobel laureate; or the history of a particular discovery or concept. Another option is to base a writing assignment on an interesting and provocative reading. Examples of both readings and assignments can be found in the book by Hatton and Plouffe.[35]

The scientific community is increasingly concerned with questions of professional ethics.[36] Scientific ethics provides a good source of writing assignments. Case studies that present real-life ethical problems are available,[37] and students can be asked to write papers that explore the issues raised in the cases and propose an appropriate course of action. Students can also be asked to write papers on recent incidents of scientific misconduct that have been reported in the popular or scientific press.

Essay Examinations. Short essays are a traditional part of chemistry examinations. Students are often asked to provide a definition, explain a concept, or rationalize an experimental result. Essay questions can reinforce a writing development program if three elements are present. First, the question should prompt a response longer than a sentence. When grading a large number of exam papers, you probably don't want to read multiple-page essays, but it is reasonable to ask for a well-constructed paragraph. Second, questions should be constructed based on the principles outlined in this chapter. Finally, evaluation must be based both on content and form. A significant fraction of the credit for the answer must be based on the quality of writing.

CONSTRUCTING A GOOD ASSIGNMENT

Because poor writing can result from a badly formulated or vague assignment, you need to consider at least four elements in developing your assignments: instructional objectives, audience, process, and evaluation. A good assignment will provide students with sufficient guidance in the first three areas so that they can direct their efforts efficiently and creatively toward producing their best writing.

Instructional Objective

The instructional objective of a writing assignment in science has three interrelated parts: the content or subject of the assignment, the cognitive and research tasks, and the rhetorical form. All three must be considered, but in any particular assignment they will be of differing importance.

Content. This first area is obvious; students have to write about something. In some assignments the content will be the primary consideration; an instructor will want the students to think through an important idea in the course and will be less restrictive about the rhetorical form. For example, if you want students to solidify their concept of acids and bases, the assignment could be a brief microtheme, a longer term paper involving library research, or even a more popular form such as an article for the "Science Times" section of the newspaper. On the other hand, if the cognitive and research tasks or the particular rhetorical forms are the more important considerations, as with abstracts or summaries, the subject might be a matter of student choice.

Cognitive and Research Tasks. The eight-fold hierarchy lays out the various cognitive tasks. The cognitive task might be closely linked to the subject. For example, it might be important for students to compare and contrast the various concepts of acids and bases. On the other hand, development of the cognitive skill might be the primary objective and the particular content to which it is applied relatively unimportant. Some rhetorical forms might be better suited to the cognitive task at hand, but usually the nature of the paper is of less importance. Another factor is the nature of the research required for the assignment. Will the student be directed to particular sources, such as the primary research literature, or will the information in the course textbook suffice?

Rhetorical Form. If the major objective is to have the student master a particular form, such as writing an abstract, the cognitive task may be dictated by the form, but the subject matter is probably less important. Part of the professional education of a chemist is the mastery of certain forms of writing, but the forms are useful in many contexts. An important consideration here is the concept of topic types discussed earlier. Is the student writing an expository, persuasive, or expressive piece?

Audience

If students do not know for whom they are writing, they are likely to be increasingly confused about the writing assignment. An article in *Discover* is intended for a much different audience than is an article in the *Journal of the American Chemical Society*. Students need to know what they can assume the reader already knows and what the reader will expect. Scientists write for roughly three kinds of audiences: experts, scientifically educated non-experts, and general readers. Each kind of audience has a different background and expectations and requires a different emphasis. Scientific prose is also much different from the kinds of papers that students write for their humanities and social science courses, where the readers are likely to have much different expectations from any of the three kinds of audiences for scientific prose. Further discussion of audience analysis and of reader awareness of self as audience appears in Chapter 4 (pp. 43–44).

Formal Process

Writing Tasks. Students must understand the formal process that the paper must go through. Will a first draft be required so that the instructor or a writing coach can make suggestions for improvement? Even if an early draft is not required, is the instructor available to read and assess preliminary efforts or to answer questions about specific passages in the draft? In a major project are there intermediate goals to be met, such as the approval of the topic or the submission of a bibliography or outline? Is the writing to be done individually or by teams? Will there be an opportunity or requirement for peer review? What final form will be expected, both the rhetorical form and the mechanics? Specifying such matters as length, margins, font size, and citation form is important. The answers to these questions will depend on the assignment, but your specifying them lets students know what to do and allows you to expect a fairly consistent appearance in a set of papers.

Academic Honesty. One other matter that your students may need help with when you make an assignment is the danger of plagiarism, the use of another's ideas and/or phrasing without acknowledging the source. Most college composition handbooks define and illustrate plagiarism and proper documentation.[38] L. Bensel-Meyers and M. Garrett offer criteria for plagiarism that you may want to share with your students. Students are plagiarizing if they

- Copy without proper documentation (quotation marks and a citation) another writer's words, phrases, or sentences;
- Summarize without proper documentation (usually a citation) another writer's ideas;
- Quote more than two or three consecutive words from a source without enclosing them in quotation marks (even though you cite the source);
- Copy part or all of a paper by another student or tutor;

- Allow someone else to correct, amend, or edit [their] work without [their] instructor's approval.[39]

Beyond encouraging your students to demonstrate integrity in their written work, you can show them how acknowledging sources places their work in the context of larger scientific endeavors and lets readers know where to find more information.

Burkett and Dunkle suggest that you can show students what plagiarism is by teaching them how to take notes and to paraphrase: taking notes by compressing text and then turning the notes into their own prose; and paraphrasing each experiment in their laboratory notebooks for the instructor to evaluate.[40]

Evaluation

Finally, students must know in advance how the writing will be evaluated. The two major evaluation methods, holistic and analytic, will be considered in detail in Chapter 4, where development and use of assessment and evaluation criteria are also discussed. It is essential that students know who will read the papers and what the reader or readers will be looking for. A clear statement of the success criteria should be part of the assignment. Careful attention to all four elements—instructional objectives, audience, process, and evaluation—will produce assignments that prompt students to produce excellent writing.

SUMMARY

As you design your writing assignments, we encourage you to anticipate the questions your students might ask and to answer them in terms of your writing assignment objectives and the potential for the writing assignment to help the students master the course material. In this process you lay the groundwork for a dialogue about writing skills that moves from your own interior conversation about your expectations and the students' needs to an exchange among students and between students and yourself and teaching assistants. In the most productive cases, the students will engage in their own interior dialogues to identify and meet audience needs. At worst, you will provide students an opportunity to strengthen their writing and thinking skills while they learn chemistry. At best, you may help some students to find their own voices and to take pride in their techniques for expressing both the content and the value of the chemistry they are learning.

REFERENCES

1. E. M. White, *Teaching and Assessing Writing*. Jossey-Bass, San Francisco, 1988.
2. M. Kiniry and E. Strenski, "Sequencing Expository Writing: A Recursive Approach," *College Composition and Communication* **1985**, *36*, 191–202.
3. See, for example, W. Zinsser, *Writing to Learn*. Harper & Row, New York, 1988.
4. R. Hoffmann, "Under the Surface of the Chemical Article," *Angewandte Chemie* (International Edition in English) **1988**, 27, 1653–63 (1988); *The Same and Not the Same*. Columbia, New York, 1995.

5. P. Levi, *The Periodic Table*, trans. Raymond Rosenthal. Schocken Books, New York, 1984.

6. R. Hoffman, *The Same and Not the Same*. Columbia UP, New York, 1995.

7. H. Beall and J. Trimbur, *A Short Guide to Reading and Writing in Chemistry*, 2nd ed. Longman, New York, 2001.

8. W. C. Booth, G. G. Colomb, and J. M. Williams, *The Craft of Research*. University of Chicago, Chicago, 1995.

9. M. Kiniry and E. Strenski, see note 2.

10. L. C. Rosenthal, "Writing Across the Chemistry Curriculum: Chemistry Lab Reports," *J. Chem. Educ.* **1987,** *64,* 996–998.

11. N. P. Shires, "Teaching Writing in College Chemistry: A Practical Bibliography 1980–1990," *J. Chem. Educ.* **1991,** *68,* 495.

12. P. Bizzell and B. Herzberg, "Writing across the Curriculum: A Bibliographic Essay," in D. A. McQuade, ed., *The Territory of Language*. Southern Illinois, Carbondale and Edwardsville, 1986.

13. A. Powell, "A Chemist's View of Writing, Reading and Thinking Across the Curriculum," *College Composition and Communication* **1985,** *36,* 414.

14. C. K. F. Hermann, "Teaching Qualitative Organic Chemistry as a Writing-Intensive Class," *J. Chem. Educ.* **1994,** *71,* 861.

15. H. Beall and J. Trimbur, see note 7.

16. M. R. Malachowski, "The Use of Journals to Enhance Chemical Understanding in a Liberal Arts Chemistry Class," *J. Chem. Educ.* **1988,** *65,* 439.

17. H. Beall, "In-Class Writing in General Chemistry," *J. Chem. Educ.* **1991,** *68,* 148; "Probing Student Misconceptions in Thermodynamics with In-Class Writing," *J. Chem. Educ.* **1994,** *71,* 1056. M. J. Strauss and T. Fulwiler, "Interactive Writing and Learning Chemistry," *J. Coll. Science Teaching,* **1987,** *16,* 256.

18. R. J. Hinde and J. Kovac, "Student-Active Learning Methods in Physical Chemistry," *J. Chem. Educ.* **2001,** *78,* 93.

19. J. C. Bean, D. Drenk, and F. D. Lee, "Microtheme Strategies for Developing Cognitive Skills," in C. W. Griffin, ed., *New Directions for Teaching and Learning: Teaching Writing in All Disciplines,* no. 12. Jossey-Bass, San Francisco, 1982; M. M. Cooper, "Writing: An Approach for Large-Enrollment Chemistry Courses," *J. Chem. Educ.* **1993,** *70,* 476.

20. A. Powell, see note 13.

21. H. Beall and J. Trimbur, see note 7.

22. J. Olmsted III, "Teaching Varied Technical Writing Styles in the Upper-Division Laboratory," *J. Chem. Educ.* **1984,** *61,* 798.

23. R. A. Bailey and C. Geisler, "An Approach to Improving Communication Skills in a Laboratory Setting: The Use of Writing Consultants," *J. Chem. Educ.* **1991,** *68,* 150.

24. H. Beall and J. Trimbur, see note 7.

25. H. Beall and J. Trimbur, see note 7.

26. D. Porush, *A Short Guide to Writing about Science*. Harper Collins, New York, 1995.

27. V. Booth, *Communicating in Science,* 2nd ed. Cambridge UP, Cambridge, 1993.

28. H. F. Ebel, C. Bliefert, and W. E. Russey, *The Art of Scientific Writing: From Student Reports to Professional Publications in Chemistry and Related Fields.* VCH, Weinheim, Germany, 1990.

29. J. S. Dodd, ed. *The ACS Style Guide,* 2nd ed. American Chemical Society: Washington, D. C., 1997.

30. Department of Career Services, American Chemical Society, *Tips on Resume Preparation.* American Chemical Society, Washington, DC, 1994.
31. M. Lomask, *The Biographer's Craft.* Harper & Row, New York, 1986.
32. C. L. Stanitski, L. P. Eubanks, C. H. Middlecamp, and W. J. Stratton, *Chemistry in Context,* 3rd ed. McGraw-Hill, Boston, 2000.
33. H. Beall and J. Trimbur, see note 7.
34. D. Porush, see note 26.
35. J. Hatton and P. B. Plouffe, *The Culture of Science: Essays and Issues for Writers.* Macmillan, New York, 1993.
36. J. Kovac, "Scientific Ethics in Chemical Education," *J. Chem. Educ.* **1996,** *73,* 26–28.
37. J. Kovac, *The Ethical Chemist,* Department of Chemistry, The University of Tennessee, Knoxville, 1995.
38. See A. Lunsford and R. Connors, *The St. Martin's Handbook,* 2nd ed. St. Martin's Press, New York, 1992; J. C. Hodges, S. Strobeck Webb, and R. K. Miller, eds., *Hodges' Harbrace Handbook,* 14th ed. Harcourt-Brace, Fort Worth, 2001.
39. L. Bensel-Meyers and M. Garrett, *The New Student's Guide to Research at UTK.* Department of English, University of Tennessee, Knoxville, 1997.
40. A. R. Burkett and S. B. Dunkle, "Technical Writing in the Undergraduate Curriculum," *J. Chem. Educ.* **1983,** *60,* 469–470.

chapter 3

Using Writing in the Chemistry Curriculum

This chapter presents strategies for using writing effectively in chemistry courses. Two interrelated issues will be considered: the uses of writing in individual courses and the systematic development of writing skills through the four years of the chemistry curriculum. For individual courses we will show uses of writing to accomplish a broad spectrum of instructional objectives. The vertically structured chemistry curriculum allows the possibility of close coordination among courses. Although undergraduate chemistry curricula across the United States share many common features, differences that do exist make it impossible to develop a four-year program for adoption by every institution. Instead, we will outline some general principles to facilitate the construction of a plan that will meet the needs of an individual department.

USING WRITING IN AN INDIVIDUAL CHEMISTRY COURSE

Every course has diverse instructional objectives. In chemistry courses, faculty are best at providing educational tasks that address the professional technical objectives of the course.[1] Exams and homework assignments are filled with excellent quantitative problems or questions about chemical structures, reaction mechanisms, or synthetic strategies. Chemistry instructors also hope that their students will develop a conceptual understanding of the subject matter of the course, as well as an appreciation of where each topic fits into both the larger structure of chemistry and the broader context of science. We assume, naively, that in the process of solving homework problems and studying for exams, students will acquire the skills of reading scientific prose and thinking critically. Our courses, however, rarely provide students with explicit tasks that address these broader objectives.

Instructional Objectives

At least four kinds of instructional objectives can be addressed by writing: conceptual understanding, skill development, reintegration of knowledge, and enrichment.

Conceptual Understanding. Asking students to explain a concept in words can stimulate them to clarify, deepen, and contextualize their understanding, and reading student explanations can help the instructor identify misconceptions. Writing about chemical concepts will also help students develop critical thinking skills. Informal writing assignments, journals, summaries, short in-class papers, and microthemes, either graded or ungraded, are useful for these purposes.[2] Short essay examination questions both allow students to demonstrate their conceptual understanding and emphasize the importance of good writing.

Perhaps the best vehicle is the personal journal, in which students regularly write to clarify their understanding of the concepts in the course material.[3] While some students will be able to use the journal as a learning tool without much guidance, most will require some structure. There are a number of possible ways to help students learn to write a journal. One possibility is to use textbook resources. For instance, most textbooks have lists of key terms followed by brief definitions. Students can be asked to write their own, more discursive explanations of these terms complete with examples. The review questions in general chemistry textbooks can also serve as the basis for a journal. If these resources are not available in the textbook, you can supply your own terms or questions. An excellent set of questions for a physical chemistry course can be found in the textbook by Castellen,[4] which is, unfortunately, out of print but might be available through your library.

Another, more flexible, possibility is to ask students to identify at least one idea from each lecture or from each major section of the textbook and write about it in their own words in the journal. Journals can be assigned as personal learning tools, in which case they should not be graded, except for completeness. If you have the time and energy, you should offer to read and comment on student journals, both for the students' benefit and for your own. In reading journals you can learn what the students are really understanding. A random assessment strategy for providing feedback to students is presented in the next section, and you can read more on journal assignments in Chapters 2 (p. 14) and 4 (p. 49).

An alternative to the personal journal is regular summary assignments. Students can be asked to write a summary prior to the major exams or at the end of a chapter or natural unit of the course. Summaries can be useful in exam preparation and can be evaluated for bonus points to be added to the exam score. Chapter or unit summaries can also be holistically graded or merely read and assessed to provide both the instructor and the student with feedback.

Short, in-class papers can serve a similar function. Again, these need not be graded, merely read to reveal what students are actually learning. The best papers can be posted on a bulletin board or photocopied onto transparencies and projected to show students your expectations. Names, of course, should be removed. One-page microthemes can also be assigned. Even for a very large class, these can be graded holistically. Chapter 6 offers a collection of assignments at all levels of Kiniry and Strenski's conceptual hierarchy.

While ungraded writing is a useful learning tool, many students will not see the connection between the writing task and their success in the course. The importance of writing can be emphasized by including essay questions requiring at least one well-constructed paragraph on the course examinations. These questions should prompt students to demonstrate their conceptual understanding and should be graded both on content and form. The number of essay questions and the suggested length of answers depends on both the amount of time required to grade the papers and the nature of the course content.

Peer review assignments are useful tools for improving conceptual understanding. A simple strategy is to ask pairs of students to exchange in-class or microtheme assignments and identify unclear or weak parts of the papers. You might also prepare a simple assessment form that asks key questions about the topic. A more elaborate collaborative learning strategy might involve three steps: (1) Ask students to use the textbook and lecture notes as resources for a brief essay (100–150 words) on a concept that is not yet clear to them; (2) in the last 10–15 minutes of class ask pairs of students to exchange papers, read about each other's problems, and then try to explain the troublesome concepts to each other; (3) end the class with this assignment: "Based on your discussion, rewrite your essay and explain the concept more clearly. Bring your rewritten paper to the next class." The instructor can then review the rewritten essays quickly to gauge what students have learned. Coppola and Daniels have developed other interesting peer review strategies for use in the structured study groups at the University of Michigan.[5]

Skill Development. Writing can also be a vehicle for skill development, particularly in reading and library research. Faculty in introductory courses commonly complain that students are unable to comprehend the textbook or supplementary material. Requiring students to write coherent extended summaries of the reading assignments can help students learn that reading science is different from reading fiction or the daily newspaper. Reading journals or structured reading logs are other possibilities. Krumsieg and Baehr[6] have developed a detailed reading methodology. The assignments can be assessed or graded by the instructor or exchanged for peer critique. To aid peer critique, you can develop a simple form that asks students to assess how clearly the key ideas in the reading assignment were expressed in the summary. While summary is the most obvious and useful rhetorical form for developing reading skills, other forms, such as listing or comparison/contrast can be used in selected situations to provide some variety in the assignments.

Few instructors, except in small colleges, have time to assess or evaluate all student reading journals or summaries, but both are important. Random assessment and evaluation can be used effectively. The first step is to provide explicit success criteria for the assignments. Students then can be required to bring their reading journals or reading summary portfolios to every class. From time to time, perhaps in the laboratory or a discussion quiz, you can quickly assess one reading summary or a page or two out of the journal for several students. Provide the students with brief written comments about both positive qualities of their work and need for improvement. The results of your assessments will spread quickly through the class. After several of these assessments, the writing exercises should show significant improvement. At the end of the term, collect all reading journals or portfolios and evaluate several of the later assignments chosen at random. To show that the skill is important, at least a small percentage of the final course grade should come from the reading journal.

As students progress in their education in chemistry, writing assignments can be used to introduce them to the chemical literature. Preparing an annotated bibliography, for example, is an effective way to teach library and information search skills. Bibliography assignments must be carefully constructed and focused, however, or they can become overwhelming. A bibliography assignment can be limited to a single journal, to journals and books published in the past ten years, or perhaps only to Internet resources. Assignments to write simple or extended abstracts can help students learn to read and digest original literature. As students progress, the two forms can be combined into a review article. Such projects can be done individually or in groups.

Learning to read a scientific paper is an important professional skill. While most research articles are beyond the reach of the average first-year student, it is possible to begin the process of developing this skill with a carefully constructed assignment. For example, in an analytical chemistry course for well-prepared first-year students, Wright has developed a collaborative team approach to understanding a research paper. Part of the process is the preparation of written answers to questions.[7] Writing assignments can be based on the less sophisticated papers that appear in journals such as *Journal of Chemical Education, Science News,* or *American Scientist.*

Reintegration of Knowledge. Writing serves well to help students grasp and internalize the connections between what they are learning in your individual chemistry course and what they are learning elsewhere, both in and outside the school. While an individual course focuses on specific content and skills, the material is connected to the rest of chemistry and to other sciences and engineering. The course material also has a history that raises philosophical questions. Finally, the course content may have implications for society and for disciplines outside of science. It is difficult to treat these reintegrative questions adequately in the lectures, laboratories, problem sets, and exams that comprise the usual chemistry course. No instructor has the time or the expertise either to reach the diverse audience in most lower-level courses or adequately to explore broader contexts. Writing assignments, however, can provide an effective solution to these problems.

Although students themselves are not likely to see immediately the relevance of a chemistry course to their own education, you can help them develop this way of thinking about your course material. In introductory courses for students from a variety of majors, lectures and textbooks can suggest certain connections of the course material to biology, geology, engineering, or other majors, but students must learn to make such connections for themselves.

While it is impossible to reach everyone, a writing assignment asking the students to explore the implications of a key concept in the course for their own major will stimulate this kind of reflection. For example, engineering students might appreciate a question such as

> Discuss the role of heat capacity in the choice of ceramic materials or metal alloys for engine block manufacturing;

biology students, a question such as

> Discuss the role of hydrogen bonding in the structure and function of DNA.

In introductory courses you can provide specific topics like these for the most common majors represented in your class. While we suggest a number of possible assignments in Chapter 6, introductory textbooks from other departments and discussions with colleagues can provide additional ideas.

A similar strategy can be used to explore the historical, philosophical, and social context of the course. Students can be asked to write a paper outlining the historical development of a particular concept or experimental technique. Students can explore contemporary societal implications by writing papers based on news articles related to the course material. Weekly periodicals such as *Science* and *Chemical and Engineering News* are good sources of articles on science and society. A good way to introduce philosophical aspects of chemistry is to use the scientific ethics cases published in *The Ethical Chemist*[8] and ask students to write short essays analyzing a selected case and proposing an appropriate course of action. A wide variety of assignment types can be developed in each of these areas ranging from a simple one-paragraph summary to detailed analysis. Reintegrative assignments make an excellent opportunity for students to practice both persuasive and expressive writing as well as to think more broadly about chemistry.

Enrichment. Reintegration of knowledge leads naturally to the matter of enrichment. Particularly in upper-division and graduate courses, chemistry faculty feel frustrated at the limited amount of time in courses. A semester seems just too short a time to explore the interesting applications and extensions of the course material. A major writing assignment can be one solution. Students can be asked to investigate the applications and extensions on their own. Both individual and group projects are possible.

Formal Writing Assignments in Individual Courses

In many courses it is appropriate to make a formal writing assignment either to introduce students to one of the professional rhetorical forms outlined in Chapter 2 or to develop further their skills in those forms. Formal assignments ordinarily require more structure than informal writing-to-learn tasks. Usually longer-term assignments, they require idea development, library research, and multiple drafts. Providing a structure that includes intermediate goals should result in a higher-quality product. Ballenger provides excellent advice on managing a major writing project.[9] Booth, Colomb, and Williams have written an excellent guide for students.[10] Guides to scientific forms include the books by Beall and Trimbur[11] and Porush.[12] Most formal writing is done by individuals, but it is also useful to introduce students to collaborative writing since much scientific writing is done by groups.

General Plan.   A general plan for managing a formal writing assignment should include the following stages:

1. Identification of a general topic: You may specify the topic for the students, or students can be encouraged to do some exploratory research to identify the area for concentration. It is a good idea to have a check point early in the semester when students have to indicate the general subject of their papers by submitting a brief description of their areas for your approval.

2. Identification of a specific topic: Narrowing the subject to a manageable size is essential. Again, it is best to require that a brief description of the specific topic along with some key references be submitted to you, just to keep students on track. You might ask them to state the topic as a hypothesis and to outline their intended research methods or their intended development of the essay. Your comments on these descriptions can help students further narrow topics that are too large or too vague, can redirect any dead-end thinking, and can identify organizational lapses.

3. First (or working) draft: All good writing goes through multiple drafts. Requiring that a working draft be turned in at least two weeks before the final deadline will encourage revision. If you have the time or the services of a writing consultant, it is useful to read and comment on working drafts to guide student revision.

4. Final deadline: The final deadline should be early enough to give you sufficient time to read and evaluate the papers at least before the course grades must be submitted but preferably before the final exam so that students can incorporate your suggestions in their exam essays. Formal writing should be evaluated carefully, even if you use a holistic method.

For formal writing assignments it is an advantage to develop a relationship with the writing center on your campus, if you have one, or with a member of the English faculty. The best circumstance would be to have the funds to hire a writing consultant to work with your students. A writing professional can help students with problems of grammar, style, and voice, leaving you to assess the technical content and adherence to professional standards.

A Collaborative Writing Approach.   A formal writing assignment can also follow one of several models for collaborative writing in chemistry courses. The simplest is a peer review strategy in which one student prepares a draft and one or more other students collaborate to review and revise that draft. Several peer review strategies are described in detail in Chapter 5. Johnson and Johnson[13] suggest a more elaborate pairing strategy in which students cooperate in both planning and revision. Pairs of students meet initially to discuss and refine their paper topics. After individual research, the pairs again meet to develop outlines cooperatively and perhaps to write the initial paragraph of both papers. Finally, the pairs meet a third time to make suggestions for revision of the first drafts.

A second model divides the students into working teams with well-defined roles. Booth, Colomb, and Williams[14] call this the "divide, delegate, and conquer" strategy. Team members are assigned to complete parts of the task. One student might search *Chemical Abstracts,* another go to the Internet, and a third search the monograph literature. The drafting and revising of the final paper, however, must be a collaborative effort. Although the initial drafting of the different sections of a paper can be drafted by individuals, it is essential that all members participate in the revision, which can be done by revising in turns. The initial drafts are circulated, and each member of the group takes a turn at revising the entire paper. At most schools today these revisions can be typed directly into the text on a word processor, and students will see immediately the impact of their suggestions. A group paper in which each student independently writes one section of the final report is not a collaboration. The final paper must reflect the best thinking of the whole team.

Collaborative writing can be time consuming for both students and instructor, but it is a skill that professional scientists must develop. Since many scientific papers and proposals are written by teams, students need to learn the skills required for successful collaboration, particularly dialogue, compromise, and project management.

Integrating Writing into the Chemistry Course

In deciding how much and what kind of writing should be used in an individual chemistry course and where in the course it should appear, the following considerations are important: student work load, grading, skill building, learning objectives, and variety.

Student Work Load. Writing is hard work. A good paper requires more than one draft, plus the research and planning. While writing-to-learn assignments such as journals and reading summaries can be simply part of a student's normal study time, larger and more formal assignments compete with problem sets and the other course requirements. If students are to write well, they must have the time.

Grading. If the writing is to be graded, someone, probably you, must do it. Holistic grading can be done rather quickly, but you do need to build grading into your time budget for the course. As with any other assignment, writing assignments are best graded and returned to students promptly. If more than one writing assignment is given in the course, the first one should be graded and returned before the students begin to work on the second one.

Skill Building. Students don't become better writers just by writing. Constructive feedback is important. Writing skills can be developed by asking students to write multiple drafts with feedback on the earlier versions from the instructor or from peers. A second method is to have the students write more than one paper in the course. Either method requires more instructor time than the typical term paper assignment, but is more effective pedagogically. Techniques for effectively responding to student writing are discussed in Chapter 5.

The conceptual hierarchy of assignments provides a framework for the building of both thinking and writing assignments within the course. When multiple assignments are used, the conceptual sophistication can be gradually increased as the semester progresses, assuming that students have mastered the earlier levels. If writing assignments based on this hierarchy have been used in earlier courses in the curriculum, you can build on those skills in choosing or designing your own assignments.

Learning Objectives. Since it is impossible to accomplish everything in a single course, it is essential that the learning objectives be clarified and ranked in priority and that the most appropriate pedagogical techniques are employed to accomplish the primary objectives. Writing is especially effective for the development of conceptual understanding, and it should be used, where possible, to approach it.

Variety. For both students and faculty, it is refreshing to have different kinds of assignments in a course. Writing can be a good alternative to the usual problem sets and exams. In addition, writing assignments provide an alternative entry point for students whose learning styles vary from the mainly quantitative flavor of most chemistry courses. Writing assignments, particularly those exploring the broader context of chemistry, can be fun, re-energizing student interest in the subject.

USING WRITING ACROSS THE CURRICULUM

In the highly structured four-year chemistry curriculum, it is possible to introduce students to all the major types of professional writing as well as develop their information searching, thinking, and writing skills. To accomplish this, a systematic plan must be developed that incorporates relevant writing into most if not all of the courses in the curriculum. Since every curriculum is different, we cannot provide a plan that fits all needs. We can, however, provide some guidelines for the core courses in the curriculum.

General Considerations

Some concerns apply at all levels of the undergraduate chemistry curriculum and should influence every proposal for a writing plan to cross that entire curriculum. The individual or group making the plan might want to incorporate the criteria listed here:

1. Writing assignments should be included in every course, if possible.
2. While writing-to-learn assignments can and should be used anywhere in the curriculum, the level of conceptual sophistication should be raised

year by year. Later assignments should call for the skills developed earlier in the curriculum.

3. Students should be introduced to all the important forms of professional writing somewhere along the curriculum. The forms more important to professional chemists should be included in the specialized courses populated mainly by majors. More widely used forms should be used in courses with more diverse populations. It is useful to have students repeat assignments, using feedback to help them to increase sophistication the second or third time. For example, a brief, highly selective literature review might be assigned to second-year students in analytical chemistry and a broader scale review given in the instrumental analysis course. Olmsted[15] gives a systematic approach for writing formal laboratory reports.

4. Reintegrative assignments connecting chemistry to other sciences and to the broader context of human endeavor are more important in lower-division courses but are still appropriate in specialized courses directed at majors.

5. Some assignments that allow students to submit multiple drafts should be given during the four years to give students practice in revising. While their appreciation of this process in your course may be minimal, their experience in graduate school and industry will exonerate you. They will learn that most of their writing energy is expended in revision.

6. Students should have at least one opportunity to participate in a collaborative writing assignment during the four years.

7. By the end of the four-year program students should be thoroughly familiar with the standards of professional style as laid out in the *ACS Style Guide.*[16]

First Year

In most curricula the first-year course is general chemistry with its highly diverse student population, most taking the course as a requirement for some major other than chemistry. Because of the large enrollments, probably only short assignments such as one-page microthemes can be graded, but ungraded or peer-reviewed writing can also be used. Because of the diverse population, writing assignments should focus on broadly applicable concepts and skills rather than narrow professional objectives. The following kinds of assignments are appropriate for the first-year course:

Skill Development. In the first year, students need to master the basic skills of reading textbooks and supplementary materials, understanding and reporting laboratory procedures, and making simple data analyses. Short summary or journal assignments can be effective in developing reading skills. Experimental procedures and simple data analyses involve seriation, so assignments at this conceptual level should be given to develop these skills.

Conceptual Understanding. Students who do not plan to major in chemistry often do not need to know how to solve detailed chemical problems, but they do need a conceptual understanding of the important ideas. Frequent short writing assignments or journals can help students clarify key concepts and develop critical thinking skills. These writings need not be graded. In fact, peer review may be a better evaluation process. Trying to explain a chemical concept in writing to a classmate gives the student an opportunity to deepen personal understanding.

Connections to Other Disciplines and Reintegration. Elementary chemistry will seem more relevant and interesting if students connect the learning to their own interests. In addition, writing assignments that explore the connections of chemistry to society and to the broader liberal arts can be effective.

Second Year

Typical second-year courses include elementary organic and analytical chemistry. While both of these courses are populated by students with interests other than chemistry, more professionally oriented writing is appropriate. In particular, assignments that begin to acquaint students with the professional literature and the norms and values of science can be introduced in the second year. As part of a four-year plan, assignments in the second year should be at a higher level of conceptual sophistication than those given in the first year.

The more sophisticated second-year laboratory courses provide opportunities to introduce students to the rhetorical forms associated with the reporting of experimental procedures, particularly seriation, and the analysis of experimental results. It is important to provide a bridge between the relatively simple laboratory reports usually required in the first year and the highly sophisticated reports associated with the physical chemistry and instrumental analysis laboratory courses usually taken in the third year.

The second-year courses also provide opportunities for students to begin reading the chemical literature. Some research literature in organic and analytical chemistry is quite accessible to undergraduate students. Annotated bibliographies or extended abstracts are good entry-level assignments. Project papers requiring a more detailed analysis of one or more literature articles are also possible.

Finally, any assignments suggested for the first year can also be used in the second year. Since many organic chemistry students are not chemistry majors, assignments to connect the subject with their proposed majors and to facilitate conceptual understanding are useful. Papers on historical and societal themes also can provide an important perspective.

Third Year

In third-year courses such as physical chemistry and instrumental analysis, essentially all the students are chemistry majors, so the writing projects can focus on professional writing skills while continuing to meet some of the broader objectives. Conceptual understanding is essential in physical chemistry where two of the major topics, quantum mechanics and thermodynamics, are difficult to grasp. Both topics also raise important philosophical questions about the nature of science and thus can provide interesting writing assignments.

Important professional rhetorical forms, formal research reports, proposals, and technical memoranda, can be introduced in the third year. For example, the instrumental analysis course is a good place to assign a literature review. The third year is a good time to introduce students to the resume, the curriculum vitae, and the professional biography, since students are beginning to think about both summer and permanent jobs and graduate school. To introduce the resume or curriculum vitae, include it as part of a proposal assignment. A junior or senior seminar, a professional skills course, or a capstone course is a natural place for students to develop both a resume and a professional biography.

Fourth Year

In the fourth year, students should be comfortable with the basic rhetorical forms. Longer papers emphasizing close reading of the literature and scientific argument should be assigned in this year's advanced courses. The shorter assignments are still useful, but the final year's goal is to make sure that the students can function in the professional world that they will be joining as either employees or graduate students. Group assignments should not be forgotten. Collaborative work is increasingly the norm in both industry and the academy. Students need to learn to write collaboratively. By this year, professional standards of citation and style should be rigorously enforced.

SUMMARY

The precise form of a four-year program of writing in chemistry will depend on the details of the curriculum as well as the interests and abilities of the departmental faculty. Cooperation and compromise will be needed to develop a comprehensive plan. The assignments presented in this handbook provide a starting point, but ultimately every instructor and every department will need to develop, revise, and refine their own assignments to fulfill the objectives of their curriculum and meet the needs of their students.

REFERENCES

1. For a discussion of the classification of educational objectives see J. Kovac and B. P. Coppola, "Universities as Moral Communities," *Soundings: An Interdisciplinary Journal,* in press.
2. H. Beall, "In-Class Writing in General Chemistry," *J. Chem. Educ.* **1991,** *148;* "Probing Student Misconceptions in Thermodynamics with In-Class Writing," *J. Chem. Educ.* **1994,** *71,* 1056.
3. A. Powell, "A Chemist's View of Writing, Reading and Thinking Across the Curriculum," *College Composition and Communication,* **1985,** *36,* 414.

4. G. W. Castellan, *Physical Chemistry*, 3rd ed. Addison-Wesley, Reading, MA, 1983.

5. B. P. Coppola and D. S. Daniels, "The Role of Written and Verbal Expression in Improving Communication Skills in an Undergraduate Chemistry Program," *Language and Learning Across the Disciplines*, **1996,** *67,* 67–86.

6. K. Krumsieg and M. Baehr, *Foundations of Learning.* Pacific Crest Software, Corvallis, OR, 1996.

7. J. C. Wright, "Authentic Learning Environment in Analytical Chemistry Using Cooperative Methods and Open-Ended Laboratories in Large Lecture Courses," *J. Chem. Educ.* **1996,** *73,* 827.

8. J. Kovac, *The Ethical Chemist.* Department of Chemistry, University of Tennessee, Knoxville, 1995.

9. B. Ballenger, "Teaching the Research Paper," in T. Newkirk, ed., *Nuts and Bolts: A Practical Guide to Teaching College Composition.* Boynton/Cook, Portsmouth, NH, 1993.

10. W. C. Booth, G. G. Colomb, J. M. Williams, *The Craft of Research.* University of Chicago, Chicago, 1995.

11. H. Beall and J. Trimbur, *A Short Guide to Reading and Writing About Chemistry*, 2nd ed. Longman, New York, 2001.

12. D. Porush, *A Short Guide to Writing about Chemistry.* Harper Collins, New York, 1996.

13. See Chapter 5 in D. W. Johnson and R. T. Johnson, *Meaningful and Manageable Assessment Through Cooperative Learning.* Interaction Book Co., Edina, MN, 1996.

14. W. C. Booth, G. G. Colomb, and J. M. Williams, see note 10, pp. 31–34.

15. J. Olmsted, III, "Teaching Varied Technical Writing Styles in the Upper-Division Laboratory," *J. Chem. Educ.* **1984,** *61,* 798–800.

16. J. S. Dodd, ed., *The ACS Style Guide,* 2nd ed. American Chemical Society, Washington, DC, 1997.

chapter 4

Grading Writing Assignments

Grading is a genuine concern of all university faculty, and the student essay inevitably compounds the concern. Even composition instructors, usually trained to assess writing, engage in lively debate over assessment approaches and the values to be applied to various writing practices. As a chemistry instructor, you are likely to have learned what you know about assessing and grading writing from the comments of English teachers and perhaps even an occasional science professor. Some of their advice will be useful as you read a set of student writing assignments, but you may feel that it's too "spotty" or too particularized.

In this chapter we lay out two different approaches to evaluating student writing: holistic and analytical. We make some suggestions about the relative importance of particular writing weaknesses. As you will see, you can make choices that will allow you to reinforce the values most important to you and will help you to manage and limit the time you spend assessing student writing. Finally, you will find some suggestions for training your teaching assistants to mark and grade student writing.

Whatever system you establish, a crucial point to remember is that no single grading standard should be used in an absolute fashion; judgment calls will always be required because of the many variables in writing and writing evaluation.

WEIGHTING WRITING

Before assessment and grading begin, you will be asked to answer the inevitable student question, "How much does the writing count?" Our experience has shown that the writing is tied inextricably to the clarity of understanding, but students seldom see or trust the connection. They will want to know percentages and will be eager to hear "bonus" or "extra credit" options. How much does grammar count? Do you give extra points to a student who uses more than the required resources for a microtheme?

Students also will want to know what *about* their writing is important to you, their audience. Do you care about spelling? Do you want article reviews in the past or present tense? Do you want examples? Are you a "neat freak"? Are your assigned lengths firmly fixed, or do you allow some latitude for excellent work?

You need to be prepared to meet some of these questions before you make the first writing assignment. You might attach a general requirements sheet to each writing assignment and include items like the following:

Required length (number of pages or words)

Margins, fonts, and font sizes (to help you measure length)

Acceptability of handwritten papers, ink colors

Features of good writing in order of their importance to you:

> Content: thesis statement (you might ask that this appear in italics), support by specific example, relevance of detail, order of information, conciseness, suggestion of topic significance
>
> Conventions of mechanics and style: spelling, sentence structure, subject and verb agreement, diction (word choice), verb tense, failure to follow format instructions
>
> Figures, tables, mathematical equations, chemical structures and equations: font sizes, use of word processing character sets and table features, legends and labels
>
> Citation form: style guide required
>
> Endorsement placement and information, i.e., student name, identification number, course and section number, date, assignment number
>
> Definition of plagiarism and statement of the consequences

This kind of information actually does more than reassure students. You make the reading easier for yourself by specifying such simple matters as font size and margins when you make the assignment. Without such minor distractions as a two-page paper squeezed onto one page, you will be more free to concentrate immediately on how well the paper meets the assignment requirements. You will receive a relatively uniform stack of papers, and you will lose less grading time to goofy fonts, tiny print, and a search for the student's name. On the general requirements sheet, you can specify a penalty for failure to follow instructions—penalties ranging from requiring the student to rewrite the paper to a deduction of a set number of points.

Plagiarism is, of course, a more serious scholarly lapse, with moral as well as intellectual dimensions (see Chapter 2, pp. 19–20). Your institution probably has guidelines for defining and handling plagiarism, and you will want to be sure that your students know those guidelines and your own additions to them. It is common to fail any paper that uses the intellectual property of others without proper documentation and to fail a student who persists in plagiarizing in the course. If you are convinced that a student plagiarized out of ignorance, you might want to ask the student to revise the paper and write a paraphrased definition of plagiarism from your general requirement sheet—with citations—to ensure the student's full understanding of the problem.

When your program has adopted writing as a requirement for all courses in the curriculum and has universalized the format and skill expectations, these general requirement sheets will be necessary only in the beginning courses. Students will internalize the writing requirement if it is applied consistently. By the fourth year of writing for chemistry courses, many students will have learned that writing can count *for* them and that even ungraded writing counts because it strengthens their comprehension and mastery of chemistry as well as other subjects.

In most cases an evaluated writing sample also serves as an assessment tool, helping the student to understand what skills need mastery and to apply more sophisticated writing techniques to the next assignment. Though students may never agree, your feedback will ultimately be more important to their writing development than the grade you assign could ever be. As students write throughout the chemistry curriculum, they should develop their own ability to use a writing handbook and to organize information effectively, in effect to raise appropriate questions for themselves before any professor sees the writing.

HOLISTIC GRADING

For some writing assignments, you may want to use a holistic approach; for others, a more analytical reading is more appropriate. The holistic approach relies on broad, general assessment of overall impact. An analytical approach assigns values to certain writing strengths and weaknesses and applies percentages or other numerical scales to the final grade.

Holistic reading allows a teacher to make rapid judgments and provides a student with a general sense of present writing ability. The process is most reliable when the students recognize that the assignment is clear and significant and when the teachers themselves are clear about their own expectations. These factors contribute to reliability in judgments. Grader judgments are then expressed in a numbered scale. We suggest using the 6-point scale recommended by E. M. White.[1] The reader simply uses the numbers 1 through 6, 6 being highest. Actually, you can use any number of points you choose, but we do recommend an even number to counteract the tendency to gravitate toward the middle number when an odd scale is used. Students can be given information about the general characteristics of the writing at each of these levels.

The 6-point scale works quite sensibly for a two-step grading process:

Step 1   Divide papers into two stacks:
Top half (4, 5, 6)
Bottom half (1, 2, 3)

Step 2   Divide each stack into three stacks:
Above average (6 or 3)
Average (5 or 2)
Below average (4 or 1)

In holistic reading, indeed even in analytical reading, it would be difficult to make finer distinctions than this process allows. The six points allow for reasonable letter-grade equivalents: 6 = A, 5 = B, 3–4 = C, 2 = D, 1 = F.

As you incorporate writing into your courses, you will establish your own criteria from experience, but the sample microtheme segments that follow may be helpful for getting started. They were written in response to the italicized portion of the following microtheme assignment for a general chemistry section:

> One characteristic feature of atoms is that their emission spectra are discontinuous line spectra rather than the continuous spectrum of sunlight. The physical origin of this remarkable observation was first explained in detail by Niels Bohr. In a coherent one-page essay, *summarize the Bohr theory* and *show how it explains the emission spectrum of the hydrogen atom.*

This general chemistry assignment evoked responses at all levels of the 6-point holistic scale.

Level 6 Criteria

1. *Content:* Clear, direct, and accurate, sensitive to ambiguities and anomalies
2. *Assignment:* Responsive to topic and intention, usually contextualizes information
3. *Conventions:* Generally mechanically and grammatically correct, with no serious grammar errors (no sentence fragments, run-on sentences, subject-verb agreement errors, or such illiteracies as "she done" or "ain't got none")
4. *Organization:* Focused entirely on the assigned topic and fluent, with specific support for ideas; logical

The response below meets the criteria for a score of 6:

> In 1913 Niels Bohr devised two postulates that account for the stability and line spectrum of the hydrogen atom. The first postulate states that electrons circle the nucleus in specific paths known as energy levels giving the atom fixed energy values and is calculated by the formula $E = R_H/n^2, (n > 1)$ where $R_H = 2.179 \times 10^{-18}$ and n is the principal quantum number. The second postulate states that an electron can change energy only by shifting from one energy level to the other in a process known as transition and the energy is figured by the formula $E_f + hv = E_i$ where E_i is the initial, E_f is the final energy level, and $hv =$ photon energy. By using the measured values for the mass and charge of the electron, together with Planck's constant $(6.63 \times 10^{-34}$ J$-$s), Bohr was able to calculate the energies that an electron would have in the allowed energy levels for the hydrogen atom. This showed mathematically how the various spectral series of hydrogen could be produced. Bohr's calculated values agreed exactly with the experimentally observed values for the lines in each series. For example, the Balmer spectral series was shown to be the result of electrons dropping from various higher energy levels to energy level 2 ($n_i > 2$ to level $n_f = 2$). Bohr's theory explains not only the emission but also the absorption of light (a reverse of the emission process).

This response presents the generalizations in a logical order with clear and useful transitions between points, then moves to an example. It is not perfect, however, and the student could be advised to lay out formulas more conventionally and to combine a sentence starting with *This* plus a verb with the preceding sentence. Both of these suggestions are matters of sophistication of style.

Level 5 Criteria

1. *Content*: Largely clear, sometimes direct, accurate
2. *Assignment*: Responsive to topic but less conscious of the intention of the assignment
3. *Conventions*: Slightly mechanically flawed (apostrophe, spelling, punctuation, etc., errors) but no serious grammar errors
4. *Organization*: Focused on topic, less fluent largely in that introductions, transitions, and conclusions are more contrived and artificial than in the 6 paper; logical

The example below is written at level 5:

> Niels Bohr found a solution to the theoretical dilemma concerning the stability of an atom. He was working with Rutherford at the time who had a nuclear model. One could show that an electrically charged particle that revolves around a center would continuously lose more energy as electromagnetic radiation. As the electron in an atom lost energy, it would spiral into the nucleus. Bohr used the simplest atom, hydrogen, to theorize the stability of an atom. Bohr formulated postulates that did two things: 1) explain the stability of the hydrogen atom including the fact that the atom exists and does not continuously radiate energy and spiral into the nucleus and 2) the line spectrum of the atom.
>
> The energy level postulate states that an electron can only have specific energy values in an atom called energy levels. Atoms can only have specific total energy values. Bohr borrowed the quantization of energy from Planck and devised a rule that could apply to the motion of electrons in an atom. From this he devised a formula for the energy levels of the electron in the hydrogen atom.
>
> In Bohr's postulate of transitions between energy levels, he borrowed Einstein's photon concept to explain the line spectra of atoms. Bohr substituted values of the energy levels of the electron in the hydrogen atom which he had derived into the equation to produce Balmer's formula exactly. He was also able to predict all of the lines in the spectrum of the hydrogen atom, including those in the infrared and ultraviolet regions.

The writer of this 5-point response offers accurate information and is fairly detailed though sometimes a bit off point. The essay gives no specific formulas, is generally more wordy than the 6-point essay, and is awkward about setting points of information in context. For instance, while both postulates are present and are eventually named, their importance does not stand out as clearly as it does in the 6-point essay.

Levels 4, 3 Criteria

1. *Content*: Usually comprehensible and technically correct, but little sense of ambiguity; simplistic

2. *Assignment*: Reveals a very general sense of topic or a tendency to veer off topic, but usually returns to it
3. *Conventions*: Mechanically flawed but no serious grammar errors
4. *Organization*: "Fuzzy" focus, stiff in introductions, transitions, and conclusions; occasional lapses in logic, but a general sense of central purpose

This example meets the 4-point criteria:

> The emission spectra lines of atoms is a phenomenon that was deciphered by Neils Bohr in 1913. Using the theories of Albert Einstein, Max Planck, and others, Bohr was able to derive an explanation which includes two postulates that interpret the phenomenon of atomic line spectra.
>
> The first postulate given by Bohr states that electrons in atoms can only have specific energy levels in an atom. This statement in turn indicates that atoms can have only specific total energy values.
>
> In postulate number two, Bohr explains that an electron in an atom can move from one energy level to another. This electron activity is responsible for the phenomenon of atomic emission spectra. More specifically, Bohr stated that when an atom moves from a higher energy level to a lower energy level the energy lost by the electron is given off as a photon with a specific wavelength.
>
> Bohr also explains how atoms move from a lower energy level to a higher energy level. Bohr states that one method through which atoms can be excited is the transfer of kinetic energy when two atoms collide with each other. Another method through which electrons can be energized is through the absorption of certain wavelengths of light. For example, when a hydrogen electron goes from energy level three to level two a photon of red light is emitted with a wavelength of 656 nanometers. On the contrary when an electron of hydrogen absorbs a photon of 656 nanometers it moves from energy level two to level three and absorbs the red light.
>
> Through a series of calculations Bohr derived a formula that related the loss of energy by an electron to a specific wavelength of light. The use of this fomrula and certain constants allowed Bohr to confirm the visible wavelengths of any hydrogen atom (known as the Balmer series) and predict the ultraviolet and infrared wavelengths of any hydrogen atom (known as the Lyman series and Paschen series respectively). Bohr's explanation of atomic spectra lines also applies to other elements if their wavelengths are known.
>
> In conclusion, Neils Bohr's theory of atomic emission spectra includes two postulates that explain this phenomenon of discontinuous spectra. The work that Bohr performed was the basis for the theories of quantum physics. The understanding of quantum physics has changed chemistry and allowed for better understanding of why atoms behave the way they do.

This essay shows that the writer's grasp of Bohr's postulates is fairly simplistic, offering little to no sense of implication or intention on the writer's part; in fact, the writer uses six paragraphs to respond to a topic that calls for no more than two. The relationships between ideas and between the postulates themselves are fuzzy but can be unraveled. Shifts in verb tense, faulty diction (i.e., *deciphered*), wordiness, and misspelling Bohr's first name mar the presentation of information. Finally, note that the weakest of these satisfactory essays is also the longest, a fairly common phenomenon when a writer is filling the page rather than attending to conceptual significance.

Levels 2, 1 Criteria

1. *Content*: Sometimes incomprehensible and/or inaccurate, sentences poorly constructed, poor word choices
2. *Assignment*: Lacking in a clear sense of central purpose, loses sense of assigned topic and method
3. *Conventions*: Mechanically and grammatically flawed
4. *Organization*: Emptiness, too little content (information, support) to achieve the intention of the assignment; illogical (i.e., lists not orderly, paragraphs unfocused, transitions confusing)

The essay that follows is written at level 1:

> Bohr has a theory that the admission of light from an atom is when an electron transfers from one energy level to another one, according to Bohr. This is when an electron goes from a higher energy state to a lower one. Basically electrons "get excited" pr gain energy to go up to a higher level. For example this can happen when there is a collision of two hydrogen atoms. When they hit each other some of the kinetic energy from one atom moves over to the electron of another atom. This makes it jump to a higher energy level. When an electron in hydrogen atom experiences a transfer in the Balmer series from $n = 3$ to $n = 2$, it gives off a photon this is red light. When light from a hydrogen gas discharge tube separates into its components by a prism, there are lines in a spectrum. Each line like a wavelength of light. The line spectrum of hydrogen is so simple that it is just four lines in visible area (red, blue-green, blue, and violet). Bohr's postulates help to explain this happening by giving (1) the stability of the hydrogen atom (that the atom exists and its electron does not continuously radiate energy and spiral into the nucleus) and (2) the line spectrum of an atom. His Energy-level Postulate is the formula for energy levels of the electron in hydrogen atom:
>
> $$E = -R_H/n^2 \quad n = 1,2,3 \ldots \text{infinity for the H atom}$$
> When you substitute the values you can get the color of the light.

The writer of this 1-point essay relies heavily on specific examples, but Bohr's theory is never pointedly summarized. While no serious errors in scientific content arise, a phrase like "surprisingly simple" in an essay this awkward suggests that the writer is trying hard to paraphrase but really has little sense of the concepts being discussed and sometimes simply copies out of the text. The individual sentences are scientifically correct, but they are arranged in almost random order. The sentence fragment, for instance, which should be included in the preceding sentence, indicates the student's inability to link ideas meaningfully for self or audience.

A list identifying these criteria or your own can be handed to the students with the first writing assignment. A cautionary note should be added to the effect that these are general characteristics of papers in each category, that no one paper is likely consistently to show every characteristic at any one level. The levels are intended to show variations in clarity (from clear and language sensitive to incomprehensibility), purposefulness (from intention to meet the purpose of the assignment to an absence of any sense of that purpose), mechanical and grammatical correctness (from essential correctness to inability to control major errors), focus on and satisfaction of assigned topic, and reasoning process. You will usually find enough consistency in a student's performance to suggest a summary score.

When you read a set of papers by this method, it is often helpful to read the entire set through quickly, making a rough sort into high and low stacks. As you read through the second time to assign scores, papers may move into different stacks. Fine judgments can be made by the "editorial hesitation" method. Writing lapses cause the reader to hesitate because they interfere with the purpose and pleasure of reading. When you face that set of papers, the best among them will be scientifically accurate, quickly processed, and easy and satisfying to read. The intermediate group will take longest to read because of the mix of clarity and confusion. The low group will leave the reader puzzled about the writer's intent, but the errors are so overt and so pervasive that scoring decisions can be made quickly.

As you follow the two-step process given on page 37, you need to judge the extent of editorial hesitation, the degree of confusion that errors cause: a minor spelling error (*occured* for *occurred*) is less intrusive than a spelling error that confuses the content (*there* for *their*); a sentence fragment or nonsense sentence is more intrusive than a simple subject-verb agreement error. At the same time you will judge the understanding level that the student essay reveals: an unclear presentation of one step in a process, for example, would cost the student less than an attempt to answer a cause-effect question by detailing a process.

Influences on Evaluation

The essay itself is not, however, the only force influencing evaluation. Freedman and Calfee suggest that the essay, the reader, and the context all influence holistic assessment and that each of these can be controlled.[2] In the case of an individual course, the controls depend largely on the reader and will develop gradually as the reader's experience develops. Your task, then, is (1) to provide students with enough information to evoke a pleasing manuscript quality, (2) to be guided by appropriate professional criteria as you evaluate, and (3) to set aside calm and productive times for reading and evaluating. Each time you apply this approach to a new set of essays, your analysis of previous experience grading student writing will contribute to greater ease and surety of judgment.

The Essay. The chapter on designing writing assignments will help you to establish controls over the essay itself. Be prepared to acknowledge an occasional failed topic and roll with that punch. Usually, though, you will know your expectations and how you want your students to achieve them. The general requirements sheet described earlier in this chapter is a second effective means to assure that you receive essays that are generally pleasing to the eye and inviting to a reader.

On this point, the English department can be helpful once again. You will want to be familiar with the grading criteria that department has established and either to reinforce those criteria or to clarify for your students any important differences in your expectations. For instance, you, the chemistry instructor, may place a far higher value on accuracy of scientific content, logical development, and grammatical correctness than on creative expression and inventiveness. Your emphasis may strike your students as "picky" or at least peculiar, and you may need to explain your emphasis to your students to help them overcome their resistance.

The Reader. Mina Shaughnessy categorizes reader expectations into three groups: awareness, improvement, and mastery.[3] Because their grades are affected, most students will be aware of the immediate importance of writing. As graded work is returned to them, you also can expect them to become more aware of you or your teaching assistants as audience.

In general chemistry courses, you can offer students an audience persona that is fairly consistent throughout a semester. In more advanced courses, with their more specialized writing assignments, like the traditional research paper, for instance, you, as reader, may be called upon to don the mask of a journal editor or peer reviewer. For a popular science article you become, instead, a comparative lay reader, a reviewer with a few undergraduate courses or an undergraduate degree in chemistry. When you assume a role, you can help your students by making them aware of this specialized audience. They need to know the following: (1) how well informed you are; (2) the vocabulary level to establish; and (3) the detail level that will satisfy you. With this information in mind, students can be expected to imagine and attempt to reach a particular type of reader.

Shaughnessy further suggests that instructors must hold realistic expectations for student improvement and mastery. In an academic term, you can reasonably expect all your student writers to improve (to reduce the number of editorial hesitations) and a few students to master certain writing weaknesses. It is easy to become defensive and even angry when student writing shows little improvement—or, on the other hand, to suffer paralyzing self-doubt. These feelings, when they do arise, intrude on a reader's judgment. Therefore it is important to recognize and control for them. A consultation with a professional from the English department at your school may be helpful in setting appropriate criteria for writing improvement.

You also can make a conscious effort to bring your best professional self to the reading. Remind yourself of the goals and expectations you expressed in making the assignment, and keep those goals uppermost in your evaluation. To accomplish this task, you will need to identify your own "hobbyhorses," or personal peeves, and hold these subservient to the primary goals and expectations. A student's confusion of *its* and *it's*, for instance, may drive you wild. Feel free to make a mark on the error, but keep your grading emphasis on content accuracy, organization, and sentence structure. The core of

Shaughnessy's suggestion is that faculty reading student essays must be self-aware and convey some of that self-awareness to the students.

Context. The place and time of the grading are both important. It helps to be in a comfortable and relatively insulated place when you settle in to assess a set of papers. Most of us are more reasonable and acute readers when we are in familiar surroundings with ready access to the tools of the trade. Interruptions can disrupt consistency and cloud the best intentions to apply clear judgment.

Choosing a calm grading time can also help clarify judgments. Immediately after a hot departmental meeting about revising the chemistry curriculum is probably not the best time to sit down to grade student writing. Neither is the end of the day when you are tired and likely to become impatient with the inevitable errors.

ANALYTICAL APPROACH

Analytical grading calls for the marking of particular weaknesses and errors. As a scientist, you will be much concerned with scientific accuracy and completeness. As you respond to the student's writing under this approach, then, you will make focus, coherence, sentence structure, exact diction, punctuation marks, and spelling your primary targets. The reader makes marginal notes and/or offers an encouraging commentary at the end of the paper (see Chapter 5) to offset the critical tone set by marking errors.

In recent years the analytical approach has come under considerable attack, ranging from charges that it is idiosyncratic by nature, to a lack of evidence that student writing actually improves as a result, and ultimately to its "confrontational air."[4] If it is to be useful, analytical grading must be supplemented with consistent and often individualized instructor follow-up on the writing assignments. A common danger of analytical grading is the tendency to "mark off" for particular errors without adding back on for overall effectiveness. An essay is more than the sum of its parts. Just as in chemistry, elements combine into compounds with very different properties from either element, so in a student essay the general impact is at least as important as the sum of its parts. Thus a survey of the list of errors must always be tempered by the general (holistic) response to the essay. You can even include a final category for overall effect.

Because analytical grading is more time-consuming than holistic grading, you may want to reserve it for student writing that passes through two or more drafts—major research papers or undergraduate theses. When you do decide to evaluate analytically, key your responses to a particular handbook—the *ACS Style Guide*, for example—and direct your students to this resource. The manual can then serve as the arbiter of grading issues, and students can refer to it when they have questions about your marking of particular mechanical matters. The manual also can be used to define technical writing terms used in the marking.

Once a manual is identified, the next task is to determine which qualities of good writing you wish to encourage most and which flaws students should be able to control or eliminate. Then, as you actually read papers, you can ignore matters of less importance to you and focus almost entirely on the selected qualities and problem areas.

You can help students prepare for this grading approach by giving them a tracking sheet that identifies the writing problems you wish to emphasize. Students can use this sheet as a checklist for proofreading and then attach it to each draft of a writing assignment. The teacher can check problem areas for the student's information, thereby signaling problems to watch for on the next draft. If revising the essay, the student can find information about correcting errors and strengthening development in the designated handbook; if drafting a new essay, the student can try to avoid specifically the marked errors.

This tracking sheet can be as simple or as complex as you want. The examples that follow show how problems can be organized and specified, first in a simple fashion most useful for large sections, then with the greater complexity required for an undergraduate thesis. Items in the checklists can be adapted to reflect your own criteria. If you mark errors in the paper text, you can use abbreviations for each criterion (see parentheses on sample checklists). Students can use the checklist for revisions or take the tracking sheet to writing center consultants. Table 4-1, a simple chart, illustrates some possible items of concern for a paragraph assignment. You can give your chart to the students when you make the assignment and require that students check off items that have been attended to and then submit the grading chart with the revision. Thus both student and teacher can use the chart to monitor writing progress from draft to draft.

If you want to use a simple chart for a short essay of more than one paragraph, you might add a column for overall form and content, with items like *introduction, organization, conclusion, insight, completeness.*

You may prefer a more complex and thorough tracking sheet like the one in Table 4-2 to show upper-division or even graduate students a wider range of errors and to give them more specific targets for revision. This chart is so detailed that it is likely to overwhelm lower-division students, but it can be useful for those who really want to develop their professional writing skills.

TABLE 4-1 Analytical Grading Chart (Simple)

Student Name _____   Topic _____

Check mark indicates need for attention.

Paragraph	D*	F	Sentence	D	F	Mechanics	D	F
Topic Sentence (ts)			Fragment (f)			Commas (c)		
Details (det)			Run-ons (cs/fs)			Spelling (sp)		
Logic (lo)			Clarity (cl)			Capitals (cap)		
Unity (u)			Combining (comb)			Abbreviations (ab)		
Authority (a)			Usage (use)			Diction (d)		

*D = Draft/F = Final Copy

Craig B. Fryhle[5] from Pacific Lutheran University evaluates student laboratory reports by a scale, adapted in Table 4-3, that can be modified as necessary for other kinds of writing projects.

TABLE 4-2 Analytical Tracking Sheet (Complex)

Student Name _____   Paper Title _____

Thesis Statement

Paper Development (Check mark indicates need for further attention.)

Format	D*	F	Sentences	D	F	Mechanics	D	F
Word Processed			Clarity (cl)			Abbreviations/ numbers (abr)		
Double Spaced			Variety (vary)			Verb tense appropriateness (vt)		
Courier (New) 12 cpi			Conciseness (wordy or rep.)			Verb tense consistency (vtc)		
Margins (1 in. all sides)			"This/There/It" sentences			Spelling (sp)		
(Style Manual) References			Fragments (fr)			Commas (c)		
(Style Manual) Citations			Run-ons (comma splice-cs/fused sentence-fs)			Apostrophes (')		
Visuals (captions, legends, source citations)			Subject/verb agreement (s-v)			Punctuation with q. marks () pq		
Numbering (3/4 in. down, rt. margin, after p. 1)			Pronoun/antecedent agreement (p-a)					
			Point of view (pv)			**Content**		
Development			Active Voice (av)			Accuracy		
Focus/Introduction			Gender sensitivity (mo)			Completeness		
Logic (lo)			Parallel Structure (para)			Pertinence		
Transitions (trans)			Dangling modifiers (dm)					
Conclusion			Introduction of quotations (iq)			**Other**		
Adequate paragraph development (dev)			Diction (d)			Obvious error (X)		
Paragraph coherence (coh)								

*D = Draft/F = Final Copy

TABLE 4-3 Report Evaluation

Course # _____ Date _____ Student Name _____

Grade _____ Grader _____

	Exc.	Good	Fair	Weak	Poor
Title Appropriateness					
Abstract (general quality):					
Conciseness					
Statement of methodology, results					
Introduction/Initial Discussion (general):					
Specific scientific background					
Establishment of context and direction					
Results/Discussion (general quality):					
Graphs, tables-careful drawing, citations					
Explanation of results					
Defense of Conclusions:					
Numerical reliability					
Comparison with literature					
Experimental Section (general quality):					
Essentials of work-equipment, source of chemicals, wt/vol./no. of moles of starting materials					
Conciseness-unnecessary details omitted					
Experimental results-m.p., b.p., yields, properties of products and materials					
References (general quality):					
Adequacy					
Format/location of citations					
General:					
Overall format (registry number section when appropriate)					
Spelling and proofreading					
Sentence structure, tense consistency, and active voice)					
Conciseness					
Flow of ideas/style					

As with the tracking sheet forms, you can make adjustments with this adaptation of Fryhle's form, naming the particular items that contribute to your general (holistic) judgment of any one aspect of the laboratory report or paper.

Remember, these are just sample tracking sheets; you are likely to want to create your own and to establish your own abbreviations if you are marking the papers. A good college grammar handbook, like *Harbrace*[6] or *Easy Access,*[7] will supply good definitions of all these marking terms and others you may want to use; the *ACS Style Guide* will define most of them.

Use a sheet that will help you to make grading judgments, for instance, pulling together the weightiest problems (which are likely to lower a grade) or placing sophistication issues (which are unlikely to affect a grade at all) at the end of the chart. As you become more experienced, you will probably make a holistic assessment and set up a point structure that reflects it.

UNGRADED WRITING

Not all writing has to be graded. Ungraded writing projects can be useful for both student and instructor. Students often gather and synthesize more information than they realize as they try to clarify a concept or describe a process; as faculty read, they develop a focused understanding of what the students actually grasp—and what they are missing. A set of microthemes may reveal which concepts large numbers of students failed to understand and also which students need help outside the classroom.

The "ungraded" option is never exercised without a price, however. Students may jump to some false assumptions about the importance of their written work. For students whose motivations are largely grade driven, ungraded work simply does not matter. They will need convincing that their good-faith completion of an ungraded assignment will influence, however indirectly, on their final grades and that the assignment can be used to improve their content grades throughout the semester. Until they mature to this position, you can motivate by assigning points for completion of the assignment.

Other students, the more obsessional ones, will be anxious if they don't know how good you think their work is. You can offer them some assurance, if you choose, by placing a check mark on the papers to indicate that ungraded work has been recorded and adding a plus sign (+) to indicate superior work. You may also post the most impressive samples from each paper assignment. You may prefer, however, to leave responsibility for writing quality with the students, which can be a useful learning experience in itself. Brookes and Grundy argue that "learner self-evaluation is ultimately more important than teacher evaluation."[8] While this statement may be true, it is difficult to get students to recognize it.

Generally, you will decide whether to grade a writing assignment on the basis of its context in your course. But one kind of assignment should not be graded: a draft of a paper to be revised later in the semester. On a draft, analytical responses, even sketchy or narrowly focused ones, can help the student to improve the paper. To measure fulfillment of the assignment, you might deduct a given number of points, say ten, from the final grade if the draft is not submitted or is noticeably incomplete. Of course, this practice should be announced long before the draft is due.

Journals make another kind of effective ungraded assignment (see Chapter 2, p. 14 and Chapter 3, p. 24). Melanie M. Cooper's assignment for large-enrollment chemistry courses illustrates clearly a use of and rewards for journal writing. She calls for a one-page analysis of a topic the student has not understood. The assignment calls for listing the key points made about that topic and an attempt to explain. Each student then exchanges papers with a peer, and each writes a brief explanation of the other's problem topic. Cooper gives credit amounting to less than 1% of the total grade for completion of the assignment.[9]

These assignments can be collected before major tests and used to shape classroom review, but their primary value is that they require students to focus their thinking about troublesome concepts. In both events the writing should have a beneficial effect on final grades. Unfortunately, since students are likely to distrust this view, some credit for writing the journals will be necessary. A relatively simple way to demonstrate both value and credit for the assignment is to require students to bring their journals to the final exam, where you will assign a holistic grade based on a spot check of each journal for both quantity and clarity of writing (or for any other quality you have asked students to establish).

As you develop the writing component of your chemistry curriculum, trial and error will help you to determine which kinds of assignments are best left ungraded. While your own time for grading writing is a legitimate factor, your goal of producing chemistry graduates who can write effectively in professional programs or in the workplace will ultimately shape your choices about this matter.

TRAINING GRADERS

If you are fortunate enough to have teaching assistants (TAs), you can train them to grade writing assignments holistically. Group training is essential to achieving three goals:

1. Clear and shared understanding of the grading criteria;
2. Maximum consistency in marking essays; and
3. Clear and shared understanding of the writing goals for the term (particularly the skills on the writing hierarchy to be developed or mastered).

Shared Grading

Kovac has used successfully a simple procedure for training TAs to grade microthemes. He introduces the 6-point scale and provides the TAs two or three sample papers at each level. He then asks the TAs to use the following procedure:

1. Read the sample papers to establish an idea of the standards.

2. Read *all* the papers in your section and divide them into two groups—upper and lower—based on the samples. The first division is a preliminary judgment. The upper half earn 6, 5, 4 grades; the lower half, 3, 2, 1.

3. Read the papers again, this time placing them into six piles corresponding to the six different grades. Don't be surprised if some of your earlier judgments change a bit.

4. After dividing into six groups, review each paper quickly to make sure you are comfortable with your decisions. But record the grades only in your gradebook; *do not* mark grades on the papers yet.

5. To validate grading, change papers with another TA (see attached assignments), and use the same procedure to assign scores to the other section. Record scores on a sheet of paper.

6. When you have returned the papers to the other TA and received the second set of scores for your own papers, compare the grades, and respond as follows:

   a. If both readers agree, that is the score.

   b. If readers differ by one score, give the higher score to the student.

   c. If readers differ by more than one score, bring these papers to the instructor for a final decision.

7. Write the final score on the paper.

8. Bring to the professor for photocopying

   a. All papers with scores of 6 and

   b. One sample paper from each of the other five scores (if you have one in your section).

9. Return all papers to the students.

Two readings by TAs will eliminate most of the idiosyncrasies. Three (or more) readings are better. With three readings the high score can still be used, but the average of the three probably provides a more refined evaluation of the paper.

Grading Exercise

If you have more time or the number of teaching assistants justifies additional effort, a more complex training procedure may help you to achieve these goals. Following the procedures listed below, you can hold a discussion on grading student writing samples.

1. Distribute three papers to the TAs, one each from the high, middle, and low ranges. Relatively short writing assignments will work best—an essay examination question, a microtheme, an abstract of a journal article, or an analysis of a journal article.

2. Give TAs the necessary materials to complete the following tasks:

   a. Read carefully the writing assignments;

   b. Review the chosen handbook or writing guide; and

c. Actually grade three sample assignments, which will be marked only by code numbers to facilitate discussion.

3. Have the assistants turn in copies of their graded samples to you before the session so that you will know and can show them statistically where they are farthest from and closest to grading consistency.

4. Ask the TAs to bring to the session(s) their own copies of the graded work, the appropriate assignment, and any handbook or general indicator of writing criteria that you have provided.

5. Use your own criteria and priorities to direct the session(s). For example, assume that you have decided that content accuracy will account for 95 percent of the holistic score. Your first task in the training session will be to guide your assistants toward a shared understanding of the specificity level and logical sequencing that you expect if content is to earn the highest score.

6. Encourage the assistants to name the judgments they applied to each sample paper and to discuss their differences with other assistants. Ask them to justify their judgments in relation to the criteria you have provided. As far as possible, help them to use discussion to arrive at a shared understanding. When they move away from your criteria, intervene to bring them back. After ten to fifteen minutes of discussion, tell the assistants how you scored the essay content and explain how you applied your criteria to arrive at that score.

7. Already issues regarding writing quality will have been raised, and you will need to give some attention to identifying organization, sentence structure, and grammatical weaknesses and deducting from the content score to arrive at a final holistic score for each paper. For this part of the training, you may want to use a consultant from your school's English department or writing center. To illustrate error significance, you can assume that you have decided that two gross grammatical errors (fragments, comma splices, fused sentences, subject/verb agreement errors) and/or sentences that don't make sense render the student writing unacceptable. Use discussion to assure yourself that your teaching assistants understand what these errors are and can identify them as they read student papers.

It is important that the TAs recognize some of the qualities of excellent writing and do not simply attend to grammatical conventions. Show them that a felicitous metaphor or an especially effective use of transitions to clarify relationships should balance out several spelling errors or a gross grammatical error. Again, encourage your assistants to identify positive qualities, which are likely to appear only in the best writing sample.

As assistants defend their judgments, the discussion may become heated. Throughout you will arbitrate, and finally you will need to insist that one or two of the assistants defer to your criteria rather than impose their own.

This sort of session is likely to consume two hours. You may want to follow up with a similar session about halfway through the term to help your teaching assistants maintain and develop their evaluation techniques. Even

TAs who have already completed a training sequence should participate in all subsequent training sessions to assure their continued application of your criteria to their own holistic grading. Eventually, as TAs gain experience, you may be able to turn training procedures over to an experienced TA.

Writing Exercise

You might prefer to ask the teaching assistants themselves to write one-page papers, which you read and then bring to a group session for evaluation. This method would certainly let you know whether any of your TAs themselves have such severe writing difficulties that more intensive training or a course in technical writing may be required before you can rely on their judgments about student writing. Indeed, if you uncover severe writing problems in any of the TA essays, you may want to avoid the group discussion and the punitive quality it might hold for the weakest TAs.

SUMMARY

Students are sometimes on the mark when they accuse teachers of preferential grading: "She just doesn't like contractions." Personal preferences do play a role in our decision making. You can control that role and minimize its dangers by declaring your purposes early in the semester, making students aware of the requirements you will place on them and the factors of their writing that will be considered. If you have revealed your own pet peeves, an occasional idiosyncrasy can be allowed.

Be open to changes in your writing requirements. Move your assessment procedures in the direction of achieving the goal: training effective professional writers for industry or the academy. Most general chemistry students need assessment focused on rudimentary writing skills, but as students move through the chemistry curriculum to graduate as "your" majors, your expectations will rise. You will help students to become more focused and concise in their abstracts and summaries; you will encourage and require critical thinking as you play devil's advocate to your students' arguments; you will convince your students that fine points in diction can have immense value in the professional biography, resume, and research proposal. And five years into their careers, your students and their employers will thank you for your efforts to assess writing skills and grade student writing.

REFERENCES

1. E. M. White, *Teaching and Assessing Writing.* Jossey-Bass, San Francisco, 1988.
2. S. W. Freedman and R. C. Calfee, "Holistic Assessment of Writing: Experimental Design and Cognitive Theory," in *Research on Writing: Principles and Methods*, ed. P. Mosenthal, L. Tamor, and S. A. Walmsley. Longman, New York, 1983.
3. M. Shaughnessy, *Errors and Expectations,* Oxford UP, New York, 1977.
4. E. M. White, see note 1.

5. Adapted from C. B. Fryhle, "Chemistry Laboratory Report Evaluation" in "A Model for Organic Cycle Reports: Based on a Typical Paper Published in the *J. Org. Chem.*" Unpublished writing assignment, Pacific Lutheran University, Tacoma, WA, Oct. 1988–Oct. 1989.

6. J. C. Hodges, S. S. Webb, and R. K. Miller, eds., *Hodges' Harbrace Handbook,* 14th ed. Harcourt-Brace, Fort Worth, 2001.

7. M. L. Keene and K. H. Adams, *Easy Access: A Writer's Guide and Reference,* 3rd ed. Publishing, Collingsdale, PA, 2000.

8. A. Brookes and P. Grundy, *Writing for Study Purposes: A Teacher's Guide to Developing Individual Writing Skills.* Cambridge UP, Cambridge, England, 1990.

9. M. M. Cooper, "Writing: An Approach for Large-Enrollment Chemistry Courses," *J. Chem. Educ.* **1993,** *70,* 476–477.

chapter 5

Responding to Student Writing

Surgeons must be very careful
When they take the knife!
Underneath their fine incisors
Stirs the Culprit—Life!
—Emily Dickinson

After you have read, assessed, and sometimes graded student writing, your response will probably determine how your students use the writing assignments to develop their writing skills. Students tend to look at a grade or a score, if one appears, and to discount all other information. This chapter suggests some ways to encourage students to review their own work, to practice identifying and assessing their own errors, and to use and develop their thinking skills to produce clear, coherent essay responses.

When you begin incorporating writing into your courses, most students will submit their first writing assignments as monologues. They have tried, usually helplessly, to figure out what you want, but they have not yet learned to view their writing project as a part of an ongoing dialogue. When you return the paper, whatever you have written on it, even only a holistic score, opens the dialogue; for most students the learning process actually begins to take effect here. You can help these students by opening the dialogue and holding it open as long as possible. Your choice of response(s) will generally focus and direct that dialogue.

The kinds of responses suggested here can be used independently or in combination and may vary depending on the general level of student writing at your institution and the percentage of students in your classes who reveal severe writing problems.

Your choice of response may also depend on how much time you can give to writing assignments and on whether you have access to teaching assistants, a writing center, or a departmental writing consultant to conduct individualized writing assistance. While you obviously will choose the type of response or combination of responses most likely to accomplish your writing goals for your students, your available time and energy may place real limits on how much you can do. Even so, you are likely to find at least a few students each term who will welcome and use any response to their writing that you give them.

WRITTEN RESPONSES

Your written responses to student papers may range from the briefest of coded messages to fairly detailed suggestions for improvement and acknowledgments of effective writing practices. You may want to try several or all of the approaches suggested here before settling on one or a combination of them to use with your assignments.

Marking Editorial Hesitations

One simple technique can be applied to holistically scored papers and requires little time. As you identify an editorial hesitation—a point at which a student's writing slows your reading or causes you to pause—mark the spot with a check mark or a circle. Use arrows to identify organizational problems. You can respond to inaccurate content with a simple "no" and to expressions that make no sense with a question mark. If you feel all this is a bit too negative, you also can offer a "yes" or plus sign where appropriate.

Here is an example of editorial hesitation marking on a paragraph from a microtheme:

> The emission of a light photon is when an atom moves from upper to a lower energy level. This is because the electron cannot move to a new energy level until it takes on energy. It gets this energy by having two hydregen atoms crash into each other, this also emits a light photon. By using the Bohr Therory formula: $h\upsilon = E_r - E_f$, the energy that comes from the light photon is in nanometers (nm). This is like the chart for line spectrum emission for hydrogen so we can find the color of the line.

Both before and after you return the papers, explain to your students that the circled item(s) slowed your reading and that the student goal is to provide you with an effortless "read." Encourage the students to review what they have written and to seek ways to clarify their meaning or correct the problems; suggest that they ask classmates or friends to review items that seem, on the surface, perfectly okay. Make it clear to the students that they should make both of these responses *before* bringing the remaining problems to you. You also can curtail the inevitable immediate and usually mindless "What's wrong with this?" by asking that students wait to bring insoluble problems to you not the day the papers are returned but before or after the next class meeting and certainly within a week.

When you return the papers, you can encourage your students by reminding them that unmarked passages did provide that relatively effortless reading experience. Since your goal is to improve scientific writing, you could even pull a few good sentences from the papers to show that a subject(s)/verb(vb)/complement(c) sentence structure is most frequently used in technical writing to clarify complex ideas for both writer and reader. The sentence below, for example, can be marked to demonstrate both normal sentence order (s, vb, c) and the value of placing parallel ideas in parallel structures (ps). The writer makes "that Bohr's did not . . ." parallel to "that it did not . . ." to introduce two limitations of the Bohr approach:

> $\overset{S}{\text{Scientists}}$ soon $\overset{vb}{\text{recognized}}$, however, $\overset{tr}{\text{that Bohr's approach}}$ $\overset{c}{\text{did not explain the}}$ spectra of atoms with more than one electron and that it did not fully explain the chemical behavior of atoms. $\qquad\overset{}{ps}$

The parallel structures promote recognition of equal importance and, in this case, will help the student review for testing since the two items lend themselves to listing for memorization. This sentence also might be used to illustrate the sophistication of embedded transitions (tr) since *however* is embedded within rather than at the beginning of the sentence.

Classroom communication should significantly reduce the number of student questions about what's wrong, but for the questions that remain, the dialogue goes on. As will be true of any response you give, a few students will not be able to figure out what "bothers" you. Even so, a student who can selectively raise questions about one or two marks out of a dozen has already engaged in the dialogue; that student's learning process is under way. Your assignment has required the student to engage in internal dialogue and has left open the avenue to further external dialogue. The few questions that remain can be answered briefly before or after the next class meeting.

This method is not likely to yield much sophistication of style, but it helps students address issues of basic sentence structure and clarity and encourages proofreading, especially if they know the process will be repeated. You can also check the results of this process by requiring students to revise right on the page, penciling in or inking in their changes above the marked glitches, marking out extraneous material, or indicating where material that is out of order should be moved to improve logic and clarity. You might withhold the score until a revision is submitted. Or you can acknowledge revisions by amending scores.

Marginal Notes

With marginal notes, you move in the direction of analytical grading to the specificity level that you choose. As you read, write messages in the margins of the paper, praising particularly good ideas or sentences and noting failures in clarity, logic, and mechanics. With this method you do open the dialogue, but it will be more difficult to trace student follow-up unless you also mark the specific point of weakness. See an illustration below:

> The emission of a light photon is when an atom moves from upper to a lower energy level. This is because the electron cannot

move to a new energy level until it takes ✗ energy. It gets this energy by having two hydregen atoms crash into each other (this)
also emits a light photon. By using the Bohr Theory formula:
$h\upsilon = E_i - E_f$, the energy that comes from the light photon is in
nanometers (nm). This is like the chart for line spectrum emission
for hydrogen, so we can find the color of the line.

[Marginal handwritten notes: CS, major grammar error, SP, SP, Avoid using This + verb, C]

Marginal notes can work well to encourage proofreading. Students often
think the "picky" points of correct spelling and comma use don't really make
any difference to a reader. Your marginal commentary can show them that
such weaknesses do evoke response.

One way to approach marginal commentary is to use a set of abbreviations,
your own or those from a college dictionary, the *ACS Style Guide,* or your college
composition program's marking chart. *Harbrace Handbook,*[1] for instance, uses
a numbering system for organizational, sentence level, and grammatical and
mechanical weaknesses. *Easy Access*[2] uses color-coded tabs to identify errors by
type. As writing moves across the chemistry curriculum, it becomes increasingly
important that chemistry professors share a departmental response code.

Marginal comment lends itself to classroom commentary in that it is
quite easy to leaf through a stack of papers to discover problems that show up
on a large number of papers. In a ten-minute class presentation, you can show
the problem codes and give examples to show the class the problem and suggest ways to repair it.

Students, however, are inclined to disregard marginal comments, feeling
that they are just picky, negative notations.[3] Therefore if you choose this
method of response you will want to emphasize in class that you have marked
only items that caused difficulty in reading. You can use the strategies outlined
under "Marking Editorial Hesitations" to evoke student consideration of your
comments and revision.

General Comment

Since preparing a general comment at the end of the paper is more time consuming than are marginal notations or circling of errors, you may want to reserve this method for use with smaller upper-division classes. When revision is
required, the general comment makes an effective supplement to the tracking
chart shown in Chapter 4.

Such a comment should include three elements:

1. A response to the content of the paper
2. Praise for demonstration of effective writing skills in the paper (Don't be
   surprised if—especially for first writing assignments—you are reduced to
   commenting on good margins for this part.)
3. Constructive suggestions for improving the paper and suggestions for
   writing the next paper

This comment should be a reasonable length, about one substantial paragraph. As far as possible, model the style you want your student to achieve as

you compose the comment, and identify specific strengths and weaknesses. For the student paragraph used earlier in this chapter (p. 49), the following comment would be appropriate:

> You seem to have a solid basic concept of how an electron moves to another energy level. You could help your reader make connections by combining sentences that start with *This* plus a verb with the sentences before them. This practice can help you to clarify the relationships for yourself as well. You might also use a topic sentence to focus your paragraph, suggesting the importance of the information you provide here.

If you choose instead to comment in a series of phrases, try to place these phrases in a logical order, to give the student the sense that you have begun a conversation about the writing, a conversation that the student can continue into a thoughtful revision of the paper.

Students revising from a general comment will need to be reminded that they can make best use of your comment by engaging in internal dialogue as they reread and revise. The students' tendency will be simply to correct specific errors and not to address the larger issues of audience appeal and conviction. You can encourage them to apply your general comments paragraph by paragraph and then sentence by sentence, raising each of your suggestions for themselves as they proceed. If you read revisions, ask students to submit the first draft with the revision so that you can use your own comments to guide your reading. In fact, some students will be motivated to revise more thoroughly if they know that you will be comparing drafts. In any event, however, initially you will be called upon to tolerate a fairly low success rate, especially in large sections of general chemistry.

PEER EVALUATION

Writing teachers frequently use peer responses to help students improve their writing. These responses can be gained in a variety of ways, from collaboration to oral exchanges about the writing to a "round robin" with a review sheet attached to each student paper. Whichever method you use, it is important to provide direction for peer response, to move students beyond their immediate urge to critique spelling and commas into a thoughtful evaluation of how the writing says what it says.

Review Dyads

Once you have decided which elements of writing are most important to you, you can provide students with a written guide for peer response. At different levels of the writing hierarchy, different criteria might appear in the guide. For example, a review of a microtheme that describes a process (seriation) and critiques it (analysis) might raise the following questions:

1. Are all the steps in the process included here? If not, what steps are missing?

2. Which steps, if any, are out of order?

3. Does the analysis of the process actually take all the steps into account? If not, what else does the student need to consider?

4. Which sentences, if any, are not clear and direct in the expression of one important idea?

5. What problems with grammar and punctuation do you notice?

_____ fragments

_____ run-ons

_____ subject/verb or pronoun/antecedent agreement

_____ commas

_____ spelling

_____ other _____

These questions are designed to require the peer reviewers to use their own knowledge of the topic to make judgments before they drop to the grammatical level. Students who conduct this review seriously may learn as much about content from it as they do from their own writing, either because the paper under review offers a clearer understanding of the process than they had yet achieved or because their efforts to explain what is missing from the paper exercise their own analytical abilities.

You might, on the other hand, simply use one of the charts provided in Chapter 4 for all peer reviews. You can then tell students your priorities and preferences as you make the peer review assignment.

Collaboration

One great advantage of collaborative writing projects is that they not only reduce the number of papers to be graded but also provide a vehicle for much revision before the papers are actually submitted. They also provide students with a writing process they are likely to encounter in the chemistry community. While it well might be argued that some students will simply sit back and let the more confident writers do all the work, you can take measures to engage every student in the course of a college term.

Short Papers. If, for instance, you ask for two microthemes in a semester, you might require that everyone do some writing and some editing/reviewing by placing students in dyads, significant pairs, for each writing assignment. Give the first paper assignment to half the class; the second assignment, to the other half. On the due dates, assign an editor/reviewer for the papers brought to class. Give each editor/reviewer a checklist or analysis sheet, and give both students in a dyad an opportunity to revise the paper before the next class meeting when they will be expected to submit it. If the assignment is graded, both members of the dyad should know that they will receive the same grade for the paper. For the second paper, you may want to change the partners to circumvent any easy reliance on the better writer in the first pair. Each student then has an opportunity to write and two opportunities to participate in revision. Both papers are submitted for grading, and each paper yields one (and the same) grade for both partners.

You can use this same process in groups of three or four for three or four parallel writing assignments. In all cases you should receive papers that already have been reviewed and revised once.

Longer Papers. For larger-scale assignments, like the scientific paper or the proposal, you can establish groups of three to five people and assign tasks to each group member. Build into your course outline the necessity for students to meet outside the classroom to discuss and merge their contributions in a final product and to negotiate to improve the quality of each contribution. Encourage each group to think critically, reminding them that all group members receive the same grade regardless of which members do better or poorer work. For a proposal writing project, for instance, you might build a group as follows:

> One member to find and review library and Internet resources for the project and to complete a reference list;
>
> One member to research and write the background for the proposal;
>
> One member to prepare and label graphics—tables and figures; and
>
> One member to coordinate group activities and write up the proposed project.

All members must be responsible for manuscript preparation and review—typing, editing, proofreading. For larger groups, you can assign two students to some or all of these tasks.

For a project of proposal or scientific paper magnitude, you will need to assign the topic and assign students to groups quite early in the semester, preferably the first week, and to require the groups to meet within a week after the assignment has been given. Generally, after some preliminary grousing about the impossibility of finding meeting times, group members do find a time and place to carry out their work together.

We recommend that you meet with each group before or after class at least once during the project to help students to resolve conflict, plan future steps in their process, and revise their schedule for completion of various tasks. You can use the meeting time to form your own impression of which students are dominating their groups or shirking their responsibilities. Then you can encourage some shifts in group behavior. If you remember that student writing contributes to a dialogue, this process makes a great deal of sense, with much of the dialogue and the drafting taking place *before* the writing is subjected to a grade.

Specialized Assignments. Collaboration also works well for preparation of annotated bibliographies or a collection of review abstracts. Students can divide up or share sections of the journal and/or book indexes, develop lists, find the materials for collection on a shared library desk, prepare the bibliographic information and write the annotations or long abstracts, then meet near the gathered resources to review each other's work, amend the content and revise the style, and organize the material to prepare the final manuscript. Again, the assignment should be made early in the semester, and students need an opportunity to discuss their progress with you as the semester progresses. If the annotated bibliographies are short, you can ask each group to prepare copies for the entire class or at least for every other group so that groups can compare the work and perhaps can even make suggestions for improvement or, even better, find ways to improve their own projects. All students in each group should be held equally accountable for the final product.

Brian Coppola and Richard G. Lawton's specific suggestion for a collaborative laboratory experiment[4] can be expanded into a group writing assignment that entails peer response. Each group can be assigned a writing project about the discoveries, and the resulting descriptions and analyses can be circulated among the groups for critique and enrichment. Other assignments appear in the sample assignment section. You may also want to read Coppola and Daniels[5] on the values of "structured group learning" and the uses of writing to promote it.

If you assign collaborative writing, you need to be prepared for a few intense personality conflicts and some absolute inability to compromise. When students bring you these problems, you tell them that they must work out their differences in a respectful, professional manner; you may work out in advance a system to refer the troubled dyads or groups to your school's counseling center for help with group dynamics; or you may accept the responsibility for arbitrating and reassigning groups as necessary. In other words, you need to decide in advance how involved you can afford to be in the group dynamics.

Oral Review

In a simpler peer-review process, you may ask students who bring their writing to class on the due date to exchange papers with a neighbor during the last few minutes of class, to read each other's papers, and to comment on topics that you have written on the board or projected on an overhead to guide responses to content, clarity, and organization before grammar and spelling. Then give the students an opportunity to take their own papers out for revision before the next class meeting. Serious students will be grateful for this opportunity to improve their work, and your own reading and responding load should be lightened.

Round Robin

When students bring in a writing assignment, you might attach a peer review checklist or list of questions to each paper and circulate these in the classroom for twenty minutes or so. Students can read and respond to several papers, and the checklist keeps them focused on important considerations about the writing. Then the writers will have to choose among differing—sometimes opposing—recommendations from several readers. You and/or your teaching assistant(s) can circulate through the room, helping to keep the papers moving.

In a large class, the round robin offers reviewers the freedom of anonymity. Sometimes students find it difficult to make serious recommendations to their friends or even to people who will recognize them in the classroom.

At the end of the reviewing session students can reclaim their papers and then revise them before the next class meeting. The first time you try this process, you may want to look over the review sheets to see whether your guide questions could be revised to evoke more helpful suggestions or whether certain pervasive writing issues could be addressed briefly in the classroom.

In all these approaches, the students are required to engage in a dialogue about their writing. They are exposed to differing learning styles, writing styles, and ideas. In the best cases, the dialogue continues internally as students decide which advice to accept and which to reject. Finally, peer review processes give students an opportunity to try the alternative approaches to learning that they encounter in the collaboration and reviews.

Posting Examples

If these approaches are too complicated for your own circumstance, at least one other and simpler way to provide peer response is to post—anonymously, of course—samples of especially good papers. You can make the posting more useful by noting in the margins exactly what traits make each paper a good one. Posting poor papers and showing what makes them poor will be equally edifying but is a bit more risky. If you choose this approach, we recommend that you post only papers from an earlier school term.

CONFERENCING

You may feel compelled to offer some one-to-one conferences to selected students. If you do so, ask each student to bring the paper in question to the conference. Whether it is graded or not, that paper is the vehicle through which you convey what you want the student to change, comparing what the student *has* done with what *might be* done. Because such a conference is likely to run twenty minutes to half an hour, professors tend to offer them sparingly, but for a receptive student the results can be astonishing.

Group Conferencing

Group conferencing can also be useful. If, for example, you identify a group of up to six students who have difficulty providing logical transitions between ideas, you can arrange to meet all these students (with their papers) together and discuss that one problem in the conference. Group conferencing provides students an opportunity to learn from each other as well as from the professor and, like individual conferencing, keeps the dialogue going. This technique works best with holistically scored papers and gives you an opportunity to demonstrate the value of writing as a way to clarify thinking. To teach logical transitions, for instance, you can ask students to identify their efforts to provide transition and then to participate in the group analysis of those efforts.

Writing Consultant Referrals

Many institutions offer writing center services, usually under the domain of the English department. The best of these work hard to provide instruction across the disciplines and welcome referrals from other departments than their own. If you have access to such a center, it may well be worthwhile to discuss your writing requirements with its director and to arrange a referral system to guide individualized response to your students' writing. The center may have printed referral forms for your use, or you may want to prepare your own. In any case, you will find it helpful to provide the center with copies of your writing assignments and, when possible, to send students to the center with a referral form that specifies the problems you want the student to address there. You can even ask the center to provide you with a record of student attendance so that you will know which students have made use of your referrals.

At most such centers a student can expect to confer with a peer tutor or a graduate student or instructor in English. The consultant discusses the items you have listed on your referral slip and usually encourages the student to bring a draft of the next writing assignment to the center for review and recommendations. If the center is adequately staffed and you request it, you may even be able to get brief telephone or written reports on topics covered at each consultation.

The center may also be able to send a consultant to your classroom to present any topic you wish. While the demands of the chemistry content may allow very little time for such presentations, you could consider asking for a ten- or fifteen-minute presentation on a writing problem that showed up frequently in a set of papers you have just read. In addition, you can encourage your students to watch for appropriate short writing workshops being offered at the writing center.

With a writing center referral, the student is drawn into the dialogue by virtue of having to make decisions about the next paper based on a synthesis of your requirements and the advice of a writing expert who is not likely to know much about chemistry. When a student is confused by what appears to be conflicting advice, you may need to enter the dialogue again to resolve the perceived conflict, but generally the center staff will be able to handle the writing response for you.

On the most luxurious end of response to student writing lies the possibility that your department will either allocate funds to appoint a writing consultant for professors and students or share such an appointment with other scientific disciplines. A part-time scientific writing consultant can be hired inexpensively. If your school is in a technology-rich area, you may also be able to contract for the time of a free-lance editor. Certainly an appointment of this kind would demonstrate your department's commitment to incorporating writing across the chemistry curriculum, and it would give you a ready means to show students that writing is not a mystical or magical occurrence but rather a matter of thinking, presenting, rethinking, and revising to achieve an end with an identified audience. Even if a departmental writing consultant is not possible right now, you may want to set a goal for hiring one and begin seeking the necessary funds.

SUMMARY

Whether you choose to rely on a teaching assistant, peer, "hired gun," or yourself, responses to student writing will depend in some measure on your desired level of control over student writing and its development. According to Richard Straub, "All teacher comments in some way are evaluative and directive."[6] Comments tend to bleed into assessment and further into grading. Awareness of the overlap and sensitivity to student readings of your comments should guide you as you try to use your comments to achieve your teaching goals.

Science students are likely to be motivated to improve their writing skills only with some teacher response, which may be as simple as asking the students to respond to their own writing in a form you prescribe. But response and dialogue are as essential to learning as is the initial composition; you can direct students toward an understanding of the content and boundaries of chemistry while teaching thought processes and communication skills they can use in all the disciplines. The suggestions here are intended to help you get started.

REFERENCES

1. J. C. Hodges, S. Strobeck Webb, and R. K. Miller, eds., *Hodges' Harbrace Handbook*, 14th ed. Harcourt-Brace, Fort Worth, 2001.
2. M. L. Keene and K. H. Adams, *Easy Access: A Writer's Guide and Reference*, 3rd ed. Diane Publishing, Collingdale, PA, 2000.
3. *The Freshman English Program*. University of Tennessee, Knoxville, Department of English, Knoxville, TN, 1989.
4. B. P. Coppola and R. G. Lawton, "Who has the same substance that I have? A blueprint for collaborative writing activities," *J. Chem. Educ.*, **1995**, 1120–1122.
5. B. P. Coppola and D. S. Daniels, "The Role of Written and Verbal Expression in Improving Communication Skills for Students in an Undergraduate Chemistry Program," *Language and Learning Across the Disciplines*, **1996**, *1*, 67–86.
6. R. Straub, "The Concept of Control in Teacher Response," *CCC*, **1996**, *47*, 223–251. See also P. Bizarro, "The Concept of Control in Historical Perspective"; J. Chandler, "Positive Control"; J. Mathison-Fife and P. O'Neill, "Re-seeing Research on Response"; and R. Straub, "Response Rethought" in "Interchanges: Reimagining Response," *CCC*, **1997**, *48*, 269–283.

chapter 6

Assignments

The authors have endeavored to gather into this chapter a collection of writing assignments for chemistry courses at all levels of the Kiniry and Strenski hierarchy.[1] Each assignment is marked with the special numerals below to designate the hierarchical levels addressed. You will find here content-specific, reintegrative, generic, and form-specific assignments. Chemistry and writing teachers from across the country have suggested many of these assignments.

❶ Listing   Display of important items

❷ Definition   Brief or extensive explanation of a word or concept

❸ Seriation   Ordered list or description of a procedure

❹ Classification   Application of specific categories to specific data

❺ Summary   Identification of important facts and ideas in a reading

❻ Comparison/Contrast   Listing/analysis of similarities and differences

❼ Analysis   Breaking down a complex idea into its constituent parts

❽ Academic/Scientific Argument   Use of facts and theories to support a proposition

Many of the more sophisticated assignments combine levels.

CONTENT-SPECIFIC ASSIGNMENTS

Acids and Bases

❶ easy: *List* and *explain* the three major theories of acids and bases: Arrhenius, Brønsted-Lowry and Lewis.

❷❹ easy: In a coherent one-page essay, *describe* the three major concepts of acids and bases: Arrhenius, Brønsted-Lowry, and Lewis. What are the essential features of each concept?

❹❻ easy: *Compare and contrast* the three concepts of acids and bases: Arrhenius, Brønsted-Lowry and Lewis. What essential features do they have in common? How do they differ?

❶ intermediate: *List* the important categories of Brønsted-Lowry acids and bases in inorganic solution chemistry.

❶❼ intermediate: *Describe* how the Brønsted-Lowry and Lewis concepts of acids and bases are used in the understanding of addition reactions to alkenes.

❸❼ intermediate: Using appropriate chemical examples, *show how* the concept of acid and base was made more general and powerful as chemists moved historically from the simple Arrhenius concept to the Brønsted-Lowry and finally to the Lewis theory. What explanatory power is gained as the concept is generalized?

❽ intermediate: *Show how* Lewis's theory of acids and bases derives from his theory of the electronic structure of atoms, the Lewis dot structures, and the rule of eight. Use examples of Lewis acids and bases where appropriate.

❸❹❼ advanced: *List* and explain the various concepts of acids and bases that chemists have used beginning with the original definition of acids as oxygen-containing substances by Lavoisier and ending with the modern concepts based on electronic structure exemplified by the Lewis theory. Describe the essential features of each concept and explain its historic origin and subsequent development (or abandonment). What are the strengths and weaknesses of each concept?

Hydrogen and Helium Atoms (Physical Chemistry)

❺ intermediate: In no more than two pages, summarize the important ideas about the hydrogen and helium atoms. Use equations and diagrams as appropriate.

For the hydrogen atom, consider at least (1) the physical model; (2) the development of the appropriate Schrödinger equation for the model, beginning with the classical energy (discuss the approximations and assumptions made in the development of the mathematical formulation); (3) the nature of wave functions and quantum numbers that result from the solution of the Schrödinger equation; and (4) the energies of the various states and the resulting emission of absorption spectrum.

For the helium atom, discuss at least (1) the development of the Schrödinger equation for the two-electron atom and why it cannot be solved exactly; (2) a description of the variational principle and its role in the approximate solution of the problem; (3) the nature of the trial wave function for the helium atom, including the important assumptions made in constructing this function; and (4) an explanation of the concepts of screeing and effective nuclear charge (What physical meaning is given to the parameter Z in the approximate wave function for the helium atom?).

Molecular Vibrations and Rotations (Physical Chemistry)

❺ easy: In no more than two pages *summarize* what you have learned about molecular vibrations (harmonic oscillator problem) and rotations (particle on a sphere). Use equations and diagrams as appropriate, and include the following points: (1) the physical model; (2) the development of the appropriate Schrödinger equation for the model, beginning with the classical energy and discussing the approximations and assumptions that are made in the development of the mathematical formulation; (3) the nature of wave functions and energy levels; and (4) the predicted spectrum.

Thermodynamics

❷ easy: In one clear paragraph, *define* the terms *heat, heat capacity,* and *specific heat,* showing how they are interrelated.

❷❻ intermediate: In an essay of one page or less explain the relationships among the concepts of *heat, work,* and *energy.* What essential *features* do they have *in common?* How do they *differ?*

Atomic Theory

❸❺ easy: From 1898 to 1908, three experiments contributed to the development of the Modern Atomic Theory. Using your textbook, summarize each of these experiments in chronological order (one coherent paragraph for each experiment). Your summaries should address but need not be limited to the following questions: (1) What motivated the experiment, and what was its purpose? (2) How was each experiment performed (use diagrams if necessary)? (3) What were the results? (4) Were these the expected results? (4) What were the conclusions? Were any numerical values determined?

❶ easy: In your own words, *list* and explain the postulates of Dalton's atomic theory.

❷ easy: Give a clear *definition* of a chemical element based on Dalton's original atomic theory. According to Dalton, what are the essential characteristics of an element?

❷❺❼ easy: One characteristic feature of atoms is that their emission spectra are discontinuous line spectra rather than the continuous spectrum of sunlight. Niels Bohr offered the first detailed explanation of the physical origin of this remarkable phenomenon. In a one-page essay, summarize the Bohr theory and show how it explains the emission spectrum of the hydrogen atom.

❺❻ intermediate: In a coherent essay, *compare and contrast* Dalton's concept of an atom with the modern concept. In what ways are they similar, in what ways do they differ? Provide a concise summary of the two concepts.

❶❼❽ intermediate: In a one-page essay, *list* the postulates of Dalton's original atomic theory and *discuss how* subsequent discoveries have caused these postulates to be modified. Have the modifications of the postulates altered the essential content of the theory?

❼ intermediate: In a coherent essay, *show how* the postulates of Dalton's original atomic theory are consistent with the empirical law of definite composition and how they explain the empirical law of multiple proportions.

Periodicity

❼ You are a principal investigator on a research project and receive the following e-mail from your chemical technician, Rogelio:

It's been a long time since I took general chemistry. I only remember the concepts of the structure of an atom, electronegativity, and atomic radius. When I did the experiments, I noticed two tendencies:

1. The chemical reactivity of alkali metal increases down a group.
2. The chemical reactivity of halogens decreases down a group.

     Can you explain why these trends occur?

Reply to Rogelio's question, bearing in mind the concepts that he knows. This reply must be 2–3 typed pages long.

Chemical Bonding

❷ easy: Write a clear, concise *definition* for a covalent, a polar covalent, and an ionic bond.

❶❹ easy: *Classify* the bonds of the following molecules—O_2, CO, NaCl—as covalent, polar covalent, or ionic and *list* the characteristics that lead to that classification.

❽ intermediate: Using your understanding of the chemical bond, construct an *argument* either supporting or refuting the statement that van der Waals interactions are bonds.

Empirical and Molecular Formulas

❷❹ easy: *Describe* the various types of chemical formulas: empirical, molecular, and structural. *What kinds* of information are conveyed by each type of formula?

❶❸❼ intermediate: In a one-page essay, clearly describe how you can use combustion analysis and gas density to determine the molecular formula of an organic compound consisting only of carbon, hydrogen, and oxygen. Briefly *describe* the experiments that must be performed, but concentrate on the *analysis* of the data. Be sure to *list* the assumptions that are made in the analysis of the data. Use mathematical equations where appropriate, but make sure that you have described the procedures clearly in words.

Inorganic Reactions

❷❹❻ intermediate: In a one-page essay clearly *define* the three major types of inorganic reactions: precipitation, acid-base, and oxidation-reduction. What are the *essential characteristics* of each type? Where appropriate, point out the *similarities and differences* among the various types of reactions.

Bond Polarity/Vectors

❷ easy: In a half-page essay, *describe* how a vector is used to demonstrate bond polarity.

❸ intermediate: In a one-page essay, *list and link* the steps needed to move from bond polarity to using vectors to determine the polarity of molecules.

❸❼ advanced: Write a one-page textbook lesson *analyzing* the use of vectors to determine the polarity of a molecule.

Data Collection

❷ easy: *Define* the terms *precision, accuracy,* and *significant figures* and show how each term operates in the _____ laboratory experiment.

❺ intermediate: *Compare and contrast* "precision" and "accuracy" as they are expressed in laboratory data. Show your understanding of similarities and differences with specific examples.

Conductors and Semiconductors

❻ easy: *Compare and contrast* conductors, semiconductors, and insulators in the context of band theory. Write an essay of less than one page at a level that can be understood by a high school student.

❼ advanced: Using HSAB theory and what is known about semiconducting materials made from Groups 3 and 5 (e.g., GaAs), propose compounds from other periodic groups that would parallel the properties of these compounds. Explain your answer fully in three pages or less.

REINTEGRATION/ENRICHMENT ASSIGNMENTS

The assignments in this section are intended to help students to analyze chemistry content in relation to other disciplines and/or to life and job experiences. A generic assignment of this type might ask students to develop a short (one-page) essay in which they apply one chemistry concept (formula, application) learned in the past two weeks to practices in their majors.

Chemistry in the News

❶❺ easy: *List* three topics in current news (within the past three months) that have to do with chemistry in some way. Giving the date and source of the news, briefly summarize each topic.

❻ intermediate: Choose one topic related to chemistry in current news (within the past three months). Find at least two additional sources from other publications about this topic: web pages, newspapers, journal articles, books, newspapers. In a one-page double-spaced typewritten paper, compare and contrast these sources in terms of detail, content, clarity, reliability, and persuasiveness.

❼ intermediate: In two to five typewritten pages, analyze the significance of a topic related to chemistry that you find in current news (within the last three months). For example, you might explain how chemical analysis contributes to the solution to an ecological problem.

❶❹ easy: List in order of importance four properties of flammable liquids that a firefighter should know. As you proceed from most to least important, defend the order you have chosen.

❶❼ intermediate: *Identify* at least four air and water pollutants most commonly found in our area, and *analyze* their local impact in terms of their sources, biological effects, and destinies. What role might chemists play in management and degradation of these pollutants?

❽ advanced: As a chemistry student, *argue* for (or against) the following injunction in the student handbook, designed to mitigate possible destructive uses of chemical substances: "On-campus students must register with the hazardous materials committee any controlled chemical substances in their possession."

GENERAL CHEMISTRY

Historical Summaries

❸ easy: Write a two-page summary of _____. (You can offer any of a number of historical topics; several examples are listed here.)

1. The discovery of fission
2. The story of G. N. Lewis's discovery of chemical bonding
3. The thalidomide controversy
4. The discovery of the cause of Mad Hatter's disease
5. Mendeleev's development of the Periodic Table

Other such assignments may be subject specific.

Literature Review

❶❺ Choose a chemistry-related topic that interests you, and find appropriate references including two books, two journal/magazine articles, two internet sources, and one newspaper article. Write a one-page abstract/*summary* of one of these sources to inform your classmates about this topic. *List* your resources, following the format provided.

Periodic Table

❶❼ intermediate: In a two-page typed paper, list and give examples of trends in the periodic table. Draw at least one conclusion from these trends.

Thermodynamics—Heat Capacity

❼ intermediate: Discuss the role of heat capacity in the choice of ceramic materials or metal alloys for engine block manufacturing.

❼ intermediate: Discuss the role of heat capacity in determining the difference between daytime and nighttime temperatures in the desert compared to the seashore.

❽ advanced: Does the theory of evolution contradict the second law of thermodynamics? Develop an *argument* to support your response.

Chemical Bonding

❼ intermediate: Explain the role of the hydrogen bond in the structure and function of DNA.

❼ intermediate: Explain the role of the hydrogen bond in the secondary and tertiary structures of proteins.

Buffer Solutions

❸❼ intermediate: Buffers are important in biological and geological systems. Pick an example of a natural buffer, such as the carbonate system in the blood or in the ocean, and explain its chemistry and the role of the buffer in the function of the complex natural system.

Chemical Elements

❸❼ intermediate: Choose a chemical element discovered after 1700, and write a biographical sketch of the scientist (or scientists) who made the discovery. In your biography, you should give pertinent details of the personal life of the scientist (date of birth, family, education, marriage), but emphasize the scientific career, focusing on the discovery of your chosen element and how it fits into the overall career of the discoverer.

❸❺ advanced: Choose a chemical element discovered after 1700 and write a paper describing the discovery process. Include a description of both the experiments and their interpretation.

❸ intermediate: A major publisher has asked your class to write a supplementary reference book on the chemical elements for use by general chemistry students. The editor envisions each chapter as a "history" of an element. Choose a chemical element and write a two-page *history* of that element that includes (1) when and by whom the element was discovered, (2) its physical and chemical properties, (3) how it was first isolated, (4) how it was named and given its symbol, and (5) its uses.

❸ intermediate: Write a one- to two-page *autobiography* of an element that can be used in a sixth-grade science class. Include how you were discovered and by whom, your chemical and physical properties that would be familiar to a sixth-grade audience, and how you are used in everyday life or in industry.

Nuclear Energy

❶❷ easy: You have been asked to write a 500-word article about nuclear energy for your school newspaper. This article must provide your readers with a conceptual definition of nuclear energy and the relation of fission, fusion, nuclei, electrons, protons, neutrons, energy, and sub-atomic particles to the production of nuclear energy.

❻ intermediate: *Compare and contrast* the energy changes in ordinary chemical reactions and nuclear reactions. Be sure to discuss the sources of any energy released or stored.

❽ advanced: Write a one-page letter to a politician using chemical arguments to express your opinion about the proposed construction of a nuclear power plant five miles upstream from your town.

Chemical Poisoning (Analytical Chemistry)

❶❷❼ intermediate: Your department is charged with contributing to the treatment plan for a baby sick from Pb poisoning. Identify and list at least six techniques to measure Pb in a sample. Choose one of these techniques and write a one-page definition in terms of concentration range, matrix (potential interferences), cost (start-up and per analysis), operator skill, time, LOD, LDR, and precision. On the basis of the information you and your classmates have uncovered, write a one-page proposal to your manager for the detection of Pb in 5ml of human baby's blood. You will need to detect Pb at the ppb level.

Chemical Warfare

❹ easy: *Classify* chemical warfare agents in terms of their impact on the human being. Identify at least three and no more than five categories.

❸❺ intermediate: In a three-page essay, *trace chronologically* the development and use of chemicals in Western warfare. The length limitation for this essay will require that you *synthesize* the wealth of information available.

❶❽ advanced: Identify at least three ethical issues raised by the prospect of engaging in chemical warfare, and use them as a basis for an argument for or against the present international accords regarding chemical weapons use.

Chemistry and Literature

Write a three- to four-page paper on Primo Levi's *The Periodic Table* to be evaluated for its scientific content, focus on the topic, organization, and use of the English language (adapted from Roald Hoffmann, Cornell University).

❷ easy: Discuss how this book is or is not a chemistry text, *defining* a chemistry text to reach a conclusion.

❻ intermediate: *Compare* Levi's *The Periodic Table* with at least one other biography/autobiography or with a history of the period.

❽ intermediate: Write an *argumentative* paper taking off from a subject in the book, for example, (1) ❼ how to *analyze* for arsenic; (2) ❸ a *historical* or social commentary—Italian history, German industry, the extermination camps; (3) ❻ a *comparison* of chemistry education in Italy and in the U.S.

❺❼ intermediate: Review (*summarize* and *analyze*) Levi's book.

❼ advanced: Write a chapter of a book, a poem, an essay, *or* a piece of a play using an idea similar to Levi's—telling a story in the context of a scientific metaphor. You may use a personal experience or write about an imagined event.

EXAM-PREPARATION ASSIGNMENTS

Summary Assignments

❺ easy: Prepare a one-page *summary* of the exam material. You may use no more than one side of one 8.5″ by 11″ sheet of paper. Although typewritten summaries are preferred, legible handwritten sheets are acceptable. You should summarize the major concepts and skills to be covered on the exam. Important formulas and equations may be included, but you need not include tables of data because all necessary data and physical constants will be provided on the exam, including tables of thermodynamic data.

Write your summary so that it can be understood by others. Don't just make random, cryptic notes that only you can decipher. Put your name and section number and the name of your teaching assistant at the top right of the page. You will be required to staple your summary to your exam. We will evaluate the quality of your summary and will add up to five (5) bonus points to your exam score. The evaluation will be based on content (whether you have included the major concepts) and clarity. While we do not expect elegant prose or even complete sentences, we do expect to be able to understand your summary. The major criterion for success is whether another student could use your summary as a study guide or reference for the exam.

Model Reading Notebook Assignment (developed by J. Kovac)

Requiring that students keep a reading notebook accomplishes three goals: (1) It gives students guidance in reading a chemistry textbook; (2) it insures that they have read the assigned material and are prepared for class; and (3) it gives them practice in writing. The general reading methodology given below can be supplemented with specific questions that direct students to the key ideas in the reading assignment. To insure that students are not just skimming the chapter and reading carefully only the sections that answer your specific questions, it is useful to put the questions in a random order rather than in the sequence the ideas appear in the chapter or section assigned.

You can give your students the following general methodology for reading a chemistry textbook, or you can use any adaptation that works for your classes:

1. **❸** Quickly scan the whole chapter to get a general idea of its contents. In your notebook, write a brief *outline* of the chapter material.
2. **❼** In your notebook, briefly and specifically *state the purpose* of reading the material. "To pass this course" is *not* an acceptable response.
3. **❶❷** As you read, identify the new terms introduced in the chapter. In your notebook make a *list* of the new words and terms, both scientific

and non-scientific. Use the glossary and a dictionary to *define* the new terms. While this list of new terms will depend on your personal background and vocabulary, the instructor will be skeptical of any reading notebook that defines no new terms.

4. ❸❺ As you read the chapter, *identify the prerequisite knowledge*, either from earlier chapters or from previous courses in science or mathematics, needed to understand the material in the chapter. In your notebook, briefly describe the prerequisite knowledge. If you feel comfortable with your understanding of the prerequisites, you do not need to do any more. If not, you should review the prerequisite knowledge in earlier chapters or in appropriate references. In your notebook, write a brief *summary* of what you reviewed.

5. ❺ As you read, make notes and observations about the key points made in the chapter. The specific questions below will guide your reading. Answers to the specific questions must appear in your notebook.

6. ❼ After you finish reading, write answers to the following general questions about the chapter: (1) How will you integrate the information in this chapter with what you have learned previously in this course and in other courses? (2) How does the information in this chapter relate to your major or projected career? What will you be able to use in the future? (3) What questions do you still have about the information presented in the chapter? (4) What insights do you have that you would like to share with other students?

Journal Assignments

❺❸ *Journal Assignment 1*: After each class meeting and before the next one, review your notes and write a half-page to one-page journal entry in which you explain briefly the most important idea about chemistry covered in that class meeting. Whenever possible link the idea developed in that class with the idea you identified for the previous class.

GRADING: Journals, worth 100 (or any number given by instructor) points, will be spot checked. Checking dates and students whose work is to be checked will not be announced in advance. The grade rests entirely on whether the student has maintained the journal regularly as assigned. Each student starts with 100 (or ?) points and loses 5 points for every class meeting not synthesized in the journal at the time it is checked. Students should anticipate at least two checks during the semester.

❼ *Journal Assignment 2*: Once each week, in a half page, identify and analyze an application in everyday life of a concept presented in the class during that week. Try to show how the chemical concept or the idea is applied and how it influences the resulting action or product. If you wish, you may use creative analogies.

GRADING: On the basis of unannounced spot checks, you will receive 10 (or ?) bonus points for each timely entry in your journal.

❶❷ *Journal Assignment 3*: After each class meeting, review your notes carefully, highlighting terms defined in lecture. Make a list of these terms on a sheet of paper, and put away your notes. Then, from memory, write a definition for each term on your list in your own words.

GRADING: On the basis of unannounced spot checks, you will receive 10 (or ?) bonus points for each timely entry in your journal.

❸ *Journal Assignment 4*: Once each week, write a half-page proposal for an application of a complicated or hard-to-understand concept presented in lecture during that week. You may be lighthearted about this application as long as your entry shows that you have improved your understanding of the difficult concept. When you finish, highlight your explanation of the concept. Feel free to seek explanation from peers, professor, or teaching assistants.

GRADING: 10 (or ?) points for each clear explanation of the concept described.

GENERAL CHEMISTRY

Sample Ungraded Writing Assignment

This two-part assignment is designed to help students master concepts that they find difficult.

The objective is to help each student to identify a concept that is difficult to understand, to clarify the point(s) of difficulty, and then to master the concept.

Part I: Distribute this assignment to the students at the end of a class meeting:

Choose one term or concept that is not yet clear to you; then write a 100- to 150-word paragraph about that difficult topic. Use your glossary and textbook as you try to explain the point at which the concept does not make sense. Bring this paragraph to the next class meeting.

Part II: In the last ten minutes of the next class meeting, ask pairs of students to exchange the paragraphs brought to class, to read about each other's problems, and to explain the difficult concepts to each other. While students do this, you may want to move through the room, listening and offering information. End the class meeting with this assignment:

Now that you have a fuller explanation of the difficult concept, write a 100- to 150-word paragraph explaining the concept. If possible, show how the concept is useful to the chemist. Bring this paragraph to the next class meeting.

At the third class meeting, collect the second paragraphs and review them quickly to see what students have learned. From these paragraphs, you can identify students in serious trouble; gain assurance that some concepts are, indeed, thoroughly understood; and select topics that might be emphasized in the classroom to fill general information gaps or reasoning lapses.

FORM-SPECIFIC ASSIGNMENTS

❺ Model Abstract Assignment (developed by J. Kovac)

Please read the attached article and prepare a 100- to 200-word abstract of its contents. A good abstract should have the following features:

1. A concise statement of the purpose of the investigation
2. A list of the major experimental or theoretical techniques employed
3. A brief summary of the major results and conclusions of the investigation

❺ Model Research Article Summary Assignment (developed by J. Kovac)

Please read the attached article, and write a summary of its contents. Include answers to the following questions. Confine your summary to no more than two typewritten, double-spaced pages, in 12-point font:

1. ❷ What is the purpose of the investigation? What problems are the authors trying to solve?
2. ❼ Why is this investigation important?
3. ❼ What is the experimental (and/or theoretical) strategy?
4. ❸ How are the data obtained? What experimental techniques are employed? (What theoretical methods are employed?)
5. ❼ How are the data (and/or theoretical results) interpreted? What methods are used to take the raw experimental data and relate them to the theoretical basis of the investigation? How are the theoretical results compared to experiment or fit into a broader theoretical context (the crucial question in any scientific investigation)?
6. ❼ What conclusions are drawn? Are those conclusions adequately supported by the evidence? Are the conclusions reasonable?
7. ❼ What is the major insight you have gained from reading this paper?

❶ In addition, prepare a list of questions that you need to have answered before you can completely understand the article. These questions should address both background material that you feel you lack and points of the argument that you find difficult to follow.

Prepare *two* copies of your summary and questions. I will read one and distribute the other to another member of the class for peer assessment.

❺ Research Article Summary Assignment (adapted from H. Beall and J. Trimbur)

Read the attached article and summarize its contents in no more than two typewritten, double-spaced pages, in 12-point font. As a guide, consider the following questions:

1. What is the central claim of the article?
2. What problem or issue does this claim address?
3. What specific questions or problems does the article address?

4. What specific approaches—theoretical, experimental, or both—were used to address these questions or problems? Be sure to identify the crucial assumptions made in the development of the experimental or theoretical approaches to the problem.

5. What are the major findings of this investigation? How do the authors portray the significance of these findings?

6. Has this investigation left questions unanswered or suggested new questions for investigation?

❼❽ To encourage students to analyze the paper critically, add the following questions:

7. What are the major strengths of this article? What new results or methods does it present? How significant are the results or the methods?

8. Are the conclusions justified by the experimental data presented or by the theoretical calculations developed? Does the article make claims that are not adequately supported by evidence?

9. State any ways in which the article might have been improved.

PROFESSIONAL ADVANCEMENT ASSIGNMENTS

Resume Preparation

Assume that you are applying for a career-opening job in industry and that one of the required attachments is a resume. As you write a chronological resume of your education and experience in the profession, follow the guidelines below.

Personal Information:

Name (often centered, bold), address, phone number(s), e-mail

No age, size, religion, gender, Social Security number

Objective (an optional feature): To establish a concise, attractive, and purposeful "paper appearance."

Use this structure to identify specifically your own immediate objectives with the company.

Start with an infinitive as above or with a noun as in "Establishing . . ."

Sections: (in order) Education, Honors, Experience, Community Service, Activities, others as appropriate, e.g., Military Service, Computer Skills, Languages, Study Abroad

References Available on Request

Major Concerns:

Be consistent.

Reverse chronological order within sections, dates first *or* last for each item

Use parallel structures (begin job descriptions with action phrases that itemize the significant details of your duties), parallel indentions

Use consistent order for job title or accomplishment, company or school name, important details

Use consistent verb tense

Be concise.

Avoid repetition.

Reduce clauses to phrases.

Reduce prepositional phrases to adjectives or adverbs.

Use strong, accurate, and varied verbs, especially in describing duties.

Be careful.

Choose precise words for your activities.

Proofread for yourself and seek proofreading assistance—your reader is likely to assume that the resume is your best work.

Keep the appearance neat—clean, unwrinkled paper, plenty of white space.

General Tips:

1. Use easy-to-read font styles, varying size according to level of information.
2. Write for your own purpose and to persuade your audience, taking care not to offend.
3. Be as specific as possible, e.g., listing specifically the computer programs or programming languages you know.
4. Use a template in WordPerfect or Microsoft Word, adapting it as necessary for your own purpose.
5. If you use more than one page, the second page should have at least twelve lines.

Some Skill Verbs:

accomplish, achieve, act, adapt, administer, aid, analyze, assess, assist, compare, collaborate, consult, coordinate, correct, counsel, create, decide, define, demonstrate, design, determine, develop, establish, examine, expedite, facilitate, implement, improve, interpret, instruct, modify, negotiate, oversee, plan, prepare, present, propose, provide, recommend, represent, revise, schedule, speak, support, teach, train, write, explain, translate, manage, survey, supervise, produce, equip

The American Chemical Society Department of Career Services has published a useful booklet entitled *Tips on Resume Preparation* (1994),[2] which contains sample chronological, functional, and combination resumes. Your students will find it helpful if you can make a few copies of this booklet available in the departmental office or through your teaching assistants.

Cover Letter Preparation

Prepare a cover letter to introduce yourself and your resume to a potential employer (specify industry or the academy). Present this letter in a plain, reader-friendly font and on one sheet of paper only. Business letter forms can be found in almost any college writing handbook; we suggest two such handbooks in Chapter 7.

Devise your own letterhead with your word processor.

Follow one of the letter formats shown in the style guide.

If possible, address your letter to a specific person; if responding to an advertisement, give the date and place of the ad.

Organize your letter into three paragraphs.

Suggest your awareness of the organization's goals and your interest in helping to achieve those goals.

Give examples of your particular qualifications to help the organization.

Express your desire to be interviewed and either provide a telephone number or indicate that you will call the organization to arrange an interview by a given date.

Close formally unless you are quite familiar with the person addressed: "Sincerely" is recommended.

Use black ink for your signature above your typed professional name.

Indicate the enclosure of your resume.

Again, the ACS booklet *Tips on Resume Preparation* gives more detailed suggestions for a cover letter and provides an example.

Curriculum Vitae (CV) Preparation

This assignment is best reserved for upper-division undergraduates or graduate students.

Assume that you have just applied for your first academic appointment as either teaching assistant or research assistant. The search committee for an academic post will be particularly interested in your experience in an academic or research setting and your professional publications and presentations. The National Science Foundation (NSF) and other federal and private funding agencies will also ask you for a CV. Unlike your resume, which will be pared down occasionally as your life experience develops and changes, the CV, which is cumulative, will grow longer with each productive year of your professional life. Review suggestions for resume preparation, and make the adjustments identified below for the curriculum vitae.

1. When you identify your degree and the date, give your thesis title and director's name and position with your institution.

2. After education information, give a brief statement of your research interests—as specific as possible.

3. List only professional societies, not clubs; give years of membership for each group. Also, identify any offices held and committee service and years of tenure.
4. If you have teaching experience, include a category for committee service.
5. List publications, then presentations.
6. State that your references will be available on request.

You will find a sample curriculum vitae in the ACS guide, *Tips on Resume Preparation*. When you have completed this project, keep a diskette copy as well as a hard copy. If you continue in chemistry, you will develop this document for the rest of your career.

Professional Biography Preparation

Write your professional biography in a paragraph of no more than 250 words. Your audience is the readers of a document you are planning to publish or the participants in a conference where you will present a paper. Include in your biography the following information:

1. Degrees earned or anticipated in the *near* future, with years
2. Current place of professional work, as employee or student
3. Academic and professional honors received, nominations for nationally important honors or awards
4. Offices held in professional organizations, especially at the national level
5. Publications, including title, co-author(s), publisher, and year

When you finish the first draft of this paragraph, revise carefully to cut the length. You will be surprised at how much extra verbiage you have added in the effort not to overaggrandize (or aggrandize) yourself.

Choose one of the following title possibilities for your biography: your own professional name, *Biography*, or *Biosketch* (a term used by Michael L. Keene, professor of professional writing at the University of Tennessee, Knoxville).

Even though you will revise this biography as requested by publishers who have accepted your work for publication or by conveners of conference sessions at which you will appear, keep this first and all other versions on diskette. You may want to trace your standing at a particular point in your career.

REFERENCES

1. M. Kiniry and E. Strenski, "Sequencing Expository Writing: A Recursive Approach," *College Composition and Communication* **1985,** *36,* 191–202.
2. Department of Career Services, American Chemical Society, *Tips on Resume Preparation.* American Chemical Society, Washington, DC, 1994.

chapter 7

Annotated Bibliography

The resources listed here range from basic writing tools to professional articles suggesting assignments and grading methods. We have marked with an asterisk the six "must-have" items, items that belong on the desk of a chemistry teacher who wants to influence student writing.

STYLE GUIDES

Any number of style guides will serve your academic purposes. We have included here a representative few of the variety available.

*Dodd, J. S. ed. *The ACS Style Guide*, 2nd ed. American Chemical Society, Washington, DC, 1997. In addition to providing much of the information you need for making effective format assignments, this book is useful enough for manuscript preparation that you might want to encourage or require all of your majors to purchase a copy.

The Chicago Manual of Style, 14th ed. University of Chicago Press, Chicago and London, 1993. The publication resources in this book are invaluable, from grammar and usage to manuscript preparation. Several documentation styles are discussed and illustrated.

Hodges, J. C., Webb, S. S. and Miller, R. K., *Hodges' Harbrace Handbook*, 14th ed. Harcourt Brace, New York, 2001. This traditional grammar and style handbook, which sports numbers or abbreviations for errors on the inside cover, is a handy tool for analytical marking.

*Keene, M. L. and Adams, K. H., *Easy Access: A Writer's Guide and Reference*, 3rd ed. Diane Publishing, Collingdale, PA, 2000. Color-coded tabs make it easy for students to find information about particular errors. The book also provides a simple chart of abbreviations for marking errors.

Strunk, W., Jr. and White, E. B. *The Elements of Style*, 3rd ed. Macmillan, New York, 1979. In addition to brief presentations of "elementary rules of usage," the authors give a handy compendium of "commonly misused" words and phrases.

DICTIONARIES AND USAGE GUIDES

The two college dictionaries listed below are highly respected. Science majors also ought to own at least one dictionary of science.

American Heritage College Dictionary, 4th ed. Houghton Mifflin, Boston, 2000. Many technical writers recommend this dictionary for its readability and usage notes. This dictionary has many illustrations.

*Barnhart, R. K., ed., *The American Heritage Dictionary of Science.* Houghton-Mifflin, Boston, 1986. This book is a standard resource for definitions and spelling of scientific terms.

Fowler, H. W., *A Dictionary of Modern English Usage.* Oxford UP, London, 1954. This old standby answers questions about exactness.

Morris, W. and Morris, M, *Harper Dictionary of Contemporary Usage.* Harper & Row, New York, 1975. The Morrises rely on a panel of writing experts to shape analyses of current usage.

Webster's New World Dictionary of American English, 3rd ed. Webster's New World: New York, 1988. This dictionary is a frequent choice of publishing companies.

INTERNET RESOURCES

Bachrach, S. M., ed., *The Internet: A Guide for Chemists.* American Chemical Society, Washington, DC, 1996. This internet guide focuses on the resources available for chemists and offers detailed information about e-mail, setting up web sites, and electronic conferencing.

National Writing Center Association. Writing Centers Online. Available: http://departments.colgate.edu/div/NWCADWLS.html. This regularly updated listing of writing centers, gophers, and OWL sites is alphabetized by school name. It is also possible to take a virtual OWL tour from the site.

Online Writing Lab, Purdue University. Available: http://ut11.library.utoronto.ca/www/writing/purdue_mirror The Purdue OWL, the best known of online writing centers, provides handouts, suggestions for writers, suggestions for teaching writing across the disciplines, and links to several other online writing centers.

Only a Matter of Opinion? Art of Writing. Available: http://library.thinkquest.org/50084/write.html Pages on introductory devices, vocabulary, and fallacies of logic can be helpful to students.

Paradigm: Online Writing Assistant. Available: http://www.wisc.edu/writing/ This site provides help for organizing several types of essays, simple and practical editing guides, and useful material on discovering and developing a writing "voice."

Prentice Hall. Companion Web Site Gallery. Available: http://www.prenhall.com/pubguide Prentice Hall's web sites to supplement their writing texts provide excellent stand-alone study guides and grammar exercises.

Writing Lab. Available: http://www.mhhe.com/socscience/english/compde/ewlab.html Extensive lists of on-line writing labs (OWLS), dictionaries, and grammar guides extend the help options available to both student and teacher. Other writing resources are also identified, including an English-as-second-language workbook.

PROFESSIONAL AND TECHNICAL WRITING GUIDES

You can choose from among many professional writing guides. The best alternative is to establish a departmental choice. If that is not possible, review a few guides and choose the one most congenial to your own goals and teaching style. A few good guides are listed here.

Alley, M., *The Craft of Scientific Writing.* Prentice-Hall, Englewood Cliffs, NJ, 1987. Analysis of overall structure for a scientific paper is the book's most helpful feature.

Day, R. A., *Scientific English: A Guide for Scientists and Other Professionals,* 2nd ed. Oryx Press, Phoenix, AZ, 1995. Day's book is brief and practical, with specific examples of the problems that most commonly plague science (and other) writers.

Ebel, H. F., Bliefert, C. and Russey, W. E., *The Art of Scientific Writing: From Student Reports to Professional Publications in Chemistry and Related Fields.* Weinheim, New York, 1987. This book, devoted to enhancing the written word in science, is particularly helpful because most of the examples come from chemistry. The authors pride themselves on showing both the "how" and the "why" of effective scientific writing.

Keene, M. L., *Effective Professional and Technical Writing.* D. C. Heath, Lexington, MA, 1993.

Keene's book provides excellent examples of the types of technical writing and the techniques for succeeding at each. He is especially helpful, however, in his suggestions for revision strategies.

OTHER RESOURCES FOR WRITERS

This short list is merely representative of the many resources available to science writers. As students become more interested in developing their writing skills, such material becomes increasingly useful.

American Chemical Society, Department of Career Services, *Tips on Resume Preparation.* American Chemical Society, Washington, DC, 1986. This succinct guide gives many useful suggestions for preparing an effective resume, curriculum vitae, and cover letter.

Beall, H. and Trimbur, J., *A Short Guide to Reading and Writing About Chemistry,* 2nd ed. Longman, New York, 2001. This book is especially helpful in its suggestions for writing the laboratory report and the scientific proposal. It also offers some assignments.

Booth, V., *Communicating in Science,* 2nd ed. Cambridge UP, Cambridge, 1993. Booth offers detailed guidelines for writing scientific papers.

*Booth, W. C., Colomb, G. G. and Williams, J. M., *The Craft of Research.* University of Chicago, Chicago, 1995. This book is the professional writer's "bible" and covers important facets of research writing: audience considerations, topic selection and narrowing, developing and qualifying an argument, and visual presentations. The quick tips can be especially helpful because they are easy to convey.

*Day, R. A., *How to Write and Publish a Scientific Paper,* 4th ed. Oryx Press: Phoenix, 1994. Among the "how to" chapters in this book is one on designing effective tables.

Elbow, P., *Writing with Power: Techniques for Mastering the Writing Process.* Oxford UP, New York, 1981. Elbow is noted for his ability to help writers establish their own writing voices.

Katz, M. J., *Elements of the Scientific Paper.* Yale UP, New Haven, 1985. Katz actually builds a short paper starting with setting the limits of the project, then collecting and organizing data, then connecting the project to the broader scientific community and polishing the draft by proofreading and refining the logic.

Lanham, R. A., *Revising Prose,* 3rd ed. MacMillan, New York, 1992. Lanham calls his set of rules "the Paramedic Method . . . a first-aid kit, a quick, self-teaching method of revision" to help people "translate The Official Style . . . into plain English."

Lomask, M., *The Biographer's Craft.* Harper & Row, New York, 1984. Chapter 11 on autobiography may help students writing professional autobiographies to identify useful resources to supplement their memories.

Marius, R., *A Writer's Companion*, 4th ed. Knopf, New York, 1998. Marius' audience sensitivity demonstrates his stylistic recommendations. This book makes it fun to read about writing.

Pearsall, T., "Interchange: What are the differences between 'scientific' and 'technical' writing?" *ATTW Bulletin* **1996**, *7*(25), 6–7. Pearsall asserts that technical writing is more varied and serves many more purposes than scientific writing, which he declares is written about science for scientists.

Penrose, A. M., Katz, S. B., Writing in the Sciences: *Exploring the Conventions of Scientific Discourse*. Bedford/St. Martins, Boston, 1998. Using a descriptive approach, this book provides students with analytical and rhetorical tools needed for scientific writing.

Porush, D., *A Short Guide to Writing About Science*. Harper Collins, New York, 1995. Porush offers good general suggestions for scientific writing. Like Beall and Trimbur, he pays special attention to scientific forms.

Schoenfeld, R., *The Chemist's English*, 2nd ed., revised. VCH, Weinheim, Germany, New York, 1986. The former editor of the *Australian Journal of Chemistry* helps readers avoid certain annoying errors but intends primarily to give his readers "an *appetite* for good English." A lively style and inventive use of language assure his achieving that goal.

Zinsser, W., *Writing to Learn*. Harper & Row, New York, 1988. Chapter 11 is devoted to physics and chemistry and offers examples of assignments and responses to writing from chemistry professors. Chapter 4 defines the concept of writing to learn.

RESOURCES FOR TEACHING WRITING

The articles and books listed here present a range of writing teacher concerns: theory and justification, assignments, and evaluation procedures.

Bailey, R. A. and Geisler, C, "An Approach to Improving Communications in a Laboratory Setting: The Use of Writing Consultants," *J. Chem. Educ.* **1991**, *68*, 150. Writing consultants can be used to help students improve their laboratory reports. The article lists essential requirements for several kinds of scientific writing.

Ballenger, B., "Teaching the Research Paper," in T. Newkirk, ed., *Nuts and Bolts: A Practical Guide to Teaching College Composition*. Boynton/Cook, Portsmouth, NH, 1993. Ballenger recommends a series of steps to completion of a long research paper. Though he recommends that these steps be carried out in the classroom, they can be adapted for use outside of class.

Beall, H., "In-Class Writing in General Chemistry," *J. Chem. Educ.* **1991**, *68*, 148; "Probing Student Misconceptions in Thermodynamics with In-Class Writing," *J. Chem. Educ.* **1994**, *71*, 1056. These articles suggest assignments and ways to use them to enhance student learning.

Bean, J. C., Drenk, D. and Lee, F. D., "Microtheme Strategies for Developing Cognitive Skills," in C. W. Griffin, ed., *New Directions for Teaching and Learning: Teaching Writing in All Disciplines*, No. 12. Jossey-Bass, San Francisco, 1982. The authors explain their uses of microtheme assignments to teach chemistry content.

Bizzell, P. and Herzberg, B., "Writing Across the Curriculum: A Bibliographic Essay," in D. A. McQuade, ed., *The Territory of Language*. Southern Illinois, Carbondale and Edwardsville, 1986. The authors analyze early material on the writing-across-the-curriculum movement.

Brookes, A. and Grundy, P., *Writing for Study Purposes: A Teacher's Guide to Developing Individual Writing Skills.* Cambridge UP, Cambridge, England, 1990. The authors recommend the ungraded approach to writing assignments, suggesting that students will learn more if they are called upon to evaluate their own work.

Burkett, A. R. and Dunkle, S. B., "Technical Writing in the Undergraduate Curriculum," *J. Chem. Educ.* **1983,** *60,* 469–470. This early article on teaching writing in chemistry courses lays out the dominant problems and suggests solutions.

Bybee, R. W., *Achieving Scientific Literacy: From Purposes to Practices.* Heinemann, Portsmouth, NH, 1997. Bybee moves toward functional and conceptual definitions of scientific literacy that might justify writing assignments and also can be used in the assignments themselves.

Castellan, G. W., *Physical Chemistry,* 3rd ed., Addison-Wesley, Reading, MA, 1983. This physical chemistry textbook asks questions that make good writing assignments.

Connatser, B. R., "Setting the Context for Understanding," *Technical Communication* **1994,** *41,* 287–291. The article addresses concerns with audience and discusses context and transition to make the audience comfortable with and confident in the writing process.

Cooper, M. M., "Writing: An Approach for Large-Enrollment Chemistry Courses," *J. Chem. Educ.* **1993,** **70,** 476–477. Cooper discusses uses of the microtheme.

Coppola, B. P. and Daniels, D. S., "The Role of Written and Verbal Expression in Improving Communication Skills in an Undergraduate Chemistry Program," *Language and Learning Across the Disciplines* **1996,** *1,* 67–86. Coppola and Daniels offer interesting peer review strategies.

Freedman, S. W. and Calfee, R. C., "Holistic Assessment of Writing: Experimental Design and Cognitive Theory," in *Research on Writing: Principles and Methods,* ed. Peter Mosenthal, Lynne Tamor and Sean A. Walmsley. Longman, New York, 1983. The authors offer suggestions for effective grading practices.

Ganguli, A. B., "Writing to Learn Mathematics: Enhancement of Mathematical Understanding," *The AMATYC Review* **1994,** *16,* 45–51. Ganguli discusses the positive impact of writing assignments on the performance of remedial students.

Gordon, C., "Socializing the Writing Process Through Collaboration" *Canadian Journal of English Language Arts* **1989,** *12,* 3–15. The first pages of this article give a strong rationale for collaborative writing assignments.

Hanson, D. and Wolfskill, T., "Improving the Teaching/Learning Process in General Chemistry: Report on the 1997 Stony Brook General Chemistry Workshop," *J. Chem. Educ.* **1998,** *75,* 143–147. The authors discuss the use of writing to teach students to explain chemical and physical phenomena.

Harmon, Joseph E., "An Analysis of Fifty Citation Superstars from the Scientific Literature," *J. Technical Writing and Communication* **1992,** *22,* 17–37. Harmon uses journal articles as a quality measure for scientific publication. The references include chemistry "superstars," which might be useful models for classes.

Hatton, J. and Plouffe, P. B., *The Culture of Science: Essays and Issues for Writers.* Macmillan, New York, 1993. The book contains examples of historical essays and profiles.

Hermann, C. K. F., "Teaching Qualitative Organic Chemistry as a Writing-Intensive Class," *J. Chem. Educ.* **1994,** *71,* 861. Hermann has helpful ideas for informal writing assignments.

Hoffman, R., "Under the Surface of the Chemical Article," *Angewandte Chemie* (International Ed. in English) **1988,** *27,* 1653–63; *The Same and Not the Same.* Columbia, New York, 1995. Hoffman, himself a prolific writer, offers a persuasive case for teaching persuasive writing in chemistry courses. Many of his works can be used as models for students.

Kiniry, M. and Strenski, E., "Sequencing Expository Writing: A Recursive Approach," *College Composition and Communication* **1985**, *36*, 191–202. The authors lay out the writing hierarchy presented in this manual.

Kovac, J. *The Ethical Chemist.* Department of Chemistry, University of Tennessee, Knoxville, 1995. This casebook of ethics dilemmas offers a wealth of possible writing assignments, either individual or collaborative.

Kovac, J., "Scientific Ethics in Chemical Education," *J. Chem. Educ.* **1996**, *73*, 26–28; "Professional Ethics in the College and University Science Curriculum," *Science and Education* **1999**, *18*, 309–317. Kovac discusses the case study method of presenting ethics dilemmas; specific cases provide fine writing topics on all levels of the Kiniry-Strenski hierarchy.

Kovac, J. and Coppola, B. P., "Universities as Moral Communities," *Soundings: An Interdisciplinatry Journal*, in press. Kovac and Coppola discuss the necessity of linking disciplines to encourage students to shape a moral framework for their academic and professional lives.

Kovac, J and Sherwood, D. W., "Writing in Chemistry: An Effective Learning Tool, *J. Chem. Educ.* **1999**, 76, 1399–1403. The authors summarize the uses of their handbook for chemistry teachers and illustrate its use in Kovac's general chemistry courses.

Krumsieg, K. and Baehr, M., *Foundations of Learning.* Pacific Crest Software, Corvallis, OR, 1996. The authors present a reading method that entails a written reading log.

Malachowski, M. R., "The Use of Journals to Enhance Chemical Understanding in a Liberal Arts Chemistry Class," *J. Chem. Educ.* **1988**, *65*, 439. The article particularizes the assignment, gives criteria for grading, and gives examples of appropriate topics.

Mayer, B. and Worsley, D., "Science Writing: Questions and Answers," *Teachers & Writers* **1988**, *19*(5), 4–5. The article answers frequently asked questions about student writing and risk.

McCleary, W. J., "A Case Approach for Teaching Academic Writing," *College Composition and Communication* **1985**, *36*, 203–212. This detailed account of an assignment based on a legal case suggests specific techniques that can be applied to a chemistry situation.

Miller, L. L., "Molecular Anthropomorphism," *J. Chem. Educ.* **1992**, *69*, 141–142. With the goals of learning to write and writing to learn in the chemistry classroom, Miller discuss criteria for evaluating a creative writing assignment that prohibits students' simply copying or rephrasing the textbook.

Moore, R., "Does Writing About Science Improve Learning About Science?" *JCST* **1993**, 22, 212–217. The thesis is that guided instruction about writing can enhance learning about science while unguided writing assignments have little effect.

Moore, R., "Writing to Learn Biology," *JCST* **1994**, *23*, 289. Moore gives excellent specific suggestions for journal assignments, evaluation, and peer evaluation procedures.

Olmsted, J., III., "Teaching Varied Technical Writing Styles in the Upper-Division Laboratory," *J. Chem. Educ.* **1984**, *61*, 798–800. Olmsted illustrates his own use of writing assignments: a detailed procedure, detailed discussion, technical report, detailed and short abstracts, journal article, and popular science report.

Parks, S. and Goldblatt, E., "Writing beyond the Curriculum: Fostering New Collaborations in Literacy," *Coll. English* **2000**, *62*, 584–606. The authors present a case for expanding writing across the curriculum to include writing beyond the curriculum, for audiences outside academic walls.

Powell, A., "A Chemist's View of Writing, Reading and Thinking Across the Curriculum," *College Composition and Communication* **1985,** *36,* 414. This article discusses uses of lecture and laboratory notebooks, abstracts, concept papers, and project papers. Powell emphasizes developing the "habit of writing."

Rice, R. E., " 'Scientific Writing'—A Course to Improve the Writing of Science Students," *JCST* **1998,** *27,* 267–272. Rice describes his own experience with scientific writing courses.

Rosenthal, L. C., "Writing Across the Chemistry Curriculum: Chemistry Lab Reports," *J. Chem. Educ.* **1987,** *64,* 996. Rosenthal introduced the Kiniry and Strenski model in chemistry.

Shaughnessy, M., *Errors and Expectations.* Oxford UP, New York, 1977. Shaughnessy is well known for her approaches to teaching developmental students to convey what they have learned in writing. She discusses the necessity for realistic expectations of student writing.

Shires, N. P., "Teaching Writing in College Chemistry: A Practical Bibliography 1980–1990," *J. Chem. Educ.* **1991,** *68,* 484–495. For the years covered, Shires offers useful summaries of articles on a variety of writing-related topics.

Shulman, G. M., McCormack, A., Luechauer, D. L. and Shulman, C., "Using the Journal Assignment to Create Empowered Learners: An Application of Writing Across the Curriculum," *Journal on Excellence in College Teaching* **1993,** *4,* 89–104. Journal writing can help the student focus on immediate analysis of class material and develop their ability to communicate the understanding.

Stanislawski, D. A., "Writing Assignments? But This Is a Chemistry Class Not English," *J. Chem. Educ.* **1990,** *67,* 575–576. Stanslawski found that students fairly readily accepted and learned from the addition of writing assignments to their chemistry courses. He encourages the use of several short writing assignments rather than one long one at the end of the semester.

Stanitski, C. L., Eubanks, L. P., Middlecamp, C.H. and Stratton, W. J., *Chemistry in Context,* 3nd ed. McGraw-Hill, Boston, 2000. This book for nonmajors contains many topic suggestions for a popular article.

Sturgiss, J., "Literacy in Science Education," *Australian Science Teachers Journal* **1994,** *40*(3), 28–32. Using the term *genre* for what we call levels of writing, Sturgiss presents another model for gradually building learning/writing processes.

Sunderwirth, S. G., "Required Writing in the Freshman Chemistry Curriculum," *J. Chem. Educ.* **1993,** *70,* 474–475. Sunderwirth presents three levels of writing assignments and evaluation criteria.

Thall, E. and Bays, G., "Utilizing Ungraded Writing in the Chemistry Classroom," *J. Chem. Educ.* **1989,** *66,* 662-663. The article discusses 15-minute ungraded writing tasks as a preparation for an essay component in the final examination.

Tobias, S. and Raphael, J. *The Hidden Curriculum: Faculty-Made Tests in Science, Parts 1 and 2.* Plenum, New York, 1997. This exposition of innovative testing practices includes the use of essay questions and other writing projects.

Trimble, L., *English for Science and Technology: A Discourse Approach.* Cambridge UP, Cambridge, 1985. Trimble's approach may be helpful not only for teaching students how to write for scientific purposes but also for teaching students to read scientific prose more effectively.

Van Orden, N., "Critical-Thinking Writing Assignments in General Chemistry," *J. Chem. Educ.* **1987,** *64,* 506–507. The article contains several examples of writing assignments that call for "practical applications of chemical concepts."

Waterman, M. A. and Rissler, J. F., "Use of Scientific Research Reports to Develop Higher-Level Cognitive Skills," *JCST* **1982,** *12,* 336–340. The article presents procedures for studying scientific literature by writing about it. The strategies suggested include peer interaction as well as the processing of data.

White, E. M., *Teaching and Assessing Writing.* Jossey-Bass, San Francisco, 1985. White presents a rationale for assignment development and offers practical suggestions. He also argues persuasively for holistic over analytical assessment and offers information about the theory and practice of teaching writing. Ideas on holistic reading procedures are particularly helpful.

Wilkinson, S. L., "Electronic Publishing Takes Journals into a New Realm," *Chem. & Engr. News,* **1998,** *6(20),* 10–18. Wilkinson explores the implications of electronic publishing for individual scholars and researchers and offers interesting suggestions for peer reviewing functions. She also offers an online bibliography on the subject of electronic publishing.

Wilson, J. W., "Writing to Learn in an Organic Chemistry Course," *J. Chem. Educ.* **1994,** *71,* 1019–1020. Wilson offers four typical assignments.

Wright, J. C., "Authentic Learning Environment in Analytical Chemistry Using Cooperative Methods and Open-Ended Laboratories in Large Lecture Courses," *J. Chem. Educ.* **1996,** *73,* 827. A team approach to understanding a research paper involves writing team answers to a set of questions.

Index

Abstract 13, 15, 18, 26, 60, 76, 87
ACS Style Guide 16, 31, 44, 48, 57, 81
Analysis 9, 11, 27, 48, 59
   audience 19, 43
Argument, Scientific 11, 33, 60, 76
Article, Journal 26, 31, 86
Article, Popular 17, 18, 43, 85
Assessment 4, 25, 37, 42, 52, 88
   analytical 44–48
   criteria 13, 38–42, 85
   goal 52
   holistic 37–42, 88
Assignment 6, 8, 87
   clarity 6–7
   design 2–4, 13, 87–88
   interest 7–8
   reliability 7
   summary 10–11
   validity 7
Assignments 65–80, 85–87
   abstract 26
   analysis 9, 11
   annotated bibliography 15, 26
   argument 9, 11
   bibliography 26, 30–31
   classification 9–10
   collaborative 31, 33, 60
   comparison/contrast 9, 11, 72
   content-specific 65–69
   cover letter 79
   curriculum vitae 79–80
   definition 9, 10
   entry-level 32
   exam-preparation 73
   form-specific 76–77
   formal 13, 15, 19, 27–29
   format 19–20, 36
   general requirements 35–36
   historical 17, 70
   in-class 13, 14, 24
   informal 13, 24, 86–87
   journal 3, 8, 13–14, 24, 29–30, 49,
      74–75, 86–87

laboratory report 16, 32, 86–87
listing 9
literature review 15, 33, 70
microtheme 14, 18, 24, 37ff, 48, 55, 59
   out-of-class 14
paragraph 45, 77
proposal 8, 16, 33, 60, 72
reintegrative 32, 69
resume 77–78
seriation 9, 31, 58, 73–74
summary 9–11, 14, 15, 24, 31
Audience 3, 8, 15, 19, 20, 35, 43, 58,
      64, 84
   lay 15, 43
   scientifically educated, non-
      expert 17
   technical 15

Beall, H. 8, 14, 16, 17, 28, 76, 83, 84
Bensel-Meyers, L. 19
Bibliography 26, 32
   annotated 15, 26
Biography 17, 33, 52, 71, 80
Bloom's Taxonomy 3

Citation 19, 33
Classification 9–10, 13, 65
Collaborative Process 26, 28, 31, 33,
      59–61
Comparison/Contrast 9–11, 12, 25, 65
Concept Paper 15, 87
Conceptual Hierarchy 8–13, 16, 18, 65
Conferencing 62
   group 62–63
   one-to-one 62
Cooper, M. M. 49, 85
Coppola, B. P. 25, 61, 85, 86
Courses 1–5, 7, 11, 14–15, 23, 30, 35, 65
   advanced 16, 33, 43
   advanced laboratory 8
   analytical chemistry 31
   capstone 33
   core 2, 4, 30

Courses (*continued*)
  first-year 31–32
  four-year curriculum 2, 23
  fourth-year 30
  general chemistry 2, 10, 11, 14, 24,
    31–32, 38, 43, 52, 58
  graduate 27
  individual 23–30
  instrumental analysis 32
  laboratory 16, 32
  lower-division 31
  organic chemistry 15, 32
  physical chemistry 14, 24, 32
  second-year 32
  specialized 31
  third-year 32, 33
Cover Letter 16, 79
Curriculum Vitae 16, 33, 79–80

Daniels, D. S. 25, 61, 85
Definition 10, 12, 17, 24, 36, 65, 68, 72
Dialogue 4, 54, 56, 58, 64
Drafts 19, 27–28, 31

Editorial Hesitation 42, 43, 55
Enrichment 3, 27, 61, 69
Ethics 17, 27, 72, 86
  The Ethical Chemist 27, 86
Evaluation 2, 3, 7, 13, 18, 20, 25, 32, 35,
    58, 84, 86, 87
  criteria 4, 6, 7–8, 14, 20, 25, 30, 38, 39,
    41, 43, 45, 58, 85, 86, 87
Examinations 17, 21, 24, 73

Feedback 29, 31, 37
Freewriting 13
Fryhle, C. B. 46

Garrett, M. 19
Grading 2, 29
  analytical 4, 44–48
  checklist 45, 46, 47
  criteria 43
  holistic 4, 37
  teaching assistants 49–52
  tracking sheet 45
  ungraded writing 25, 48–49

Hoffmann, R. 8, 72

Journal 13, 24, 25, 31, 49, 69–70, 86
  reading 24, 69

Kiniry, M. 3, 9, 24, 86
Kovac, J. 14, 49, 73, 76, 86

Laboratory Report 16–18, 31–32, 87
Lawton, R. G. 61
Levi, P. 8, 72
Listing 9, 11–12, 13, 25, 44–45, 73

Microtheme 14, 24, 31, 38, 48, 55, 59
  samples 38–42
  TA grading 49–52

Objectives 3, 18, 23–27, 30, 52
Obstacles 2

Paraphrase 14, 20, 36, 41
Peer Review 4, 13, 25, 31, 58–62, 85, 86
  checklist 58–59
  oral 61
  Round Robin 58, 61–62
Plagiarism 19–20, 36
Planning 28–29, 30, 36
Proofreading 45, 56, 60, 78, 83
Proposal 16, 72

Reading 23, 24, 25, 26
  faculty 16–17, 36, 42–43, 48, 55, 86–87
  log 86
  notebook 73–74
  persona 43
  scientific 26
  student 23, 24, 25–32, 29, 31, 32, 42,
    51, 73–74
Reintegration 26, 28, 69–70
Research Paper 16, 44
Response 54ff
  oral 61–63
  peer 58–59
  written 55–58
Resume 16, 33, 77–78
  Tips on Resume Preparation 78,
    79, 80
Revision 28, 29, 45, 57–58

Seriation 10, 15, 31, 32, 58, 66
Shaughnessy, M. 43, 87
Sherwood, D. W. 86
Stafford, William 1, 2
Strenski, E. 3, 9, 24, 87
Summary 10–11, 14, 15, 25, 31, 70

Teams 25
    dyad 58–59
    pairs 25, 75
Tests, Standardized 3, 4, 6, 7
Thinking 1–2, 11, 23–25, 26
    critical 1–2, 20, 24, 52
    dead-end 28
    focus 49
Topic 7–8
    expository 8
    expressive 8, 27
    failed 42
    general 28

narrowing 28
persuasive 8, 27
specific 28
Training 49–52
Trimbur, J. 14, 17, 28, 76, 83
Tutor, Peer 63

Writing 1–2, 23–28
    center 45, 51, 54, 63, 82
    consultant 28, 63–64
    creative 86
    expository 9
    expressive 8, 27
    formal 2, 13, 15, 31
    in-class 14, 24
    informal 24
    persuasive 8, 27
    process 19, 27–28
    reintegrative 26